NO PLACE TO BE SINGLE

NO PLACE TO BE SINGLE

a novel

FELICIA KINGSLEY

TRANSLATED BY HILLARY LOCKE

Previously published as *Non è un paese per single* by Newton Compton Editori in Italy in 2022. Translated from Italian by Hillary Locke. First published in English by Amazon Crossing in 2026.

Published by Amazon Crossing, Seattle

www.apub.com

EU product safety contact:
Amazon Media EU S. à r.l.
38, avenue John F. Kennedy, L-1855 Luxembourg
amazonpublishing-gpsr@amazon.com

ISBN-13: 9781662533457 (paperback)
ISBN-13: 9781662533440 (digital)

Cover illustration and design by Mumtaz Mustafa
Cover image: © Vector World / Adobe Stock; © MikhailPopov / Shutterstock

Printed in the United States of America

NO PLACE TO BE SINGLE

PROLOGUE

Elisa

It is a truth universally acknowledged that a single man in possession of a good fortune must be in want of a wife.

Except this isn't Hertfordshire, and it's not 1812. This is Belvedere, in Chianti, a small village of about thirty-two hundred inhabitants between the provinces of Florence and Siena. And it's the twenty-first century.

At least that's what the calendar says, though certain conversations might suggest otherwise.

Take the one unfolding now, at the bakery—swarming with housewives like every morning. It's a conversation in which Elisa Benetti finds herself engaged entirely against her will.

"When is he coming?" Fiorella asks Giliola.

"How old is he?" adds Viola.

"I must immediately tell him about my Sara!" exclaims Angela, as she rushes toward the exit, nearly trampling Mamma and me. "Sorry! Didn't see you there."

"Morning, Pietro. The usual two loaves, please," Mamma says to the baker, who attends to her, clearly amused by the chatter. "So who's coming? The new parish priest?" She's as bad as the others when it comes to procuring the latest gossip.

For a little village where nothing ever happens, even a new parish priest has people buzzing for days.

"A parish priest? After Caterina's niece put an end to the last one, the diocese won't send anyone under fifty. The next man who heads up the parish will need a nurse rather than a housekeeper."

In Belvedere, no celibate man is safe, not even a man of the cloth. Here, with just a handful of bachelors under retirement age, nothing is sacred: Mothers, grandmothers, aunts, and daughters are all equipped with a precision radar capable of detecting a potential husband from miles away. Mamma is no exception.

Don Marzio, fresh out of the seminary, lasted all of four months before Caterina's niece Greta cooked him up in a brief courtship to the tune of homemade pappardelle with wild boar and then proceeded to marry him.

"This person must be important," Mamma presses, her curiosity piqued. This is what I get for volunteering to cart home her groceries on my Vespa.

"What?" Viola spits. "You of all people don't know? Gianni Vanucci, the notary, just went to see Ricasoli's nephew. He's inheriting his uncle's estate!"

Oh. That's why they think we would know: We live and work on the estate in question, Le Giuggiole. Count Umberto Ricasoli died a month ago, a heart attack relieving him of his arduous life of leisure at all of fifty-six, and we've been awaiting directives from the heirs, who are as yet unknown.

"I didn't know a thing about it," says Mamma, annoyed. "It went from the Ricasolis of Poggio a Caiano?"

Count Umberto didn't have children, so Gianni had to track down his next of kin. There are loads of Ricasoli-Guicciardis in Tuscany; with regard to selecting an heir, there'd be no shortage of candidates.

"My cousin lives in Poggio and didn't say a word. Maybe it went to the ones in Pontassieve," says Giliola.

"There are a few Ricasolis in Pisa too," says Fiorella.

"I'd rather have a corpse in my house than a Pisan at my door!" announces the pharmacist, parking his bike on the sidewalk and stepping inside. "Good morning, ladies! What are you all going on about? Who is this nitwit from Pisa?"

"Ricasoli's nephew is inheriting Le Giuggiole, if they can figure out which one he is." Pietro explains.

"What does that have to do with Pisa?" Duccio says. "I know who it is: Gianni's neighbor Fernanda told me when she was in buying a balm for her calluses."

If anyone would know, it would be Duccio. Everyone talks to the pharmacist about everything. Absolutely everything.

"Who is it? Who is it?" squeal the ravenous mothers in chorus.

Duccio, pleased at the attention, puffs out his chest under his white coat. "It's old Lanfranco Ricasoli's great-nephew—the one in London." Lanfranco was Umberto's father and the prior owner of the estate. "The son of his niece Elena."

Duccio's announcement catches me so off guard I take a step back. "You mean Carletto?" In reality his name is Charles. His mother, Elena Ricasoli, married an English cloth merchant, Richard Bingley, and Charles and his twin sister used to spend summers at their great-uncle's estate.

"That's the one," Duccio confirms. "Gianni caught a flight out of Florence last night."

I'm about to reach for the bread, when I'm assailed by the band of sprightly housewives of Chianti.

"Do you know him? Is he handsome?" asks Giliola.

"Is he rich?" wonders Fiorella.

"Is he spoiled?" Angela, who had stepped out moments earlier, is back on the threshold, ravenous for details. What did I say about the Belvedere women having a radar when it comes to men?

"I actually haven't heard from him in years," I say, trying to extract myself from their circle.

"Let's just hope he's not gay; otherwise, you ladies will be left salivating."

"If he's *a homosexual*, he can stay in London," Viola declares. "We have no time to waste here."

From what I can remember, Carletto was not, in fact, *a homosexual.* At least he wasn't fifteen years ago.

"Mariana"—Giliola pulls Mamma by the wrist—"could you do us a favor? Tell us when he arrives."

"Tell you what?" Mamma feigns confusion, but she knows exactly what they want. "Why?"

"So we can come to Le Giuggiole with an excuse to meet him!"

"Great idea," says Fiorella. "My Paola can make him some *cantucci*!" Ah, Paola's famous cantucci, better described as *reinforced concrete.*

"And I'll make him some profiteroles!" echoes Angela.

These women are in "take him by the throat" mode. In other words, if he doesn't ask their daughters out, they'll strangle him.

"Oh, just listen to yourselves. We have work to do. We hardly have time for this nonsense," Mamma says, bristling. Knowing her, she's hardly eager to share such precious information.

"Of course. Elisa, tell your mother to do us the favor. Mariana, don't be selfish," Viola insists.

"I'll talk to her," I lie, to neutralize them, knowing that otherwise I'll never get out of here.

"Good girl."

As we leave, Mamma links arms with me and whispers thoughtfully into my ear: "Don't say a word to anyone. We need to go straight home and start cleaning, including under the furniture, and prepare the primary suite, and bake two cakes—no, three—and warn Giada so she can get her hair done . . . And we need to iron her lace dress, the one that brings out her eyes. And you, Elisa, get busy and make yourself presentable, for once."

"Mamma, please don't you start too," I sigh.

No sooner have we left than Fiorella tracks us down and slips me a rolled-up ten-euro bill. "Make sure I'm the first to know," she says, eyeing me with complicity.

I can't take any more.

I hop on my blue Vespa Rally without bothering to fasten my helmet and speed off at full throttle. The sputtering muffler releases a cloud of gray smoke and the stench of burned oil, invoking a "Mamma mia!" from the elders sitting outside Mario's bar, while Mamma shouts after me from the bakery door: "You forgot the bread, dear!"

But I don't dare turn back for it.

1

Michael

"This had better be important, making me run here from the office like it's a national emergency." That's how I greet Charles, my best friend, as I join him on the treadmills at the gym.

"It's Saturday, for the love of God. Do you ever relax?"

"It's Saturday?" I ask, stunned.

"See? You're so strung out on work, you don't even know what day it is."

I'd been sure it was Friday. So that's why my assistant, Penny, was so annoyed when I dragged her out of bed at seven this morning with a barrage of urgent messages.

"I have a new client, and this morning was the only time I could meet him." This is only half true—I've been courting Ernest Havisham for months, and yesterday he officially hired Saxton & D'Arcy to manage his sizable investment portfolio. This morning I was trying to get some work in, even though Saxton, my partner and honorary father, strictly forbade me to stay in the office past nine in the evening. And on weekends. And on national holidays . . .

"Okay, enough about your addiction to work. I have some news."

"Oh yeah?" I'm surprised by the enthusiasm in his voice. Charles is a man of habit. He doesn't like it when his plans change and consequently hates anything resembling news. He hasn't had any real news to share since he got his adenoids out in third grade.

"Do you remember my great-uncle Lanfranco? The one with the villa in Tuscany?"

"Of course I do." Charles's parents became legal guardians for my brother and me when our parents died twenty-nine years ago; George and I lived with the Bingleys until we were adults. Charles's mother was from Florence, at home they spoke Italian, we went to a bilingual high school, and we spent all our summers in Italy at Charles's great-uncle's villa.

"His son just died with no heirs," he says, "so the estate goes to my sister and me."

"Are you serious?"

"Yesterday a notary from Belvedere served me all the heirship documents."

"Are you going to accept?"

Charles shrugs. That's another thing he hates: to make decisions. "I don't know." The expected response.

I'd bet my right arm he's going to ask what I would do in his place. Three . . . two . . . one . . .

"What would you do in my place?"

I'm no psychic. I just know him like the back of my own hand. "I should have known you'd put the ball in my court, Bingley-Boggley!"

"Don't call me that. We're not at school anymore."

Bingley-Boggley, the wavering Bingley, was the nickname our PE teacher had given him because he was always the last to join the line for anything that involved jumping, running, climbing, or diving.

"How should I know what I'd do? I guess I'd be weighing the pros and cons, wouldn't I?"

Cornered, my friend snorts. "It would be a nice property, and I have a lot of happy memories there. The issue is I wouldn't know what to do with it. Now that my dad is retired, I have to represent the company: Today I'm here; tomorrow it's New York or LA . . . It would be a big expense for a place I'd never have time to visit." Charles stops the treadmill and rests his right hand on his hip. "My spleen hurts. Let's do some weights."

The fact that I didn't share my opinion may be among the chief causes of his aching spleen.

We position ourselves on the benches, lifting our barbells in sync.

"I told the notary I'd think about it; if I refuse, I have to send him a formal renunciation," he says in the break between sets.

"Who would own the property if not you?" I ask.

"Some cousins seventeen times removed from Pontassieve, who I think would be more interested than I am."

"More interested than I am, that's for sure," a woman's voice interjects.

I look up from my supine position to see Caroline, Charles's twin sister, towering over us.

"Hi, Carol," says her brother between huffs. "I was just asking Michael his opinion about the estate in Tuscany."

"Good," she says, loosening her bun and letting her long copper hair cascade down her back. "Michael, convince him to let it go."

"Charles, let it go," I parrot.

"There's nothing more boring than the countryside," she goes on. "If only it were a penthouse in Nice, on the Promenade des Anglais! A casino, a vibrant social life, and with the Mediterranean climate, we could enjoy it all year round. Don't you think, Michael?" she asks me.

"I prefer Spain," I shoot back between lifts.

"Of course you do," she says. "Too many French people in France, plus all that butter in everything. Spain is the new Costa Azzurra: Benalmádena, Marbella, Estepona. Perfect for spending your days by the sea."

"I'd rather visit the backcountry," I reply, sitting up and dabbing my sweat.

"Oh, um, yeah . . . the backcountry." She nods. "Wow, Michael, that barbell is heavy; you must be quite strong to lift it."

"It's only forty kilos, the same as Charles's," I point out.

"Yeah, but he doesn't train like you do."

"We're on the exact same program," I reply.

"I appreciate your respect for me, Carol," Charles replies. "You also seem rather knackered from your training . . . Wait, no! You've just come from the spa, judging by your robe."

"I did water aerobics before that."

"Yes, quite the workout."

Charles and Caroline have a love-hate relationship. More hate than love, really.

"Hey, Charles! Ciao, Michael." One of the female trainers stops to greet us.

"Oh, hi, Zoe." Caroline's acid tone betrays her annoyance at having been ignored.

"Sorry, Carrie. Didn't see you there," Zoe shoots back. She who lives by acid dies by acid. "Next Friday, we're doing yoga under the stars, followed by hot oil massages, vegan finger food, and an herbal tea tasting," she says, extending a flyer to Charles and me. "Will you join us?"

"Am I not invited?" says Caroline.

"Sorry," says Zoe, with a cutting smile. "Limited capacity on the terrace."

"As if."

"Very interesting," says Charles.

"Interesting," I mimic. I don't want to be rude, but it's not my kind of evening. "Afraid I have plans."

"What a pity." Zoe seems disappointed. "No chance of changing them?"

I can't change something that doesn't exist. "Work dinner."

Zoe lights up, and I realize I've just scored a goal. "On a Saturday night? How stressful! You know what you need to relax? Hot yoga." She leans down to my level to write something on the invite she just handed me, revealing her breasts squeezed into her top. "I do private lessons too. Here's my number. Call me anytime."

She says bye to all of us and gives me a look.

"Shameless," says Caroline. "I can't stand women like that."

"What do you mean, women like that?" asks Charles. Sometimes I can't tell if he's really that clueless or if he does it on purpose.

"Vulgar," his sister retorts. "God, Michael! She practically hurled herself at you. And the way she dresses! I bet she's not even wearing underwear under those microscopic shorts."

"Want me to go check?" I can't resist the joke.

"Michael!" Caroline looks scandalized. "She's not your type, is she?"

Charles laughs through his teeth. "Michael has a lot of types."

"You know what? I've had enough of you both. Ciao," she says, turning to leave.

"Here." I extend Zoe's invite. "Take mine."

She snatches it and turns on her heels, then tosses it into the trash bin on her way out.

"Is your sister still in anger-management therapy?" I ask Charles.

"She never started."

"Hence the lack of progress."

We change stations and proceed to work our shoulders and backs.

"Anyway, Zoe's fit. You could take her to dinner, Michael," Charles suggests.

Christ! "Charles, you're the last of the romantics. Zoe isn't looking for dinner."

"Maybe she'd appreciate an appetizer and a glass of wine *beforehand*," he emphasizes. "Oh, sorry, I forgot you're not into courtship, foreplay, or anything else that could make a date resemble the beginning of a relationship."

"A relationship isn't among my priorities at the moment."

"Is that why you're seeing two different women?" he shoots back. "Sheila and . . . Denise?"

"Danielle," I say. "Eyes for everyone, heart for no one." That's my motto, and it's worked well up to now: Sheila is a masseuse at a spa in Maida Vale. She's sweet and attentive, with absurdly long shifts that prevent a social life, and I see her whenever I need a cuddle. Danielle is a copilot for British Airways who I see on her two days off every week for forty-eight hours of practically uninterrupted sex. I've never stepped out in public with either of them. Neither of them has been to my place. And they know nothing about my private life.

"I, on the other hand, am starting to feel ready for the old 'May death do us part.'"

I almost drop my weight. "Huh?"

"You heard me. Marriage, children . . ." Charles insists.

"A Labrador retriever, full pension plan, and a Volvo," I laugh. "Come on!"

"You'll wake up one day wanting the same thing, and then it will be my turn to tolerate you, Michael," says Charles.

"I can't bear to be in a relationship with someone who can't keep up with me. I don't want to spend my life with a woman who indulges me all day long just to keep me happy and whose whole world revolves around me. If it's going to be forever, I want it to be with someone who isn't afraid to push back against me; I want someone who can put up a good fight instead of just agreeing with me all the time, someone who makes me want to wake up every morning just to hear what they have to say."

"You wouldn't last a week with someone like that." Charles looks at me skeptically. "You're too proud to apologize after an argument. You'd break up before you even got together."

"Better than the generational anxiety you have. Mister 'All my friends from uni are getting married and having children, and I'm still cutting the crusts off my toast.'"

"Sebastian, Duke, and Ashford all seem rather happy with their married lives. Harring is getting married too! And in any case, that doesn't mean I don't feel ready of my own accord."

"Whatever makes you happy." I dismiss the topic.

"What do you think happened to all those kids we spent the summers with in Tuscany?" he asks me out of the blue.

"Why?"

"They're more or less our age. It would be nice to know how they've landed. Giada, for example."

So that's where he's going with this. One point for Charles. "You're really desperate if you're fantasizing about your childhood crush," I say.

"I'm not fantasizing. I just remembered our summers in Chianti, and she was part of them. The end." At the estate, in addition to the four of us, there were also the children of the count's employees, and all together, we were a little gang of terrors.

"I won't believe it even if you swear on your life."

"In spite of your cynicism, you must admit we had fun. Do you remember Elisa, her younger sister?"

Click.

Charles unlocks a memory for me. "Elisa!" I exclaim, with a little too much excitement.

She and I were complicit in every Machiavellian plan, like Chip and Dale, like the cat and the fox. At night, we went to the neighbor's farm to steal watermelons, we took showers under the jet of the garden sprinklers, we played vet with the chickens and rabbits on the estate, we opened roadside kiosks to sell slimy mud pies, and we played hide-and-seek in the barn. When one of us had a thought, the other said it, and vice versa . . .

"Michael? Michael?!" Charles calls me back to reality.

"What is it?"

"Are you possessed? You've been in a trance for five minutes."

"Who, me?"

"Do you see any other Michaels here?"

"Ah, um, no . . ." It's true, dammit. I was lost in my head. "I was resting. What?"

"What do you think I should do? Accept or decline?"

Accept or decline? Five minutes ago, the answer was crystal clear. "I . . . I don't know," I say.

2

Elisa

Evenings at Le Giuggiole are always the same. Mamma tidies up the kitchen, polishing the copper pots that hang from the ceiling beams, and Donatella, the housekeeper, sips her jasmine tea laced with rum. She suffers from an irritable throat, or so she says. "I have delicate vocal cords. I was a mezzo-soprano. Have I ever told you about the time I sang at the Paris Opera?" Yes, at least twenty times.

Next to her is my older sister, Giada. She's Belvedere's beautician-hairdresser-mani-pedicurist, and at the moment she's hard at work on Donatella's nails.

Linda, the youngest in the house, does her summer-break homework sitting at one end of the long oak table. It's homework that she invented for herself because, unlike her friends who wait until the last minute, Linda finished all her assigned summer homework by August.

We observe in amazement as she tackles *rosa-rosae-rosae* from her Latin textbook. She's studying on her own to give herself a head start on the year after this one, when she'll go to high school.

She's the only thirteen-year-old who sulks when school ends in June.

I'm in charge of the vineyard. Donatella and Mamma manage the interiors. I do the exteriors, and with the harvest approaching, I'm completely preoccupied with harvesting times, grape ripening, grading, and bottling. I check the weather for the next few weeks, the humidity levels, the soil mineralization analyses, and the temperature forecasts, day and night.

Now that the days are getting busier, by evening I'm exhausted and struggle to keep my eyes open and focused on my laptop. This armchair is so comfortable . . .

"Eyes a little heavy, dear?" Donatella sings. She always addresses me with names like "joy," "dear," or "star," because she insists it adds emphasis.

"What? No, not at all," I say, jolting out of my thoughts.

"You were staring at a blank screen," Linda points out. She never misses a beat even though she never takes her eyes off her books.

"I'm just a little dazed from the sun . . ." I say, picking at my cuticles. I hate showing that I'm tired: Mamma always used to tell me how demanding my job is, how I should pursue something less tiring, how this is no occupation for a woman.

"Want a manicure?" my sister asks me.

"I'm good, thanks," I reply.

"What do you mean, you're good?" She seems to disagree with me. "Look at those nails! Are you still biting them?" Her tone is severe.

"No, I stopped," I lie. Actually, I'm trying to stop, but old habits die hard.

"What about a nice gel polish? Which do you like best?" she asks, waving two bottles under my nose. "You can choose between London by Night blue and Thames petrol." Giada has a minor obsession with London. When she was nineteen, instead of taking the train to Rosignano, where she was supposed to work in a hotel, she secretly went to London, where she took a beautician course, paying for it with the money she'd earned harvesting grapes right here at Le Giuggiole.

"Neither, Giada. What's the point? I work in a vineyard, not in fashion." Solid argument, I think.

"Nail polish doesn't have a *point*." She stands behind me, massaging my neck and shoulders. "It's a way to pamper yourself and relax."

"In the meantime, how about finishing my left hand, treasure?" Donatella calls to her.

"It *is* finished," Giada objects.

"But it doesn't match my right hand."

"Asymmetrical nails are the latest trend in Soho."

Donatella looks horrified. "Among the lunatics of Soho, you mean."

Giada rolls her eyes. "Can't you ever just humor me?" she says, and points to me. "You're neglecting yourself. And you," she says, now turning to Donatella, "have always been a downer. I'm going to fix you both. I'm setting up profiles for both of you on MatchMe," she exclaims, waving her cell phone in the air. "Just let me find a spot in this fortress where I can get a signal." She wanders around the kitchen with her phone in the air.

Giada is obsessed with MatchMe, a dating app. She spends her weekends going from Lunigiana to Maremma to meet her matches. She's on the hunt, not for just any ring but for a true, great love.

The problem is, she's looking for love but only finding duds, perhaps because her sole criteria is no men from Belvedere.

"There we go! Behind the fridge you get another bar. Hey, I have three matches!" she gloats, scrolling through her notifications. "Lorenzo from Cecina . . . Jacopo from Pisa . . ."

"For the love of God!" exclaims Mamma.

"Oh, this one seems nice: Simone from Viareggio. Too bad his photo's a bit blurry. I'll ask him for a better one in the chat. I'm not going to Viareggio in the dark."

"Remember what happened with that guy from San Macario in Piano," I remind her. The guy in question had given her a photo of a model downloaded from Google, and since then Giada's been harder to fool.

"Ugh, Gherardo. Bastard," she grumbles. "Oh! He just answered!"

"Let's see!" orders Donatella, whose opinions on the male universe are quite radical: No one is up to her standards.

Giada clears her throat, feigning embarrassment. "It's not exactly a photo of his face."

"Show us!" Donatella, Mamma, and I exclaim in chorus.

We all huddle around Giada, stunned and incredulous.

"What is that? An obelisk?" says Donatella.

"They put that thing in with anesthesia, right?" I add.

"That's not a man," says Mamma. "That's a horse."

"What's not a man?" asks Linda, looking up from her books.

"Nothing," the four of us reply, in unison.

"Can I see too?" she insists.

"Um, it's getting late!" I exclaim. "Linda, it's time for bed."

"But it's only nine o'clock," she objects.

"Yeah, but somewhere in the world it's late," I say.

But she doesn't give up. "I'm on summer break."

"You have to get used to your new school schedule." I approach her and give her a kiss on the head. "I'll be up in a little while to say good night, okay, Little Cub?"

"Such a drag, Mom," she mutters. "And don't call me Little Cub! It's a child's nickname!"

Yes, I'm "Mom." Little Cub is what I've always called her because of a tattered stuffed bear she's had since she was little.

Linda grumbles, collects her books, and heads toward the annex. I can tell our conversation is about to get spicy, and even though she's thirteen, I'd like to protect her innocence for as long as I can.

"Come on, Elisa, you could have let her stay," Giada scolds me. "She's going to see one sooner or later."

"I hope nothing that big, or she'll be damaged for life. And in any case, not until she's eighteen."

"So you're imposing compulsory chastity until she's an adult?" Mamma snaps.

"Of course, Mamma!" I reply. "Look at me! If you'd done the same, I wouldn't have had Linda at seventeen."

Donatella shrugs. "She's so shy she'd run away at the sight of one."

"One can only hope," I say. "So . . . how did you reply to Fury the Stallion?" I ask Giada, changing the subject.

"I asked where and when we'll meet," she says, typing.

"But you don't have a photo of his face!" objects Donatella.

"This time I decided to trust him."

"Trust? Is that what it's called now?" I tease her.

"I hope this one's closer than Viareggio. You're always chasing after these far-flung men," observes Mamma.

"Where do you suggest I look for them? Here?" Giada sounds horrified. "The most eligible bachelors here are Colli's son, the funeral director, and Ceccarelli's son, the plumber."

"Even in the darkest crises, people don't stop dying or shitting," Mamma reminds her.

"Belvedere is no place to be single," I agree.

"You can say that again. I would never stay here forever. As soon as I have the money, I'm going to London. If I have to look for the love of my life, I'll take my chances in a city of nine million people. Anyone in their right mind got out of here as soon as they could."

"Ahem," I say.

"You mean everyone who didn't become teenage mothers, dear," Donatella observes abrasively.

"And in any case, while I'm waiting to escape, I don't see why I should lock myself in a convent."

"Let's see the photo again," orders Donatella.

We all gather round Giada's phone to gawk at the outsized work of Mother Nature.

"My God, it's swollen!" exclaims Mamma. "Do you think he has enough blood to make it work at the same time as his brain, or does he faint?"

"Can he find underwear that fits?"

"Maybe he has them custom made . . ."

Knock, knock, knock.

We jump in surprise at a knock at the door.

"Who could it be at this time of night?" Mamma grumbles, opening the door.

"So, what's the news?" asks Giliola, who, arm in arm with her daughter Regina, steps inside without even bothering to say good evening.

"My God," Donatella scoffs. "If I'd known you were coming, I would have spiked my tea with a double shot."

"What do you mean, news?" replies Mamma sharply. There's bad blood between her and Giliola—their rivalry in the kitchen is legendary.

"Is he here?"

"Who?"

"What do you mean, who?" insists Giliola in her nasal voice. "Ricasoli's nephew!"

"No sign of him yet," Mamma snaps, waving them away.

"What a shame!" exclaims Giliola, ignoring Mamma's invitation to leave. She surveys the kitchen, while Regina lowers her eyes to the tart in her hand, disappointed.

"Did you make apricot jam?" asks Giliola inquisitively, nodding toward the row of steaming jars lined up on the shelf.

Mamma sighs nervously. "What does it look like to you?"

"You waited too long!" Giliola immediately criticizes her. "They were at their best last week."

"We made some on Saturday, and I put it in the tart," adds Regina.

"Did you remember to use sugar instead of salt this time?" Donatella asks pointedly. Last year, she'd made half the village sick.

"What were you all on about, anyway?" asks Giliola, evading the dig.

"Horses," we hasten to say.

Giliola shrugs, disinterested. If she only knew . . . "Let's hope Charles arrives in time for the Schiacciata Festival. We should tell the Pro Loco committee to include him on the jury as an honorary judge."

The Schiacciata Festival is a no-holds-barred competition: sabotaged leavening, ingredient theft, broken ovens . . .

Until five years ago, we made the *schiacciata* at home and brought them to the jury for a tasting, but Giliola accused Mamma of presenting a schiacciata so perfect that it must have come from the baker, and since then the whole process has taken place publicly in Belvedere's little square. Much to Giliola's dismay, Mamma won again the following year, effectively proving that hers was the best of the best.

"Oh, I'm sure he'll be here for the occasion," observes Giada acidly. "I bet he can't wait."

"Men like women who know how to cook," replies Giliola. "But what do you know about cooking, Miss Priss? And those fingernails! You couldn't even peel a potato."

"Then I'll be going in style, because I'm not the least bit interested in peeling potatoes," Giada retorts, and I applaud her in my head.

There's another knock at the door. Giliola and her daughter perk up, but when Mamma opens the door to Angela and her daughter Sara holding a tray of liver crostini, their faces twist into a disappointed grimace.

"Is he here?" asks Angela anxiously.

"No," Donatella replies dryly.

"Oh, we thought he'd be here by now. He and Vannucci the notary were supposed to arrive this evening."

"And somehow they've yet to appear," reiterates Mamma. Angela and Sara join us inside, exchanging resentful glances with Giliola and her daughter. "Fancy seeing you here."

"Indeed," replies Giliola.

"What a beautiful, relaxed atmosphere," I comment ironically. "Anyone want some chamomile tea? A sedative? A horse tranquilizer, perhaps?"

"Do you have any glue?" Giliola asks. "That way we can seal Angela's mouth shut once and for all."

"Whose mouth would you of all people like to shut?" protests Angela.

"You heard me. I know you say I'm cheap behind my back, you old bat."

"It's the truth. You asked me for your old aluminum cannelloni mold back, and when I told you I'd thrown it out, you got mad and demanded I buy you a new one," Angela replies.

"Okay, I lent you my cannelloni mold, and *I'm* the cheap one!"

"You made yours with eggs from my chickens."

"You gave them to me!" replies Giliola, increasingly flustered. "You gave them to me because you had too many and were going to throw them away."

Donatella gets up from the table, her tea in hand. "I think I still have time to add an extra shot to my tea after all."

Knock, knock, knock.

This time, it's Fiorella and Paola, with her famous quick-setting *cantuccini*.

Mamma quashes their enthusiasm before they can even open their mouths. "No, Charles isn't here. We have no idea when he's coming."

As if the initial disappointment weren't enough, as soon as Fiorella spots Angela and Giliola, she gives me a hurt look as if to say, *I thought we said you'd call me first.*

Wedding fever has spread through Belvedere once again, and at this rate I wouldn't be surprised if there was a run on *Bride Magazine* down at the newsstand.

The air in the room is saturated with estrogen: daughters on the hunt, mothers competing, and we—an awkward quartet in the form of a grumpy widow, a bitter auntie, a former teen mom, and a party girl—are bearing witness to the carnage.

At the fourth knock at the door, Mamma, exhausted, seizes her rolling pin. "I'll take care of this," she threatens.

But, to our amazement, instead of yet another mother-daughter duo, it's Vannucci, the notary. "I'm not armed," he says, defending himself from Mamma, hands in the air.

"Oh, Vannucci, finally. Welcome to the circus. Come tame these tigers. We give up."

He enters, intimidated, looking like someone who would rather be elsewhere. "Good evening, everyone."

The mothers and daughters attack him with a barrage of questions: "Where is Charles?" "Will you introduce him to us tonight?" "Has he eaten dinner yet?"

Vannucci scratches his head, hesitating. "Well, actually, I'm here to inform Mrs. Donatella and Elisa that Charles has decided to decline his inheritance."

An ominous silence falls over the kitchen. Only Giliola, after several seconds of disbelief, has the courage to open her mouth. "So he's not here with you?"

"He's in London. He's handing over the estate to his closest relatives."

"I knew it!" mutters Mamma. "Those hideous Ricasolis of Pontassieve! Then again, between the broken gate, the boiler, the garage, and the clogged flue, they will really need to shell out; otherwise, everything here will go to pieces." Mamma, as befits a housekeeper, always sees the practical side of things and doesn't even think about the girls' shattered dreams, even as their long faces practically stretch to the ground.

"I'm sorry. I should receive his formal renunciation in a few days. I have to go. Good night."

But his hopes of quietly slipping away die when the convoy of mothers follows him out, bombarding him with questions about why and how it could be that Charles didn't accept.

Mamma, Giada, Donatella, and I are finally left alone, in the newfound peace of the house, but instead of calm, I feel a burning in my chest.

The moment I heard about Charles's hypothetical return, my mind immediately flew to Michael, his best friend. He and his older brother, George, always visited the Bingleys in the summer, and Michael and I were very close. We had the same instinct for trouble, were both incapable of sitting still, and were constantly on the lookout for a new adventure. And we always dragged poor Carletto—Charles, now that he's in London—along on our escapades.

As silly as it may seem—fifteen years having passed—I found myself thinking that Michael might have come with Charles, just like when we were kids.

3

MICHAEL

Two weeks later

What I thought was the exception is now the rule: I'm woken by the phone and the unamused voice of my assistant, Penny: "You're late. Again."

I leap out of bed, scolding myself for having slept through my alarm. Or should I say, my alarms—all four of them.

The triple espresso I down has no effect, so, before going out, I quickly pop a fourth capsule of the ultra-strong and hyper-concentrated blend into the Nespresso machine while I button my shirt.

No time for a shave or a tie today; there are six messages on my phone from Saxton, the last of which is a terse *We're waiting for you.*

The taxi ride from Grosvenor Square to Marylebone, though short, only heightens my anxiety.

"Saxton started the Bradford meeting without you," Penny informs me when I arrive at the office. "They're in the Windsor Room."

Perfect, on the opposite side of the building. I reverse course like a rocket, but she grabs my jacket. "Necktie. Cologne. You're a mess," she says, handing me the silk Drake's that I keep in the office and that I tie as she sprays me with her Eau de Guerlain.

"That's women's perfume," I protest.

"You'll live. Go."

I burst into the Windsor Room, eliciting a gasp from everyone seated at the polished mahogany table. The Bradford brothers look perplexed, while Saxton just looks like he wants to kill me.

"Sorry, traffic was a mess this morning," I justify myself.

"Not a problem, D'Arcy," replies the eldest Bradford. "We're practically done. Lawrence answered all our questions regarding the portfolio diversification proposal."

Ah, they're already done. Even though the delay is on me, I'm annoyed I wasn't able to present my proposal myself. "If you have any other questions, don't hesitate to call me," I reply affably.

We shake hands and they leave. Before I can go, Saxton stops me. "Sit down, Michael. We need to talk."

I obey, pretending I don't have a concern in the world. "What's on your mind?"

"This isn't good."

"The Bradfords seemed satisfied with my investment plan," I bluff.

"You're too smart not to understand what I'm talking about." Saxton sits in front of me. "But if you really want me to, I'll enlighten you: At Friday's briefing, you were falling asleep."

"I was thinking."

"You were asleep, Michael."

"Okay," I admit. I struggle to keep up with my own relentless schedule, and I'm caving under the exhaustion. I didn't think it was that obvious, though.

"At the HSBC meeting, you presented the wrong draft of your presentation."

"But I killed it," I defend myself.

He gives me a cold look. "Stop talking back. You're trying my patience."

I raise my hands in surrender, and he continues with his litany of grievances. "You missed two meetings this week and . . . how long has it been since you shaved?"

"I'm resting my skin."

"Do it this weekend."

"Okay, I realize I've been underperforming ever so slightly as of late, but I can assure you my business instincts are intact."

"You're the best, Michael. You're even better than your brother—may he rest in peace—but if you're not at the top of your game, you're of no use to me."

At the mention of my brother, I clench my jaw, annoyed. Everyone thinks it's a compliment to compare us, but no one realizes there's nothing that offends me more.

"Do you want to fire me?" I ask directly.

"Never. We're equal partners, but we can't go on like this." Saxton stands up, shoves his hands in his pockets, and saunters around the table. "I'm old; I want to enjoy my final years, my grandchildren, and my money. I shouldn't be telling you this, but I think it's best you know: When I retire, I intend to gift you my entire share. You'll be the sole proprietor."

My jaw nearly falls to the floor in amazement. "Are you serious? Sax, I don't know how to thank you, I . . ."

"But not in your current state," he interrupts me, serious.

"What state?"

"You're addicted to work, but you can't handle the massive load you've taken on. You're so obsessed with the company, with our business, that you don't even understand what you're doing anymore. You work in the evening, you work on the weekend, you work while you eat, you work while you sleep . . ."

"That's why I'm so good!" I protest.

"No, that's why you're so exhausted. You're not capable of taking on the burden alone, and if you don't get ahold of yourself, I'll start looking around for someone else to take my share."

"Are you threatening me?"

"Not at all. I'm trying to push you to take care of yourself. You could be my son, God knows I think of you as one, but if you can't hear what I'm telling you, I'll be forced to make decisions on your behalf."

"If you don't want to dismiss me, then what do you have in mind?"

Sax comes to a halt right in front of me. "Take a holiday."

Huh? "I don't understand."

"How long has it been since you took a break? When was your last vacation?"

"A few months ago," I guess. I always promise myself I'll take a break, but I put it off every time an interesting deal or a new client appears.

"It was four years ago," he replies. "I had HR check this morning."

"Time flies when you're having fun," I comment sarcastically.

"You think you're invincible. I thought so too at your age, but I have bad news for you: You happen to be human and, like everyone else, you need a rest."

"Are you forcing me to go on holiday?"

"I want you back one hundred percent, not at half-mast, tired and sloppy. A distraction here can cost our customers millions of pounds and us our reputation. It's my responsibility to ensure the business isn't exposed to risk."

This lecture is starting to annoy me. "Don't you think you're making a big deal out of a little tardiness, Saxton?"

"Maybe, but at sixty, I know a problem when I see one, and you're a ticking time bomb. As of today you're on leave for a month, and that's an order, Michael."

"May I object?"

"No."

Giving up, I look down at the table grain. "Fine. But only because you leave me no choice—not because I agree."

"And when I retire, I will give you my share, not because I have no choice but because you'll deserve it."

"How can I prove I deserve it if you shut me out of the office? It's so . . . humiliating."

"Spare me your pride and self-pity and be smart enough to admit you're not at the top of your game. You may not see it now, but believe me, I'm helping you. Tell Penny to transfer your schedule to me and go home."

"So what does this mean, a mandatory holiday?" Charles asks me over a sushi lunch at Nobu. "Are you complaining? If only I could have one! The closest I get to a holiday is a trip to see clients in Milan the day after tomorrow to show them samples for next year's autumn-winter collection."

"Saxton says I'm exhausted." Just thinking about it notches up my blood pressure. "I told him I wasn't remotely fatigued—do I seem exhausted to you?"

"No, not in the slightest," Charles replies with a sarcastic grin.

"What have you decided to do with the inheritance?" I ask. He'd asked me for advice, but I decided to let him think about it first.

"I declined. As much as it pains me, the cons outweigh the pros."

I could have predicted as much: If Charles's future plans didn't include a house in Tuscany, he wouldn't be one to change them. "Makes sense . . . Wait a minute . . ." A thought we hadn't considered comes to mind. Well, it's normal that Charles wouldn't have considered it. He has no eye for investments, but that it didn't occur to me is downright shocking. Maybe Saxton is right—I am exhausted.

"What is it?" he asks me with his mouth full.

"Have you already sent the formal renunciation?"

"I signed it, but I still have to send it," he replies, chewing.

"Don't do it," I tell him slowly.

"Why?"

"Because you need to accept."

"Do I?" Charles says to me in a surprised tone, after swallowing. "But I just told you—the cons outweigh the pros."

"You accept and then sell the estate to the highest bidder," I exclaim, seizing a nigiri and brandishing it at him like a weapon. "Listen to me: Why give away the property to relatives you don't even know? With the profit, you can get a nice house in Primrose Hill, where you can raise your future family, and Caroline, with her share, will buy her penthouse in Nice, and you can finally get away from her."

"It does make sense," he concedes. "But selling is also a chore I don't want on my hands: Finding a realtor, buyers who make offers and disappear, months of waiting, endless negotiations . . ."

"Saxton & D'Arcy is full of potential buyers for an estate in Chianti."

"Seriously?" he asks me, relieved.

"Seriously. Let me handle it, and I'll find the fastest and best way to get it off your hands."

"You have carte blanche, Michael. You know I'd trust you with my life."

"The only thing I'd ask you is to do an inspection for me and check the building regulations to see if there's any potential for renovation."

"Me? I deal in fabrics, not real estate investments."

"You'll be in Italy next week, right? Extend your stay and take a detour to Tuscany."

"You'd have to come too! You have a month's vacation. Spend it on the estate and take advantage of it to close the deal. If you can really find me a buyer that quickly among your clients, think what a great impression you'll make when you return."

"Honestly . . ." I'd like to object, but his proposal is unassailable. He has a good reason, and it's not like I don't have the time now.

"Don't say no, Michael. You know I'm right. How do you want to spend this time? It will be over before you know it. You always make fun of me for being a creature of habit, but you are too. It's impossible to extract you from your routine. Go, see it, sell it. End of story."

Indeed. How else could this end? I'll go, see it, sell it. End of story.

4

Elisa

It's almost sunset when a speeding red sedan almost hits me out of nowhere.

A middle-aged couple gets out of the car as soon as it parks on the edge of the driveway, right on top of Mamma's beloved begonias. She's already glaring at them.

"We've come to take possession of the estate," the man announces, taking off his sunglasses like he's some kind of movie star. "I'm Ferdinando Armaroli Ricasoli, and this is my wife. You are the servants, I imagine."

The famous Ricasolis of Pontassieve.

Donatella, Mamma, and I stare at them rigidly from under the colonnade. We're employed here, but describing us as servants doesn't exactly curry our favor. We can't be bought and sold.

"Welcome to Le Giuggiole," Donatella greets them coldly in her capacity as *keeper of the house*, as she likes to call herself.

"Ferdy, am I wrong or is the villa smaller than in the photos?" asks the woman, with her lips puckered in disapproval. "I thought it was a noble palace."

"I can assure you, as someone who cleans every inch of it, it's not exactly small," Mamma replies.

"And you are?" asks the woman, looking her up and down.

"Mariana Monteleoni, cook, waitress, and second housekeeper."

"Very good. I'm Graziana Armaroli Ricasoli, but everyone calls me Graziella."

"More like Drisella," I murmur, but Donatella hears me and elbows me in the ribs.

"Easy, dear," she hisses.

Graziana holds out the back of her ringed hand to us. "Well?" she asks impatiently.

"Well, what?" repeats Donatella.

"I'm a countess. Are we no longer kissing hands?" Graziana, outraged, turns to her husband. "Ferdy! They won't kiss my hand."

"Women don't kiss other women's hands," points out Donatella, an etiquette teacher.

"What about a bow? Or a curtsy?" asks Ferdy.

"We never once bowed for Count Ricasoli," I point out. "And in any case, the title lapsed with Umberto's death—he had no direct heirs."

"What?" Graziana doesn't like this news at all. "Ferdy, do something! I've already ordered the business cards and a letterhead. Write to the prime minister. Indeed, no, to the president of the Republic!"

"Don't hold your breath waiting for an answer," I say.

Graziana withdraws her hand in a huff. "We have a lot of work to do here when it comes to manners," she comments, throwing her cigarette onto the pavement and crushing it with her sky-high heel.

Le Giuggiole isn't mine. I have no rights to the property, but I grew up here and the Armarolis' lack of respect is already making me hate them. I wish I could make her pick up that cigarette butt with her tongue.

"So?" she says brusquely, clapping her hands as if we were dogs. "Are you going to show us the house or not?"

Donatella scrutinizes them icily. "Follow me."

Mamma and I join the convoy, a few steps behind.

"If these are the new owners, I'll resign," she mutters. "I'll definitely resign."

"Why waste such an excellent opportunity to spit on their plates?"

"I actually have some soup on the stove."

Donatella leads the way into the reception room. "This is the foyer. Behind that door is the private living room."

"What a hideous painting," comments Graziana, indicating the object of her disgust hanging over the fireplace.

"It's a Chagall," Donatella points out, annoyed.

Graziana frowns. "Who?"

"Marc Chagall," she repeats, edging toward implosion. "I had the honor of meeting the maestro in 1978, in Saint-Paul-de-Vence, during my honeymoon."

"Well, tell him to come take it back; it's awful. There should be a portrait of Count Armaroli Ricasoli in the foyer. And maybe some leopard-skin rugs instead of these old carpets."

Not surprisingly, Ferdy nods. "Darling, you have impeccable taste, as always."

Donatella sighs, trying to maintain control of herself. "If you'll go upstairs, I'll show you the primary suite."

"I'd rather go downstairs," Ferdy objects. "I'd love to see the legendary cellars."

"I look after the cellars," I say. The cellars are my sanctuary, the idea of letting this troglodyte down there annoys me to death. I could turn off the lights, push him down the stairs, and make it look like an accident . . .

"Ah, a woman," he notes with a skeptical air.

"What an eye," I can't help but reply.

He doesn't understand my sarcasm. "You know something about wine?"

"I only have a degree in agriculture and a concentration in enology," I reply. "Nothing serious."

"Ah, from school!" he exclaims in a voice tinged with reproach. "Wine isn't learned from books. You have to travel and I—if I say so myself—I've seen the world. I'll have a lot to teach you. Come with me to the cellar."

I lead the way while he babbles on about what an expert he is at tasting, and I pray that God makes me momentarily deaf.

"Here we are," I say, opening the heavy wood and wrought iron door.

"Huh," Ferdy moans, scanning the room through the dim light, with the lanterns barely illuminating the rows of bottles. "That's all?"

"There are hundreds of wines," I reply with bewilderment. "All rare labels." I approach one of the racks and remove a bottle worth over a thousand euros. "This Amarone della Valpolicella is practically impossible to find. And this Barolo Riserva too."

"Yes, but where are the champagnes?"

"Champagne?" I ask.

"What kind of collection has no champagne?"

I cross the cellar, unnerved by his attitude.

"And among the French bottles, here we have very fine DRC Romanée-Conti. The count highly appreciated the Sauternes Château d'Yquem." But the labels I mention, which would normally send any connoisseur into a fit of rapture, have no effect on him.

"No Dom Pérignon? No Cristal?"

I could get into it with him, but I prefer to mock him instead. "I can let you taste a wine from a case that cost the count almost half a million at a Sotheby's auction. He won an all-out bidding war against a Saudi emir."

At the mention of the words "half a million" and "Saudi emir," Ferdy's antennae perk up. "Interesting."

"Wait here. I'll fetch it from the vault."

Ferdy almost faints at the word *vault*. Obviously there is no vault nor, much less, is there a case of wine bought at auction. I go into the pantry, take the very cheap carton of wine that Mamma uses for cooking, and pour it into an empty bottle.

I put my index finger between my lips and imitate the noise of a powerful cork pop, then I leave the pantry with the open bottle in one hand and a cork in the other, which I pretend to smell.

"Is that it?" he asks me eagerly.

"Yes," I say, placing it theatrically on a barrel. "It is a Crétin Casse Couilles from 1868 that belonged to Emperor Napoleon III, one of six bottles found in the basement of the Louvre. Do you see how the label is worn?" If it's worn, it's because this bottle has been washed, filled, emptied, and washed again dozens of times. "Perfect hygrometric storage conditions."

"A wine for royalty. Now you're talking," he gloats, without even realizing I've just called him a *crétin casse coullies*, a pain-in-the-ass idiot.

I make a production out of pouring it for him. "It has a complex bouquet. Few palates can truly appreciate it . . ."

But Ferdy, who is excited at the idea of tasting a wine that belonged to the royal family, snatches it from my hand. "Give me the glass."

"If you allow me, I'll pour myself just a taste, to check that the organoleptic structure has not been altered." I bring a second glass to my lips and pretend to savor it in a considered manner. "Forest notes of juniper berries and pine, woody but fragrant aroma," I say, completely at random. "Full bodied, slightly sweet, with a tannic finish." If he were truly an expert, he would debunk me here, since I'm talking about tannins in a white wine, as opposed to a red.

Ferdy takes a sip, then two. "Excellent," he comments. "The juniper is lush, aromatic. And then, the tannins, so . . . powerful."

"Indeed," I agree, laughing to myself. What an imbecile.

A heated uproar upstairs draws our attention, and we go back up.

In the hall, Mamma, Donatella, and Graziana are arguing.

"It's out of the question," says Donatella in her typical icy tone.

"Never, ever," decrees Mamma with folded arms. "Over my dead body."

"What is it, Cicci?" Ferdy asks his wife.

"The servants refuse to wear the uniform with the white apron, gloves, and crest."

Ferdy shakes his head. "How could that be?"

"I cook, I clean, I tend to the garden; it would all be impossible dressed as a mannequin."

"What kind of counts will we be without uniformed staff?" Graziana whines.

"You'll just have to find other staff." Donatella would never abandon her Chanel-style suits and pearl necklaces.

The uniform battle is interrupted by a loud knock at the entrance.

Donatella, who has zero interest in a debate, goes to open the door, ignoring Graziana, who threatens her immediate dismissal.

On the doorstep there is a young man dressed in a dark suit and tie, with slightly disheveled red hair and lively blue eyes, accompanied by a woman with the same coloring and a decidedly more affected air.

"Good evening, everyone," he greets us in an Italian that's beyond rusty. The "good evening" is addressed to everyone present, but I notice that his gaze has fallen on my sister, who has emerged from the kitchen.

"I beg your pardon. Who are you?" asks Donatella.

Before he can answer, I beat him to it. "Carletto!"

5

Michael

I never thought I'd set foot in Chianti again, and yet here I am.

In the taxi to Belvedere, the golden hilltops undulate before my eyes and the cypresses stand thin and pointed under a rosy sunset. It all comes back to me.

To avoid an hour of small talk with the taxi driver about why I'm here, if I like Italy, the usual chitchat, I pretend not to understand a word of Italian and instead scroll through old emails.

I told Saxton I'd take a holiday, but in reality, I've secretly arranged to keep working through Penny, with whom I've set a very tight schedule of webcam meetings with all my clients. I bought her silence with a Chelsea lifetime season ticket.

When I see the sign that says "Welcome to Belvedere, Chianti," I give the taxi driver the address of the estate, but he takes at least five wrong turns, given that there are no signposts along the main street.

As he reverses for the sixth time, I spot an unmarked private lane just off the provincial road. There, a familiar clue sparks my memory.

"Turn right," I tell him, forgetting I shouldn't speak Italian. I point to a little brick pillar supporting a small enclosure with a flickering candle inside. "I recognize that votive column to the Madonna."

"You've been here before?"

"A long time ago," I admit.

The driver turns, and we climb the hill up to an elaborate but ramshackle wrought iron gate that's hanging open.

"Here we are," he announces.

"The house is at the end of the drive," I tell him.

"I know," he replies. "But this path isn't paved. It's all rocky and full of potholes. This is a car, not a tractor."

"How do you expect me to get there?"

"On foot, of course!" he replies, as if it were the most natural solution in the world.

"But it's half a mile away!"

"Get moving! It's good for your health," he encourages me. "That'll be seventy-two euros."

During my hike along the dusty drive, as I lug my suitcase over the stones, I think *Who got you into this mess?* And immediately after: *Damn you, Charles.*

I mentally list all the alternatives to this drudgery that I could have chosen for my month off:

1. A holiday in the Caribbean, under a palm tree, a mojito in hand

2. A trip on the Trans-Siberian Railway from Moscow to Vladivostok and back

3. Volunteering in India

4. A quantum physics class

5. Collecting tangerines on a kibbutz

After a thousand curses, I arrive at the villa. It looks exactly the same. I grab the aged brass ring hanging from the jaws of the lion and knock. Nothing.

I knock again, harder, but nothing. Tired, dusty, and impatient, I pick up the phone to call Charles but realize it's still in Airplane Mode. As soon as I switch it off, I find a message from him.

We're all in town for the Festival of the Assumption. Meet us there.

At this moment, my desire to take part in a village festival is zero. But since the alternative is to stay here, perched on the steps until my friend returns, I decide I might as well join them.

6

Elisa

"How many more years do you think they'll have us manning the drinks station?" I ask Lucia, my faithful sidekick for every tedious village social gathering.

"As long as we can tell red from white through our cataracts and Alzheimer's doesn't stop us from counting change," she replies, replacing an empty barrel.

The mid-August festival is one of four cardinal points of Belvedere's social life, together with patron saint's day, the spring fair, and the grape harvest.

Those considered undesirable for marriage, like Lucia and me—me because I wear the scarlet letter of single motherhood and Lucia because she's too close to forty—are made to set up the gazebos or serve drinks while the village's aspiring brides show off on the dance floor, hoping to catch the eye of a fellow reveler. From here, at least, I can keep watch over the corner where my daughter has gathered with her classmates, even though she always tends to be a little left out. It's partly my fault, since I don't let her go out in midriff tops and cutoffs like the other girls, but she's only thirteen, for goodness' sake!

"The smiling singles are somehow never stuck behind the counter all evening," I observe. "Their looks would be ruined by tomato jelly–stained aprons and hygienic hairnets."

Belvedere village festivals tend to attract curious people from San Casciano to Castelnuovo Berardenga and even from as far as Florence: a truly great opportunity to trawl for a husband.

It's not rare, in fact, for someone to end up showered with rice within six months of one of these events.

"Pity the wives seem to overlook the fact not all the men dance, but they all have at least one drink," Lucia giggles.

"Not Carletto," I say, nodding toward my rediscovered childhood friend, on whom everyone was transfixed. "He doesn't drink."

Lucia raises her eyes to the sky, making the sign of the cross.

"Begone, Satan."

"He was always a good boy . . . too good. He used to take the blame when Michael and I stirred up trouble. He was incapable of lying and gave in to the slightest questioning."

"Handsome, rich, and a little dumb: everything it takes to win golden bachelor of the year. Though from the looks of things, he only has eyes for your sister."

My sister usually dodges these village festivals like stones; on Saturdays she has a nail art masterclass in Florence, and when it's over, she goes with her classmates around the city, as she calls it. Tonight, however, not only is she here but she's dragging Carletto onto the dance floor song after song. "She looks like she's never had so much fun in her life."

"The Cozzi cousins are definitely not having fun."

The three Cozzi cousins are at the head of the singles pack and seem none too pleased that Charles is giving Giada all his attention.

My sister has always exceeded the aesthetic standards of Belvedere; it's lucky for her local contenders that she's not looking for anything more than a change of scenery.

"He's certainly grown out of the name Carletto," observes Lucia. "He used to be long and lanky like a Panini figurine; now he looks more like a man."

"'Carletto' is perfect. He may look different," I say, stacking the paper cups, "but after chatting with him last night, I can assure you that his Labrador puppy personality is still intact. By the way, do you know who's meeting him here? Buckle up . . ." I pause briefly to create suspense.

But I don't have time to finish the sentence before a strange buzz spreads through the crowd like a current of electricity.

"What's going on?" asks Lucia. "Did two wives get into a brawl?"

Her question isn't rhetorical. Two years ago it actually happened: Piera and Luciana got into a fight because one claimed that the other had cheated in the parish lottery. What some people won't do for a rosary blessed by the pope.

I crane my neck over the counter to identify the cause of so much commotion.

Everyone is staring at an unmissable newcomer: In addition to his considerable stature, his clothing is not exactly ideal for a village festival involving a suds soccer tournament and a sausage-eating competition.

He's wearing a shirt and tie with a clip and a perfectly tailored jacket and trousers.

"Oh, that man is prime marriage material," muses Lucia.

"Michael," I whisper.

"What?"

"That's Michael."

I haven't seen him for fifteen years, but I know it's him: I know from the way he combs his fingers through the soft brown curls that fall across his forehead. And those big eyes, shadowed by his knitted dark eyebrows, still retain the same sly spark that used to tell me when he'd cooked up a good scheme. "Michael D'Arcy is here."

I stare at him in disbelief, my heart jumping into my throat. Can one single moment erase half a life?

"Mamma mia! That's Maicolle?" Lucia exclaims. "He sure turned out all right. Enough man there to make three or four women happy."

I turn to her, panicking. "What should I say to him?"

"What do you mean?"

"How should I greet him? How should I break the ice? Should I hug him? Or maybe a handshake is better?"

"I'm sure you'll think of something—you're never exactly at a loss for words. Find them quickly, though."

"Why?"

Lucia nods toward the counter. "Because he's here."

I gulp, my heartbeat accelerating so much I can feel it in my ears. I inhale forcefully, trusting in the surge of oxygen to recover my faculties. I walk toward Michael with my lips stretched into an uncontrollable smile.

"Finally," he says. Like Carletto, his Italian is still in good shape, even if his accent betrays years of no practice.

"Hi," I whisper so quietly that I can barely hear myself. Where has my voice gone?

"What is there to drink here, apart from watered-down wine on tap?" He doesn't look particularly happy; in fact he seems annoyed.

"Michael, how good to see you."

He cocks his left eyebrow, scrutinizing me with a smug look. "Have we met?"

The answer sticks in my throat, not so much caught on his words but on his arrogant demeanor, as if I should feel honored to be in his presence.

"Anyway," he says as he scans the board behind me with the drinks written in marker, "is the Colli Senesi in a bottle?"

"It is," I reply like an automaton. Why does he seem so changed?

"Then I'll have a glass, not hot out of the dishwater, if possible."

Petrified by his attitude, I lose all enthusiasm for our reunion. "Coming right up."

I disappear inside the tent that we use as a galley, where the smell of fried dough permeates our clothes, our hair, and even our souls.

"So?" Lucia asks me, coming in to fill the ice bucket.

"He didn't recognize me," I say dejectedly.

"Really?"

"He's cold, rude . . . I don't find him particularly impressive."

"Maybe he's just tired from his trip. Get a little wine into him and then say, 'Are you sure you don't recognize me, you idiot?'"

I nod, reassured. "Maybe you're right. Come on, help me get the Colli Senesi out from under all these cases."

As we unstack the boxes, our ears catch a conversation on the other side of the tent.

"D'Arcy! Don't you feel like you've gone back in time?" We immediately recognize Carletto's voice, also no one else here would be speaking English.

"A little too much. In fact I'm quite sure absolutely nothing about this place has changed."

"Instead of being so critical, try to enjoy the change of scene and have some fun."

"Excuse me, Bingley, are you trying to tell me you're having fun?" Michael's tone is tinged with skepticism.

"Have some of these fritters; they'll bring you back from the dead."

"No, thanks," Michael declines.

"And look at all the girls! Not bad, eh?" Carletto says, undeterred by his friend's constraint.

"Right. Certainly none up to par. In London, I can find all the beautiful women I want."

"There's Giada over there. Do you know she and her family are still at the estate?"

"Oh yeah?"

"She's wonderful, D'Arcy. I remembered she was beautiful but not like this!"

"Are you talking about the estate?"

"No—Giada. Look at her! Can you blame me?"

I am going to remind my sister of this conversation every time she takes a selfie and loads it with ridiculous filters because she doesn't like herself enough.

"You're not wrong."

"And her sister Elisa is cute too!"

Hearing the compliment makes me blush. Ultimately, it's nice. Especially when I'm dressed like a recycling bin.

"If I remember Elisa correctly, time certainly can't have done her any favors."

I wasn't exactly expecting praise, but Michael's comment still takes me off guard.

"You were friends," objects Carletto. "And she's changed a lot."

"Yes, Bingley, but Elisa was always a tomboy, not some great beauty. I can see why you'd fancy Giada, but Elisa's personality is all she has going for her."

I stare bitterly at the bottle of Colli Senesi in my hands. In three blows, Michael has managed to strike down what little self-esteem I had.

"Hey," Lucia consoles me, lifting my chin. "You don't care what someone you haven't seen in fifteen years thinks of you, eh?"

"Noo! Why would I?" I wish I really believed that, but inside I'm burning with rage. All-consuming rage.

I leave the tent but without the bottle.

"Sorry, my wine?" Michael asks arrogantly.

"I'm sorry, all I have to offer is my personality, but I'm sure one of your beautiful London ladies will fetch it. Asshole."

I tear off my apron emblazoned with the words "Pianigiani Award-Winning Charcuterie" with the motto "Even a shoe is delicious if it's fried" and throw it at him. My shift is decidedly over.

7

Michael

"Michael, what's with that face?" Bingley asks when I join him.

"I think I've just made what Oxford might define as 'a total ass of myself,'" I snort. "Do you remember when I said all Elisa had going for her was her personality and that in London I can find all the beautiful women I'd ever want?"

"How could I forget? That was all of five minutes ago. Why?"

"Well, Elisa heard me. She was the woman at the drinks counter who took my wine order."

Rather than commiserate with me, Bingley bursts out laughing. "And you didn't recognize her?"

"Who can recognize a person after fifteen years, especially when they're disguised with an apron and a hairnet?" I reply, piqued.

Bingley picks up a spade leaning against the wall and hands it to me. "Here."

"What do you expect me to do with this?"

"Dig yourself a grave," he says, laughing. "Or smack yourself in the head."

"I appreciate your support."

"Among other things, Elisa is more than a wee bit touchy. If you offend her, you might get a deathbed pardon."

"I can imagine," I mutter.

"Sorry!" he offers.

"You know I'm no good at apologizing," I reply. It's just not in me. I hate apologizing, and even if I did it, it should be spontaneous, not out of obligation.

"You're allergic to three phrases: 'Excuse me,' 'I'm sorry,' and 'I made a mistake.' But know that just because you never admit you're wrong doesn't mean you're never wrong."

"I'll think about it," I murmur through gritted teeth.

"Come up with a nice speech and deliver it tomorrow," Charles exclaims, impervious to my sarcasm. "And if I don't see you around tomorrow, I'll call the homicide detectives, because when Elisa's done with you, there won't be anything left to do but identify your body."

8

ELISA

"He didn't recognize you?!" asks Mamma, barely looking up from her hand of cards. She and Donatella left the party before I did, and I arrive home to find them playing burraco in the living room of the annex.

"Yes, but that's not all!" I proclaim. Here I was, worried about how to break the ice. I should have broken the ice on his head. "He spoke to me so arrogantly, as if I were his servant. And then, thinking I couldn't hear him, he called me a shrew."

"Did he actually say that?" asks Donatella, perplexed.

"Not exactly," I correct myself. "He said all I had going for me was my personality. Same thing."

"You surprise me, dear," she replies. "You've never cared about compliments or beauty standards. Why let this get to you?"

"I think most people would take it the same way." I don't know if I'm more hurt by his comment about my looks or by the fact that he didn't remember me. I never forgot him. He's in some of my favorite memories. "He made me feel like a nobody."

"Who made you feel like a nobody?" Linda interjects as she appears in the kitchen. I thought she was already in bed.

"Nobody," I snap back. Sooner or later, she'll give me a heart attack. "Are you hungry, Little Cub? Do you want some biscotti?" I say, hoping to change the topic.

"No, I had some when we got back."

Mamma lifts the cloth from the pan. "They're the ones with chocolate chips that you like so much!" she insists.

"Okay, I'll take two more," Linda says, holding out her hand. Good thing my daughter didn't inherit my metabolism.

Deep down, Mamma is happy to be able to feed my daughter. That's how she shows her affection, by fattening people up. And boy did she show me a lot of affection.

"Hey, Little Cub, do you want to sleep in the big bed with me? We can watch a *Ulisse* rerun on Rai Storia."

"I don't feel like it," she flatly dismisses me.

"Did you have fun at the party?" I ask. Dialogue with her is growing increasingly difficult.

"Yeah."

"What did you and your friends do?"

"Nothing," she replies, following what has by now become a script. "Okay, I'm going to bed."

"Oh, Linda, I wanted to let you know there's a new guest joining the Bingleys."

"Michael D'Arcy," she tells me.

"How did you know?" I ask her in surprise.

"Belvedere's Facebook page. Everyone's commenting on the photos from tonight."

Good heavens, is there anything in this village that doesn't enter the rumor mill in less than twenty seconds?

"Well, if you meet him, tell him you're Donatella's great-niece," I say.

"Why would I do that?"

"Because . . . because . . . I don't quite trust him." It's not exactly the truth, but it's not a lie either. "Tell him your parents travel abroad a lot, and you stayed to study here in Italy."

Linda shrugs. "Whatever." In total indifference, she disappears up the stairs. I wait to hear her bedroom door close, then I turn to Donatella and Mamma. "You two as well: not a word to Michael, understand?"

"Elisa, that child is your spitting image. How do you plan to pretend she isn't your daughter?" Donatella scolds me.

"He's not exactly observant. After all, he didn't even recognize me."

"You're so harsh," says Mamma, who has always had a soft spot for Michael. "You've changed a lot over the years, and he has too. If Carlo hadn't introduced me to him, I wouldn't have recognized him either."

"But he didn't give you the cold shoulder," I reply.

"The cold is great for anti-aging, dear. If the boiler at the villa actually worked, maybe we wouldn't look so fabulous," comments Donatella.

"I came looking for some female solidarity, but I see you're all Team Michael, so I'm turning to my only source of consolation," I announce, plucking a carton of ice cream from the freezer. "Good night, everyone."

I go up to my room and throw myself on the bed to start shoveling my *stracciatella*. I don't generally use food as an outlet, but tonight I need it. Plus it's soy, and soy doesn't count.

As a child I had weight problems. I liked to eat, especially junk food and especially between meals. I'd have seconds for every course, and I never left the house without sweets in my pocket. My fat rolls may have inspired tenderness, but I wasn't doing myself any favors. I had to straighten out and lose weight, if for nothing else than for my health.

Saying goodbye to bad habits was hard, but I'm proud of every pound I lost, of every inch I lost, of being able to run for more than a minute without collapsing on the ground panting, of living in a body that finally gives me one hundred percent.

I know I haven't exactly become a top model—it was hardly the goal—my size 4 jeans are a tad too snug before my period, but when I look in the mirror, I can say I like myself.

I've learned to love myself, if not in the same way every day. I feel affection for that clumsy, chubby teenager because she managed to discipline herself, and I don't tolerate anyone making fun of her. Not even Michael. Especially not Michael, because as kids he never, ever dared to comment on my appearance.

So what's changed? How did he forget about me?

Instinctively, I grab my phone from the bedside table, and just like Giada, I start wandering around the room, looking for a signal. Nothing, as if we were in a submarine.

I go up to the dormer in the attic, which seems to be the only place blessed by Saint Telecom, and sit on the wooden windowsill with the phone pointed to the sky.

I type "Michael D'Arcy" in the search bar and click on the first result. It's the About Us page of a London company, Saxton & D'Arcy, investment stuff, and under Michael's photo, there's the word *partner*. The bio summarizes his brilliant academic and work achievements, but I focus on his image.

He's not disheveled like he was in tonight's heat. He's dazzling, with his brown hair artfully cascading over his forehead like he just got out of bed, the half smile of someone who knows he's in the right place at the right time, and a tailored suit.

I find myself struggling to see my childhood friend's face in his chiseled features, his sharp jaw, and his sculpted cheekbones, which are decidedly masculine and have nothing to do with Michael's innocence as a child.

I focus on his eyes, on his changing irises that are still blue or green, depending on the light, always lit by a funny little spark, as if he were devising another prank to pull or holding a secret that, back then, he would have shared only with me.

This man has the same eyes as my Michael, but I wonder how much of him is left beyond that.

One thing is certain: A man like Michael hasn't set foot in Belvedere for years, and in t-minus twenty-four hours, every mother and daughter in the village is certain to have him in their crosshairs.

9

Michael

Cock-a-doodle-doo.

Cock-a-doodle-doo.

Cock-a-doodle-doo.

I wake with a start, dazed from my interrupted REM cycle.

What the . . .

Cock-a-doodle-doo!

Through the window, the piercing crow of the rooster is amplified as it reverberates off my bedroom walls.

I rub my eyes and grope around for my watch on the bedside table. Five a.m.?

No chance. I refuse to get up at five. I don't wake up that early for work, let alone when I'm on holiday.

I flop back down again, but as soon as my head hits the pillow, the bird is back at it.

Cock-a-doodle-doo.

I take two pillows from the mountain surrounding me and muffle my ears. Okay, now we're talking.

I'm about to drift back to sleep when the *cock-a-doodle-doo* erupts more violently than before. What's happening? I lift my head to find that perched on my windowsill is . . . a parrot?!

That's right, a bright-green parrot with a red head singing *cock-a-doodle-doo*.

I start to question my grip on reality.

Undaunted, the parrot looks at me first with one eye, then with the other, and . . . *Cock-a-doodle-doo* . . .

Bam!

"Take that!" I exclaim, hurling my pillow at him as he flies away.

Okay, so I won't be going back to sleep. Why not check the news. I open the app on my phone, but there's no network.

I search for a Wi-Fi signal, but my brand-new phone detects nothing. No network, no Wi-Fi . . . maybe I need to update the operating system.

I turn on the old tube TV, which looks like some kind of antique prop, though the remote control on the bedside table suggests it might actually work.

The speaker crackles as flickering images appear on the faded screen. I flip through one channel after another. "Where on earth are the international channels?"

I have millions in investments to manage. I can't not have access to the news in real time!

I'm not one to give up, but the only channel I can get is the local home-shopping network.

"Eat whatever you like, whenever you like, and watch the kilos melt away! Ladies and gentlemen, finally, straight from Brazil, a miraculous musk ointment found exclusively in the rainforests of Manaus. Just for today, two for one at the extraordinary reduced price of not three hundred, but two hundred euros! Just a slather before bed, and you'll be half a kilo lighter by morning, guaranteeeeed! Do you understand?" shouts the seller.

I switch off the TV, unnerved.

I need a shower. I drag myself to the bathroom, which, I'm relieved to admit, is up to par. For all intents and purposes, it is a bathroom, with a big Carrara marble bathtub, a long vanity, a shower that might as well be a fairground, and a stupendous coffered ceiling with all its original details.

When we came here as kids, we slept in the more spartan rooms. Not that we cared much about luxury back then.

I open the tap and jump in, but after less than two minutes, it goes from lukewarm to cool, to melted snow directly from the Himalayas. "Fuck!" I exclaim with a jump. I turn the knobs but nothing happens. It's still freezing, and my mood takes a definitive nosedive.

I dry off and go back to my room to get dressed, only I don't see my suitcase anywhere. Where did I put it?

I replay everything I did yesterday, but I can't remember putting it in my room. Maybe I left it downstairs. When did I last see it?

So . . . I had it in the taxi at the Florence airport, dragged it with me on foot to the villa, then dragged it back into the taxi when I reached the fair in Belvedere and . . . "I left it in the trunk!" I shout, punching the bathroom door.

All I need now is coffee.

I pull on my clothes from yesterday, except the jacket, and go downstairs, but on the way down, I notice something I hadn't before: The house looks neglected. For such a historic villa, I'd expect to see signs of age, but this place actually seems as if it's been abandoned, with cracked walls darkened by dust, warped doors, and threadbare curtains, not quite as I remembered it.

In the kitchen I find Mariana, already busy at the stove, and a girl sitting at the table. She gets up, takes a banana from the fruit bowl, says goodbye and leaves, as Mariana says: "See you at lunch, Linda."

"Good morning," I say as I enter.

"Oh, hello, Michael. You're up early!"

"Yes . . . a parrot with an identity crisis came to cock-a-doodle-doo on my windowsill at dawn."

"So you've met Renato!" she gushes.

"Renato?"

"Count Umberto's parrot. He always carried him on his shoulder, like a pirate, and taught him to speak."

"And to act like a rooster."

"Renato repeats everything he hears."

"I hope he got the message not to wake me at five again. Oh, I think my shower is broken—last night everything was fine, but this morning the water was freezing."

Mariana sighs. "The boiler broke; it doesn't heat much water. We have to get a new one. In reality, we need a whole new system. It leaks everywhere, and that's just for starters."

Very good, this is good news, Charles will be happy about it. "Speaking of things to fix." I turn practical. "Is there a cell phone repair shop in town? I can't connect to the Wi-Fi; my phone must be broken."

"We don't get Wi-Fi here. They don't service us. There's a data signal, though, but it only works outside because the walls are too thick. Are you hungry?"

"What do you mean, no Wi-Fi?" I ask, horrified, hoping I've misunderstood. "And what do you mean I can only get data outside?"

"It can feel a bit isolated here, but you'll adapt."

"I can't adapt. I have things to do. I have to work. How can I do anything without Wi-Fi?"

"You'll rest," she replies peacefully.

"What about TV? Where can I watch cable? BBC, CNN, Fox, Bloomberg . . ."

"At Mario's bar. He has a satellite dish so they can watch the games. Would you like a fresh, hot raisin roll?"

"I have to make myself a coffee," I say in an attempt to maintain control, which I feel is one short step from slipping away. "Where's the Nespresso?"

"The what?"

"The Nespresso," I repeat. "The coffee machine."

"We only have a percolator here."

"Everyone uses Nespresso," I say, amazed that Mariana doesn't even know what it is. "Compact machines, coffee on demand, special blends . . . Nespresso—What else? Even George Clooney says so in the ad!"

I'm starting to panic: no Wi-Fi, fickle data, no satellite dish, the boiler doesn't heat enough water, and I can't make a coffee. I have to get on the first flight back to London.

Mariana shrugs. "Donatella and I drink barley coffee, Giada doesn't drink coffee, and Linda is still too young."

"Was Linda the girl who was here before?"

"Yeah. She's Donatella's . . . great-niece, she's in eighth grade, and she practically grew up here since her parents go abroad so much for work. She's very quiet, very studious. You'll barely notice she's here."

"I see." I'm not very enthusiastic about the idea of sharing my living space with kids. I think I lack any paternal instinct whatsoever. In fact, I know I do, given my preference for child-free restaurants and hotels.

"She's staying with us in the annex," she specifies, handing me a steaming roll.

From her look, I know she's picked up on my hesitation.

"Speaking of children, I heard you saw Elisa last night . . ." I can tell from her suggestive tone that she *knows*.

"More or less," I waver.

"I heard it didn't go so well."

How can I blame her? "Is Elisa still mad?" I ask.

Her look says my question is futile. "Believe me, Michael. She's changed a lot over the years, but her character is the same as ever. She's a sensitive one."

"She never moved away?" I ask. "I remember she wanted to study literature in Milan and get a master's degree in publishing."

"Let's say life had other plans."

"So what did she do?"

"She studied enology; now she manages the estate's vineyards."

"Ah, so she—"

"You'll be seeing her often, yes," Mariana finishes my sentence for me, since I'm speechless with embarrassment. "Maybe you should apologize."

I'm about to retort that I have better things to do, which is a hard sell, given that I lack the technological means to do anything, when Caroline arrives in the kitchen doorway, already fully dressed and made up.

"What does someone have to do around here to get breakfast in bed?" she asks angrily. "I've been buzzing the intercom for thirty minutes."

"The intercom, like so many other things around here, is broken. We need to fix it," Mariana replies.

"We're off to a great start," she comments, rolling her eyes. "I'd just love a slice of wholegrain bread toasted for a minute and a half, a fat-free yogurt and an unsweetened mango, papaya, and pineapple juice. I'll eat in the dining room. Michael, will you join me?"

"I've already eaten."

"Let's chat. I need to vent to someone who understands me. What a farce last night's fair was! It was just missing a ring with a mechanical bull. Another planet to Grosvenor Square, don't you think?"

God, save me. "Where can I find Elisa?" I ask with almost too much enthusiasm, jumping up.

Mariana looks amazed by my sudden change of heart. "She's at the stables, but she'll be leaving for the vineyard soon."

"Maybe I'll bring her a roll," I say, wrapping a pastry in a white-and-blue checked napkin. "As a peace offering."

"Oh, so you're an optimist."

"Wish me luck, Mariana."

"Wait!" she stops me, pouring a dark, steaming liquid into a cup. "Coffee. You're gonna need it."

I take a sip and don't know if it's too hot or too bitter. "Is this substance even legal?" I gasp, my throat scalded and my eyes and nose watering.

"Not even the devil has a roast like mine. I grind the beans to dust. You're welcome! Anyway, off you go to face the beast."

10

ELISA

August is a month of joy and anxiety: joy, because the grape harvest is approaching and we get to see the fruits of a year's work; anxiety, because of everything that could go wrong.

Parasites, viruses, fungi, hailstorms . . . and every kind of plague in the Bible and beyond.

Four years ago we had a tough time—like so many other winemakers—with *Scaphoideus titanus*, a sneaky little insect we soon referred to as *Syphilis titanus*, with the unfortunate superpower of attacking the vines with an incurable infectious disease.

This morning Foliero and I are studying some of the leaf samples he collected yesterday, which have jagged edges and brownish spots.

I'm examining them under a microscope so we can anticipate any issues like downy mildew; an increase in humidity can make it easier to attack the vine.

"So?" Foliero asks me, anxiously.

"I don't see the typical mosaic marks, nor do they have the characteristic polygonal shape, delimited by the veins," I say, observing the sample on the slide. "But let's collect some leaves from the same row and neighboring ones every evening to see if they appear. We have to stave it off for a few more weeks to get us through the harvest."

"May God give us a good one!" he exclaims, mounting his horse. "I'm going to tell Carlo and Angelo."

Carlo and Angelo are two other winemakers who work with us. A few years ago, Count Umberto bought the neighboring land, so the estate's holdings almost doubled, and we hired both of them. They could easily be retired, but they grew up working the earth, and they hate sitting around at home.

I'm afraid to say I get it. I can't imagine spending my days doing crosswords.

While I am still observing the leaves in what I call the office—just a makeshift cubicle at the entrance to the stables—I notice a dark shadow stretching across the table.

"Mariana just baked some raisin rolls. They're still warm. I thought you'd like a snack," says a man's voice behind me. "Elisa."

I turn and see Michael behind me.

Hearing him say my name has an unexpected effect on me: My breath catches in my throat. Luckily I'm sitting down.

"Hi there. So do you finally recognize me? A little slow on the uptake, don't you think?" I reply defensively, once I've recovered from my shock.

"I never could have imagined our first meeting after fifteen years would be so—"

"Grotesque?"

"Confusing," he corrects me.

"I wasn't confused at all," I counter.

"You can't expect me to have recognized you straightaway. You're quite a bit—"

"Thinner?" I interrupt him again.

"Stop finishing my sentences. I was looking for a better way to say it, but yes, you have lost weight. Plus you were disguised by that apron and hat." He holds out the raisin roll. "It has vanilla sugar on it."

"Still incapable of saying sorry, huh?"

He leans against my desk, arms folded. "You're the only person I know who would make assumptions over a pastry roll."

One thing I've always envied about Michael is that he's practically bilingual, which has made it difficult for me to win our verbal duels. That much, at least, doesn't seem to have changed.

"I already had breakfast," I reply indifferently. Feigned indifference, because I'm hungry and the roll smells like heaven, but I won't accept it out of pride. I can't let him buy my forgiveness with pastry.

Michael places it on the table in front of me. "Maybe you'll want a snack later."

We stand there, staring at each other in silence, me sitting on my stool, him standing with his hands stuffed in his pockets.

"Is there anything else?" I ask.

"I think we got off on the wrong foot," he says.

"Certainly not my fault," I tell him.

"We could talk."

I stand up, even though it gives me no height advantage whatsoever since he's still several heads taller than I am. "I have to work," I reply matter-of-factly. "The vineyards are waiting for me."

"Let me go with you. I'm curious to see Le Giuggiole again after so many years."

"I'm going on horseback," I point out.

"So what?"

"Have you seen yourself? You can't ride dressed like some city boy in your suit trousers and leather shoes."

"I'm not going to work in the city."

"It doesn't matter; you know what I mean. You're not dressed for it." I'm pushing him away, be it out of spite or as a defense mechanism I'm not sure. On the one hand, I would like to reconnect; on the other, I'm afraid to discover that Michael is no longer the person I used to know.

"I'll change," he replies, shrugging. Now, this is totally an "old" Michael thing: never give up and persist until he gets what he wants.

"You mean you brought battle clothes as well as suits and shirts?"

"Actually I have nothing at the moment. I left my suitcase in the taxi, but if things haven't changed, there should be some extra work trousers and boots here in the stables. Or am I wrong?"

He's not wrong. "Yeah, well . . . you don't want to wear someone else's dirty clothes." I try to dissuade him.

"I don't mind. Where are they?"

"In the bathroom, right here next to the office," I relent.

He closes the creaking door behind him, leaving me alone with my thoughts. Or rather, my only thought: I'm not ready for this.

What will we talk about? Weather? Traffic? I'm a literal kind of person. I'm no good at small talk. I realize I'm biting my nails, so I quickly stick my hands in my pockets, as if Giada herself were breathing down my neck. Of course that roll does look rather inviting, and it's fragrant and warm . . . Maybe I'll just take a bite while he's gone.

The butter and the sweetness of the raisins slide from my tongue straight to my heart. Delicious.

The truth is that Michael knows sweets make me feel safe, and they've always been his way of apologizing to me. When he tripped me at the stream, he offered me a slice of peach tart; after tearing a page from my math notebook, he brought me a chocolate cream puff; after he used my bike without permission and bent the wheel, he gave me a jar of Nutella.

Come to think of it, he bears some of the blame for my weight as a kid.

They say the way to a man's heart is through his stomach, but I'm no better. The first bite whets my appetite, so I take a second, then a third, more and more voraciously, until I devour half of it.

I'm about to take another bite, but the bathroom handle clicks, and I have just enough time to rewrap the roll in the napkin and put it back where he left it.

"Ready," he announces enthusiastically.

"Do you still remember how to ride?" I ask.

He gives me a sharp look, with poorly concealed malice. "Do you remember how our fights always ended?"

"You're in no position to brag, Michael. We still have an apology in play."

"Don't worry; I'll choose my next move wisely."

We weave through the vineyards on our horses, light-years away from the time we'd both ride Arthur—may he rest in peace—me in front and his arms encircling me to hold the reins.

"Not that it's any excuse for my behavior, but I have to admit I didn't expect to find you here," he offers. "Plus you've changed a lot. I didn't put it together right away."

"And where did you think I'd be?" I ask him.

"In Milan. You always said you wanted to work in a publishing house."

Ah, yes . . . sweet teenage dreams of yore. "Well, I changed my mind. Plus, moving away would have meant leaving my father."

"Ah, yes, how is Alfio? I don't think I've seen him around."

"He's dead," I say, flatly.

"Oh, sorry. I hadn't heard that either."

"Aren't there phones in London? You could have spared us a call if you were that interested in how we were doing," I hit back.

"I didn't call," he admits. "But neither did you."

Touché. I can't argue with that one.

"End of play, ball back to center. But if it's not too painful, can you tell me what happened? Was Alfio ill?"

"It happened twelve years ago, but he'd already been ill for a few years. He had heart problems and high blood pressure. I'd been helping him with the vineyard for a while, and when he got worse, I took over. Then suddenly he couldn't get out of bed."

"How old was he?"

"He was around sixty-four, but a lifetime working on the vineyard added a good ten years to his age. Luckily he didn't suffer too much, less than a month." In hindsight, knowing he had so few years left, it was the right decision to stay, though the real reason I didn't go was Linda. Where was I going to go at eighteen years old, with a little girl? "What about you?" I ask, to avoid sharing more.

"I graduated from Eton and then read economics at Oxford. I got a master's degree in New York, and then I went back to London. My brother George died four years ago, and I took his place at Saxton & D'Arcy, the family financial management company, and now I manage the assets our parents left."

The indifference with which he says "My brother died four years ago" does not escape me.

I heard about it from Count Umberto, but I pretend it's news to me. "I'm sorry—my condolences."

"I stopped mourning him years ago, if I ever was. But thanks anyway."

"How did he . . . ?"

"Car accident," he says succinctly, and I don't press him further. He and George hadn't been on good terms as children either.

The conversation dead-ends on George. I try again, hoping to be luckier. "And what exactly do you do at Saxton & D'Arcy?"

"I manage the investments of important people who are too busy to do it themselves. They put their assets in my hands, and I grow them."

"Compelling," I comment with a hint of sarcasm.

"If you look at it from the outside, it's a fairly monotonous job. Basically all I do is sit at a computer, looking at graphs or reading strings of numbers, though in reality I'm collecting data so I can make the best decisions. And I can assure you that as the assets grow, it can be quite compelling."

"Michael, the money-making slot machine. I never would have thought you'd end up becoming a cold-hearted businessman."

"And what did you imagine I'd become?"

"As a kid, you talked about adventures, discoveries, an exciting life . . . At ten you were obsessed with archaeology. We dug holes in Mamma's garden pretending to look for treasures, and she chased us with the spade. Then, at twelve, you wanted to become a skipper so you could travel the world on a sailboat, and we spent a month sanding and painting that old hull we found down by the springs."

"*Splinter.*"

"Do you still remember it?" I ask in amazement, seeing the old Michael emerge for the first time.

"We wore our fingers raw on that wood."

"And at thirteen . . . at thirteen, you wanted to be a mechanic, and we spent the summer trying to fix that decrepit yellow Cinquecento in the shed."

"Mauro the squire's Cinquecento!" he exclaims nostalgically. "Whatever happened to him?"

"Mauro retired and moved to a little house in Follonica so he could spend winters by the sea. The Cinquecento, on the other hand . . . I think it's still in pieces in the shed. Do you remember what you said? You promised to take me to Florence when you got your license."

Something we always said we'd do, but then we didn't because Michael stopped coming here, well before he could even get his learner's permit. Silence falls between us again, both of us unsure about what terrain to explore next.

"Aside from work, do you have a girlfriend back in London?" I venture. I don't know why I've brought up matters of the heart, but part of me is curious. In reality I want to know if Michael is dating Carletto's twin sister. Caroline, now as ever, is not too thrilled to be here and does her best to let it be known. She's always had a soft spot for Michael, and with her strong will, perhaps she's managed to conquer him over all these years.

"Zero! Girlfriends require time and energy I don't have. Plus, a serious relationship leads straight to the altar, and that's not where I'm aiming."

"Well, don't say that too loudly around here."

"Why?"

"You're about to find out," I reply cryptically.

"What about you? Fiancés? Husbands?"

"Let's just say I'm married to the vineyard," I sigh, stretching out my hand to caress the trellis with its lush leaves.

"Does it take up that much of your time?"

"I am the giver in the relationship, but the love is mutual," I say. "We have twenty-five hectares of vines and olive groves . . . but I don't want to bore you."

"No, go on. I want to hear more."

"Good to know. Le Giuggiole needs someone to take an interest in it, and Carletto is the perfect person to bring it back to its former glory. He told us you'd help him appraise the estate."

"He has no experience in property matters and I do, so I'm lending him my skills. Talking about real property value, do you have a range in mind?"

"With regards to land, I can tell you that ours is zoned historic, appraised at around one hundred and fifty thousand euros per hectare—that alone would be around four million. If you add the seventeenth-century villa with twenty rooms, I think we're closer to around five million."

Michael's grimace contorts into a look of admiration. "I didn't imagine that a vineyard would be worth so much."

"It's not just any old vineyard in some random place," I say. "Maybe in London you have other standards, but I can assure you that this is a very respectable property."

"Yes, sorry, that didn't come out right."

"Yeah," I agree. "That happens to you often, it seems."

"I'm more of a city guy."

"You don't say." I roll my eyes. "Do you remember when I was nine and got my appendix out? You drove me around in the tractor bed all summer. You drove it for miles, back and forth across the estate. Have I jarred your memory or did they brainwash you?"

"It's true, but you can't deny that at least then, even though I was only twelve, I was a real gentleman."

"It's true. In fact, I think I prefer the twelve-year-old Michael. As an adult, you leave a lot to be desired."

"And you don't even try to hide your disdain."

"Nor did you last night."

"You haven't forgiven me yet?"

"I'm thinking you should do some kind of penance," I retort.

"I sense a certain sadism in your voice. Should I be worried?"

"Mmm . . . maybe." I still don't know what to make him do, but I'm thinking about it.

"Like that time you made me put nettles in my underwear?"

"You remember that?" I ask, amazed.

"How could I forget it! I couldn't sit for a week. I had a big purple butt like a macaque."

"You deserved it. You put salt in my goldfish's bowl! Poor Pallino, he died such a horrible death."

"I thought he'd be more comfortable in salt water."

A crescendo of shouts from the villa interrupts our conversation. I can't tell what's happening from where we are, but I sense a strange commotion.

"What's going on?" asks Michael.

"I have no idea. Let's go see," I suggest, turning my horse around. "I hope it's not the cousins from Pontassieve, back with an army of lawyers to claim the property." As we get closer, my suspicions are proven wrong. "Oops . . . well, Michael, maybe the cousins from Pontassieve would have been better. You're about to find out why firsthand."

"That doesn't sound very reassuring," he says, dismounting from his horse.

Gathered in front of the villa are all the flittering mothers and their dolled-up daughters. They erupt in a stadium cheer at Michael's presence.

"Maybe you still have time to . . ." I say, but not even two seconds later, one of the wives intercepts us and points her finger at us.

"There he is! It's him!" Her battle cry unleashes the horde in our direction.

"Who are they?" Michael asks me, somewhere between astonished and alarmed.

"The Belvedere welcoming committee."

"The commit . . . Help!"

One woman grabs his right arm while another takes his left, both tugging in opposite directions.

"Gud mornin', ar iu? Mai neim is Giliola!" one of the ladies of charity shouts in his ear, attempting to speak English.

"Hai, Maicolle. Du yu laic cantuccini?" Fiorella yells in his general direction, making the gesture of eating with her hand. "Dis is Paola," she shouts, pointing to her daughter. "Biutiful gorl; sci is singol."

They all pounce on him, offering him bruschetta, Prato biscuits, and chestnut cake in an orgy of food and screams that makes me giggle. I could put an end to this frenzy, but I won't.

Revenge is so sweet.

"Oh, you idiots, why are you shouting?" yells Mamma, appearing on the staircase, rolling pin in hand. "Away, away! What's all the fuss about! The Englishman is not deaf, and he happens to speak Italian very well. Let him go!"

Mamma makes space between the wives and delirious daughters so as to allow Michael to get up, his borrowed shirt all spattered with dirt.

"Sorry . . . but who are you people?!" he blurts out, annoyed.

At his question, all chaos breaks out again, so much so that he doesn't even know which way to turn to shake hands.

The barrage of invitations continues: Some invite him to breakfast, some want him over for dinner, some are expecting him as a guest of honor after Sunday Mass. Every aspiring mother-in-law fights over the days on the calendar.

Michael turns to me, his eyes pleading, hoping I'll tell him what to do.

And I get an idea.

I jump off my horse and stand next to him. "Please, ladies, don't fight. Michael's not going anywhere. He'll be delighted to accept your invitations."

He turns to me, stunned. "What? Are you nuts?"

"Do you know the little penance I said I'd make you do? I found it."

An expression of terror takes over his face. "You don't think . . ."

"Oh, yes. You will indulge in dates with three damsels. No need to thank me."

"Don't you think this is a little extreme?"

"Don't tell me a man who can have the most beautiful women in London is scared off by some gastronomic tête-à-tête in Tuscany? Where is your confidence from last night? Could it possibly be that . . . you're scared?"

"Are you scared?" has always been our way of throwing down the gauntlet, and neither of us can resist the challenge.

"I'll show you." Michael grabs the saddle pommel and gets back on his horse. "Ladies, it was a real pleasure." He mimes a bow in their direction and then moves closer to my ear. "Did you enjoy that raisin roll? You know, Elisa, I think I see a few crumbs on your lip," he says, pointing.

Fuck.

11

Michael

It's after nine when Bingley comes strutting back to the estate. Is he drunk or something?

Caroline and I are in the living room partaking in Mamma's fruit tart.

I'm instantly relieved to see my friend arrive—I've spent the last half an hour listening to Caroline drone on about her day of shopping in Florence, where she was privately chauffeured to La Rinascente, the famous department store. Sometimes I wonder how Charles and Caroline can be twins, different as they are.

"I hope you saved me some tart," Bingley says, smiling from ear to ear.

"Here, take mine." Caroline holds out her untouched plate. "Too much butter and sugar for my taste."

"Seems perfect to me," he replies, practically inhaling the slice in two bites.

"Where have you been all day?" I ask him. "I thought we were going to start appraising the property."

"Giada and I took a trip to Volterra."

I try to keep my eyebrows from arching incredulously. "And it took you this long?"

"You know how it is, one thing leads to another; we got a little lost in the city. Tomorrow afternoon, we want to go to Monteriggioni. Want to come?"

"Absolutely not," Caroline replies. "I booked a week at a spa in Cortona with limited availability, and you can feel free to leave me there. Michael, I'm feeling generous, let me save you from all this provincial nonsense: Come with me."

I could give her the same response she gave Bingley. "I don't want to intrude."

"What do you mean, disturb?"

"You've booked for one. They might not even have room for me."

"I booked a double room."

That's one for Caroline. Now I'm forced to resort to the universal answer that begs no further replies. "I have to work."

"Speaking of work," my friend interjects, "have you seen the estate, Michael?"

"I have, and if you have ten minutes, I'd like to speak to you about it."

Charles nods. "Gladly, but at least let's go outside! It's a splendid evening."

"You already know what I think. I don't want to bore myself with it. I'm going to bed," announces Caroline, to my great relief. "These beds are not ergonomic; I'll need physical therapy when we get home. Plus, the pillowcases aren't even silk. I can already feel my skin shriveling!"

"Let's go," I exclaim, jumping from my seat, irritated by her blathering.

I follow Bingley into the kitchen, where he grabs two beers from the fridge, and we go out the back door that opens onto Mariana's vegetable garden.

As we sit on the stone steps, the evening breeze tickles my nose, carrying with it the fragrance of rosemary and basil.

We are immersed in silence and darkness, except for the chirping of crickets and a swarm of fireflies dotting the box hedge. I could tell Bingley he's right, it is a splendid evening, but I won't.

"Remember when you said I should extend my trip to Italy and come here? Well, Michael, you were right; I needed this break," he sighs, taking a sip of beer.

"Something tells me Giada has something to do with it," I venture.

"Giadaaaaaa, Giadaaaaa," croaks Renato, the parrot-rooster who glides between us repeating my words.

"More or less," my friend says.

"You've got a crush on her again, huh? Assuming you ever got over the one you had as a kid."

"It's not a crush," he replies, seriously. "When we saw each other again, something clicked. We go well together."

"So, is that what this is? Are you together?" I ask, horrified.

"We are spending time together," he corrects me. "We enjoy ourselves. We like each other."

"You're a fucking suicide mission," I comment, shaking my head.

"Speaking of suicide missions: Have you apologized to Elisa?"

"Let's just say I did my best."

Bingley elbows me in the side. "I'll take that as a no."

"I did it in my own way," I insist.

"You mean, badly."

"Even you must admit Elisa was unrecognizable, and not just because she looked like a juvenile prison warden," I defend myself.

"You're right about that," he agrees. "But she practically exudes femininity now."

"Well, *exudes* is a big word. She wasn't exactly a paradigm of beauty this morning in her overalls, but I'll admit that she has remarkable eyes—large, bright . . . truly expressive. And a very sensual mouth, even if she mainly uses it to insult me."

"You kind of deserve it, Michael."

"Anyway, let's get to the point." I cut to the chase. "She and I discussed the estate. I also spoke with Mariana and Donatella to get a sense of how they manage the property, and I have two rather negative concerns to share. For starters, the late count let the estate fall into disrepair; he was more interested in his idleness and eccentricities than in taking care of his property. Elisa, Mariana, and Donatella have done everything possible to keep it up, but its general neglect is apparent—inevitable when an owner doesn't address maintenance. Apart from the vineyard, everything here needs to be redone, and I don't think that would work for you, given that you've repeatedly emphasized that you don't want to live here full-time."

"Exactly," my friend agrees. "What's the second thing?"

"It's worse: Everyone is convinced you will be the owner who brings Le Giuggiole back to life, that you'll move here and transform into Sting, walking through the vineyards barefoot and doing tantric sunset yoga."

"Oh." This time he sounds more laconic. "Perhaps I should clarify my intentions to avoid misunderstandings."

"I wouldn't. You'd risk starting a conflict before we can start negotiating with a buyer."

"Do you already have someone interested?"

I nod, satisfied. "Yeah. I told you to leave me to it and it's done."

"Who is it?"

"Sergei Bogdanovic, the billionaire owner of the Green Star international golf courses. He's a Saxton & D'Arcy client, and he's looking for another golf project. He doesn't own anything in Italy yet and has been looking at land in Veneto but hasn't closed on anything. This property would be perfect: He could convert the vineyards into a golf course and use the villa as a clubhouse. If he likes it, he won't haggle too much on the price."

"Sounds fantastic to me."

"If you want, he can come as early as tomorrow," I say, satisfied with myself. "But to keep everything to plan, things need to stay calm around here. I have a feeling they won't be too fond of the idea, especially not Elisa. Just this morning she was talking to me about wanting to plant more vines."

"She said as much to me yesterday at lunch, but I must admit I didn't really follow her point."

"Was Giada there too?" I ask, already knowing the answer.

"Yeah."

"Enough said."

"You see? I was right to make you come. You've been able to take care of all this better than I could have. I know how to produce quality fabric efficiently, but I really don't have a head for real estate."

As we walk back inside, there's a knock at the main entrance. Donatella goes to open the door, and from the kitchen threshold, we spot another delegation of women asking if we're in.

"I can't believe it," I mutter. "Again."

"Do you think we can escape?" asks Bingley, looking around.

"We have to cross the foyer to access the stairs."

"What if we went out the back again, took a ladder from the garage, and climbed up to one of the second-floor windows?"

"Are you mad?"

"It was just an idea."

Donatella unsuccessfully continues her attempt to dissuade the visitors.

"Mr. Bingley and Mr. D'Arcy aren't in."

"But Elisa told us Michael was here," says one woman, not taking no for an answer. "We'll wait. They'll be back sooner or later."

Damn Elisa, she was serious today.

"Let me guess," Bingley murmurs. "Revenge underway?"

"On second thought," I whisper to him, "let's try that ladder thing."

We're about to leave when a "Pssst, hey!" behind us makes us spin around.

The whisper comes from the cupboard, and for a moment, Bingley and I look at each other as if we were hearing things.

"Pssst! Here!" we hear it again.

The cupboard moves away from the wall, opening like a door, and a dark-blond head peeks out. "Hey, you. This way."

Bingley and I look at each other in surprise, remembering one of our favorite tricks when we were kids. "The secret passage!" we whisper in unison.

The belly of the villa hides several secret passages that connect the rooms to one another, and the accesses are hidden behind the furniture or camouflaged between the boiserie panels.

When the villa was a stately home, the servants used these passages so as not to disturb the main rooms.

This one in the kitchen, specifically, has a spiral stone staircase that connects all the floors. If I remember correctly, the other passage connects the greenhouse to the living room . . .

"Come with me," the girl urges, and we willingly follow her. "Once they get an idea into their heads, no one can stop them."

"Stop who?" I ask.

"The three Cozzi cousins: Regina, Intemerata, and Pompilia, also known as 'the three clams' because once they attack, they're impossible to shake off," she explains.

So that's why Elisa chose them; she really does want to make me pay. "You know them well, then," I comment.

"Everyone knows everyone here. Belvedere is tiny. The arrival of two handsome, rich bachelors under forty is a rare event in these parts. They won't let you leave without marrying one of the brides-to-be, even if it means tying you to the village hall gate. Even if it seems one of you is already taken."

"You certainly know what's up around here, don't you?" Bingley chuckles.

"I'm an attentive observer."

"In addition to being an attentive observer, do you also have a name?" I ask her as we climb the steps of the winding spiral and she lights the way with the flashlight on her cell phone.

"Linda."

"Donatella's great-niece, right?" I ask.

"Y-yeah."

"And what were you doing in the secret passage?" I insist. "Just out of curiosity."

"I was studying in the library. Count Umberto always let me use it since he never did but only on the condition that I wasn't seen or heard, so I use the secret passages."

"What are you studying?" Bingley asks in a gentle tone generally reserved for children.

"Everything. There's not much else to do around here. You can study or leave town, or you stay and wait to get married. And considering the current state of the male population, I imagine when I come of age, there will only be farm animals left."

Okay, this little girl is strange. "So you want to leave?"

"I won't stoop to the level of the Cozzi cousins, and if I want a way out, I won't look for it in a husband."

Strange, maybe, but I like her. "You're right."

"Mr. Bingley." Linda blinds us with her flashlight. "Can I keep using the library?"

"Sure, until we se—ouch!" he interrupts himself when I thump him.

"Until when?" she asks.

"Until you find a better place to study," I say.

"Right," Bingley agrees.

"Thank you."

"And don't worry about disturbing us; you can use the main staircase," my friend insists.

"No," Linda replies. "I like secret passages. The adults behave differently when they don't know they're being watched."

What a slippery little bugger. I like her, but I'll have to keep an eye on her.

"Here we are!" she announces, releasing a latch that opens one of the cue panels in the billiard room. "Your rooms are on this floor, right?"

"Are you asking us or do you know?" I ask.

"I know."

"That's what I thought."

"Well then . . . good night. Thanks for your help," Bingley says, setting off for his room. "Aren't you coming to sleep, Michael?"

"I think I'll take a couple of shots to help me sleep," I reply. He's already out the door as I start arranging the billiard balls on the table.

"Good night," Linda says to me.

"'Night and thanks for the shortcut."

She, however, instead of leaving, remains planted there in front of me with her palm outstretched.

"Ah, sorry," I high-five her.

"What was that?" she asks, perplexed.

"I high-fived you," I explain, bewildered.

"I didn't want a high-five."

Oh no? "So . . . what did you want?"

"Did I just save you from the clams or not? I think a tip is in order."

Strange, slippery bugger, extortionist. I like her, but I have to keep an eye on her, and I refuse to give her a cent. "Look, young lady, you didn't invent the secret passage. It's always been there. We used it as kids."

"Yeah, but you didn't remember it was there."

"We would have."

"But I reminded you first. Do you prefer I inform the Cozzi cousins of your presence?"

The terror of the scene freezes the blood in my veins. "Are you blackmailing me?"

"Let's say I'm trying to make you understand how much my help is worth."

"Fine," I grumble, taking out my wallet. "How much do you want? Is ten okay? Let's make it twenty . . ."

"Fifty euros," she shoots back decisively.

"Fifty?!"

She stares me down, unwavering. "The network connection doesn't pay for itself."

"Pfff, fine. Fifty." I give up, handing her the bill that she tucks into the pocket of her jeans. "How old did you say you were?"

"I didn't say. Anyway, I'm thirteen and a half."

"If you manage to leave Belvedere in a few years, send your CV to Saxton & D'Arcy," I tell her. "You have what it takes."

"I'll think about it. Assuming the company is up to my standards."

Does she hear herself? "Get out of here, kiddo, before I take my money back."

"You're going to need me again." Her parting sentence sounds like a veiled threat.

"Hey, wait a minute. You talked about connecting to the network . . . How can that be? My phone doesn't get a signal anywhere around here."

"Oh, there's a signal. But only on the roof of the annex," she replies, her voice fading in the darkness of the staircase.

12

Elisa

When I go to the bathroom to brush my teeth, I find Giada busy putting on make-up.

It's nothing new. Her make-up and hair are perfect every morning, but today something seems different.

Her hand trembles as she struggles to apply her eyeliner, something she can usually do in the dark.

"Elisa, look at me: Are my eyes the same size, or is one bigger than the other?" she asks anxiously.

"They look perfectly identical to me," I reply, squeezing the toothpaste tube. "But I just woke up three minutes ago and haven't had my coffee yet."

"Is the line too thick? Is it too long? I don't look like Cleopatra, do I?"

"No, you're beautiful enough to stop traffic, as always," I reassure her. "This toothpaste tastes strange . . ."

My sister snatches the tube from the toothbrush holder and holds it up to my face. "Um . . . Elisa . . . You didn't use this by any chance?"

"Yeah, why?"

"Because it's eyelash glue!"

"Whaaat?!" I spit and rinse with a liter of mouthwash.

"Never ask me anything before I have my coffee. And keep your things on your half of the vanity."

"I'm sorry. I'm not thinking straight today," she says.

"I can see that. What's going on with you?" I ask, even though in my mind, I'm thinking of all the horrible ways that eyelash glue could kill me. Will it be a sudden death or a slow and painful one?

"This afternoon Charles and I are going to Monteriggioni, and I don't know if I'm dressed right, if it's too much or too little . . ."

"You're getting ready now to go this afternoon?" I ask, even more amazed. She cares a lot about her appearance, but she usually gets ready last-minute for her dates. She even has an app for her outfits so she doesn't waste time. This version of Giada, insecure and anxious, is completely new to me.

"This morning I have three clients. I don't want to be pressed for time and then find myself with hair that won't style, bad make-up, and nothing to wear."

"Hon, your closet is so full you take up half of mine. Are you sure you're okay?"

"Okay? I'm fine!" she exclaims, cheerful, her eyes gleaming. "It's just . . . promise you won't make fun of me for what I'm about to tell you."

"I promise."

"I think Charles is the one."

"That's what every mother in Belvedere thinks. Only Michael could beat him with how filthy rich he is, if he didn't take such pride in having become such an arrogant asshole. He's always been proud, but the years have brought out the worst in him."

"You talk about Michael's money as if it were his fault. He didn't choose to be born into one of the wealthiest families in England."

"No, his fault is insisting he's better than everyone else."

"Look who's talking," Giada sprays a jet of hairspray in my face. "Miss, 'No one here is good enough for me.' It's no coincidence that the only person to whom you extended the gift of your pristine flower was—"

"Shh!" I silence her with a hand over her mouth. "Are you crazy? Linda is in the other room! What if she hears you?"

"If only she did. That kid has every right to know whose daughter she is."

"It's irrelevant," I cut her short. "And anyway, we were talking about you. How did we end up on me?"

"You were the one who mentioned Michael," she retorts. "Actually, ever since he made his appearance here, you somehow manage to slip him into every conversation."

"That's not remotely true. In any case, you were saying that Carletto is the one . . ."

"As soon as we saw each other again, a spark lit up inside me, and now I feel like I'm on fire!"

"Pepto-Bismol," I say, taking the box from the medicine cabinet. "Four times a day after meals. Works like a charm."

"You take the antacid," she retorts. "It'll do you good. He and I, on the other hand, are on the same wavelength. We get each other, and he's kind, and thoughtful, and a romantic dreamer with his feet on the ground. He's my ideal man."

"I wish I had a euro for every time you've said that." I'd be richer than the Aga Khan. "Like the time you fell in love with that poet, whatshisname? The one who dedicated all those sonnets to you. It was supposed to be forever until he disappeared."

"I've uninstalled MatchMe and all my other dating apps," she exclaims, showing me her phone.

I don't believe it. Someone call a doctor. "Are you serious?"

"Serious as a tax collector."

I believe her. I'm used to her crushes, but I've never seen her quite like this: She's literally emanating light. "I'm happy for you, even though Carletto will take you around the world from New York to Singapore like you've dreamed of all your life, and I'll basically never see you again."

"It's still early to think that far ahead, but I think he feels the same about me. If we do end up together, I'll find a way to visit often . . . Even if it's just to make the wives and their poisonous daughters seethe."

I'm about to reply that it would be a scene I'd happily watch with popcorn and a Coke, when, in the silence, I hear someone talking.

"Giada, listen," I say.

"What?"

I point my finger toward the ceiling, in the direction of the voice. "Do you hear a man speaking?" It's definitely a man, judging by the baritone.

Giada nods. "Yeah, I hear it. It's coming from outside, though."

We open the window and now the voice seems as if it's coming right from . . . the roof?!

I can't quite make out what they're saying, just something about a Bogdanovic, or rather, I think it's Bogdanovic. Giada and I open the shutters and hear a scream followed by a figure falling right before our eyes.

We look down, and on the pile of enriched fertilizer bags Mamma uses for her geraniums is Michael, splayed out with his cell phone in one hand. Next to him is an overturned ladder.

"Do you think he's dead?" Giada asks me, worried, though he answers by letting out a hoarse moan.

I race down to the courtyard, where Michael is still recovering from his fall. "Were you trying to kill me?" he asks as soon as he sees me.

"What the hell were you doing up there?" Luckily the annex only has two stories, and Mamma always has a nice supply of fertilizer ready to go.

"I had to send some work emails and take a few video calls."

"And to do that, you decided to climb a ladder to our roof?"

"That's the only place there seems to be a signal."

"How did you know that?" I ask him.

"Linda, Donatella's great-niece. Big help around here."

"Too big." If I superglued my daughter's lips together, would child services come after me? "So you're making millions on our roof?"

"No . . . it was nothing important . . . a regular call. Hey, how about you and I get a pizza tonight?"

He comes out with this invitation so casually, out of nowhere, that it catches me off guard. "What?"

"To chat, catch up on all these years we've missed. Weren't we friends once, or am I mistaken?"

"You're not mistaken, but we'll have to do it some other time."

"Are you busy?" he asks, finally getting to his feet.

"I'm not, you are," I reply cryptically.

"I am?" Michael frowns, confused. "I have absolutely no plans."

"You're having dinner at Regina Cozzi's," I reply with a devilish grin.

"I haven't planned any dinner, and I assure you I haven't lost my memory in the fall."

"You're right; you didn't plan a thing. I did."

"You?"

"Yeah. And tomorrow you're having an aperitif with Intemerata and then a picnic with Pompilia."

"I don't have any suitable clothes," he replies with an obvious excuse. "I still don't have my suitcase, and my only shirt has now been fertilized."

"At the local store, they'll be more than happy to outfit you with a brand-new wardrobe. You won't find any Armani or Prada there, but Regina will still like you just as you are."

"Great," he replies sarcastically. "How can I ever thank you."

"Look at it this way: Once your dates with the three Cozzi cousins are over, we can go out for that pizza. And don't try to cancel. You'll offend the ladies."

"Don't worry, I can handle all three at once."

Yes! If the Cozzi cousins deliver the best of their worst, I think they'll make Michael think twice about strutting around the way he does, I muse as I watch him leave.

As he walks down the path leading out of the courtyard, he takes off his shirt and stops at the fountain, where he takes the hose and showers the fertilizer from his body.

I could go back inside, but for some reason I'm stuck there, in the doorway.

"Maremma infoiata!" Mamma exclaims, planting herself at my side. "Is that Michelangelo's David right here in our courtyard?!"

Giada materializes on my left. "Two, four, six . . . eight!"

"What the hell are you doing?" I ask my sister.

"Counting his abs."

"I thought you were all about Carletto?!" I reproach her. "And you, Mamma, aren't you a little old for . . . for . . . for . . ." I would like to conclude with "drooling," but I can't bring myself to say it.

"I'm old, not blind!"

"Whose abs?" Linda interjects, peeking out of the kitchen window, but fortunately Michael is already too far away to hear her.

"No one's," I say, more to myself than to her.

I may be out for revenge, but I start to feel a tinge of annoyance at the thought of Michael out on those romantic dates I've arranged.

13

Michael

"Have some more *tortelli*," Regina's mother suggests, gunning to pile a third portion onto my plate.

When Elisa told me about dinner with Regina, she failed to mention it would be with her entire family. Her *entire* family.

Mother, father, grandmother, grandfather, younger siblings, and pets.

"I'm really quite full." I stop her, but I can see she's offended, so I give in. "But I'll take two more because they are so good."

Brief, sad story: These tortelli filled with potatoes are accompanied by a more than abundant ragù, and I must have eaten about a pound of them. The end.

"Regina made them this morning," remarks Giliola, her mother. "By hand."

"I made the stuffed peppers too," replies the daughter, who has done nothing but bat her eyes at me all evening.

How do I tell them that peppers don't agree with me?

We're still on first courses, but before this, they stuffed me with appetizers like crostini with glazed onions, fig and pecorino jam, artichoke pâté, Maremma-style pork rinds and tripe, goat cheese with a honey-and-egg sauce . . . now, after this tortelli ragù, I can vaguely see the Madonna.

As a kid, I ate cuisine from all over the world, but my digestive system seems to prefer English food.

Unfortunately, I'm also too English to offend my host at her table.

"We would have liked to host Carletto too, but we never see him around!" Giliola grumbles, sitting back down at the head of the table. It's obvious who's in charge here.

"I think he had plans," I say vaguely.

"It seems he went to Monteriggioni," she replies.

"With Giada," Regina points out. Is it me or is there a not-so-subtle contempt in her voice?

I see that my attempt to keep him out of village gossip was futile. "She went to show him around," I say, to dilute any resentment.

"Oh, I doubt that Giada would interest him. She's so . . . how should I say it . . . flashy." Giliola purses her lips in clear disapproval. "Of course I'd never allow *my* little queen to go around the way Giada does."

"The peppers are excellent," I say, trying to change the subject.

"Regina is the type of girl who takes certain liberties from time to time," she goes on. "But Giada, on the other hand, is well known in the village for her . . . friendships. Let's just say if she had to hold a banknote between her knees, she wouldn't have a cent. My daughter is a serious girl. No man would want to marry a woman who's been around, don't you think, Michael?"

All I can do is nod. I don't know Giada well enough to say more.

"Plus, it's clear she's looking to marry rich," echoes Regina. "She wants to live the life of a city lady. She never left because she couldn't afford it, but if the right lottery ticket appeared under her nose, she wouldn't pass it up."

"So you, Regina, you're not looking for marriage, then . . ." I venture. Whyever would I be here if not?

"It'll be a lucky man who marries my queen! She's a good girl. Our family is one of the most prominent in the region, the Cozzi ancestors are among the founders of Belvedere. Glass of wine?" she asks me. "My brother-in-law makes this Vermentino on the Bolgheri vineyard."

"I don't . . ." The answer gets stuck in my throat because the respectable queen in question has reached a foot under the table toward the crotch of my trousers.

I try to move it with my knee, but Regina perseveres, whereupon I give her a look that I believe to be rather eloquent but which she, instead, takes as encouragement, and in three seconds her other foot is next to the first.

"You know what, Mrs. Giliola, I'll happily have a glass of that Vermentino," I say, hoping Regina's mother approaching to pour the wine will embarrass her enough to move her foot, except Giliola passes the task on to her daughter.

"Regi, dear, would you pour Michael some wine?"

"Gladly," she exclaims enthusiastically. All she'd have to do is pass me the bottle, but instead she gets up and comes to my side. She tops up the wine for the other guests, and when she reaches my side, she pours the wine onto my thigh instead of into the glass.

"Oh my, how careless of me! I'm so sorry, Michael. I'll dry you off right away," she exclaims, grabbing the napkin to dab me.

Since I wasn't born yesterday and until a minute ago she seemed like a girl in full possession of her faculties (mental, I wouldn't know, but physical for sure), I'm sure her move was anything but accidental, so I jump up to prevent her from enacting whatever fantasy she has in mind.

"Ugh, what a shame!" I say, unconvincingly. "I really must go home and change."

"Come on, Michael. It'll be dry in no time," says Giliola.

"Yes but the stain will set. They're new trousers; I got them today. I'd be sorry to see them ruined."

"We'll wash them, and in the meantime, you can wear a pair of my husband's."

"I can't possibly take advantage of your hospitality any further," I say, trying to ward off the attempts to stop me.

"But we still haven't eaten the drunken pig or the tart," protests Regina.

"You've all been very kind, really, but there will be another time," I reply hastily. The door, where the hell is the door? As soon as I spot it, I rush toward it as if my very life depends on it. "Everything was excellent, really. Fantastic. Dishes worthy of the best restaurants . . ." I insist. Then I take off like Usain Bolt.

I take a taxi back to the estate, where, miraculously, I actually feel safe.

The heat has lifted, so I find myself lured by an old deck chair under the wooden gazebo surrounded by wisteria and the elderberry shrubs Mariana uses for her famous syrup. I could use a glass of something now.

I flop down, exhausted from the buffet, and for a good half an hour, I fall into a heavy sleep, from which I am awakened by laughter in the distance.

I crane my neck to see who it is and spot Bingley and Giada.

They're practically waltzing up the path that leads to the garden at the back of the estate: He twirls her around, her skirt flaring, then he pulls her in for a kiss. Yes, that was irrefutably a kiss, and certainly not a shy one.

Well done him. Although . . .

I don't like to give too much credence to gossip, but what Giliola and Regina said about Giada is ringing in my head, all this about Giada looking for a winning horse to bet on.

Bingley has already ended up in the crosshairs of a few social climbers, and he's the perfect prey for that kind of huntress: generous by nature, a good Samaritan by vocation, always assuming people have the best intentions, and ready to trust anyone with a smile.

I got his ass back on track twice and don't intend to stand by while some vampire sucks up his soul along with his bank account—first there was Brielle, from his company's design department, and then Kelly, the physical therapist who helped him heal after his ski accident two years ago. And they say trouble comes in threes . . .

Not that I'd enjoy shattering his fantasy, but I learned to recognize slimy opportunists from a young age—my brother, George, was a master social climber. And Charles, unfortunately, is a magnet for these types.

Within a few minutes, Charles and Giada disappear, probably to a more secluded corner of the sprawling garden.

I return to the villa, and right as I'm about to go upstairs, Donatella surprises me from behind, taking two years off my life.

I turn, and next to her there is a brunette girl with very straight hair and bangs that fall like a curtain over her eyes.

"Mr. D'Arcy, it pains me to interrupt your plans for the evening, but Miss Ballini has come to see you," she announces with the funereal voice of someone who has fought and lost, and a look that says *I've tried everything, and there was no way out.*

I sigh and hold out my hand to the girl. "Pleased to—"

"My name is Chiaraluce. I'm Regina Cozzi's neighbor," she interrupts me, overwhelming me with her machine-gun speech. "I heard you were at Regina's for dinner with her family. What a shame we didn't meet there. I stopped in to bring you this black cherry cake, but they told me you'd already left, so I thought I'd come straight here so we could enjoy it together."

Eat more?! God, please no!

"I'm full," I apologize.

"Come on. There's always room for dessert. Plus we could get to know each other better."

"Mr. D'Arcy." I recognize the thin voice calling from the kitchen: Linda. "You're finally back. I was waiting for you to help me with my English homework."

"Your homework . . . ?" I ask, confused.

"English," she repeats. "Remember? That extremely difficult translation you said you'd help with?"

Linda, what a little genius you are. "Of course! The translation!"

"Can't that wait?" Chiaraluce objects, annoyed.

"I'm afraid not," I insist. "Otherwise, Linda could get a bad mark. It's full of idioms that can't be translated into Italian. You have to be a native speaker."

"And Mr. D'Arcy was so kind to offer his help." Linda plays along.

"Forgive me, Chiaraluce. We'll have to save it for another time," I say.

Linda and I disappear into the kitchen, where, however, no translation awaits.

"I told you you'd need me again," she starts.

"How much will it cost me this time?" I ask, my hand already on my wallet.

"I actually wouldn't mind your help in English. This year I'll be in eighth grade, and then I want to go to high school in London."

"Ambitious."

"An ambitious person knows how to live; everyone else is just existing," she states confidently.

"Plato?" I guess.

"No, me." Linda sits down at the long oak table and from under a white linen cloth takes out a biscuit in the shape of an S. "My . . . Mariana made them, for tomorrow's breakfast. Want one?"

"For goodness' sake. Isn't there any Alka-Seltzer, baking soda, or, I don't know, Liquid Plumbr here in the house?"

"Did you eat too much?"

"I had dinner at Regina Cozzi's," I explain. "With her entire family."

"They stuffed you like a turkey, didn't they?"

"I'll be fasting for days."

As we sit facing each other, she with her biscuits, me with a glass of lemon water, I decide to ask Linda a few questions. "Do you know Giada well?"

"Just a little. Not like I grew up under the same roof as her or anything."

"Would you say she aspires to live the high life? I mean, with a financially well-off man?" I ask, echoing Giliola and Regina's suspicions.

"Who wouldn't? At least she can afford herself the option. There's no one more beautiful than Giada around here."

"Would you say she's the faithful type?" I insist. It's my sense of protection speaking; I feel more like a brother to Charles than I did to George. "Giada, I mean. I know these are questions you don't normally ask a thirteen-year-old, but you seem like a smart girl."

Linda shrugs. "She's always had her flings, but she gets tired of people quickly. To be faithful I guess you have to be with someone for a while, so I'd say she has the potential to be faithful."

"Are you sure you're really only thirteen years old?"

"Do you want to check my ID?"

"And all you do is study? Don't you have any friends? A boyfriend? Or a girlfriend?" I hasten to add. You never know.

"Yeah, I just study. I have friends, but I'm kind of boring, so no one's really dying to hang out with me; as far as a boyfriend goes, I'm not pretty enough," she replies with a disillusioned tone that almost makes me sad. "At least not for the guy I like."

I focus. Something tells me that under this tough scholarly dispenser of maxims hides an insecure little girl who would trade an afternoon in the library for an outing with friends, perhaps with that boy she likes.

And the moment I see her dejected expression, I understand that I not only made a bad impression with Elisa, but that I was truly a giant shit.

Beauty aside—because that's relative—it's the "enough" that hurts. And I of all people should know about not being enough.

"Who is this boy you like?" I don't know why I ask, but I want to know.

"Tommaso Ghirardi, son of Giampaolo Ghirardi, the lawyer."

"Does he know you like him?"

"Are you kidding? All the girls in school drool over him. I hardly plan to join them."

"Are you in class together?"

"No, Tommy is a year older. He just finished eighth grade. He's a striker on the Siena youth soccer team and just got an offer to join the Tottenham Academy as soon as he turns fifteen."

Another piece of the puzzle falls into place. "He's going to England in a year, and you want to go to high school in London in a year. That's not a coincidence, is it?"

"I'd been thinking about it for a while, actually; then when I heard about Tommaso's offer, I took it as a sign, even if I don't think he'd care much."

"Don't be so pessimistic."

"I'm a realist. But thanks for the encouragement."

I'm about to give her some valuable life advice, when the kitchen door swings open and Elisa appears, red in the face. "You!" she exclaims in a tone that is anything but friendly. "You lying, lazy, cowardly traitor."

"You talking to me?" I ask, pointing to myself.

"Do you know anyone else who's trying to convince Carletto to sell Le Giuggiole to a Russian billionaire so he can build a golf club?"

She delivers the information so bluntly that I just sit there, stunned, like the time at Eton when Harring hit me between the eyes with a ball during a tennis match. He never had a great sense of the court . . . "Wha . . . huh?"

She closes the ten feet that separate us in two steps, her face an inch from mine. I confirm: beautiful eyes. Angry as hell but dazzling.

"Did you or did you not come here to convince Carletto to sell the property to one of your clients?"

14

Elisa

I actually wouldn't have minded joining Michael for a pizza, but as Mamma always says, if I hit a wall with my head, it would be the wall that cracks, so I refused to compromise: penance first. I set him up on three dates with the Cozzis and only after he's atoned for his sins will I grant friendship benefits.

For Giada and me, the Cozzis were a real problem in high school: a cohort of snobs and bigots that showed blatant contempt for us.

In truth, they harbored a poorly concealed envy toward Giada: There wasn't a boy in school who wouldn't have thrown himself at her feet.

While toward me they were downright disrespectful—though I was the one stupid enough to get myself pregnant at sixteen.

Those three managed to embody a true living punishment.

I'm sure that in London Michael is surrounded by hordes of Kate Middleton clones—beautiful, tall, pure, and light—but as long as he stays here, he'll have to deal with Belvedere, and Belvedere doesn't overlook a single man under forty. There's a toll to be paid.

These memories, however, don't have any power over me when I'm off in my peaceful little corner: like now, in the annex's garden, reading Kinsella's latest novel—which I went to pick up in Florence especially, just so I could have a signed, limited-release edition—lying in the hammock stretched between two olive trees, equipped with a miner-style headlamp and a bowl of watermelon cubes resting on my stomach.

Giada is out and about with Carletto, Linda is studying in the library, and Mamma is watching a rerun of *Il Ciclone* with Donatella. So I have a moment of total peace that I intend to savor until the last second. If my exhaustion doesn't catch up with me first, I might even be able to finish this book in one night.

It wouldn't be the first time I've fallen asleep in the hammock with a book on my face.

Tf-tf-ft-tf-tf-tf.

A flutter tickles my head.

Tf-tf-ft-tf-tf-tf.

"Renato, are you still awake? Go to your birdhouse. Be a good boy," I order, as the parrot pirouettes happily on top of me.

"Golf in Chianti," he croaks. "Golf in Chianti."

Huh? "Renato? What are you saying?"

"Golf in Chianti," he repeats. Then I understand him. "Golf in Chianti."

"Renato, come here," I say, holding out my right arm as a perch. "Say it again."

"Sergei Bogdanovic."

"No, the first thing you said."

"Sergei Bogdanovic, Sergei Bogdanovic," he croaks again with conviction before flying off.

What on earth was that?

"Golf in Chianti and Sergei Bogdanovic," I repeat, while feeling a little stupid for listening to a parrot with multiple personalities. "Golf in Chianti and Sergei Bogdanovic . . . Bogdanovic . . . Bogdanovic," I muse. "Bogdanovic!" That's why it sounds so familiar; it was the name Michael said this morning on our roof during his call.

I leave Kinsella in the hammock together with the watermelon and go up to the attic, which, despite the open skylight, is still boiling from the day's heat. I intercept the network signal and type the words *Bogdanovic* and *golf* in the search bar.

Two million results. Not bad. But the first one tells me all I need to know.

This Sergei Bogdanovic is not a golf champion but a Russian billionaire who built his immense fortune in the early nineties by dealing in the oil import-export business. After he moved from Moscow to London, the tycoon extended his interests to the world of sport, in particular golf, of which he is a great enthusiast and proud owner of an international circuit of exclusive clubs called Green Star.

The circuit website lists all his golf clubs: Scotland, the Emirates, Singapore, Florida, California, South Africa, Beijing, but there is nothing in Italy and definitely not in Chianti.

I go back to the search results and see the media mostly reports on the parties on his stratospheric yacht in Monte Carlo, complete with superstars landing by helicopter.

The *Nastasya*, baptized with his wife's name, comes up immediately in an image search.

I click on his wife's birthday photoshoot and feast my eyes on the parade of glamorous guests toasting on the bridge of the megayacht. While I think about the sidereal distance that divides my world from the one I'm observing, my gaze falls on one of the many photos in which Bogdanovic is shaking hands with guests. There's one man I recognize, not because he's a celebrity but because he's . . . Michael!

A strange suspicion is creeping up in my chest, so I continue to scan the results.

On the Saxton & D'Arcy website, Bogdanovic is listed as a client.

A cold shiver runs down my spine, and I start putting it together: all Michael's questions about the value of the estate, the video call to the Russian this morning on my roof, Michael's unexpected presence in Belvedere, his golf mogul client . . .

What until a moment ago seemed like a far-fetched idea now makes horrific sense.

Without even considering a strategy, I rush to the villa, prepared to drag Michael out of bed if necessary.

When I enter the kitchen, however, I find him sitting at the counter and—God forbid—in deep conversation with my daughter.

"Linda, go back to the annex," I say, without even looking at her, too busy looking straight through Michael.

"But, Mo—"

"Now." I cut her off her before she can finish the word *Mom*. She recognizes my tone, and leaves in a sulk.

"So, Michael, I'm going to ask you one last time: Are you here to convince Carlo to sell Le Giuggiole to Sergei Bogdanovic so he can develop his next golf club?"

"First, lower your voice; second, how dare you eavesdrop on a private conversation?"

"I couldn't care less about your precious conversations. It's Renato who evidently heard you talking about it. He just landed on my head, croaking, 'Golf in Chianti' and 'Bogdanovic, Bogdanovic.' I may not be an Oxford graduate, but I know how to process information."

"Ah, Renato," he comments with the tone of someone who has been caught in the act.

"You better watch what you say when he's around; he repeats everything he hears. So?"

Michael sighs, rubs his face darkened by the shadow of evening stubble, and nods. "That's right."

The confirmation stuns me. I don't know why I was hoping for a no, but I was holding on to the faint hope that I was wrong. "Who are you?" I ask, looking at him in horror.

"I don't understand the issue. It's business, not personal."

"Not personal? Of course *for you* it's not personal, *for you* it's business. But *for me*, my life will be ruined. For me and for my whole family," I say.

"Forgive me, but your life is not my responsibility, nor is it Bingley's." Michael stands up, angry. "He has no clue what to do with the estate, and I, his best friend, intend to help him make the decision that most benefits him. That's my job; report me!"

"And it seemed appropriate to do it behind our backs? When would you have told us? After the sale went through? Good morning, the estate has been sold, and tomorrow the vineyards will be razed to the ground to make way for a golf course for fat billionaires? Would you please gather your rags and leave the premises?"

"Did you come to talk or to be dramatic? Because in the second case, I'm not interested," he replies, starting to leave.

"Hey, listen up, Michael. Just because you come here from London dressed as an heir to the throne and waving credit cards around doesn't mean your time is worth more than mine. In fact, as far as I'm concerned, you have a lot to learn about the value of time."

"Maybe, but I don't owe you any explanations," he cuts me off coldly. "Are you quite finished? I'm here to do my job and to do it well."

"What if Carlo changed his mind about selling? Maybe he'd like to stay, now that he's seeing Giada."

"Then great! But what if Giada has no intention of staying stuck in this godforsaken hellhole, like . . ."

His sentence hangs halfway in the air, but it's too late, because I know what he meant anyway. "Like me. Of course."

"Elisa, I don't—"

"Let me guess. You didn't mean to hurt me, right? How strange, you never want to hurt me and yet somehow you always manage it." And I understand that now we really have nothing left to say to each other.

"Elisa," he calls to me when I'm halfway out the door. "Wait."

"For what, for you to offend me again?"

"This was the wrong way to deal with this," he offers.

"You're right; we shouldn't have had to deal with it at all." I'm so enraged that I'm trembling. "But it's done. You know what, Michael?

At first I was happy to see you again. I really would have gone for a pizza with you, just the two of us, but now I curse the day you came back here."

And I go back to the annex, thinking that he and I have never been further apart from each other than in this moment.

15

Michael

I spend the night wavering between "What the hell does Elisa expect from me?" and "Maybe she has a slight point."

I just have to lay it out for her as rationally as possible, given that her open resistance could put this entire operation at risk.

I shower, and as I'm pulling on a gray T-shirt and a pair of jeans I bought yesterday at the only clothing shop in Belvedere, Renato perches on my windowsill.

"You and I have a beef," I threaten, pointing my finger at him.

"Kill me, Levante! Kill me if you love me!" he replies.

"Oh, shut your beak," I mutter as I leave the room.

When I arrive at the annex to talk to Elisa, I find the door open with no one there, and no one answers when I shout.

I decide to proceed upstairs, even though there doesn't seem to be a soul there either.

As I follow the corridor punctuated with doors, a fireball stops me short, nearly hitting my left temple. I bend down to pick up the unidentified flying object: a blue-and-yellow cardboard box.

I turn it over in my hands and . . . Tampax? Did I almost get killed by a box of Tampax?!

A "Fuck you!" precedes the launch of a second box, the same as the first, which I dodge by ducking.

The flamethrower in question is Linda.

I approach the bathroom door and stick my arm inside. "I believe these are yours."

"Keep them," she growls angrily.

"I appreciate the thought, but I can't use them," I reply.

"Aaargh," is all she manages to utter.

"Everything okay?" I ask more out of politeness than anything else.

"No," she snorts.

"Um, okay . . . I'll . . . I'll just put them here," I say, squinting my eyes closed and placing them on the vanity.

"Now get out of here," she orders.

Given the current situation, I don't think twice about removing the object of her disgust. As I'm walking toward the stairs, however, Linda stops me again. "Actually, no. Come here."

Oh God.

"What do you need?" I ask from outside.

"You can come in; I'm dressed."

I open the door and find her sitting on the edge of the tub, sulking, her arms crossed. "Maybe this isn't the best time."

"This is the perfect time," she replies. She looks down at the tiles, huffing. "I got my period. For the first time."

This was *decidedly not* the best time. "Ah, well, shall I go find Giada or Elisa? Or would you like to phone your mother?"

"For goodness' sake, no!" she stops me, rolling her eyes.

"Perhaps a female point of view would be more useful."

"I don't need anyone's point of view, least of all my mother's. She'd insist on giving me the famous 'talk.'"

"The talk?" I ask, dazed.

"You know, all the things I need to know now that I'm a woman. How babies are made. Mortifying."

"I agree." We men have no similar rite of passage, fortunately.

"As if I even need it!"

"Ah," I say, taken aback, as I sit next to her. "So you already know how babies are made?"

"Obviously. By having sex," she replies naturally. "The man's penis penetrates the vagina and ejaculates seminal fluid, then the spermatozoa fertilize the egg as it descends the fallopian tube."

Described like this, the act rather loses its appeal, coming in second only to a cricket match in the rankings of tedium. "And do you know what all these things mean?"

"Of course, I read the anatomy book in the library. My mother still sees me as a seven-year-old girl, she'd just recite the story about the birds and the bees. She doesn't realize I've grown up."

"And don't you think that telling her that you've got your . . . er . . . menstruation . . . would be a way to make her understand that you're growing up?"

"No way! She'd just get paranoid and keep me miles away from any male animal or plant being. I'm not allowed to go out with boys until I'm eighteen."

"Might you be exaggerating just a little?"

"Look, Michael, what's the appropriate age to have sex?" she asks me point-blank.

Am I the only one who hears the fallout sirens? What do I say now? Linda looks at me with the same serenity with which she might have asked me the difference between a hedge fund and an investment fund.

"I don't know if there is a right age," I venture. "I can speak for myself: My first time was when I was nineteen. Even though I was considered 'late' compared to my peers."

"Why did you wait so long?"

"I was in love with a girl who didn't love me back, and I needed time to forget her," I admit. "It took me years."

"But if she had loved you back, you would have had sex with her much sooner, right?"

What torture. "I don't know, but I certainly would have enjoyed it much more than I did with the girl with whom I actually lost my virginity."

"You didn't like her?"

"She was nice, but we didn't have any chemistry. And without chemistry, the first time is a mess. It's like speaking two different languages: slobbering, toothy kisses; bras that don't come off and the embarrassment of not being able to ask for help; nails that scratch in places that should never be scratched; tension when putting on the condom that slips all over the place, falls, unrolls; you take another one, then that one breaks; and then you panic because you only have one left. Your hands shake; you're both kind of embarrassed . . . Looking back on it now, it's almost comical, but in the moment it was terrifying."

"Go on," she urges. "This is all very interesting."

"What I'm trying to say is that your first time should be with someone you're comfortable with, because you need to feel like you're 'together,' not like two strangers who happened to be in the same room by chance."

"Maybe your experience was so bad because you hadn't completely forgotten the girl you were in love with and in your subconscious you were thinking about how much you would have preferred to be doing it with her."

"Okay, Freud, that's enough. As for your, er, situation, I don't think I can be terribly helpful to you."

"But you can be!" she exclaims. "I need normal pads, and there are only tampons here. Can you buy some pads for me?"

"Me!" I exclaim, terrified. "Couldn't Mariana or Donatella do it?"

Linda arches an eyebrow. "I'd like to keep this to myself for as long as possible."

"I can accompany you. You go into the supermarket, get what you need, and I'll bring you home," I propose, just to avoid the painful task.

"On a Saturday?! It's the wives' big shopping day. If they see me in that aisle, the entire village will know I've got my period before dinner."

She looks at me with pleading eyes. "Please, Michael, it'll only take a minute. Have mercy on me. I'm sitting here with balled-up toilet paper in my underwear . . . don't make me walk around like that."

"This is moral blackmail," I reproach her.

"Is it working?"

"Unfortunately, yes," I say, standing up. Now look what I've gotten myself into.

When I see the packed supermarket, I turn around and opt for the pharmacy, which has a more reserved and discreet air.

I enter the small, immaculate shop and queue up behind an elderly lady who wants a tube of denture paste.

How do I know? Because the pharmacist recites the lady's request out loud. So much for discretion.

I face my turn by hesitating. Perhaps I can try to make myself understood without openly declaring what I need.

"Next," calls the pharmacist.

"I'm next," I say.

"Good, good. A new face . . . Which happens to be one of the Englishmen staying at Le Giuggiole? The friend of the count's nephew?"

He got me. "Yes, but that's not important."

"What do you need?"

"I need a box of those things that you put . . . down there . . ." I say, pointing to the crotch of my trousers.

"Suppositories?" he asks, in a tone six octaves higher than mine. "What kind? Mucolytic? Analgesic? Laxatives? My mother-in-law uses this kind with glycerol and chamomile."

"No, no." I stop him immediately. "It's not a medicine I need. It's not for the back, but for the front, those things that are only needed at *special times*."

"Understood! So Viagra then." At his announcement, all the other customers in the pharmacy look me up and down.

"Viagra? No, this isn't for me."

"That's what they all say: 'It's not for me.' Look, you shouldn't be ashamed, you know? You're not the first. Do you see that gentleman over there?" he asks me, pointing to a man in his seventies who is having his blood pressure tested. "He is Belvedere's official tester of erectile dysfunction drugs: Viagra, Cialis, Levitra, Spedra . . . nothing scares him! Oh, Beato!" he calls him. "Did you take Viagra last night?"

"Good lord!" he replies. "I lasted three hours!"

"Good for you, Beato! You're not a man. You're a power tool!" replies the pharmacist, who then turns to me again. "He's our local impotence influencer."

"I have no impotence to speak of!" I exclaim, this time careful to make myself heard by those present. "Look, it's really very simple. I need a pack of pads, okay?"

"Oh, well why didn't you say so?" he blurts out. "What kind?"

"What do you mean?"

"What kind of pads?"

Wait a minute, no one told me there were different types of pads. That is, of course I know how they're made, I've seen the adverts on TV with women who claim to go skydiving, save cats from rooftops, and defuse bombs thanks to whatever miraculous pad they're wearing, but I've never paid particular attention to the object itself. "I have no idea. What types are there?"

"I can give you these for medium flow," he says, placing a package on the counter. "These are for heavy flow, and these others are for lighter flows."

Flows? What do I know? "What is the difference between flow and leakage?"

"Plus," continues the pharmacist, "we have a contoured variety, with simple wings, or night wings, lady wings, thin with wings, cotton with wings."

I am overwhelmed by the wings. "I, here . . ."

"The cotton ones are the best," interjects a lady who, if I recall, is among those who came to the estate the day after my arrival.

"I prefer the contoured," says another, placing herself to my right.

"You should get the heavy ones. You never know," advises a third.

In short, the supreme court of mothers gathers around me, and instead of clarifying things, they confuse me even more, inundating me with questions.

"Who are they for?" "What do you need them for?" "Are they for a period or for incontinence?"

"They're for . . . for . . ." Oh, to hell with it. "They're for me!" I exclaim.

"For you?" the pharmacist asks me, amazed.

"Yes, they're for me, because I wear them . . ." Where do I put them? What am I saying? "I . . . I . . . I put them under my armpits to stop sweat stains, that's it!" I declare. I'm not even sure if that makes sense. I take advantage of the moment of general perplexity to take a box at random and slap it in the pharmacist's hand. "These'll work great," I say.

I have no idea which ones I chose, but I have to get out of this hell immediately.

Just as I've left the pharmacy, the elderly lady who bought the denture paste intercepts me. She pulls me by the hem of my T-shirt, motioning for me to bend over and listen to her.

I don't know if I have the patience to tolerate the intrusion of yet another meddler.

She holds out a vial of capsules to me. "Lady's mantle and chaste tree," she says. "It's a natural but very effective remedy," she adds with a wink.

"Look," I snort, "you're very kind, but I'm not helpless. I don't need chemical or natural remedies. I'm functioning wonderfully, thank you."

"They're not for you. They're for Linda."

At the sound of Linda's name I freeze in the doorway. "Linda?"

"To counteract the typical PMS symptoms, lower-back pain, headaches, cramps. It's just a supplement, but it makes a big difference. Trust me."

"I'm sorry . . . but how do you know Linda got her period?" It turns out these village housewives really do have antennae.

"You are Michael D'Arcy, are you not? They haven't stopped going on about you in this village since you arrived. I'm Giovanna Tersilli; nice to meet you. I was Linda's pediatrician. I retired when she was five, but since they can't find another doctor for the clinic here in Belvedere—you know, there are so few of us, it's hardly a desirable position—I continued to treat quite a few patients privately, especially for minor annoyances, so they wouldn't be forced to go to Greve or Radda. Her mother brought her to see me earlier this year because Linda was feeling tension and pain in her chest. Her breasts had begun to develop: A period will usually arrive in the following six to ten months, so that's how I know. Linda is very reserved. I'm not surprised she sent someone to get pads for her."

Reserved? Are we talking about the same person?

"So you're telling me that the last time Linda saw her mother was in January, and she's been abroad this whole time?!" I exclaim. No wonder she has such a difficult relationship with her if she never sees her.

"What do you mean, abroad? Elisa never left."

Hold it. "What do you mean, Elisa?"

"Elisa, Linda's mother, has never gone abroad that I know of."

"Elisa. Linda's mother," I repeat in a trance. Elisa. Linda's mother. Elisa. Linda's mother.

I leave the pharmacy stunned and hail a taxi back to the estate.

Elisa has a daughter?! When did she have her? Elisa's thirty now, Linda is thirteen, so she had her at . . . "Holy shit!"

The taxi driver gasps. "Beg your pardon, sir. I can't avoid the potholes. The asphalt's practically disintegrating."

"Sorry, I was thinking out loud."

Elisa had Linda at seventeen! And she didn't tell me shit!

I arrive at the estate and take off toward the annex without even waiting for the change from the fifty euros I give the taxi driver. On the driveway, I cross paths with Elisa.

"They said you were looking for me this morning," she says icily. "Is there something you need to tell me?"

I don't know. Maybe there's something she needs to tell me too. "Not now, sorry," I cut her short. "Can we talk later?"

"I have plans," she replies sharply.

"I'm sure you have many," I suggest. "But we have several things to talk about."

She snorts, smugly. "I'm going to the stable. When you've finished your business, you can find me there."

I wait for her to walk away before I dash up the steps of the annex, taking them three at a time, to find Linda still perched on the edge of the tub.

"You took your time, didn't you?"

"Not a word," I warn her, handing her the bag. "I think we're even now."

And while I watch her unwrap the pads, I realize that Linda is the spitting image of Elisa.

How the hell didn't I notice before?

16

Elisa

I pace around the stable, distributing hay around one of the stalls with a pitchfork, and every time I furiously thrust the fork into the stack, I imagine I'm performing a voodoo ritual on Michael.

In my mind, he's no longer my childhood friend but an enemy intent on depriving me of security, of everything I've built through years of sacrifice.

He's become cold, cynical, ruthless . . .

"I'm here," he says, surprising me from behind.

"Good evening to you too," I reply without even turning to face him.

"I came to talk. I have some things I need to explain to you, and you have some things to explain to me as well."

"Good intentions, bad timing," I reply with a hurried glance.

"It's never the right time for you, Elisa," he replies. "Avoiding me won't change things."

"I'm not"—I huff—"avoiding you," I lie.

"Maybe if you stopped for a second—what the hell are you doing?" he asks, furrowing his brow.

"Do you want the serious answer or the sarcastic one?" I reply, leaning on the pitchfork to catch my breath.

"As much as I'd love a dose of your sharp wit, I'll take the serious answer."

"I'm preparing Dolly's stall," I explain.

"That can't wait?"

"No," I shoot back. "Important as you think you are, Dolly is about to give birth, so I have to get her stall ready now. Unless you want to do it."

"Perfect," he says, surprising me to the point that the pitchfork handle slips from my grip and falls to the ground with a loud clang.

He rolls up the sleeves of his denim shirt, bends down to pick it up, scoops up a much more generous load of hay than I ever could, and looks at me defiantly. "Where should I put it?"

"In the box at the back."

Michael nods, satisfied. "Sure thing." He goes back and forth, giving me smug looks like: *See? You think I couldn't do it?*

"It's just hay, Michael, not lead," I scoff.

"Can I ever do anything right in your eyes?" he asks, planting the pitchfork in the haystack.

"Not yet," I reply dryly, crossing my arms over my chest.

"Shall I keep going, or is that enough?"

"It's enough," I reply through clenched teeth. I bring Dolly to the foaling box where I untie her, with Michael still at my heels. I retreat to the sidelines, out of the mare's field of vision so as not to make her nervous, and sit on the ground, my back against the wall. "Well, now all we have to do is wait. I have all the time you want to talk."

"Is the vet here?"

"The vet doesn't come for births. We only call him when there's a complication, and let's hope there aren't any, given that the closest one is in Gaiole."

"So you're saying . . . ?"

"I'll take care of it," I say.

Michael looks at Dolly and then at me. "Very good. Since you're not going anywhere, I guess now's my chance," he says, sitting next to me. "I'll stay too."

"To witness the birth?" I ask in disbelief.

"In case you need a hand. And since you can't escape, we can talk like adults."

"Fine, but we need to be quiet," I say to silence him. "We can't distract Dolly."

"Are you sure she's okay?" he asks, nodding toward the mare, who is stirring restlessly. "She collapsed."

"Yeah, the contractions have started. She'll alternate between calm and agitated for a couple of hours before entering the second phase."

"Okay."

"So? What do you have to say that I don't already know?"

"I feel bad about how you found out about the sale of the estate."

"Considering I'm the one who manages it and a parrot still found out before I did, I'd say I have every reason to feel offended."

"It wasn't my intention to leave you in the dark about everything and then have you evicted in two months. I was waiting for the right time to talk to you."

God, I wish I had that pitchfork handy now. "How about the moment you arrived, for example?"

"Sure, perfect entrance," he blurts. "'Good evening, everyone. I'm here to sell the estate for Charles, and you're all going to end up under a bridge. Can you show me to my room now?'"

"Brutal but honest."

"What did you expect? That Charles would be jumping for joy at the idea of inheriting a decrepit old villa with crumbling facilities, holes in the gutters, mold in the attic, a broken TV antenna, peeling plaster, no Internet . . . ?"

"Why sell it if it's so disgusting? Better to raze everything to the ground, right?"

"Let's not exaggerate. The property has potential, but Charles and Caroline are not interested, so the fact that the estate needs so much maintenance is just an incentive to pass the ball to a new owner."

"Pass the ball?" I repeat astonished. "Me, my mother, and Donatella are not balls to be passed."

"It's a figure of speech, Elisa!"

"It's a figure of speech that sucks, as if we've been included in the negotiation like furniture. Out of curiosity, how did you plan to sell to us? By weight? By years of seniority? Or as a lump sum?" I provoke him.

"Elisa, my God, no one ever proposed anything of the kind. You're free to go elsewhere whenever you want."

"Sure. The world is full of vineyards waiting just for me! Not to mention Donatella and Mamma—one is sixty-five and the other sixty-three. Do you think there's a line out the door waiting to hire them?"

"So stay. What do you want me to tell you?" he replies. "Listen, Elisa, I know you think it's crazy that someone doesn't love this place enough to move here right away, but Charles has a different life. *I* have a different life, and if I were him, I'd do the same without thinking twice."

"Of course, you only care about money."

"I'm a businessman. I do business, whether you like it or not. Which includes the sale of this property, since my best friend knows nothing about real estate. I won't lie and tell him it's a good investment just because you don't want to lose your vineyard."

"All right. I'll try to speak in a language a businessman understands." I change strategy. "When you make investments, what do you base your investments on?"

"Market prices, stock trends . . ."

"Numbers," I summarize.

"They have meaning."

"Let me give you some numbers. Let's start with five hundred and four."

"Five hundred and four, what?"

"The number of different types of vines grown in Italy; in France they have just two hundred and seventy-eight. We also have five hundred and thirty-three varieties of olives. Spain, which is the second largest producer in Europe, has seventy. We produce two hundred and eighty-two DOP and IGP specialties recognized at the EC level, and we hold the green record in Europe with almost fifty thousand organic farms, including Le Giuggiole. We're small, yes, but here we are. Owning an agri-food company in the most sought-after country in the world is an immense privilege. 'Made in Italy' is a brand whose value I'm sure you know well, businessman that you claim to be. Le Giuggiole is not just a crumbling old villa. It's an investment." I don't know if I'm terribly convincing, but I will argue my position as long as I can breathe.

"It's just not the kind of investment I know how to manage, you know?".

"At least now you have something to reflect on."

"There's another thing I'm reflecting on."

"Oh yeah?" I ask, curiously and with a hint of hope. Maybe it's not a done deal after all.

"Why didn't you tell me Linda's your daughter?"

Oh shit!

17

Michael

Elisa gasps in surprise. That was the last thing she was expecting.

"You . . . how . . . who . . . ?" she stammers, swallowing dryly.

"Belvedere is a small town," I snap. "All that matters is I know now. You lied to me. I wonder why."

Elisa keeps her eyes riveted on the toes of her boots. "You didn't seem like the type of person I should be sharing my private life with. And even less so now."

"Were you afraid of being judged?"

"That too."

"Christ, Elisa! I don't live in the Middle Ages. Do you really think I would have been shocked by the fact that you had a daughter at seventeen?"

"I was sixteen when I got pregnant."

"Ah, sixteen! Well, that changes everything," I comment sarcastically.

She shrugs, becoming defenseless in a way I've never seen before, dropping the armor she's worn since the day I arrived. "Being a single mother in a village of three thousand, two hundred inhabitants wasn't exactly easy. Everyone stared at me, whispered, called me a bad person behind their Cheshire cat smiles. At least many of the mothers were happy to note that there would be one less rival for their daughters' future husbands."

"Why?"

Elisa turns to look at me with a quirked eyebrow. "First of all, I was no angel, and second, I already have a daughter. I'm demanding, very absent, and unappealing. But I don't care. There's no one in town whose wife I aspire to become. I don't aspire to become a wife in general," she explains.

"But why were you and Linda left alone?"

She lets out a nervous laugh. "Is that an indirect way of asking who the father is?"

"If you want to tell me. Do I know him?" I ask. Maybe he's one of the guys from our gang of terrors. "Is it Lapo? Or Cosimo?"

"No way! Lapo married Margherita." Both were part of our daredevil group.

"The girl with the red hair?"

"Yes, her. He's the village accountant; she works at the post office."

"And Cosimo?"

"We can't even mention Cosimo's name in public. He betrayed all the mothers."

"How?"

"He came out four years ago: He's with a man from Fiesole, and they opened an artisanal perfume shop in Florence, in San Frediano."

"That's why as a child Cosimo always wanted to pretend to be a seamstress, a hairdresser, a concierge . . ."

"The mothers really had their hopes up over him. It was a real drama."

"We were talking about you," I remind her.

"Anyway, you don't know the father. He was an Australian exchange student we hosted at the estate for a few weeks. He was on a trip to research Chianti production."

"A long-distance love?" I hypothesize. Although the question is completely harmless, I'm surprised to have a strange fear of the answer.

"Just a summer crush. He was hasty and selfish; I was gullible and superficial. The night before he left, having sex seemed like the natural conclusion to our flirtation. Then, about three weeks later, I realized our connection wasn't over at all."

"Did you tell him? Are you still in touch?" The questions come pouring out of me.

"I wrote dozens of emails but never sent them. What could he have done from the other side of the world? And we barely knew each other," she sighs, shrugging her shoulders.

"So you decided to do what you always do, fend for yourself," I conclude.

"Yeah."

At least in this way, Elisa hasn't changed. "You always refused to ask for help, even for the dumbest things. Do you remember when that swallow's nest full of eggs fell from the lime tree during the storm, and you almost killed yourself on the ladder putting it back on the branch? You must've been all of nine. Or when your mother had a frozen back and you worked all night so she wouldn't have to help you make preserves? How old were you?"

"Thirteen."

"You boiled, pureed, and potted half a bushel of tomatoes," I remind her.

"And I burned myself."

"But the worst was when you cut yourself with a billhook during the harvest and tried to sew up the cut with a needle and embroidery thread so your dad wouldn't freak out."

"Yeah, that was probably a mistake."

"A big one: You got an infection and almost lost your hand," I say, taking her left hand where I can still see the scar from her heroic experiments. "You were never afraid of pain."

"Maybe now I'm paying with interest for the lack of fear I had as a kid. I learned what fear was from the day that pregnancy test became positive."

"Was it hard?"

"Giada was the first to know; she took the test with me. She helped me hide it while I decided what to do, but then Mamma found out because she was the one doing the laundry, and she hadn't found stains on my underwear for two months. When I uttered the fateful words 'I'm pregnant' for the first time, I was so terrified. I was trembling. Mamma was understanding, but Dad spoke to me in monosyllables for weeks. I thought about myself, about my future, about the child being without a father, and I decided to terminate the pregnancy."

"It seems like you changed your mind, which isn't very like you."

"I was very clear about what I wanted for myself: college in Milan, a master's degree in publishing, working at a big publishing house, and then at the first ultrasound, I heard the heartbeat and was overwhelmed. I respect anyone who has the courage to end their pregnancy, but I just couldn't do it. When Mamma and I got home, Dad gave me a sandwich and said, 'Here. You and the baby both have some growing to do.' He already knew."

"I always knew Alfio was only gruff on the surface."

"School, however, was a different story. I no longer had a name. I was just 'the pregnant one.' I felt everyone's eyes on me as I walked through the halls, the buzz spreading through them, the sidelong glances of the parents at the front doors, all of them thinking, 'Thank goodness that didn't happen to my daughter.'"

"Vapid gossips," I comment, horrified by their cowardice.

"When Linda was born, I realized none of it mattered. I went into labor in the seventh month, at the beginning of July; Mamma was in Sarzana, helping her sister recover from surgery. Giada was on holiday in Lloret de Mar after graduating from high school, and my father, a good man but one who only knew about land and vineyards, had no idea how to handle the situation. There was only me, barely seventeen years old, after an emergency C-section with a sore incision, my nose pressed against the incubator to see a shriveled little bundle weighing three pounds that could barely move. After three days of crying and no one to talk to, I knew I had to steel myself and fight for both of us."

"If you were anything like the Elisa I know, you had strength for five people."

"But since then I've also been paralyzed by fear of everything. I look at Linda and not only do I feel guilty for having brought a child into the world in a totally irresponsible way, I feel constant performance anxiety: Am I educating her the way she deserves? Am I missing something? Does she feel loved enough? How much does not having a father weigh on her?"

I look at Elisa, and she seems tiny curled up next to me, her knees up to her chest, and I feel the unstoppable instinct to hug her. I even make the gesture of stretching out my arm, but before I can wrap it around her shoulders, she gets up and starts walking in circles through the hay. "I wasn't able to provide much security, but until now she at least had this house, Mamma, Giada, Donatella, and all the other workers became her family. Now she'll lose all that as well. I understand your choice from a business perspective, but as a mother, I can't help but hate you for the consequences it will have on my daughter."

From listening to her, I begin to doubt she knows Linda wants to study abroad, but I don't think I should be the one to tell her. "I understand," I reply simply.

"No, you can't understand, but you don't have to."

Dolly lets out a neigh, catching my attention. "Look, speaking of births, didn't you say that phase one, or whatever the hell it's called, lasts a couple of hours? Because that passed a while ago, but I don't think anything has changed . . ."

"Oh shit!" Elisa exclaims, looking at the clock. "You're right." She enters Dolly's box, checks her, and shakes her head, worried. "Her water broke, but she's having trouble pushing."

"Is that bad?"

"Enough." She gestures for me to get up. "We have to intervene."

"We?!" I blurt out.

"No, the pope! Yes, us. The vet wouldn't get here in time. Come on, Michael. You said you'd stay to lend me a hand if I needed it. So, great. Now I need it."

"Okay." I go stand next to her, but she looks at me impatiently. "Your hand, Michael."

"My hand?!"

"Yeah," she says, taking my right hand and pulling the sleeve of my shirt up to my shoulder. "It's not a figure of speech. I really need your hand. In fact, I need your whole arm."

A shiver of terror runs down my spine. "Sorry, to do what?"

"This." She hands me a thick, long latex glove and makes me kneel behind the mare. "Stick your arm in and find the colt's hooves."

I really hope she didn't just say what I think she said. "What do you mean, 'inside'?"

"You need to check whether the foal is face-first, which is a big problem, or if you can feel its hooves. If you can, just pull it by the hooves when the mare pushes, to help her get it out," she explains to me politely.

"And why do I have to do that?" I protest, annoyed.

"Because you have more strength and a longer arm. Come on, we can't sit around, knocking on mussels before we open them."

I have other complaints to present with a wealth of arguments, but I can't bear the mare's pained neighing. By God, we English may have some deficits when it comes to human relationships, but let it never be said that we don't care about horses. Or dogs. Horses and dogs arouse an overwhelming tenderness in us.

"Okay." I breathe in, steeling myself, and with one eye closed and one open, I stick in my arm up to the elbow. "Better my arm than my head . . . Aaah! Fuck!"

"What is it? What do you feel?"

"Bad, by God! Bad! I think the mare had a contraction and crushed my arm."

"You're such a crybaby," she grumbles.

"You can say that because it's not your arm."

"Come on, stop protesting and tell me what you feel."

"I haven't the faintest idea," I mutter, confused.

"Use your imagination!" she exclaims.

I resist another contraction and try to feel the sensations that come to me. "I feel something hard."

"Are there any holes? Like nostrils, or a mouth?"

"No." At least, I don't think. "It's knobby . . . next to the first there's another just like it."

"It's the legs!" Elisa exclaims. "Thank goodness. Okay, now grab them and pull on the next contraction. As soon as its head is out, I'll free his nose."

On the first try, nothing happens. On the second, I risk getting kicked in the teeth. On the third, two dry, oblong hooves slip out, followed by a snout, all covered in a translucent membrane that Elisa tears with a quick gesture.

"Done?" I ask, the hooves still in my hand.

"We still have the shoulders, the widest part. Keep pulling," she instructs me.

I comply without question, and the colt slides out. The mother welcomes him next to her, smells him, and then bends over him, covering him with her robust neck in a protective gesture.

"She knows it's her daughter," Elisa explains to me. "Woe to anyone who touches her."

I look at the image of the mare and her foal, enthralled. Somewhere in my head, a neuron starts up my mental record player, and I can hear "Love Is All Around" by Wet Wet Wet.

"Now we have to do the enema," Elisa announces briskly.

"You're sucking the poetry right out of the moment," I reply.

She looks at me impassively and hands me an enema bulb. "First the enema, then the poetry."

"Me again? You could do this part."

"Meconium—the plug of hard feces formed during gestation—has to be expelled as soon as possible, or the foal won't eat. Since one doesn't need particular expertise to administer an enema, you can go ahead—unless you know how to dress the umbilical cord and inject it with a tetanus shot."

"Say no more." I take the enema, surrendering. What a day.

While Elisa plays nurse, I'm basically the janitor. I hardly have time to finish the purge before the foal reacts.

"Ugh, gross!" I exclaim.

"What happened?"

"That creature put it right in my hand," I say, waving it in her direction.

Elisa is not the least disgusted. "It brings good luck."

"What's the little guy's name?" I ask her.

"Little guy? It's a girl," she corrects me. "You name her—after all, you delivered her, right? The honor is yours."

Damn. I am now realizing that I, Michael D'Arcy, financial adviser at one of London's leading firms, have just delivered a baby horse.

"Splinter," I say. "Let's call her Splinter."

Elisa turns to me with the first sincere smile I've seen since I've been here.

We had wanted to name our damaged little boat to suggest something slight and agile, but in reality we just ended up with splinters in our fingers. "We used to like doing things together," I say.

Elisa and I sit next to each other on the hay, exhausted, silently observing Splinter nursing from Dolly. "It's not that bad, huh?" she asks me.

"What?"

"Doing something good, lending a hand, making a difference."

"I must admit you have a point."

"You're a businessman. I have a deal for you."

"What's that?"

"Stay until the harvest is over. Study the estate, look at what we do and try to determine whether we're a good investment," she says resolutely. "Then and only then can you properly advise Charles on whether to sell or not. One month, that's all I'm asking."

"You seem confident you'll change my mind."

"I have no doubt," she says, staring at me with those shrewd eyes of hers.

"It seems more like a challenge than a deal."

Her quirked left eyebrow tells me it's a yes. "What's the matter, you scared?" she replies.

Me? Never. "Absolutely not."

"So." Elisa holds out her hand with a mocking smile. "Do we have a deal?"

I look at her hand, then at mine, which is still in the latex glove covered with amniotic fluid and foal poop. Almost . . . I snatch her bare palm, and before she can escape, I squeeze it. "We have a deal."

18

Elisa

"I want to buy Le Giuggiole," I announce at breakfast. Giada's toast slides sideways from her hand; Donatella drops her spoon into her instant coffee, and Mamma spills the pot full of diced vegetables for the minestrone.

I made my decision last night, after talking to Michael. If the Bingleys want to sell, I'll be their buyer.

"Does anyone know the number to call to have someone involuntarily committed?" Donatella asks.

"Hilarious," I reply, miffed.

"Darling, didn't you just say you wanted to buy Le Giuggiole?" asks Mamma. "This estate?"

"Do you know of any others?" Nice to know they take me so seriously.

"And why on earth would you want to do that?" Donatella asks.

"Well, for starters, I give my lifeblood to the vineyards, I work weekends and holidays, I get no vacation, and if I have to dedicate all my time to it—which I love—I want it to be for me, not for someone else. Secondly—and here's where this applies to you—Michael is negotiating the sale of the property on behalf of the Bingleys to a Russian mogul, a client of his."

"He'll still need a housekeeper, a maid, and someone to manage the vineyard," objects Donatella, unperturbed.

"That's where you're wrong. The Russian wants to turn the estate into a golf club. He plans to tear out the vines to make a golf course, and the villa will become a luxury clubhouse for members of the circuit," I explain. "And we'll have to take a hike."

"I didn't know about any of this," stammers Giada.

"Why should you have known? Bingley is making Michael do everything, and you've never made a secret of your desire to leave Belvedere," I reply.

"But they can't do that!" Mamma exclaims, her face now transfigured into a mask of terror.

"They can, unless the new zoning plan for Belvedere and Collalto is approved, and that probably won't be for another six months, after the new council is elected. The current regulations allow it, so as the Romans said: 'We're screwed.'"

Silence now reigns in the kitchen of the annex.

"Now do you understand why I want to buy the estate?" I say, hoping I won't get any more sarcastic remarks from them.

"What do you want? Who knows what future Donatella and I have ahead of us, but I worry about Giada, you, and Linda," Mamma interjects. "Giada will be all set with Carletto. And you, instead of worrying about all this, should find yourself a good man, with a good job, who wants to be a father to your daughter."

"Unfortunately I don't want to be 'all set,' as you put it. It would be the simplest solution but not the right one. I will not mortgage my life on a loveless marriage just for the sake of financial security," I declare.

"What about Altamio's son? He seems like a nice guy, and he's always had a crush on you, even though . . ." she stops, unfortunately not in time to avoid my piqued reaction.

"Even though what, Mom?" I blurt out. "Linda?"

"Yeah. Even though you have Linda. Whoever decides to be with you would be taking her on too, and it's not the kind of two-for-one men are looking for. Elmo has always courted you with full awareness of your situation."

"But Mamma, Elmo Colli is an undertaker!" I object.

"So what? People will never stop shitting or dying," she replies with her unassailable maxim.

"He doesn't even live here anymore." I shrug.

"But he always comes to visit his parents, and he happens to be here this weekend. You could pop in for a coffee, my picky girl."

"No, thanks," I cut her short. "You go, Mamma, if you care so much."

"Do whatever you want, Elisa, but remember that you have a daughter. It's her security you have to worry about," Mamma urges me.

"I'm very much worrying about it. And I've found the best solution."

"Where on earth do you think you're going to find the money to do this? It would take a fortune to buy this place!" she protests.

"At the bank! Where else? Italy is a democratic republic founded on mortgages, loans, and leasing."

"Of course," insists Mamma. "Nowadays, who wouldn't give you a million-dollar loan?"

"The winery is profitable; it's good collateral. Plus I found a European Community RFP for five-year nonrepayable grants for expanding organic farms. I'll apply for it—we meet all the requirements."

"How much time do you have?" asks Giada, the only one who hasn't tried to demolish my idea.

"I got Michael to give me one month—oh, and he knows Linda is my daughter, so there's no point in continuing to pretend. I'll try to get this rolling as soon as possible."

My sister takes my hand, and her perfect, enameled fingers intertwine with mine, which are tattered by manual labor. "Do you think you can do it?"

"If I don't try, I'll never know."

We are interrupted by the doorbell, and I get up to open the door, mostly to get out of the situation.

"Hi, Elisa. What a pleasure to see you."

Dark, greasy hair raked across his forehead to hide his receding hairline, sunken cheeks, hooked nose, drooping shoulders, and a prominent paunch in spite of his lean physique.

It's Elmo.

19

MICHAEL

The second punishing date awaits me at the village bar, in Belvedere's main square.

The Cozzi cousin of the day is already sitting at one of the plastic tables shaded by a faded Cinzano umbrella.

As children, we used to come to this bar to have ice cream after breathy bike rides up and down the hills; over on the wall there's still an old metal etching with the different types of cones and popsicles and the prices in lira with euro stickers over them.

"Hi," I greet her, holding out my hand. "Have you been waiting long? You must be Inte . . ."

"Intemerata," she says. "No, I just got here. I stopped by the rectory to pick up the new songbook. I am a catechist. I direct the children's choir."

"Interesting, Intemerata. What an unusual name," I observe, looking for something to break the ice. We English are masters of small talk.

"In honor of the Madonna," she replies.

"Isn't her name Louise Veronica?"

"No, Madonna the Virgin mother of Jesus."

"Sorry, I tend to confuse them."

"From the Litany of Loreto, you know? Immaculate Virgin, pray for us. Praised Virgin, pray for us . . . Virgin Intemerata. It means 'absolute purity and moral integrity.'"

I stop to study her for a moment and notice details that should have been a tell: Intemerata is wearing a long skirt, ballet flats with white stockings, a blouse buttoned tightly to the last buttonhole, and a heavy crucifix around her neck. She's practically a nun.

"I see . . . Shall we have a drink then?" I propose, nodding to the waiter who is serving the three old men playing cards at the next table. I think they've been here as long as the ice cream sign. "What would you like? A glass of wine?"

"I don't drink wine. It reminds me of the betrayal of Jesus at the Last Supper. I only allow myself the wine blessed at Mass on Sundays."

This is going well. "What about a spritz?"

"No alcohol for me," she replies firmly. "Alcohol leads to sin. When I was sixteen, on holiday at the parish house in Pontremoli with the Little Virgins, we drank Bacardi Breezers and played spin the bottle, and I kissed Massimo, a boy from the Young Apostles of Jesus," she explains to me in a low voice so as not to let anyone else in on her shameful secret.

"You could go straight to hell for that," I observe with a hint of sarcasm.

"I know." Sarcasm she evidently didn't catch. "I couldn't sleep from the guilt, so I woke up Don Pietro so I could confess."

"All's well that ends well. So, two glasses of Coke?" I ask.

"I can't; it has sugar. I've given up sweets for Sant' Antonio," she explains. I must look perplexed, because she delves deeper. "Women who pray to Saint Anthony will find a husband. I lit a candle on June thirteenth and made a vow: I will not eat or drink anything sweet if he finds me a husband. I wouldn't want to ruin everything now that I'm verging on success."

"I'm sure it will work," I encourage her with veiled irony. "Two . . . apple juices?" I venture.

She shakes her head in denial. "Eve."

"Two sparkling waters," I finally say to the waiter.

"Would you like ice and lemon with that?" he asks, with a look that I interpret as heartfelt pity.

Intemerata nods and I give the okay. "Ice and lemon! Let's splurge." This is going to be a long date.

"You speak Italian very well," she comments.

"I grew up in a bilingual family and went to an Italian-English school." I feel knowledgeable enough about education to keep the conversation on this track.

"I studied with nuns," she replies. "What about religion? Are you Catholic or Anglican?" she asks me.

"I'm not religious." Her eyes narrow into two angry slits. "But I prefer Catholics to Anglicans." Betrayal. I don't deserve to be Her Majesty's subject. But my life is at stake here.

The waiter comes to rescue me with the two glasses of water, and I practically dive into mine, hoping to drown in the cup.

"What do you think about sex before marriage?"

"Uh, umm . . ." I mumble. What do I think about sex before marriage? That train left the station a while ago.

"I think that sex should be reserved for having children," she decrees seriously.

"But children are born out of wedlock all the time," I object, regretting it a second later.

"Who would be so cruel as to give birth to a child in sin? And then how would you dare to have them baptized?" she blurts out.

"Yes, that's quite the dilemma."

"I'd like to have four girls and four boys. I'd call the girls Maria Chiara, Maria Benedetta, Maria Gioia, and Maria Incoronata. And I'll name the boys after the four evangelists: Matthew, Mark, Luke, and John. What do you think?"

"I might prefer John, Paul, George, and Ringo . . ." But her hardened expression makes me realize she didn't get the joke. "But your names are beautiful too."

"Well, parents should be in agreement on what to name their children."

Stop right there! Whose children? I don't have time to pour cold water on her enthusiasm before I'm distracted by two figures that enter my field of vision.

One of them is Elisa, in a light-blue flowered dress that skims her thighs with every step, her long, dark-blond hair swaying freely on her back. I refrain from abandoning Intemerata only because Elisa is not alone.

"Who is that?" I ask, pointing to the lanky man in a black suit next to her.

"Elmo Colli," she replies dryly.

"Do you know him?"

"His family runs the local funeral home. He's in business with his father. They've expanded to other towns too. A real shame he doesn't come to visit more often."

"Why is he with Elisa?" I ask, still without looking away from the couple, as if I were a sniper keeping them in range.

"I don't know, but Elisa and her sister will take anything they can get."

"Are they dating?" I ask.

"Why do you care?"

I don't know, but I care.

Elisa and Elmo disappear inside the bakery, and I, inexplicably, feel very annoyed.

"We were saying: We agree on names for the children. Now, I think we might have some issues with the ceremony. I have so many relatives, if I don't invite them all, they'll get offended. And then there's my mother's side, from Grosseto, who I absolutely must invite, in part because her sister-in-law Matilde is my godmother . . ."

"Do you know if Elisa went out with anyone after she had Linda? Did she have any boyfriends?" I no longer have any interest in conversing with Intemerata—not that I had any before.

"I never!" she blurts out. "Why are you only interested in discussing Elisa? Here we are, deciding our future. You could at least do me the honor of participating."

Okay, it's time to call it quits. To hell with English manners. "Look, Intemerata, I don't know what made you think I came here with a ring in my pocket. I've known you for half an hour, and that's already enough for a lifetime. I don't want eight children, I don't care about your relatives in Grosseto, and above all I very much enjoy sex outside of marriage!" I explode.

"Bravo!" the old men at the table beside us cheer with applause. "Candidate for mayor!"

Intemerata looks at me in shock, her right hand clutching her rosary. She jumps up, snatching away the songbook so threateningly that I think she's going to hit me with it. "I'm leaving. You don't deserve me!" she shouts, and then strides off toward the church.

Maybe she'll go ask divine justice to punish me.

"Oh, look at Mr. Hot Stuff over there. You have a lot of fun with the ladies, don't you?" comments one of the old men.

"I have a certain talent," I reply, bringing the glass of melted ice and water to my lips.

"We're missing a fourth player. Want to join us?"

"Why not?" I have two very good reasons for accepting. The first is that I really want to drink something other than water. The second is Elisa: She hasn't left the bakery with what's-his-name yet, and I wonder what they're up to.

I change tables and sit with the three players. Two are much older, and the other is at most fifteen years older than I am. He's wearing mechanic's overalls with a T-shirt that says "OfficeMax."

"Nice to meet you, I'm Vanni. I deal the cards because Max doesn't know how to shuffle them, and Luciano has Parkinson's. If he deals, the three of cups might end up in Pistoia."

"I may not be good at dealing cards, but my wife is one happy woman."

Okay, I feel much more comfortable at this table. "I'll have a Manhattan," I order. "Neat."

"A what?" the bartender asks me. "I have some grappa. At most I can make you a Negroni."

"Oh, Mario, what are you saying? You can't say 'negroni' anymore. It's 'men of considerable stature from sub-Saharan Africa.'"

"Negroni is the surname of the person who invented the drink, you ignoramus!" replies the bartender. "So, what will it be? Grappa or Negroni?"

Grappa? This early? "A Negroni is fine."

Vanni deals the cards and puts the trump in the center. "Fuckers win with swords," he announces.

"You made that poor girl take off running," comments Luciano.

"We had irreconcilable visions for our futures," I reply. I drop a card and lose my hand.

"Belvedere has a strange air. The good women always leave," replies Max. He's joking, but I think I can hear a hint of regret.

"Not all of them," I observe, my thoughts already turning to Elisa. Even with all her flaws, I can't help but appreciate her tenacity. Vanni takes another hand with the three of swords, rejoicing with a blasphemy through gritted teeth.

"My wife and I have been married fifty-six years," says Luciano. "And she's still the most beautiful woman I've ever seen in my life."

"The Lollobrigida of Belvedere," comments Vanni, mimicking a busty chest with his hands. "We were all vying for her, but she married this scoundrel here. She said he made her laugh."

"Laughter is the way to a woman's heart. Beauty fades, money comes and goes, but if you know how to make your woman laugh, she'll never leave you."

"Oh, what a poet! Who do you think you are, Dante?" Max mocks him. "Drop your card and shut the hell up!"

"You have a lot to learn from me, dufus." Luciano swipes back.

"And while you two were busy philosophizing, I won," exults Vanni. "I told you: Fuckers win with swords."

"In your dreams. You can barely take it out to piss!" Okay, Luciano is a genuine romantic.

"Ask your sister if that's true or not." Vanni shuffles the cards, proud of his victory, and deals them out. "Cups, the drinkers. That's you, Max! On the table."

"Go ahead and laugh," he says. "Alcohol may not have the answers, but at least it makes you forget the questions."

While the three men continue to make fun of each other, my eye falls on a couple sitting next to us: They must be around my age, they're wearing wedding rings, and she's caressing her belly.

But what caught my attention was her thick, curly hair: I remember there only being one redhead in Belvedere.

"Margherita?" I ask without wanting to seem intrusive.

She turns. "Yes?"

Then the man must be Lapo, the famous climber. There was nothing he couldn't climb as a kid: trees, gutters, tractor tires, hay bales . . .

"Lapo, Maggie!" I greet them with more conviction, leaving the card table. "I'm Michael. Michael D'Arcy."

Their previously suspicious faces brighten. "Oh my goodness! What are you doing here?"

For the first time, I sigh with relief in seeing that my arrival was not the subject of gossip for everyone. "I'm here with Charles to evaluate the estate."

"Ah, did he inherit it in the end?" asks Maggie.

"Yes, well . . . I don't think they're talking about anything else in the village."

"We came back from Massa yesterday. We were at the seaside for one last peaceful holiday. Sara will be born at the beginning of September."

"Congratulations, guys . . . Elisa told me you got married."

"Yeah." Lapo nods with an ear-to-ear smile. "Just think that I went to study in Madrid, and she went to do a master's degree in dance in Toledo. We met in Barcelona and had an instant spark. Sometimes there's no need to go and look for destiny in God's house when you have it just a stone's throw away."

"I'm very happy for you," I say. I really am, because the two of them are the picture of joy.

"What about you? Married? Kids?"

"Free on all fronts," I reply. I usually recite this line with lively and vibrant satisfaction, as if I were a heroic survivor of a catastrophe, but it makes me feel incredibly lonely at the moment. No women, I systematically reject them all; no children, and no prospect of having them. "But never say never," I find myself adding.

"Maybe we should organize a dinner while you and Carletto are here, with Elisa and Giada, like old times!"

"I would very much like that." I really would like that.

We say goodbye, and I go back to the game. "Sorry, two old friends of mine."

"Maybe the only two who actually came back to Belvedere," comments Max. "And over the years, I have seen a lot of people leave. I win again," he says, closing the game.

"Have you always lived here?" I ask him.

"Yeah. I took over my father's workshop," he replies dryly.

"And you never got married?" This piques my curiosity, because according to the standards of the village, he would have been quite the catch.

"He missed the kind of train that only comes once in a lifetime, and he's still standing on the tracks, crying," Vanni interjects.

"There was a woman I would have taken to the altar with my eyes closed. I proposed to her, she said yes, but she wanted to go live in Florence. She'd studied languages and had a good job there as a guide. That year my dad had a lung problem, and so he had to decide whether to pass the workshop on to me or close it. He knew Laura wanted to move and urged me to go with her, but I knew that it would kill him to close up shop, so in the end I chose to stay."

"And Laura married someone else," concludes Luciano.

"You never forgot her, did you?" My question is more a statement than a question.

"You can't ever forget someone like that," admits Max. "But it's the harsh law of the village: As kids it seems like the whole world is here. Friends that meet every day; Wednesday nights watching Real Madrid matches on the TV at the bar; the summers, when the most important event of the week is the open-air cinema in the parish courtyard; racing up and down the hills two at a time on our Ciao bikes without helmets. When someone came back from Florence with a pair of Roy Rogers, he was so cool, a rock star. People talked about him for a week. Those years seem never-ending, like nothing will change, and you'll all be friends until you're old. Then it happens."

"What happens?"

"One after another, they all leave, and when you run into them later, you're missing something. Just like you, before, with Margherita and Lapo. I saw it on your face."

"I didn't have any face," I reply, even though Max's speech touched a nerve I didn't think I had.

"The beautiful ones go home rich," says Luciano, winning a third game. "And with your ugly faces, there was no competition."

Vanni deals another round of cards. This time he trumps clubs, and in my hand I have the ace and the three.

"In life, it's better to have remorse than regret," reasons Max. "Remorse is over something you regret having done. Regret, on the other hand, is about the things you never did, all lost to time."

As we continue to play one round after another, I notice Elisa and Elmo coming out of the bakery, his hand on her back. *"Maremma impestata ladra!"* I blurt out, dropping my ace with a violence that makes the cards on the table jump.

"Oh, you old farts, in less than an hour, he's already become as bad as the rest of you!" the bartender remarks, hearing me.

"No, no, he's bothered about his own problem," says Luciano.

Irritated for no apparent reason, I stare at the edge of the table and force myself not to follow Elisa with my gaze and—dammit—I couldn't have made a bigger mistake as to where to look.

MICHAEL + ELISA FRIENDS 4 EVER

The crooked letters we scratched into the plastic table with the tab of a can, now tattooed in my brain. It's barely legible, but to me it's like a neon sign.

"This hand is mine!" I exult. I count the points, and I hit the jackpot. "Sorry for putting you to shame! Gentlemen, it's been a pleasure. Whenever you need a fourth, you can find me at Le Giuggiole. Now, I regret to say I must be off," I excuse myself, with fire under my shoes. "Oh, who wins with clubs?" I ask, turning back toward the trio.

A satisfied grin appears on Vanni's face. "With clubs? Fools win!"

Not this time.

Where the hell did Elisa go?

20

Elisa

I swear I'll get Mamma back for this. I don't know how yet, but I'll find a way.

This morning Elmo invited me to go for an aperitif when I was done in the vineyard. I told him I was supposed to help Mamma with the vegetable garden, but she interjected and insisted she'd do it herself.

She ignored my pleading look that said *Please don't do this to me*, and told us we should go to dinner as well.

"Elisa really needs to relax," she said. "She's always working so hard in the vineyard."

And now here I am with Elmo, sitting at the village bakery, stuffing myself with pretzels while he monologues. It started the moment he picked me up—in his hearse, a brand-new Maserati—and it hasn't stopped yet.

"So, I said to my father: 'Let's expand. Italy is full of funeral parlors, but how many specialize in extra-luxury services?'"

"I don't—"

But he doesn't even give me time to finish the sentence. "So I opened a parlor in Forte dei Marmi. We had to invest quite a bit, but a good entrepreneur always knows how to evaluate risks and benefits."

He's overflowing with self-satisfaction: "Did you hear that Saverio Colli & Figlio was just mentioned in an article in *La Nazione*? Did you know our cinerary urns come straight from Japan?"

While he talks to himself, I keep my gaze fixed behind him, beyond the window, where in the distance I can see the table where Michael and Intemerata are sitting.

Maybe karma is making me pay for the nightmare dates I forced him to go on.

At a certain point, Intemerata strides away, piquing my curiosity: What happened?

"Elisa?" Elmo demands my attention.

"Huh?"

"So?"

"So, what?"

"I asked how things are going with your daughter."

"Well, Linda's a really good kid, and she studies a lot. She's learning Latin now—"

"Whoa! Did I tell you we also offer funeral services in Latin? It's coming back in style . . ." The self-congratulatory *blah blah blah* continues. He only stops to greet the deputy mayor. "Mrs. Melli, how are you? You look so wonderful! Does your son still play the piano? If I recall correctly, he's a little Mozart!"

Elmo is so slimy. He sucks up to anyone with money or power, without worrying about appearing false or pandering.

"Sorry for the interruption, Elisa. It's public relations," he says, turning to me again after the deputy mayor leaves. "By the way, I was thinking that my agency could use some new staff. We're expanding, and I need someone I can trust as a partner . . ." He takes my hand in his, with a soft, moist grip. "And not just at work."

Oh God. "Elmo . . ." I stammer.

"I have a gorgeous house in Versilia. It's not seafront—it's closer to the highway exit—but the shore is only a few miles away. You should come and see it. How about next weekend? Of course, I have to be available for work twenty-four hours a day, but I hardly ever get a call at night." The wink he adds at the end of the sentence sends chills down my spine.

"My goodness, it's late!" I exclaim, jumping up. "I have to . . . I have to . . ." I need an excuse and quickly. "I have to go to the pharmacy before it closes."

Elmo frowns. "Can't you go tomorrow?"

"No!" I exclaim. "It's for . . . something a little intimate," I whisper. The discomfort on his face confirms I chose the right tactic. I could go further . . . "I have this annoying itch. I hope it's not herpes."

At the word *herpes*, Elmo retreats a foot, as if even our proximity might expose him. Come to think of it . . .

"Sorry, Elmo. I'm mortified to have to interrupt the evening like this."

"Of course, in fact, I just remembered I also have to run to . . . to . . ." He rushes to the register where he pays at lightning speed, ignoring my offer to split the bill so as not to stay a second longer than necessary.

Unfortunately, I rejoice too soon. He must have realized that perhaps he was too explicitly disgusted, so he pauses in the doorway of the bakery and turns to me again. "I'll walk you to the pharmacy," he insists.

"It's okay."

"No, I'm happy to come," he reiterates, even though his tone betrays him.

We go out, and he puts his hand on my lower back, a demonstrative gesture I'm sure is aimed at showing everyone what a gentleman he is, but in reality he barely touches me, as if I were radioactive.

We say goodbye with a generic "See you soon" and, to my relief and his disappointment, I enter the pharmacy. I don't need anything, but while I'm here I can't leave empty-handed. I start wandering aimlessly among shelves and displays, enjoying the air-conditioning.

"Was I seeing things or did I just witness you on a romantic date?" Michael surprises me from behind, making me jump.

"Michael! Are you trying to kill me?" I exclaim, my heart in full fibrillation.

"No, I wish you a long and prosperous life. But you didn't answer my question," he insists with that mocking half smile.

"Are you really that interested?" I ask, crossing my arms.

"Now that you're being so mysterious, very much so."

I could tell him the truth, but his surprised tone irks me. Furthermore, it's both scandalous and immoral that he manages to look like he stepped out of a high-fashion catalog even while wearing clothes bought at the store known to sell clothes that don't suit anyone. They sell garments to cover oneself, not to dress oneself, and my outfit is a good example of this: a little girl's flowery dress. I probably wore something similar to my first communion . . . So, instead of explaining to him that Elmo Colli was foisted on me by Mamma, I take up his challenge. "I know the most I have going for me is my personality, but it just so happens that someone else likes it. You're not the only one in line, my dear."

"A *yes* would have been good enough for me, but apparently someone's feeling a little touchy. Let me ask you something: Doesn't being so thin-skinned hurt your liver?"

"Why do you think I'm at the pharmacy?" I reply.

"You might be looking in the wrong section." Michael nods at the display on my right, the one with intimate lubricants: cherry, long-lasting, warming, refreshing, aloe . . .

This time, too, cheek wins over truth. "No," I reply. "I need . . . this!" I grab a tube at random and wave it under his nose.

"Thai massages?!" he reads on the label with a wink. "Now I'm interested."

Thai massages? What exactly is a Thai massage? "Exactly."

"Who's the lucky one? That gloomy guy who was just with you?"

"I don't intend to share any further details with you," I reply, as I head for the cash register.

But he follows me. "We men love details," he insists.

"I know. And we women like to torture you. Use your imagination." If this is a last-ditch skirmish, I don't intend to lose.

"I know that you like torturing me; the date with Intemerata was exhausting."

"If you think you have my pity, you're wrong."

"I'm not asking for your pity, but I would like to remind you that you and I have a pending pizza. I have my last date later tonight, then we'll be even."

"If you survive Pompilia Cozzi, then we can discuss the pizza."

"You can count on it. Don't make any plans for tomorrow night," he replies, winking in a way that would instantly make every woman in Belvedere swoon. Every woman except for me.

21

MICHAEL

I arrive at the lake, better known as The Puddle, an artificial basin too small to have a real name, mostly used for agriculture and the occasional scenic backdrop for a date, like tonight. It's about a twenty-minute walk from the estate, and I can't say how many times Elisa and I have been here together.

When I arrive, I find Pompilia waiting for me, holding a basket.

"Hi, I'm Pompilia, Lilia to my friends," she introduces herself. "I've prepared a picnic. I hope you're hungry."

I don't see any spare relatives or crucifixes. So far everything seems normal, which in itself seems strange to me.

"I didn't know what you liked, so I made a bunch of things," she announces cheerfully. "Kebabs?"

"They look delicious," I say, taking the plate she hands me.

"So, you went out with that stick-in-the-mud Regina and Intemerata the nun. I bet you're scared to death now," she says. "Jacket potato?"

"At Regina's house, the main topic was Regina herself; with Intemerata, it was God."

"Whoever marries Regina also marries her mother; whoever marries Intemerata, on the other hand, marries the Vatican," she comments, having a laugh at her cousins. "But we're not all crazy here in Belvedere."

"I'm happy to hear it, they were two somewhat . . . unusual dates."

"There's no need for you to be an English gentleman with me. There's no polite way to say those two should be committed."

"Committed, yes," I confirm. "Why did you stay here in Belvedere? It seems like anyone with a chance runs off as soon as they can."

"I don't think it's so bad here. I mean, in the end, I'm not held captive at home by my parents like Regina, nor have I been forced out into the world with only my faith like Intemerata. I can work from home, and I have my financial independence."

Perfect! I like talking about work. "Right! What do you do?"

"I am a digital entrepreneur. I sell my underwear online."

This is getting interesting. Maybe Elisa set up a good match for me after all. "Ah, so do you actually make it by hand or are you the designer?"

"No, no, I sell *my* underwear. Underwear I've worn."

There's a lag between my ear and my brain. "I mean, so you . . . you sell the underwear you've already worn? Dirty or washed?" The question seems stupid, but at this point I can't help it.

"Dirty, obviously. For example, I wore a pair yesterday, and tomorrow I have to send it to a guy in Lugano. Shipping at his expense, of course."

Perhaps it's time to focus on the practical. "So this is a good business, the . . . the . . ."

"Fetishes? Of course! I sell everything: bras, socks, shoes—one guy even asked me for a toothbrush. They tell me how used they want the pieces to be, what color they should be, whether they want a photo of me wearing them—at an added cost, of course—and I send it registered mail from the local post office. My customers are incredibly loyal. Do you have any particular interests? I can give you a good discount," she asks me with the same ease she might have offered me a coffee.

I was wrong. This date is definitely the most shocking. "No, thanks. I think I'm okay."

"Suit yourself," she replies, shrugging. "There's a waitlist for the thongs anyway. Hey, don't you like the tomato soup?"

"I'm so full." In reality, my stomach closed of its own accord.

"No one in all of Belvedere makes it like I do." She hands me a small bowl. "I'm offended."

"Okay." I taste a bite, and for a moment I think I'm going to choke to death. It's spicy—testing the limits of human consumption.

"Do you like it?"

"Y-yes," I whisper, my voice struggling to escape my burning throat. "I just need some water," I say, stretching out my hand toward the cup, tears streaming from my eyes.

"Anyway, know that I'm not here to extort a marriage proposal from you. All I'm after is a little fun. No commitment. You know what I mean . . ." Pompilia's expression is nothing if not suggestive.

"I'd never dare take advantage of you like that," I lie. Normally I'd be happy to consider a proposal like this, but her used underwear business is a total turn-off.

"What do you think, that we women don't want exactly what you men want? That we don't have the same desires as you?"

If eyes could undress a person, hers would have stripped off my second skin. How do I get out of this now? "I'm honestly quite tired this evening."

"If it's a question of energy, I have enough for two. Not to mention, my tomato soup is an aphrodisiac. Aphrodisiacs are my specialty," she says, dipping her finger into the soup and sliding it into her mouth while she stares me down. "And do you know what else is my specialty?"

"I don't dare guess." I admit at this point I'm genuinely scared.

She crawls across the blanket toward me and, without much ceremony, unbuttons my jeans with one ninja move. "I'll show you."

I shrink back, but she's already grabbed the waistline of my boxers. "Pompilia, I was serious . . ."

"So was I."

"I don't think that's true . . . We barely know each other . . ." I try to dissuade her. "We just ate . . ."

"Leave it to me," she whispers, before leaning down and taking me between her lips.

This is where sexual awareness activists might talk about consent, but although I've said no with my lips, my lower half is responding quite enthusiastically to her stimulation. And that, in turn, is influencing my brain.

Lying on the blanket, I abandon myself to Pompilia's care, who does her best with her lips, tongue, and hands for my well-being. My male nature has prevailed over common sense; I'll hardly lose sleep over it.

But boy, do I.

Once I have my happy ending, and before Pompilia can request a favor in return, I fake an urgent work call and make a run for it.

My animal instinct won out over reason. I may have been as excited as a macaque in mating season, but I'm also the kind of man who appreciates the discretion of hygiene.

That's why I had a bidet installed in my London flat.

By the time I get to the villa, a flash of volcanic heat has ignited the front of my underwear and its contents, followed by a persistent burning sensation.

I take a total of three ice-cold showers—for once, the broken boiler isn't an issue—but once the cold water's temporary numbing effect wears off, the burning flares up stronger than ever.

The chili pepper. I have a mental flashback in which Pompilia, before launching into her oral performance, sucked a finger dripping with her demonic tomato soup.

Around three o'clock in the morning, my penis turns lobster orange; at four o'clock, it's red; at five, Pompeian red; and over the following two hours, it reaches shades of cardinal purple and gangrene. At seven thirty, just before it's about to turn dark blue, I get dressed and rush to the pharmacy.

I enter with an embarrassing waddle, and with a good dose of stoicism, I await my turn while the pharmacist and the baker chat about this and that, as if I weren't there.

"I'm so sorry," I interrupt them. "I have an urgent request."

"Oh, good morning. Even our English friend here has become a loyal customer!" he exclaims in his usual booming voice.

"Yes, well, you happen to be the only pharmacy for miles," I say.

"Good, good. Wyddayaneed?" he asks, in a thick Tuscan accent I can hardly make out.

"What?"

"Wyddayaneed?" he shouts again, as if I hadn't heard.

"I don't understand. Can you speak more slowly?"

"Wa-d-ya-need? What do you need?"

"I need something for . . . for a burning sensation," I say, refraining from clutching the crotch of my jeans in desperation.

"A burning throat? I have this spray, just spritz as needed," he decrees, slapping the package in my hand.

"No, it's not my throat," I say, pushing it back to him.

"Ah, so it's a stomach problem. Then you need Gaviscon. This will take care of it, but you have to eat bland food for the next two days."

"I think you've misunderstood. It's a burning sensation further . . . further down."

The pharmacist claps his hands. "Hemorrhoids! Eh, Preparation H," he announces, waving a yellow box in the air that you could see from the main square.

"I don't need Preparation H."

A lady intervenes. "Preparation H is great, you know! I use it for wrinkles. Look how smooth my skin is."

"Ma'am, would you mind standing back to wait your turn?" I blurt out. "I don't have hemorrhoids," I reiterate through clenched teeth.

"So what's the matter?" ask the pharmacist and the baker in unison.

I lean forward so no one can hear me. "It's my penis," I whisper.

"Why didn't you say so?" asks the pharmacist.

"I tried."

"What happened? Did you polish it a little too much?" asks the baker.

"I think it got burned."

"Burned?" the two ask, even more incredulous.

"Someone gave me . . . they gave me some . . . some oral sex. A woman," I hasten to specify.

"Who was it, then? The Fire Breather's daughter?" laughs the pharmacist.

"That's not relevant. This woman, before she . . . well, you know . . . she'd eaten this spicy tomato soup she makes."

"It's Pompilia!" exclaim the baker and the pharmacist in unison.

"She's famous for her tomato soup. Tastes like it was cooked by the devil himself!" adds the baker.

"Excuse me, but can you explain what this has to do with anything?" I ask him, taken aback by his intrusiveness.

"I'll give you a second opinion."

"I don't need a second opinion," I explode, exhausted. "I need an ointment, something to put on my dick because it's on fire, and it's about to fall off!" I can feel all the customers in the queue staring at me. "And I'll take these fruit chews as well," I add, sheepishly.

The pharmacist wraps up a tube of ointment for me. "Store this in the fridge and apply it every two hours. Put on some nice, loose cotton underwear and get yourself an ice pack. Tomorrow you'll be good as new."

22

Elisa

"You'll never guess what I just found out," exclaims Giada, rushing into my room, where I'm sitting on my bed with my laptop on my lap, surrounded by piles of papers, folders, and notes.

"Please don't mess up my papers. I'm working on my business plan for the EC grant," I say, turning the computer toward her. "May I present, Le Giuggiole Agriturismo!"

Giada blinks her long eyelashes in amazement. "What about the vineyard?"

"We'll keep producing Chianti, but once the villa is renovated, thanks to the regional fund for the restoration of historic-artistic assets, we can make it a wonderful farmhouse with a restaurant and lodging, where we can host events and ceremonies."

"Like the Relais & Château?"

"Maybe," I sigh. "But let's start small: An *agriturismo* is required to serve drinks and food that are at least forty percent its own production. So in addition to Chianti and Vinsanto, we'll use our oil, honey, elderberry syrup, jujube syrup, and all the jams that Mamma makes with our fruit trees; the preserves and sauces will be made with vegetables from the garden. We can even make the soaps ourselves. It may be just a hobby of Donatella's for now, but why not exploit it."

"It sounds nice, but you keep saying 'ours, ours, ours.' There is nothing of ours here, Elisa."

"Not yet," I point out.

"What if they don't give you the loan? What if they deny you the funds?" she says, her big blue eyes shining with anxiety. "You're already so invested in this, and I don't want to see you disappointed."

"We'd be the only agriturismo in Belvedere! Everyone else is gone; no one we knew thought about how to reinvent what they already had, they all went looking for new things elsewhere. There's no competition, and the proposal is solid. Why would they deny me funding?"

"I'm just saying you should prepare yourself in case something goes wrong."

"I appreciate your concern, Giada, but I know what I'm doing. I could give Linda a solid future, which is a lot more than I've done for myself."

"Have you come down with irresponsible single mother syndrome again?" she reproaches me. "I thought you were over that!"

"I don't know if I'll ever get over it completely."

"You did a great job with Linda," she reassures me.

"I also made a lot of mistakes."

"The only people who don't make mistakes are the ones who never do anything in the first place," she says, repeating her life mantra to me.

"Hey, why the hell am I talking to you anyway? You're the one who let Mamma sell me to Elmo Colli without the slightest objection. What good is a sister who doesn't come to my aid in times of crisis? It was a terrifying date," I reproach her for her complicit behavior from the other morning, when she sneered at me behind my back.

"Ah!" she exclaims, with a bounce that shakes the mattress. "Speaking of scary dates, I almost forgot what I wanted to tell you . . . although I don't know if I should . . ."

"Too late to back out now." I close the laptop, because it's clear I'm done for the evening. "Do tell."

"Charles told me that Michael had a spicy date with Pompilia yesterday."

"Okay, I don't think I want to hear the rest," I announce, throwing my hands up. "Keep me out of sordid hardcore romps."

"What do you mean hardcore romps? You can't even imagine what happened to him, poor thing," she insists. "So, Pompilia, as soon as she saw Michael, jumped on him and proceeded to practice her specialty."

"So far, I certainly wouldn't describe him as a 'poor thing.'" On the contrary. Honestly, I'm also a little annoyed. "He must have enjoyed his 'mic check.'"

"Well, unfortunately, Pompilia had eaten her famous spicy tomato soup just before her performance." Giada winks at me, as if to say the best part of the story is yet to come. "The result? The oral exam irritated Michael's nether regions to the extent that he's now lying in bed with an ice pack in his underwear."

So that's why we haven't seen him all day. "Karma's real!" I exclaim with a treacherous hint of glee.

"Don't you feel the slightest bit of guilt? You're the one who inflicted these three terrible dates on him!" Giada asks.

"I may have forced the dates on him, but I certainly didn't push Pompilia's open mouth on him."

"What do you care what they did or didn't do?"

"I don't." Really, I don't care . . . but . . .

"Then put an end to this feud. Remember he's the one managing the sale of the estate. If you want them to sell it to you, tone down your animosity and start talking to him like a friend you've known for ten years."

It pains me to admit it, but Giada's right. "Did Mamma make pizza tonight?" I ask her.

"Like every Monday: one with sausage; one with ham, mushrooms, and artichokes and a white one with bacon."

Okay, let's do this. I get out of bed and pull on my All Stars. "Perfect, that ham, mushroom, and artichoke is mine," I say, and I head toward the villa to get the hot pan.

23

Michael

Lying in a bed, in pain, naked, with a bag of diced frozen vegetables on my crotch, I stare at the canopy, wondering what I've done to deserve this.

I'd love to be Googling the possible consequences of this incident on my genitals, but with no Wi-Fi, I can't even self-diagnose any terminal complications.

Two knocks on the door snap me out of my catastrophizing. "Come in," I say, pulling the sheet up to my waist.

"May I?" Elisa peeks through the crack. "I've come in peace."

She enters the room holding a pan covered with a tea towel. "Have you by any chance hidden a knife so you can finish me off down there?" I ask.

"No." She lifts a corner of the white linen towel and a sublime aroma fills the air. "We had a pizza date pending, if I remember correctly: ham, mushroom, and artichoke. Is it still your favorite?"

Just the smell of it opens up a chasm of memories: Here at Le Giuggiole, pizza Mondays were sacred. Mariana baked an industrial quantity of pizzas in the large wood-fired oven in the kitchen, and we rascals polished them off while holed up in a tent pitched in the garden.

We'd camp out, eight of us in a four-person tent, and stay up until morning playing Uno.

"As long as I have teeth to eat it," I reply. I move over to my left and motion for her to sit on the free half of the bed.

"Since you can't go to the pizzeria in your state, I brought the pizzeria to you."

"Ah, did you hear . . . ?" I ask her sheepishly.

"Yes. No detail spared."

Damn. "So are we good now?" I ask her.

"No. Not now, *for* now. It's different," she objects. "We're in a temporary truce."

"Ah, yes, one month to reevaluate the estate and tie up Bingley to stop him from selling it."

"If it can happen to me, there's a good chance it can happen too to you," she says.

"What do you mean?"

"Don't you remember? I wanted to go to Milan, get a master's degree in publishing, work with a large publishing house, travel . . . Then Linda was born, and I had to give it all up. I haven't always loved this place, you know? In fact, I even hated it for a while."

"From the way you talk about it now, you wouldn't think so."

"When my daughter was born, I didn't know how to be a mother. I wanted her, I kept her, I felt sorry for her while she was hospitalized, and then, after they discharged us, I was overcome by this wave of negativity. What was I thinking? How could I love a daughter who was the obstacle to all my dreams? And this village with all its gossip had become so suffocating. I knew what a mess I'd gotten myself into, and I felt doubly shitty because not only was I a failure, but I'd also implicated this little girl who hadn't asked to be born. I did nothing but walk around the estate in the grip of my demons, so much so that in two months, I lost all the weight I'd gained during pregnancy."

"What changed your mind, then?"

"It was my *babbo*. One evening he took me by the hand and asked if he could walk with me. And I just started sobbing, because I felt like I'd hit a dead end. What else could I do with my life, besides be a mother?" Elisa sighs, and I can see in her eyes how much she misses her dad. "He was a simple man, a farmer, and I mean that in the best way possible. He was grounded in the earth, he spoke the same language as nature, so he started talking to me about the vineyard. 'Do you know that a vine takes seven years to produce its first grapes after it's planted? Seven. Like a child going to school. Before that, nothing or very little. But over those seven years, it must be cared for every day. A winemaker isn't born a winemaker, and a vineyard doesn't immediately bear fruit. Patience is learned, Elisa, and love grows along with it.'"

"Your dad was a man of few words, but I think he was wise enough to speak only when he knew the right thing to say," I observe.

"That's how he was. Then he broke a leaf off a vine and put it in my hand. He said it was a plant that represents devotion, protection, and strength because it's robust and resists everything, like life. Then he said, 'As of tomorrow, you'll come to the vineyard with me. You're not made to stay at home and stare at the wall.' Babbo was right: I learned patience, and day after day, seeing the bunches ripen, I fell in love with it too."

"You've always been tenacious," I reply after polishing off my second slice of pizza. "I had other plans too, but my brother's death scuppered everything."

"You two never ended up getting along, did you?" Elisa knows that from the time we were kids, there was no love between George and me. We were like strangers forced to share space and time against our will.

"It got even worse as we grew up. He was always a shrewd and calculating opportunist, eager to take advantage of anyone he associated with. He had those blond curls and blue eyes, that angelic face with so much charisma. He knew how to sell himself. The Bingleys had a way of keeping his bluster in check when they were our guardians. But once George turned eighteen and got his inheritance, he started traveling all around Europe, squandering his capital down to the last penny on luxury cars, yachts, casinos, 'expensive' women, and then, finally, drugs. It started as a way of fitting into his social circles, then it became a habit, and it ended with addiction."

"Drugs? I . . . I had no idea," Elisa gasps.

"He ended up broke, came back to London, and when I inherited my share, he asked me for money. Being the eighteen-year-old idiot I was, I gave him a property in Dorset. He sold it and was penniless again within six months. He begged me for more cash, and after I said no, we basically stopped speaking. We agreed that I'd manage the D'Arcy properties, while he would head up the financial consulting firm. It could have been incredibly profitable had he not squandered it all on gambling, coke, and whores. In the last year, I never saw him sober; he was doing a hit every hour because he couldn't handle the comedown. One night he thought it was a good idea to join a drag race and slammed into a wall at two hundred miles an hour with his McLaren P1. To protect Saxton & D'Arcy, I passed it off as an unfortunate accident. I worked hard to clean up his mess and took over the company. I would have probably done something else if I'd had the choice, but life had other plans."

Elisa nods with a sad smile. "Our lives have been more similar than we thought."

"But, like you, I've learned to appreciate change," I say.

"But your whole life isn't on the line. If I can't convince you that Le Giuggiole is a valid investment, you'll sit Bogdanovic down in front of Carletto with a million-euro check, and I'll be left homeless with a mother and daughter who depend on me."

"That's why you have my utmost attention. When do you start persuading me?"

"I've already started: with a pizza," she replies, pointing to the last slice.

"I could be convinced if you leave me that last one," I insinuate.

"What happened to that famous English gallantry?"

"There's not enough gallantry in the world to resist Mariana's pizza," I reply. "But since I'm feeling generous, we can split it," I say, handing it to her.

"I'm in." She grabs a corner of the crust to tear, and in that instant our fingers touch.

It's only for a second, but it unsettles me and leaves a strange tingling sensation on my hand. It's our first physical contact, skin on skin, as adults.

She also looks strange, but I don't dare ask why. I stare at her in a daze, studying her features until I find the Elisa I knew. I'd never noticed how thick her hair was, because as a girl she wore it very short, and since I returned she's always worn it pulled back. Her thick eyebrows that she furrows when I make her angry are still there, more expressive than ever, together with the eyelashes that always made her big brown eyes seem softer than she wanted to appear, especially when she wanted to seem tough at all costs. Her straight nose gives her the look of a determined woman, but in the very rare times she laughs, she scrunches it up, and her sprinkling of freckles makes her look like a cheeky little girl. And when she laughs, her lips curl in a spectacular way . . .

"Michael?" she asks me.

"Huh?"

"Why are you staring at me?"

Good question; the explanation might be embarrassing. "Why . . . ?"

"Do I have pizza on my face?"

Thanks for the assist. "Yes, you have a bit of tomato right there," I say, pointing to an imaginary stain on her cheek. "I'll take care of it," I find myself saying. I reach my right index finger toward her face and slide it across her skin.

There it is again, the same feeling as before. "Got it," I announce, to lend credibility to my colossal lie.

"Thank you."

A strange silence hangs in the room, not the empty, awkward kind, but as if something were about to happen, only neither of us know what.

"So, when do I get a tour of the estate? A serious tour, I mean, from entrepreneur to investor," I say to break the tension.

"Michael, we'll go on horseback. Do you feel up to it . . . in . . . your condition?"

"Absolutely, yes! Give me a few days, and I'll be ready for the Palio di Siena," I exclaim boldly. I can't be sure, but if I'm wrong, I'll suffer in silence.

"Okay. I'll have Mamma pack us a lunch—nothing over the top, just a quick bite to eat. And dress comfortably and coolly. We'll be out all day. Think you can handle it even if it's not a Michelin-starred tour?"

"It sounds perfect." I'm serious.

"Okay, then, I'm off," she says, taking the pan and throwing the napkins onto it. "Wait a minute . . . what is this?" she asks, bringing something up to her eyes.

"This, what?"

"Is it a . . . piece of zucchini? What the hell is it doing in your sheets?"

This is *definitely* going to be a hard one to explain.

24

Elisa

"Doing yourself up?" Giada asks me, invading the bathroom as usual. The concept of personal space goes right over her head.

"I wouldn't say that," I reply, studying myself in the mirror as I get ready for the estate tour.

"If what I see in your hand is my MAC illuminating foundation, purchased for the modest sum of seventy-eight euros, I would say you are, in fact, doing yourself up."

"I can't find my sunscreen, and this is SPF 30, so it's perfect."

"And I was born yesterday . . . Come here. You're making a mess," she says, snatching the bottle from my hands. "You have to apply it to your neck and collarbones too. Sorry, Elisa, but since when do you wear such low-cut shirts to work on the vineyard?"

"My work clothes are all in the wash."

"Yeah, but this happens to be my shirt!" she replies.

"It is. The most serious-looking one I could find in your closet." Giada's wardrobe is a riot of pink, sequins, and ruffles—nothing wearable on a farm, except this white, ribbed short-sleeved shirt, which she must have bought after a blow to the head. It's low-cut and a little tight for my standards, but by hers it's practically a nun's habit.

"Something's going on here," she mutters under her breath, "and if you won't tell me, I'll find out on my own. Don't frown, or you'll crease the foundation."

"I'm showing the estate to Michael today."

"You sure all you're showing him is the estate?"

"I don't know what you're insinuating, but yes. I have to be credible. I don't want to look like a walking dumpster."

"So this is all for credibility's sake?" she asks teasingly.

"What else would it be for?"

"Nothing. Maybe you want him to see something else besides an entrepreneur, but I could be wrong."

"You're wrong," I confirm.

"So, you don't see Michael as a beautiful man desired by every woman in town, from whom you wouldn't mind a little attention—is that right?"

"Is that what this looks like to you? Anyway, I'm not into him, and he's not into me."

"People attract what they hate."

"What nonsense! I have to go. I've heard too much out of you." I end the conversation by leaving the bathroom.

"Are you sure you don't want a hint of lip tint?" she calls after me over the stairwell. "It's long lasting and never smudges, whatever you end up doing."

I arrive at the stables, where Michael and I have arranged to meet, and he surprises me by having already saddled and bridled D'Artagnan, his horse.

"Good morning," he greets me. "I took the liberty of preparing Soldatino for you. I know you usually ride King, but the blacksmith is shoeing him."

"Soldatino is great. Thank you."

"My pleasure." The moment he smiles at me, I thank my lucky stars that I wore Giada's shirt. Despite Michael's "comfortable" clothes, he looks like he could be at a polo match.

"You're an early riser," I observe.

"Renato wakes me up at dawn. Ready to go?" he asks me with an unexpected burst of enthusiasm.

"Sure."

"I'll give you a boost up," he offers.

I'm about to brush him off with a "No, thanks, I'll do it myself." But he's already behind me, wrapping his hands around my waist and lifting me into the air. I don't know if it's the sudden upward momentum, but for a second I go dizzy.

Don't even go there, I say to the voice in my head, which has already raised its finger to remind me that the same thing also happened the other evening, when our fingers touched over that slice of pizza. I couldn't say what happened then. It certainly wasn't a drop in blood pressure, because I was already lying down, nor was it a neck pain, because I've been sleeping with an orthopedic pillow for years . . . and then it happened again when Michael wiped the tomato smear from my cheek. Could it be he has some kind of effect on me? "Absolutely not!"

"Absolutely not what?" he asks me, confused, from D'Artagnan's back.

Oh, Christ. Did I say that out loud? "Um . . . we absolutely . . ." I don't know what the hell to say, so I prod Soldatino, who takes the path straight ahead of him. "We absolutely shouldn't go around the other way. If we do, we won't even be halfway there by noon."

"All the land you see is planted with vines to make Chianti. The vineyards cover twenty hectares; sixteen are Sangiovese, and the remainder are Ciliegiolo, Malvasia Nera, and Sagrantino," I explain, gesturing with a broad sweep of my arm toward the rows on different slopes. "There are also five hectares of olive groves. We make oil in addition to wine."

"I didn't know you grew four different grape varieties," observes Michael.

"Chianti is made of eighty percent Sangiovese and the remainder is a combination of the other red grapes—that's according to the August 9, 1967, regulation." The year of the regulation is totally irrelevant for Michael, but I want to impress him. Oh God! Did I seriously just think that? Do I really want to impress him?

Well, of course I want to impress him—as a competent entrepreneur. Nothing more.

"The southwest exposure of the land is ideal. The grapes are protected from cold winds while the sun exposure optimizes ripening and sugar concentration. The soil is composed of a bedrock that slows down the vegetative growth, drains the soil, and retains heat, plus clay that acts as a water reserve." I haven't talked so much about land stratification since my pedology exam. Thank you, Professor Landucci, for making me work for that A+. "Moreover, the soil in this area is around four hundred meters above sea level, which means lower temperatures at the beginning of the season, but in turn, smaller bunches that ripen slowly with almost no health problems."

With a click of my heels, I urge Soldatino to take the path that goes down through the vineyards, and Michael follows me.

"So then, what do you do all day in the vineyard until harvest?"

"We check the hygrometric state of the soil, make sure there are no insects or weeds, and monitor the health of all two hundred and twenty-five thousand vines."

"How many?!" he exclaims, surprised.

"It's so we can select only the best bunches. What's more, we harvest by hand. For better grapes, we keep our yield low compared to the potential of the land. It is the price for producing an excellent wine."

"I didn't imagine all this study was behind it."

Bull's-eye! "Do you also imagine we still stomp the grapes with our feet?" I tease him, pondering whether to deliver a final blow by explaining spurred cordon cultivation.

"I wouldn't go that far, but seeing you stomp grapes would be an interesting sight."

"Sorry to disappoint."

"What a shame," he replies with a strange half smile, which makes me wonder if there was a subtle mischief in his suggestion.

At midday, with the sun shining and the cicadas chirping, we get hungry and take a break in the middle of the olive grove.

Michael unfolds the rough cotton mat in the shade of one of the trees with the thickest foliage, and I unpack the basket that I had secured to the saddle.

"I haven't asked you yet if the ride bothered you," I say, sitting down next to him. "You know, after the incident with Pompilia . . ."

"Those diced frozen veggies worked miracles," he announces, uncorking the bottle and pouring the wine. "Let's toast."

"To your newfound virility," I exclaim, holding out my glass to him.

"It was never lost, just momentarily tested," he says after we down our glasses in a single gulp.

I set out all the treats prepared by Mamma: focaccia with *finocchiona* and pecorino, an egg-and-artichoke tart, and a pie with ricotta and candied orange. "You can relax today; there's nothing spicy here."

"Will you stop bringing that up? It wasn't a good experience."

"Oh no," I exclaim with mock regret. "Does that mean you won't be asking Pompilia on a second date?"

"No. Not her, or Regina, or Intemerata."

"Was I too horrible to you?" I ask, taking a bite to hide a satisfied smile.

"Quite. Maybe I wasn't the epitome of gallantry that night we met again, but I don't think I deserved that much suffering."

"Look at it this way: You've earned a credit for the next time you're rude to me," I warn him.

"I have no intention of being rude. In addition to apologizing for what I said, I take it all back and repeat: In reality, I find you rather beautiful."

Okay, maybe the glass of wine on an empty stomach is talking for him. "Don't be a cad, Michael."

"It's the truth. I think you're the most beautiful woman in all of Belvedere."

"Giada is the most beautiful," I reply, my basic sense of reality preventing me from accepting the compliment.

"It's not just a question of looks. You're not exactly one to be without words."

"Is that a polite way of saying I can't keep my mouth shut?"

"I've always known you have no filters, but that's not what I mean. You're one of the few people who always has something interesting to say."

"Oh, so you liked my lecture about the cultivation of Chianti?"

"I don't know if I'll retain any of it, but I can say that today I know more than I did yesterday. You're a beautiful person, Elisa."

I shrug, stuffing my mouth with tart so I don't have to talk. "Oh, um . . . thanks!" I stumble.

"For what?"

"I don't know how to respond to compliments. I'm not very used to it."

"Just accept them. But if you really want to repay me, you could smile. You never give me enough of those." Michael brushes aside a strand of hair that's escaped from my bun, and when he touches my forehead, I feel dizzy again.

I stop to look at Michael and realize Giada wasn't wrong. Even though I'd like to think of myself as being indifferent to what others say, I'm flattered by Michael's attention. And I find myself shamefully hungry for compliments.

Vanity is a sin, but no one has ever come back from hell to say how bad it is, so I'm willing to take the risk. I don't need anyone to notice my looks or my skills, something like "You have such a natural talent for breathing" would do the trick at this point.

Damn this wine!

"Is everything okay?" Michael asks me. "You seem like you're somewhere else."

"I'm fine!" I hasten to say, before he manages to read my thoughts. "I think I'm just a little tired, between the ride, the sun, and the wine on an empty stomach."

"Why don't you take a little nap? Here in the shade, with this breeze, it's so nice."

"Maybe . . ." I lie down on the mat, with my head resting on the knotty root of the olive tree, which is anything but comfortable.

"You can lie on me," Michael invites me to move my head onto his shoulder.

I could act tough, as usual, but what would it cost me to say yes just this one time?

Human beings are defined by their propensity for mistakes, and even though I know a polite but firm no is the correct answer, I feel irresistibly attracted to the wrong one.

Besides, it's not like I'm doing anything wrong . . . It's just an innocent nap; nothing to see here.

I wake after a deep sleep that's lasted for who knows how long.

I squint and notice that the light has changed, so it was a little more than just a nap.

I'm still lying on Michael's shoulder, but my face is burrowed in the crook of his neck, the tip of my nose against his skin, and, when I inhale, his scent intoxicates me more than the wine at lunch.

He wraps his left arm around me and rests his hand lightly on my waist.

My hand, however, has risen to his chest, as if I were clinging to him, and is moving up and down to the slow rhythm of his breathing.

Michael is also sleeping, and I notice the sinfully sensual profile of his parted lips.

I squeeze my eyes shut so I can force my thoughts off the slippery road they're starting to take.

However, with my eyes closed, the scent of Michael's skin grows even stronger. It's fresh and masculine, and my nose, trained to recognize the bouquets of wines, is delighting in torturing me: notes of rosemary, anise, orange blossom . . .

The ringing of my phone interrupts my conscience from its orgy of senses.

Still dazed, I stretch out my hand on the mat until I find the infernal device, which with its ring has also awakened Michael, and I answer.

"Elisa, where are you? Are you okay?" Foliero asks me in a panicked voice.

"Yeah, why? Has something happened?"

"You tell me: Soldatino came back to the stable on his own. When I couldn't find you, I thought something had happened to you."

"What? Soldatino?" Still confused, I scramble to my knees and notice there's an empty space next to D'Artagnan. I rewind the mental film of our arrival and see it again: I was hot, I was thirsty, and I was hungry. I unhooked the picnic basket in a hurry and . . . "I didn't tie him up. I forgot to secure Soldatino's reins to the tree."

"Thank goodness. We were all so worried."

"It's okay. I was just a little careless. In any case, we're in the olive grove; we'll be back soon," I reassure him.

"Everything okay?" Michael asks, stretching in a way that lifts his polo shirt an inch, revealing the grooves of his obliques that continue down beyond the waistband of his riding trousers, which I only now notice are tight enough to reveal *everything*.

God or whoever's up there, make me blind . . . or at least not completely dazed.

I slap a hand over my eyes in a last-ditch attempt to end the hormonal surge. "I didn't tie up Soldatino, and he went back to the stable," I say in a voice that comes out higher than I intended.

"Okay . . . and why are you covering your eyes?"

"Um . . . the . . . the light bothers me. I have a little issue with the tear duct in my right eye, and it burns when the light hits it at a certain angle." Yes, of course, and what other nonsense should I throw at him now?

"Maybe you should see an ophthalmologist. Lasers work miracles."

"You're right. I'll make an appointment for September." I'll make an appointment, all right—with a psychologist. "Anyway, I think that pretty much does it for today; let's go back. You're probably tired and want to shower . . ." And at the word *shower* a still frame of him reappears in my mind, in the courtyard of the annex, shirtless, rinsing himself with the hose to the soundtrack of "You Sexy Thing." Why wait until September? I'll call the psychologist tomorrow.

"A shower sounds great. Let's go!" Michael unties D'Artagnan, leaps onto him with the agility of an Ascot jockey, and holds out his hand to me. "Come on, get up."

"I like walking," I say, before I can even formulate an intelligible sentence.

"All the way to the estate?" he asks me, confused.

Listening to myself again, I process the idiocy of what I've just said. Miles of dusty hills? What was I thinking?

The fact is, right now, the last thing I need is to have my body pressed against Michael's on horseback.

"I don't know if D'Artagnan can carry us both. You know, he's getting up there in age . . ."

"Foliero rides him, and he's well over two hundred pounds." He waves his hand, inviting me to join him. "Come on up. I know you don't want to be a damsel in distress, and you would never let me trample your girl power, but I'm not offering out of chivalry. It's because if

I go back without you, they're going to think I murdered you and hid your body."

Too bad—a bit of chivalry would have been nice . . .

"If you don't do it for your own feet, do it for my criminal record. I don't know any good lawyers in Italy."

I squeeze his hand and grab the pommel with my other. In a second, I'm on D'Artagnan's back, my back resting against Michael's chest and . . . Oh my God, it's even worse than I thought!

25

Michael

"Hey, Elisa, relax," I say. We've been on the horse for all of ten minutes, and she's stiff as a board.

"I'm afraid of falling. I don't feel safe when I don't have the reins."

"Am I that bad? I thought I was doing pretty well."

"No, you're very good. I'm the one who's a bit of a control freak."

I put my left arm around her waist. "Is that better?"

"It's better if you hold the reins with both hands."

I carry out the order reluctantly. Right now, all I want to do is hold her close and bury my face in her hair, which, after she has slept, has escaped from its bun and now falls softly over her shoulders. And those shoulders! Defined and tanned, just waiting to be bitten.

Similar thoughts have been crossing my mind—and not only my mind—since this morning, surprising me each time my imagination takes another leap forward.

Before, when we were riding through the vineyard, I couldn't take my eyes off her breasts wrapped in that tight top, bouncing up and down to the rhythm of the horse.

Then, after lunch, with her sleeping on me, I started to think I might kiss her. It would have been so easy, her lips were just a breath away from mine. All I had to do was turn my head. When she put her hand on my chest, I almost did it . . . but then I didn't. I closed my eyes and recited all the principles of economic theory from Arrow to post-Keynesian thought and fell back asleep.

Maybe it was for the best, because she doesn't seem to be on the same wavelength as I am. Or maybe she's just more lucid.

Listening to her talk about viticulture surprised me, I liked it and . . . I don't know how to describe this, because it's the first time it's happened to me. I didn't understand a thing she was saying, and yet I still wanted her to keep talking.

"Are you still seeing that guy from the bakery?" I ask her out of the blue.

"Elmo and I were never seeing each other," she replies with a shrug. "I only went out with him because Mamma made me. I can barely stand him."

She can't see me now, but my face is the picture of relief. "So, that massage gel you bought wasn't for him?"

"Do you need a man to use massage gel?"

I force myself to erase the mental image generated by her sentence before the animal instinct I kept at bay a few moments ago takes over, because this time there is no Keynesian theory that can hold me back. "So, is the tour over?" I ask, changing the subject.

"Oh no. You still have to see the production facility and cellars, but it's too late now. We can do it tomorrow if you don't have any plans."

"What else would I be doing here?" I reply, in an attempt to hide my enthusiasm, because the idea of spending another day with her makes me rejoice.

We arrive at the stables, and to my great disappointment, our ride together comes to an end.

"I hope you enjoyed today," she says, as we dismount. "I know you probably have no interest in most of it, but I'm sure the more you know, the more you can understand that Le Giuggiole can't be thrown away."

"You're right. It shouldn't be thrown away. Call me crazy, but Belvedere shouldn't be thrown away either: It's the classic postcard village, but it needs to enter the twenty-first century. There isn't even a sushi restaurant, and there's sushi everywhere nowadays."

"You miss sushi here?" she asks me with a skeptical look.

"It was just an example. A gym wouldn't be bad either. Isn't there anyone who wants to keep fit with a run on the treadmill?"

"Of course there's a gym!" she exclaims.

"Really?" I ask, shocked.

"Follow me." She motions for me to leave the stables with her and spans her arm across the landscape.

"Here are our treadmills. There's no LED screen to watch the news, but you can enjoy this incomparable view of the hills. No heart rate monitor either, just the sound of your breathing."

"Aren't you being a little too poetic?" I challenge her.

"And aren't you a little too blind?" she replies. "Race me to the villa?"

I didn't expect this. "Do you seriously want to compete?"

"Why, you don't?"

"It wouldn't be a fair competition," I protest.

"Do you mean for me or for you?" She doesn't stand aside. In fact, she gathers her hair into a high, tight ponytail, like a runner.

"Do you really want me to tear you to shreds, Elisa?"

"And do you want to run or stand here and chat?"

"I think you're teasing me."

"And I think you're scared."

Here it is, the magic phrase. Like when we were kids, whenever she wanted to push me to do something, all she had to do was utter those words to awaken my pride.

"Me, scared? I'll even be chivalrous. After you."

"Okay. Take your marks," she says, tracing a starting line on the dirt road with her heel. "When I say 'three.' One . . . Two . . . Go!"

Elisa rushes forward without even saying "three." Just like I used to do—I'm stupid for forgetting.

I catch up with her, and we run down the path side by side, shooting each other competitive glances.

I have to admit she's in better shape than I thought.

When I gain ground, she catches up quickly, and to my surprise, as soon as the road steepens, she passes me.

I concentrate on overtaking her, but my gaze, initially riveted on her shoulders, lingers down on her round and shapely buttocks and her sinuous hips that sway left and right in a hypnotic motion.

"I win!" she exults, slapping her hands down on the railing of the staircase. "Remind me who was supposed to be torn to shreds?"

"Maybe I let you win," I suggest.

"You? You wouldn't even let a blind, lame person on oxygen win!"

She's right. "I got distracted by the view."

"Nice, isn't it?" she asks breathlessly, her breasts rising and falling.

"Incomparable." Luckily, she has no idea what I'm referring to.

26

Elisa

This afternoon I'm taking Michael to visit the enology lab, but I arrive at the villa to find a scene that leaves me speechless: He's sitting at the large kitchen table, speaking English with Linda.

She's telling him about the last book she read, and I wonder how he could possibly be interested in some plot about insecure high school girls whose biggest problem in life is finding a prom date.

"Let me guess," I interject. "In the end, the ugly loser who's beautiful on the inside impresses the coolest guy in school and becomes prom queen?"

"Actually, the loser is only elected prom queen as a joke and her classmates bully her, but then she gets possessed by Satan, sets fire to the gym, and everyone dies," replies Linda.

"It's *Carrie*, by Stephen King," Michael explains to me.

"Sounds fun, right Little Cub?" I say, giving her a kiss on the head.

"Come on! Don't call me Little Cub," she grumbles, avoiding my attempt at affection. "Mom, can I have a sleepover here with some school friends on Saturday?" she asks me imploringly, her big eyes shining, as if she hadn't growled at me a second earlier.

"Why not? Great idea!" I say, relieved at her rare urge to socialize. She has a group of classmates she sometimes sees when she's not hunched over her books, but Linda isn't exactly the life of the party. She prefers to keep to herself, though it's probably at least partly my fault since I don't let her take part in more "grown-up" initiatives organized by her friends. Like the time they wanted to go to the water park one afternoon, but I nixed it when she said there wouldn't be an adult with them. A sleepover at home seems completely innocent to me. "Let's have Nonna make her famous pizza. And we can go buy snacks and gummies." What kind of sleepover would it be otherwise? I'm happy to risk being named crappiest mother of the year if it means I can push my daughter into a healthy social life with junk food banned by the Geneva convention.

"Speaking of invitations," Michael jumps in, "I ran into Lapo and Margherita, and they proposed we all have a reunion dinner before Carletto leaves again. What do you think?"

"We can do it in the garden. Maybe I'll call Cosimo and Lucia as well," I add enthusiastically. More than anything, I'm thrilled that Michael actually wants to do something enjoyable here, rather than counting the minutes until he goes back to London. "But Carletto leaves on Sunday, so that just leaves Saturday."

"Saturday's perfect." Michael downs his orange juice and stands up. "Shall we go? Linda, you can finish telling me about *Carrie* tonight."

"Mom, isn't that one of Aunt Giada's dresses?" Linda asks me with a suspicious look.

"No, it's mine," I lie. "We bought the same one." Today I've borrowed another of Giada's pieces: a red dress with white polka dots and a sweetheart neckline, a bit like a 1950s pin-up, which I think she wore for a *Grease*-themed party.

Like yesterday's shirt, this is a tad too modest for her.

"And since when do you go to work dressed like that?" Linda insists.

"So many questions this morning, Linda," I reply without answering, certain she has at least ten more shots lined up.

Michael and I go out to the lab on the electric cart built by the late count, who used it to zip around the estate like some kind of furious madman.

"Your daughter looks a lot like you," Michael observes.

"I hope that's a compliment."

"She's frighteningly intelligent for her age."

"I wish she'd learn to make friends," I sigh. "She's so lively and expressive with adults but very shy with her peers. They aren't really drawn to her."

"It's a shame, because she has plenty of personality. Have you ever thought about finding a different school for her? Maybe she'd find it easier to socialize in a more competitive environment that can nurture her skills."

"And what school would that be?"

"There aren't any options besides the village school? What about in Milan? Or in Switzerland? In London, there are high schools that would give a scholarship to a student like her."

"If there are options, they're either too far away for a thirteen-year-old girl or too expensive for me," I reply. "Plus, the idea of sending her who knows where kills me inside. Linda and I grew up together. She slept in my bed until she was ten. Next year she'll be in high school; maybe another year will bring her out of her shell."

"I thought perhaps she needed to broaden her horizons."

"Everyone's a good parent with other people's children."

"You're right. Sorry, I didn't mean to come between you and Linda."

"No problem. If you ever want to be a father, you're welcome to take her for a few weeks."

"Thanks but not for me. So, what did you want to show me today?" he asks when I stop the cart in front of the long brick building that until a few centuries ago was the farm workers' quarters.

"How harvested grapes become Chianti." I invite him to follow me inside, where the machines are now stopped, though in a month, they will be running at full capacity. "We select the bunches based on their quality, after which we run them through these machines that separate the grapes from the stalks."

"And from the peels," he adds.

"The skins are precious: They contain the polyphenols that lend color, aroma, and structure to the wine," I say, entering the next room.

"These polyphenols pack a punch."

"They do. Plus, they contain flavonoids, which are now known for their numerous properties, including as an aphrodisiac."

"Aphrodisiac?" He winks in a way that makes me feel as if the buttons on my dress might explode out of their buttonholes. "And you say this because you personally experienced it?"

"Harvard, which conducted the study, says so."

"I feel a sudden need to know more about enology."

"I won't leave you hanging. Here," I say, moving on to the next room, "the grapes are pressed to extract the must."

Michael looks at the machine I'm pointing out to him. "I much prefer the image of you crushing grapes with your feet, the old-fashioned way."

"And why is that?"

"It happens in a lot of Sophia Loren films, super sexy."

"Sophia Loren?"

"No, you."

His response, as direct as it is unexpected, leaves me shocked. Does Michael seriously see something sexy in me? Not that I don't consider myself sensual. I can be very sensual when I want to be, but I was convinced—and I still am—that if there is one man on earth incapable of seeing sensuality in me, it's Michael.

Nearly breathless, I continue my explanation of the winemaking process. "The must then passes into these steel vats for fermentation. Our wine is organic. We don't add sulfites because reds are naturally protected from oxidation by tannins, another gift from the precious skin."

"This professor's dress of yours is also rather interesting, you know."

Wham! Another blow below the belt. This time, however, I manage to respond with a worthy joke. "And make sure to stay in line; otherwise, I'll have to punish you." For added authority, I grab a long blackthorn twig that we use to turn the must and tap it on my palm.

A thin, mischievous smile tugs at the left corner of his mouth. "Really interesting."

"Careful, there will be a quiz later," I threaten him, turning my back to him and proceeding at a brisk pace between the vats. With a quick and shameless little shimmy . . . He started it, right? Rise to the challenge or succumb. And this dress I stole from my sister accentuates my every movement. "After two weeks, we filter the impurities out of the wine and . . . follow me." With a pirouette that flares my skirt, I enter an arched passage carved into a wall at least half a meter thick, "We transfer it into these oak barrels."

"Splendid."

"What do you think?" I say, spreading my arms as if to embrace the whole room. "It's the most beautiful part of the property, besides the cellar, of course."

"Actually I was referring to you, but yes, I like the winery too."

This time I speak up, because otherwise I'll have false hopes. Michael is showering me with compliments, and even though I'm an adult and practically immune, I'm not only listening for them a little too much, but liking them a little too much. "Please, Michael, that's enough."

"Enough, what?" he asks with an innocent tone that defies his earlier malice.

"Stop making fun of me. It was funny the first few times, but I don't want to be the butt of your jokes while I'm trying to work."

"Am I joking?"

"Sexy, splendid, exciting teacher dress . . . Come on. I know very well what you think of me."

"I assure you, you have no idea," he replies. "But if I'm out of line, I'll stop. Message received: No more personal compliments."

"Thank you," I reply, reassured. "Professional comments are more than welcome."

He takes my arm, escorting me through the tunnel. "I'm impressed. I didn't know so much work went into a bottle of wine."

I can finally relax. "It's normal. You don't know how hard it is until you're in it." I listen to myself again, and Michael's sidelong glance tells me that there is no way to escape this blatant double meaning. "Work," I specify unnecessarily. "In the work."

"I really appreciate your invitation to let me in," he replies without hesitation. "To your work, of course."

Michael and I walk solemnly in step between the two rows of barrels towering over us, as if we were walking down the nave of a cathedral, the sound of our footsteps reverberating against the vaulted ceiling.

"This is where the wine ages, right?"

"Matures," I correct him. "*Aging* sounds like something is getting worse. *Maturing*, however, means it's improving. In eight months, the acids and tannins balance; the wood barrels enrich the bouquet; and the oxygen that penetrates the oak stabilizes the wine."

"Where are all the bottles?" he asks when we reach the end of the barrels. Michael's voice reveals a sincere curiosity that amazes me and quickens my heartbeat. Not even the most pyrotechnic compliment can match a man who simply shows he's listening.

"Here," I reply, pointing to a wooden door with a worn look and a heavy latch. I unhook it and take one of the flashlights hanging on the wall. "Do you want to see where the magic happens?" I ask, pointing to a stone staircase that disappears down into the darkness.

"That's the best part, isn't it?"

"Nothing better." We step inside, and I close the door behind us, plunging us into darkness. "There are no lights here. There's nothing that can disturb the wine." With a click, I turn on the flashlight, which illuminates a flight of worn stairs.

The staircase is long and narrow, and as we go down, the temperature gradually cools. When we reach the bottom, I illuminate the endless cellar with its low ceiling, one cross vault after another, the sides lined with wooden racks packed with bottles.

"Here's the Chianti Classico Gallo Nero: One hundred thousand bottles come to rest here every year in the dark, cool, silence," I say whispering. I take out a bottle of Count Ricasoli Riserva Oro and place it on a barrel where we keep the tasting kit. If I want to impress Michael, I have to uncork the best we have. "2015 was an excellent year," I say, pouring it into two glasses. "The winery's most prestigious selection."

"Are you trying to bribe me?" he asks, taking the glass by the stem, his fingers near the base, giving me a mental orgasm. Practically everyone I see drinking wine holds the glass by the cup, unaware that heat from the hand alters the flavor.

"If I'm going to convince you that the company has great potential, you have to taste it for yourself, and the potential, right now, is in that glass. But yes, I'd also like to bribe you. Am I succeeding?"

"We shall see," he replies cryptically.

We bring the glasses to our lips and take a sip, in silence, locking eyes in the dim light, our faces barely illuminated. God, why does it look like he's thinking about anything but wine?

I wanted to impress him by reeling off tasting notes worthy of *Wine Spectator*, but everything I ever knew about wine analysis just went out the window. I could have drunk some flat Fanta and not realized it. "What do you think?" I ask him.

"Superb."

"I'm responsible for all this," I exclaim, exhilarated, taking the flashlight again and illuminating the cellar. "Time doesn't exist here. Wine doesn't care; you can't rush it. Every second, every hour, every day, every year that passes, it improves."

"I think you've improved," he says out of nowhere, putting the glass down. Here we are again on that slippery ground from before. "In every way."

"Not that much," I say, a strange pang in my stomach.

"You're just too hard on yourself to admit it." In the dim light, I don't notice his hands moving over the bare skin of my arms. A shiver runs down my spine, and it's not because the cellar is cold.

The shudder turns into a tremor that makes the flashlight slip from my hand. It falls and goes out, leaving us in the dark, at the mercy of our four remaining senses.

Hearing: Our breathing echoes slow and heavy through the brick vault.

Smell: Orange blossom and rosemary—the intensifying scent makes me realize he's gotten even closer.

Touch: His chest exerts a warm, solid pressure against my breasts. I'm in his arms, and even though I'm forcing myself to remain still under his touch, my body doesn't care and reacts by responding with equal and opposite pressure. If one thing is sure in life, it's the third law of motion, and it applies here too. Damn you, Sir Isaac Newton!

And finally, taste: My lips meet the sweet and decisive flavor of berries and an enveloping vanilla: Chianti Riserva, 2015. Michael's lips caress mine with slow and sensual movements to the point that I feel my knees buckle, and I have to clutch his shoulders to stop my fall.

His sweetness gives way to an impetus that is impossible for me to resist and that I welcome with equal enthusiasm, my mouth giving him free access.

We're kissing.

Michael and I are kissing.

He holds me by the waist, his hands leaving a hot trail wherever they go. I breathe him in; he breathes me in. The echo of the vaults, which previously amplified our breaths, now gives voice to our gasps.

"What the hell was in that wine?" he whispers into my mouth, licking my lower lip.

"Flavonoids," I moan, unable to break away long enough to respond.

He lifts me onto the barrel and raises my skirt to my hips, finding space between my open legs.

His mouth descends cheekily below my low neckline, where he finds access, and which I don't even dream of denying—on the contrary, I lower myself backward to make things easier for him, as if they weren't already easy enough.

Crack!

The clang of breaking glass startles me. We've knocked over the glasses and bottle.

It's a fraction of a second, but it's enough for me to summon my mental faculties and shout, "What the hell are we doing?"

He is about to pull me back to him, but I push him away. "No, Michael."

"No?" his voice holds a mixture of surprise and uncertainty.

"No . . . it's . . . it's all wrong."

I don't even give him time to reply before I turn and sprint up the very steep steps four at a time.

With my heart pounding in my chest and my pulse thudding in my ears, I go outside into the blinding sunset.

What have I done?

27

Michael

"What if I told you I kissed Elisa?" I ask Charles, while we indulge in a game of billiards after dinner.

"Are you saying you've realized there's more to her than her personality?"

"Well, I didn't really get to confirm it . . ." She spared me little mercy, but I admit I keep wishing we'd taken things further.

"So, you like her?"

"I don't know. It's all very confusing. One minute she's a witch who can get on my nerves like no one else; the next minute the only thing that stops me from jumping on her and tearing her clothes off is the violation of at least nine articles of the penal code."

Charles, with the cue resting on his shoulders, in his typically indolent pose and the expression of someone who is not remotely surprised, shakes his head mockingly. "Is that so?"

"I can't define the gray area we're in." Damn! I just shot at one of Bingley's balls.

"Did she kiss you back?"

"What kind of question is that? Of course she kissed me back. Who are we talking about here?"

Bingley reaches across the table, aiming for the yellow billiard. "Was she active or passive?"

I retrace those few long and torrid moments in the cellar. "Active." Damn, she was active. "Just that . . ."

"Just, what?"

"Eh . . . we still had more left to explore," I say, my thumb and forefinger clutching the blue chalk. "But she stopped, said it was a mistake, and ran out."

"What the hell did you do to her?" he asks me, amazed.

"Me? Nothing! Not yet, at least. I don't know what happened."

"The classic last-second change of heart," says Charles, with a mock-pained tone.

"Oh, will you stop playing Dr. Strangelove?"

"If you didn't care, you wouldn't be here, talking to me, would you?"

"Guess not."

"Change of heart about what?" a third voice interrupts. It's Caroline, returning from the spa.

"Nothing. Charles is nervous about turbulence on his flight to New York," I say. If there's one person I want to keep out of my business, it's her. "You know how much he hates flying."

"I wouldn't care if I had to fly in cargo," says Caroline. "Landing in New York after this week in the middle of nowhere will be like coming back to earth."

"At least one of us is happy about it," Charles mutters, missing his shot.

"Why do you want to stay here?" she asks, dazed.

"Not why, but for whom," I say.

She raises an eyebrow in confusion. "Is there something I should know?"

"No, but if you really must, I'm seeing someone, and it's serious," says Charles.

"Giada," I point out.

Caroline bursts out laughing. "The words *Giada* and *serious* cannot be used in the same sentence. Charles, please, she's so cheap!"

"You think anyone who doesn't wear Dior from head to toe like you is cheap," he dismisses her. "Plus, I'm the one who has to like her, not you."

Caroline looks at me, annoyed. "Look, Michael, you've seen them together, what do you think?"

"I think our Charles has had a nice trip, as usual. You know how he is, right? He floats three feet off the ground, his eyes turn into hearts, he daydreams . . ."

"Just because you've never been in love doesn't give you the right to make fun of me," he replies. "When it happens to you—when, not if—you'll be even worse."

"I doubt it."

Donatella interrupts us with a light knock and enters with a tray. "Passionflower tea for Miss Bingley, with house honey."

"Thanks, pour me a cup. No honey," she replies without even looking at her. "Please, Charles! Think about it—what's the point of being in a relationship with someone who lives in Chianti?"

"It actually won't be long distance. We talked about it. She's not particularly fond of Belvedere either and would love to broaden her horizons; at the end of the year, she'll come be with me in London."

"There you have it." I stop him, after Donatella has left us. "You may be perfectly over the moon, but are you sure she isn't with you because you're a walking, all-inclusive one-way ticket to London?"

Okay, maybe I'm coming across as an asshole, but Bingley is soft as they come, and a smart woman could easily eviscerate him. I'm his best friend. It's my job to warn him about these things.

"He's right," Caroline echoes. "For a broke country beautician, you're practically a diamond mine in South Africa."

"You two see bad intentions everywhere," he replies, leaning on the edge of the billiard table. "Saturday night, we're having a reunion dinner with friends from when we were kids. Watch us together, and you'll see Giada and I are serious."

Caroline rolls her eyes. "Sounds like torture, but I'm happy to sacrifice myself for the cause."

"It won't be a sacrifice and there is no cause," he replies.

"Maybe, but someone could make eyes at you over a petrol pump and come away with something. You're also not bad-looking; I'm sure it wasn't a stretch for her to indulge herself," insists Caroline, much more ruthless than I would ever dare to be.

Although, if the rumors are true, Giada has extended her graces to just about everyone, though I won't say this to Bingley.

"Look"—I intervene to calm things down but still try to keep some leverage—"we may be wrong, but just in case we're not, why don't you slow it down a little?" I suggest. "Now it's intense, you're seeing each other all day, every day, maybe it seems bigger than it is. You have a few trips over the next few weeks. Put some space and time between you and Giada and see if anything changes. You always throw yourself into these things from the high dive, holding your breath until you bottom out. Listen to me: Come to the surface and get some air. Maybe you'll realize that what you mistook for an ocean is just a kiddie pool." I lean over the table and take aim. "Purple in the corner pocket."

Bingley, however, puts the cue back in its brass holder with an annoyed huff. "You two can play, I'm done," he snaps. But first, he stops in the doorway and points his finger at me. "If I were you, I wouldn't be feeling so superior. You have your own problems to solve."

"I don't know what you're talking about," I say, angrily.

"You know exactly what I'm talking about, Michael. You're too smart not to have noticed."

28

Elisa

Linda and I are driving back from the village, where we picked up some things at the market for her pizza night and our reunion dinner. It's a big day at Le Giuggiole.

Tonight I'll be cooking for everyone. I haven't suddenly come down with a case of Belvedere tradwife syndrome, but I need to keep my hands busy to avoid thinking about what happened in the cellar.

Yesterday I was in the vineyard all day, but today I have no escape.

"How many of you are there tonight?" I ask Linda.

"Six."

"Who did you invite?" I press, in an attempt to extend the conversation.

"Alice and Valentina Pini, Laura Bolli, Enrico Quinti, and Tommaso Ghirardi," she says the final two names quietly, almost inaudibly, though it doesn't help that the old Punto I drive has a punctured muffler and you almost have to scream to hear over it.

"Boys?" I exclaim, petrified.

"Yeah. So what?"

"We didn't talk about boys the other day," I protest.

"I told you I was inviting classmates. I never said if they were boys or girls."

I guess I took that one as a given. "So, why on earth did you choose them?" I'm afraid to ask, but I have to.

"Valentina likes Enrico and would only come if he was there, but Enrico doesn't go anywhere without Tommaso, and Alice always goes out with her sister," she replies concisely. Smooth as butter, without hesitation.

"Are you still doing homework for Alice, Valentina, and Laura?"

"What's the harm in it?"

My daughter is as good as it gets. Those three take advantage of her. "You do know that real friendship isn't based on trading favors? If you keep doing their homework, you'll never know if they're your real friends." But I want to go back to the question that worries me the most. "And Enrico and Tommaso are okay guys? Are they well behaved?"

"No, Mom. They're two felonious junkies," she replies, annoyed.

"You know what I mean, Linda," I admonish her for her tasteless joke.

She's only just started adolescence, and I already can't wait for it to end.

"Neither of them will rape us, you can rest assured."

"In the meantime, tone it down, please. You know I trust you. I just don't trust kids I don't know. And you weren't exactly transparent when you told me you were inviting your classmates."

"So are you saying I have to uninvite them?" she asks bitterly.

"No, it's too late for that now, but remember, I'll be in the next room . . ."

"Ready to spoil our sleepover. Got it," she concludes, crossing her arms over her chest.

"I don't want to ruin anything for you, Little Cub. I'm the first to want you to have fun with your friends, but I also want you to behave yourself," I warn her. "So yes, I'll come check on you if I think that's necessary." I can't help but grasp the subtle irony in the fact that I'm lecturing my daughter when, yesterday, in the cellar, I was about to launch into a scorching performance with Michael.

"G-o-o-o-o-d, Mom!" she snorts, jumping out of the car as soon as we stop in front of the annex.

As I leave all the junk I bought her for her party in the kitchenette, my eye falls on a garbage bag overflowing with pastel-colored objects outside the door. I peek and recognize some of Linda's things: Winnie-the-Pooh pajamas; playdough necklaces; the photo of her at Gardaland with Prezzemolo the mascot; a Barbie blanket that used to be Giada's, then mine, and then hers; and at the bottom is a faded, mangy pink rag: her teddy bear, the one she has slept with every night since she was a year old.

Instinctively I pull it from the bag and put it in the laundry basket.

Mentally advising myself to address the "kid" issue with her another time, I take the groceries to the villa's kitchen. I have two hours until guests arrive, and I haven't even started cooking.

I had the unfortunate idea of getting dressed and putting on make-up beforehand without thinking that between kneading and baking, when I've finished I'll have runny make-up and a ruined dress, plus the gladiator sandals I'm wearing are already coming loose and sagging around my ankles.

As I'm contorting myself to pull up the evil laces with one hand, holding the hem of my long white linen dress between my teeth, with the two shopping bags in my arms, Michael appears.

He greets me with a wave of his hand, and I nearly spill the market bags on the floor.

He has quick reflexes and catches the one with the eggs. "Can I help you?"

"No, I can manage," I say, stiffening, careful not to let him touch me.

"That doesn't appear to be the case." He insists, taking the other bag from my hands. "Let me make myself useful." And without further hesitation, he takes the shopping bags to the kitchen.

"Okay, um . . . just put everything on the table," I stammer. "Thank you."

We stand there, staring at each other in silence. The clock made from an old copper pot hanging over the fireplace marks the seconds of silence between us.

"Listen . . ." he begins.

"Listen . . ." I say at the same time.

"You first."

"No, you go ahead, Michael." I may be a coward, but I don't dare open my mouth without knowing what he's going to say.

"I wanted to talk to you about the cellar," he continues in a near whisper. "About what happened."

"There's no need," I reply, randomly taking something out of a bag to pretend I'm busy and hide my face, which is already flushing.

"I think there is," he insists. "Why did you put the dish detergent in the fridge?"

Oops. "Surfactants work better if they're cold when the hot water hits them."

"Really?"

"Yup. I studied it in chemistry. A+," I reply with the confident air of Count Mascetti.

"Anyway, I think we might have gone a little too far."

Oh. "Absolutely," I lie. Or rather, I agree that we went too far, but the fact is I didn't mind it.

"From the way you ran off, I realized it was a mistake. I don't want to complicate things between us."

A mistake. It was just a mistake. "Of course."

"I think I just got a little carried away. I was so taken by your words, by the atmosphere, by the flirtation that started as a joke . . . Anyway, I'm sorry for making you uncomfortable."

"You don't have to apologize. I didn't behave any better."

"You knew how to stop yourself."

"It's just so . . . strange." It's not the exact word, but it's the only one that comes to mind.

"I know. That's why I wanted to be sure we're on the same page. Better to pretend it never happened, right?"

"And it won't happen again." I say it aloud, but in reality I'm addressing my irresponsible conscience.

"Well then, as for tonight, has everyone confirmed?" he changes the subject.

"Yeah," I reply, relieved at the idea of being back on safe territory. "Lapo and Margherita, Cosimo and his partner, and Lucia, who asked me to add another place because she's bringing someone. Then there's the five of us: me, Giada, you, Carletto, and his sister."

"Eleven people? And your mom is doing the cooking?" he asks, amazed.

"No, Mamma is at the annex, making pizza for Linda and her friends. I'm cooking for us."

Michael looks at me in amazement. "Not to doubt your abilities, but eleven mouths is a lot to feed."

"I chose an easy menu: a preprepared charcuterie board; bruschetta with sausage and provola from Mugello; cherry tomatoes, burrata, and basil for the vegetarians; and a main of *pici* pasta with vegetable ragù."

"I'm already hungry," he says, licking his lips. I look away, staring intently at the loaf of bread, because if nothing more is going to happen between us, I have to avoid every temptation.

"Well then, leave me to it, if you want to eat. If we keep talking, we'll be having toast for dinner."

"I can do better than leave you to it," he says. "I can help you."

I swallow dryly. Oh God. I have the feeling that these will be the longest two hours of my life.

29

Michael

It took me a while to convince her, but in the end Elisa gave in, but only because I swore not to say a word—both literally and figuratively—and to follow her orders. She prepares the toppings; I slice the bread. It's not exactly a Cordon Bleu–level skill, but hey, even at Her Majesty's court someone has to clean the toilets.

"Three slices each," she orders, dicing the cherry tomatoes. "One finger thick. Then put them on the trays and brush them with oil."

"Yes, Chef," I shout like Gordon Ramsay's underlings in Hell's Kitchen.

"Are you teasing me?"

"No, Chef."

"Careful, or I'll make you eat the crumbs."

"I'm happy to lick the pots." I realize that after our truce I should stay away from double meanings, but the look I give her at the word *lick* escapes my control.

She responds to my provocation by dipping her finger into the bowl of cherry tomatoes with burrata and sucking off the juice. "Then I won't leave any of these for you, either." It's getting bad.

The dress she's wearing, though it's floor-length, is so revealing, with thin straps and semi-sheer linen through which I can just glimpse the pattern on her panties. But she's not wearing a bra because, well, she just isn't.

I was very convinced about what I said to her before—key word being *was*. Now I don't know.

"Nooo!" she exclaims. "This traitorous cherry tomato just stained my dress. My hands are dirty—can you do me a favor, Michael? Can you get my mother's apron over there on the door and help me put it on?"

I carry out the harmless order without batting an eye until I'm behind her tying the apron at her waist, and I realize there's nothing innocent about it at all.

How do I put this on her without touching her? I'm not Houdini! Among other things, in this position and from my height, I have the best possible view of her breasts . . . Michael, concentrate!

I complete the mission with my eyes half closed and using only the tips of my fingers, which tremble as if I were defusing a bomb. "Done," I announce with a parched mouth and Olympic gold–worthy pride.

"Thanks. Let's season the bruschetta and set them aside since we'll bake them last. Now for the pici—I'll need your hands here."

No, Elisa; you can't say these things. I can't take it. "Okay."

She pours some flour into a bowl. "Now, so we don't make too much of a mess, you slowly pour in the warm water while I stir."

We get to work, and in a short time a nice white, soft dough thickens in the bowl which she then greases and wraps in plastic. "While this goes in the fridge, we repeat the process two more times."

I'm about to tell her we can do this as many times as she wants, but I hold back. The problem is that when I offered to help her—and it was a sincere and disinterested proposal; I'm not the type of man who thinks that a woman's place is in the kitchen—I underestimated the seductive power of cooking together.

The way she moves her hands, the way she smells the ingredients, the way she tastes them, the closeness of her . . . it's the stuff of fantasies.

Once the dough is finished, we take the first bowl from the fridge.

"Now comes the best part," she announces. "Making the pici." She divides the ball in two with a knife and passes half to me on the large floured cutting board. "Watch how I do it."

It's easier said than done for someone who always just orders off the menu, and she certainly doesn't make it look easy. Roll out the dough with a rolling pin? Who uses a rolling pin in the twenty-first century? Then, with impressive knife skills, she cuts a series of strips and rolls them on the cutting board, transforming them into something like spaghetti, all with the same length and diameter.

I give it a try, but my hand-eye coordination, which is infallible on the squash courts, abandons me here. "I give up," I say, raising my hands in front of my first bunch of pici, which look more like worms that have been crushed by a truck.

"Come behind me," she says, positioning herself in front of me. "And don't snort in annoyance."

I'm not annoyed—far from it! But is she really so naive to think that after yesterday there can be an entirely innocent connotation to the phrase "come behind me"?

"Place your hands on either end of the rolling pin, next to mine," she says. "And roll out the dough like this: forward, backward, forward, backward."

All fine, except that her body—specifically, her lower half—is rocking back and forth, rhythmically touching my pelvis.

I'm dangerously approaching the limit to my best intentions. And that's my best—not my worst . . .

"Now let's cut the strips and roll them up, like this." As she stretches out the innocent pici, our hands touch.

It's dangerous skin-to-skin contact, with her bare neck caressed by a few wavy strands falling from her bun and the sweet scent of her rose water perfume teasing my senses. I just want to bite her . . .

I could . . .

I know there's a huge chance she'll give me an epic slap but . . . who cares. I'll take the risk!

30

Elisa

Good thing I decided to cook to distract myself! Michael and I are candidates for the Palme d'Or for liars of the year. It took us half an hour to get from "Let's pretend it didn't happen" to making allusions, to physical contact which, I admit, I also encouraged.

I'm afraid I like Michael more than I want to admit. The worst is that I'm knowingly throwing fuel on the fire in the hopes that he'll take this flirtation to the next level, because I don't have the courage to make the first move myself.

Right now, Michael is behind me. We're practically spooning, bent over the cutting board making—or, at least, attempting to make—the pici.

His hands, which until now were next to mine, move up my arms and stop around my shoulders, and a warm pressure on my neck triggers an internal shock.

"What are you doing?" I whisper breathlessly.

"Tasting you," he replies.

"Do you like what you taste?"

His mouth continues, impertinent and brazen, up to my ear. "It's to die for."

We've taken the plunge. If I'd wanted to push him away, this would have been my chance. I turn to face him, my hands on his chest. "I thought the new rule was no touching," I murmur against his lips.

"Rules are made to be broken," he shoots back, brushing my lips with his. "Where did we leave off yesterday?"

"On the barrel."

And just like yesterday, he lifts me up, but this time it's onto the floured cutting board. "Let's pick up where we left off." He unclips my hair, letting it fall down my back. "You drive me crazy."

We're all over each other, ravenous, our flour-covered hands traveling everywhere. The straps of my dress fall down, revealing my breasts, while I wrap my legs around Michael's waist and hook his T-shirt with my fingers to lift it.

Our goodwill agreement was short-lived. Only this time I have no intention of running off . . . on the contrary! I lean back until I'm almost lying down, pulling Michael on top of me, without any thought for the dough.

"The pici!" he pants.

"We can order pizza," I say, imploring him not to stop kissing me, my hands gripping his hair to prevent him from moving more than a millimeter away from me.

He lifts my dress and grabs my buttocks firmly, his fingers already hooked on the edge of my panties; I'm busy fiddling with his belt buckle when the thud of the front door and the echo of lively chatter in the hall surprises us.

We freeze, looking into each other's eyes with a flash of terror. "Did you hear that?" he asks me, petrified.

"Yeah. Are they here already?" I ask, recognizing Lapo's and Margherita's voices. "What time is it?"

"Seven," he replies, checking the clock.

"They're early!" I exclaim, looking around. "Shit."

"Shit!"

I jump off the table, and we brush the flour off each other. "How do I look?"

"You should pull your hair back."

"Your jeans, zip them."

We clean ourselves up just in time for the merry gang to make their entrance.

"So, are you the chefs tonight?" asks Giada, followed by everyone else.

"Did you manage to make something edible, or did you spend the evening just working yourselves up?" jokes Carletto.

Cosimo approaches the table, from which he plucks one of the pici we steamrolled. "Judging by this, I'd say tonight we're having nothing but bread. But it's a pleasure to see Elisa has finally learned to dress herself as God intended."

Michael and I exchange a sideways glance, as if to say, *Just in time.*

"Well, there's dessert: We brought a ton of Buontalenti!" Lapo announces, waving the tub of gelato. "What can we do? Shall we help you set the table?"

"Sure," I nod. "I'll bake the bruschetta. You guys can set the table under the pergola." Practical things—I have to concentrate on practical things to cool off.

While guests swarm around the kitchen with their respective tasks, Michael approaches me, touching his head to mine. "It's just a setback," he whispers in my ear. "I have every intention of finishing what we started."

Someone call 9-1-1. There's a fire!

We're about to sit down at the table, Giada and Carletto hand in hand, Caroline with her perpetual annoyed look, Lapo showing off his repertoire of jokes and Margherita scolding him for the vulgar ones. Cosimo and his partner Andres have brought each of us one of their personalized essences, and Michael and I end up accidentally finding ourselves next to each other. Of course, this only fuels the tension from the kitchen. Not to mention that tonight I have to keep an eye on the bunch of wild teenagers down at the annex . . .

We're only missing Lucia and her companion, who are coming up the path.

"I thought we were eating at your place, not here at the villa. So, it's an event! Good thing I wore my new dress," she jokes. Her mysterious plus-one appears a few steps behind her . . .

No, it can't be!

This must be a joke.

"Elmo?" I ask, unable to contain my shock and earning a kick in the shins from Giada, who is sitting across from me.

"I told you I wouldn't be alone," she replies with a serene smile. "Did you set an extra place?"

"Of, of course," I stammer, still stunned.

Elmo Colli? What the hell is Lucia doing with Elmo Colli? Charity work?

"Sit down!" Giada trills with enthusiasm. "There was a mix-up with the pici, but the *bruschettoni* are plentiful, there's charcuterie for days, and we have crudités and dip with veggies from the garden. And what we don't have in food, we'll make up for in wine." She welcomes them over by holding out two full glasses to them. She gives me a big-sister look, and I down my entire glass of red in one gulp.

Food and alcohol liven up the conversation, and Cosimo and Andres hold court with updates.

"Let's toast! We have an announcement to make," exclaims Cosimo.

"Are you getting married?" asks Margherita, who, like a good Belvedere native, is always thinking about wedding rings.

"That's coming, but not yet. On September 15, a selection of our perfumes is going on sale at Selfridges! In London!"

We all burst into applause. It is extremely rare for a person from Belvedere to venture over the county line—not to mention the Alps.

"How did you do it?" asks Giada.

"Pure luck. In April, a buyer from Selfridges was pickpocketed right in front of our store," explains Andres.

"Lucky for you," Carletto jokes.

"Not so much for her. In any case, we helped her, took her to file a complaint, and tried to make up for the loss of her brand-new Gucci tote with a gift of three of our fragrances."

"Gangsters," Michael taunts them. "You hired that pickpocket, didn't you?"

"We had no idea who she was. She hadn't told us what she did, and we thought she was just another English tourist. But the next day, she came back and introduced herself, telling us that the following month was the Paris Parfumeur, the largest international perfumery fair, where she and the warehouse managers decide what new products to bring to the shop. She said if we had a stand, she'd do her best to convince her buyers, so . . ."

"And so we used all our savings," Andres takes the floor.

"The cash we would have spent on a wedding reception, basically," emphasizes Cosimo.

"You sound like you regret it," his partner scolds him.

"Never! But yeah, it took us a long time to make that money . . . sorry. I'll stop. Go on."

"Well, we invested in everything we needed for the fair—the stand, the logistics, the samples, the travel. At the end of the week, Selfridges offered us an exclusive deal for part of our line. In short, we're potential future billionaires."

"Who are currently totally broke. Cheers," says Cosimo, smiling tipsily.

"How wonderful, guys," I say, sighing in admiration. "I'd love to get our wines on the international market."

"Then do it!" he replies, as if it were obvious. "Take your best bottles, sign up for the most important fair you can find, and introduce the label to anyone who matters."

He's not entirely wrong. I know we make excellent wine, and if I found good buyers, I'd certainly have more leverage with the bank. "I'll think about it," I say with conviction.

"Oof," Margherita snorts, leaning forward as we all look at her wide-eyed.

"Everything okay?" Giada asks.

"Yes, it's these fucking false contractions. Anyway, it passed. All jokes aside, looks like we're all in relationships—it's just you left, Caroline," she chirps cheerfully.

"Better alone than in bad company," she replies dryly. "And in any case, you're wrong. Michael is also happily single," she points out with a smile that I feel is directed at me.

"Ah, I must have misunderstood. Cosimo and Andres, Lapo and me, Lucia and Elmo, Carletto and Giada, and then seeing Michael and Elisa sitting so close, I just assumed . . . The two of them have always been like chalk and cheese. Anyway, don't mind me. It's a shame, though, you'd make a nice couple," comments Margherita, biting into a bruschetta.

"I'll go get the dessert," I say, standing up suddenly. I don't want this conversation to escalate. Michael and I are already walking on the edge of a fiery ravine. All we need is for people to start speculating.

Would we make a nice couple? I don't know. Maybe we're one of those beautiful ideas—brilliant in theory but disastrous in practice. It's almost certainly the latter. And in terms of disasters, we'd be like Fukushima.

But what if we did work out?

No, it would be a one-in-a-billion chance. He and I can't stay in the same room without arguing or jumping on each other; it certainly doesn't bode well . . .

But . . .

Okay, that's it. Enough of these mental movies—there is no *but*! I take the tray with the *zuccotto* and stride out toward the pergola.

"Dessert!" I announce.

"I think we have to go," says Lapo, helping Margherita to her feet.

"These aren't false contractions. They're real," she pants. "We have to get going."

"No!" Cosimo jumps up. "We'll take you. Come on!"

"I'm off to sleep. I have a headache," Caroline announces, in the tone of someone who has generously given her time to inferiors.

In short, the table empties, but not quite enough to leave Michael and me alone, and with the risk we took earlier, neither of us dares to make a move.

From this dinner, I seem to have emerged in more of a bind than ever.

31

Michael

I watch Elisa clear the table, but she doesn't even spare me a glance; or rather, she does, but as soon as I intercept it, she looks away. It's making me crazy.

I have to find a way to be with her. Alone, just the two of us.

32

Elisa

I'm rinsing dishes to load into the dishwasher, when I hear footsteps in the kitchen.

My first thought goes to Michael.

I turn around to find it's actually Lucia.

"I'll give you a hand," she offers, placing the empty serving plates on the table.

"It's okay. I can do it."

"Fine, but I want to know what's up with you."

"Me?" I say in a voice so shrill it's suspicious. "Nothing."

"You hardly spoke to me all evening."

"We were at opposite ends of the table," I justify myself, knowing that it's a lie the size of a house.

"Come on, be honest. I don't want something hanging between us."

Okay, let's address the issue. If she wants me to be honest, I will be.

"Come on, Lucia! Elmo Colli?! I hope he's a mercy date," I blurt out, doubting myself immediately afterward. "Please tell me you brought him out of pity?"

"No, Elisa. Elmo and I are dating. We're a couple."

At her reply, I find myself with so many things I want to say to her that in the end I don't know which to choose and I'm left gasping for air.

"Don't make that face."

"I don't know what to say," I say, stunned.

"Do you have to say anything?"

"You do realize who we're talking about, don't you? Elmo Colli! The most unctuous, pompous, presumptuous, and all the other worst adjectives ending in *-ous* a person can be. How on earth can you bear to date him?"

"He also happens to have some good qualities, if you care to look for them," she objects.

"Don't you realize he's only here with you to get to me? Because I rejected him?" I wasn't too subtle, but it was a safe bet that, slimy as he is, he would choose my only friend in Belvedere as a way of taking revenge.

Lucia's expression darkens, and she looks down. "Yeah, Elisa, I'm well aware that I'm his fallback, a miserable second choice and that he would have preferred you a hundred times over, but you know what? I'm not offended because I know the truth and I accept it. I harbor no illusions."

"Lucia, do you think maybe you've caught the local wedding fever? I thought at least you would be immune to such anachronistic nonsense."

"I am also a nearly forty-year-old woman who still lives at home with her parents."

"And the only alternative is Elmo?" I insist in disbelief.

As we raise our voices, she closes the door so no one can hear us.

"Let me tell you about my situation. Ever since I got my philosophy degree, I've been hanging by a thread at the university, which decided not to renew my research grant. I tried to move to Florence, but with the odd jobs I picked up, I barely made the rent and was living in an illegal garage studio apartment, waiting for someone to call to offer substitute teaching work. Like so many others, I was full of hope when I left Belvedere, but I came back because, unlike the others, I didn't make it."

"Sooner or later, you will get a permanent position," I reply.

"Yeah, but when is this 'later'? Did you know that the average age of entry into a teaching job in Italy is forty-four? Forty-four! I want a job, I want my own money—I want my own family and a real life; I don't want to wait any longer. I am one hundred and ninety-fourth on the national teacher's list, which means one hundred and ninety-three teachers have to be placed before I can get a job. How many philosophy teachers could Tuscany need?"

"You speak like someone who has no choice."

"Do I have one? I've tried everything. I can't keep tutoring for a pittance, plus Elmo offered me a good position."

"In his company," I point out.

"What's the harm? It won't be the carnival in Rio, but someone has to care for the dead."

"So that's all there is to it? You're seeing him because he offered you a job?"

"I happen to like Elmo too. He is an honest, polite man, and he's relatively cultured, which doesn't hurt. He may not be Brad Pitt, but at least he is not the type to abandon his own kid."

One shot, one target. She aimed straight for me and didn't miss.

"I'm not asking you to jump for joy, but at least respect my choice, Elisa. Or if you can't, at least avoid criticizing me—you're in no position to do so."

"Lucia, I just want to see you happy."

"Well, I will be. Much happier than I am now."

I shake my head, not understanding the path she's decided to take. "I thought you were stronger than this."

"Oh, sorry, Elisa, have I disappointed you? You know what? Have you ever wondered why it's so hard to get along with you? Why you hardly have any friends? Because you are judgmental. You look down on everyone from your ivory tower, deciding who is worthy and who isn't, but you never question yourself."

"Sorry if I expressed a doubt."

"No, you didn't express a doubt. You've openly insulted me and the person I'm with because we don't have the same grandiose plans for our future, as if you have it all figured out. I don't want to have to be mean, but I'll say this: Look at your life with a little less arrogance and you'll see that it's not too different from mine. And decide if you're okay with being alone and working on a vineyard that isn't even yours."

"It is fine with me," I state with conviction, crossing my arms assertively.

"Perfect, then there's nothing left to discuss," she decrees with the same severity with which she calmed our arguments as kids, back when she used to babysit us. "I'm happy with my life, you're happy with yours, so we're all happy. I have to go. Tomorrow morning, if you feel like it, we can have breakfast, calmly, at the bakery, before I start moving my things to Forte."

She leaves without another word, and I remain there, frozen in place, in the middle of the kitchen that looks like a battlefield.

Feeling a little dejected, I start to scrape leftovers into the dustbin so violently that it tips and spills part of its contents.

"Damn it," I mutter to myself, bending down to clean up the mess.

Among the crumbs, lettuce leaves, crusts, and celery stalks, I find a balled-up piece of paper, which I open.

I don't know if we can be a good couple, but we certainly have some good times together, you and me.

I also like it when we fight.

If you want, I'll wait for you in my room tomorrow morning, early, while everyone is still asleep.

Michael

"Am I judgmental?" I ask Giada as soon as she turns on the light and enters her room, where I've been waiting for at least an hour.

"God! You scared me!" she exclaims with a leap.

"You didn't answer my question."

"Um, yes, you are," she says bluntly.

"Gee, thanks," I reply resentfully.

"Why do you care? I thought it was your most prized character trait."

"I think I criticized Lucia a little too freely for dating Elmo," I confess.

"No offense, Elisa, but it's really none of your business," she says, undressing. And as she takes off her dress, I notice that she's naked underneath.

"What happened to your underwear?"

"That's none of your business either," she replies, sticking out her tongue. "If you must know, Charles has it. He's leaving tomorrow, and I'd like him to remember me."

"What a refined souvenir . . ."

"We were just saying a second ago how judgmental you are."

"I'm sorry, but you don't find it strange that she and Elmo got together?" I ask, returning to the main topic.

"Believe it or not, they seem like a pretty balanced couple to me: She's patient, sweet, maternal, and introverted, and Elmo needs someone like that. And he's old-fashioned and over the top, which makes her feel safe and appreciated. His fake compliments may disgust you, but evidently that's what she needs. I'm not a psychologist, but that's how I see it." My sister flops down on the bed, her legs propped up against the headboard to "reverse the circulation," as she always says, and fight cellulite.

"I'll try to be less judgmental," I sigh.

"And maybe less touchy," she adds. "By the way . . . why was your lipstick all smeared when we arrived?" she asks me with a sly smile. "Confess."

I narrow my eyes and clench my fists as if what I'm about to say could hurt me. "Michael and I kissed."

"What!" she exclaims, jumping up. "And this is how I find out?!"

"And it wasn't the first time," I add.

She grabs a pillow and throws it at my face. "You're such a coward. You couldn't even tell your own sister!"

"I have no idea what the hell we're doing."

Giada raises her hand like a telephone receiver to her ear.

"Hello? I'd like to talk to Elisa's libido. Can you pass the phone? I have to explain what two healthy and robust adults do when they're attracted to each other."

"Not funny."

"When was the first time?"

"Thursday afternoon," I sigh. "In the cellar. I dropped the flashlight, the darkness and the wine did the rest . . ." I trip on the words, thinking back to that moment.

"The rest, what?" Giada urges me. "This is no time for suspense."

"If the broken glasses hadn't brought me to my senses, I'm pretty sure we would have gone far beyond a kiss."

Giada looks at me with a mischievous expression. "More than a kiss, huh? Then I guess it wasn't such an innocent little thing."

"*Innocent* is the last word I'd use to describe him."

"And then what happened?" she urges.

"Nothing. I ran away."

"Very mature," she observes.

"It wasn't supposed to happen again."

"Until tonight."

"I never thought making pici could be such an erotic experience. At a certain point he slammed me onto the floured cutting board and . . . and then nothing, then you arrived."

"How did you leave it?" she asks, gripped by curiosity.

"How did we leave it? Halfway through, Giada. Halfway through."

"Once is a mistake, twice, on the other hand . . . you know what they say: Things come in threes."

"With a fourth sure to follow," I conclude. I decide it's best I don't tell her about tomorrow morning's secret rendezvous.

33

MICHAEL

The note was a tad middle school, as in, "Do you want to be with me? Check *yes, no, maybe,*" but I didn't want to leave things unresolved.

Did she find it? Did it work?

I wondered about it all evening, thinking about the bad timing of it all; if she hadn't had to supervise Linda's sleepover, we could have ended the night here, in my bed . . . Finally, just as the sun is rising, I hear a light knock on my door.

"Come in," I say to Elisa, as I settle down to welcome her, the sheet barely covering me. "I was waiting for you."

"I highly doubt that," says Donatella, surprising me with her aplomb.

"Shit!" I exclaim, pulling the sheet up to my chin. "What are you doing here?"

"There are visitors here for you, Mr. D'Arcy."

"I'm not expecting any visitors," I reply dryly. I can't handle another sister, cousin, or tenth-degree relative of the three Cozzi cousins. I'm done with that.

"Your girlfriend is here with your other girlfriend," she says, unfazed.

Her sentence sends me scrambling to sit up, alarmed. "Whaaat!"

"Miss Sheila and Miss Danielle are waiting for you in the living room."

Exactly as I feared. But how is this possible?! Grasping for words, I find myself speechless. If Elisa finds them here, it will be such a mess! Shit!

"Shall I tell them the gentleman will come down, or shall I send them up to your room? And in the latter case, do you prefer to receive them one at a time or both together?" I seem to detect a vaguely sadistic streak in Donatella's serious and competent tone.

"I'll go down," I grumble.

"Very good. I'll make some coffee."

"Donatella," I call her back before she disappears. "I don't have a girlfriend," I say.

"Okay, then you should probably share that information with them."

I quickly pull on my clothes and go downstairs to the foyer, where I find Sheila and Danielle sitting next to each other on the sofa, arms crossed and livid.

"I'll just be taking this," Donatella announces, entering and snatching away a vase from the coffee table. "It's a Ming." She must have noticed things are looking ominous. "Would you ladies like anything?"

"Cyanide," Danielle says through gritted teeth, staring at me.

"I'll leave you to it, then." Donatella hands me over to the firing squad.

"Surprise, darling," Sheila greets me sourly.

"Yes, quite." This isn't the time for sarcasm, but my nerves get the better of me.

"Did you think we were idiots?" she attacks me, surprising me with an aggressiveness I've never seen from her.

"No, I just didn't imagine . . ." I didn't think they'd ever cross paths.

"That we'd find out you were screwing two women at once?" finishes Danielle. "You nearly got away with it too. Except my sister gave me a voucher for a massage at a new spa near her place in Maida Vale, and guess who gave me the treatment?"

"Me," Sheila replies, raising her hand. "You know, Michael, it's quite normal for masseuses and clients to chat about this and that during a session, and it turned out we both had a boyfriend named Michael, they both worked in asset management and that—get this!—they were both in Italy for a month to close a real estate deal. A few too many coincidences."

"I can explain," I defend myself, behind my open hands to protect against any forthcoming blows.

And since God hates me and wants me to know it, he chooses this very moment for Elisa to make an entrance.

"Explain what?" she asks from the doorway, confused by the strange scene.

"Looks like she's the third," Danielle exclaims, elbowing Sheila.

Although she's only just arrived, Elisa knows English well enough to have understood. At Danielle's mention of a *third*, her gaze changes, her eyes filling with disappointment.

"The third what?"

"It's not a business trip," spits Sheila. "He's sleeping with her too."

"It's not what it seems," I say to Elisa, in a tone that's hardly reassuring. It's not what it seems—it's worse.

"Who . . . who are these women?" she asks me with a tremor in her voice.

"I'm Michael's girlfriend," Sheila says quickly.

"So am I," adds Danielle. "What about you? He's with Sheila during the week. He's with me during the weekend, so where do you fit in? What are your shifts?"

"I can't believe it," Sheila moans with tears in her eyes. "I trusted you. We've been together for six months. When did you start seeing other women?"

"Well, Sheila, that's the point. I never started seeing other women, I've always seen other women," I confess, ashamed to the core. "I didn't think we were exclusive . . ."

"Well, instead of thinking it, you could have bothered to say it," Danielle confronts me. "You know what? You're just a big dick with a little man attached to it. You don't offer anything a nice vibrator doesn't, so you can go fuck yourself, Michael," she shouts, as she coldly brushes past Elisa, who is watching me silently.

Sheila, Elisa, and I remain, immersed in a chilling silence.

"You know, I can see why you're into Danielle. She's a beautiful woman, classy, she holds herself well for forty-three—but her?" Sheila asks, pointing to Elisa. "You go for slobs now too?"

"Sheila, please don't insult someone who has nothing to do with this," I stop her. "It's my fault."

"You're right, it is your fault. I was wasting my time with you. We could have been a family one day!" she says, grabbing a glass ornament and hurling it at me, though it misses and hits the mantelpiece. "Don't ever speak to me again," she shouts, before walking away.

Elisa looks at me and shakes her head.

"Please, I . . ." I implore her. "I can explain."

"What is there to explain? I saw it all with my own eyes, and in any case, unlike these two unhappy people, you told me. In fact, you wrote it down in black and white that we are not a couple. You don't owe me any explanations. I'm sure you can easily find some other naive lady to add to the notches on your bedpost."

"Elisa, I know I'm not in any place to speak, but you're not a notch. Not you."

"Look, we're okay. Anyway, what else could there have been between us, if not a one-night stand? At least this way, I've had the chance to make an informed decision and still maintain a modicum of dignity. It wasn't a great way to find out, but I still prefer it to believing lies." She turns and walks out, her shoulders hunched like someone who suddenly has a heavy burden to carry.

"Elisa—wait!" I chase after her, but she stops me with a wave of her hand.

"That's enough. I don't want to hear your pathetic and hypocritical excuses. You're ridiculous."

She exits the villa, and I'm left standing alone at the entrance, contemplating the vastness of my idiocy and looking for a nonexistent way to turn back time.

I only come out of my haze when Donatella appears from the kitchen, carrying a breakfast tray.

"Your coffee, Mr. D'Arcy," she says, handing me a cup. "I see there are some pieces to pick up."

"Yeah, Sheila threw an ornament at the fireplace. I hope it wasn't valuable."

"Oh, it was just a Bohemian crystal bear from Otto von Bismarck's collection. But that's not what I was referring to," she replies with her characteristic nonchalance.

"In any case, I'll reimburse Bingley."

"You know, Mr. D'Arcy, I've been with three men too."

I look at her, amazed. "Really?"

"Yeah, but not at the same time," she replies with a vague tone of regret. "At a certain point, we either learn to choose or life chooses for us, only in the second case we have to take what it gives us and not what we would have chosen."

34

Elisa

I slink back to the annex with my tail between my legs. Giada is still sleeping, so I won't wake her for a postmortem—also there's very little to discuss.

I go to my room, take the note from Michael that I stupidly stowed in my bedside table, tear it into pieces, and throw it in the toilet.

When I flush, instead of feeling relieved, I'm devastated.

35

Michael

I messed up big-time. Intergalactically big. I stare into space, walking around the grounds of the villa, extremely disappointed in myself for not realizing how much I'd messed up my life until it hit me in the face.

I wouldn't have been able to be in a relationship with either of them: Sheila is too clingy and Danielle is too effusive.

But what I did to them reminded me too much of the worst person I've ever known in my life: my brother, George.

Snooty, profiteering, reckless George.

He would have behaved like this and been proud of it. I'm starting to disgust myself.

Plus, I think I've completely ruined my chances with Elisa.

I need to talk to Bingley, but he's already gone. We barely had time to say goodbye.

As I walk, I hope in vain to run into Elisa. I wander aimlessly with my gaze lowered until I see the darkened imprints of two small hands in the concrete walkway. It was the summer of my tenth birthday, and the old count had had the crumbling walkways around the agricultural buildings rebuilt. Elisa and I had waited for the workers to leave after they poured the concrete, and then we pressed our hands into it with all our strength.

It's so poignant to see the imprints all these years later. This memory immediately unlocks another: I'm behind the old shed, one of the many outbuildings on the grounds, a place forgotten by adults but that Elisa and I, as children, used as a refuge.

I walk around it—it doesn't seem anyone has kept it up in all these years—until I reach the wooden plank door.

I force the rusty bolt, which no longer glides, but when I manage to open it, it's as if I've entered a portal in time.

Everything is as I remembered it.

Our bikes, the tires now deflated, are tossed in a corner; the out-of-tune guitar and the rickety drums from when we decided to start a band—a cover band of an Italian duo . . . Jasmine . . . No! Jalisse! And we always sang the same song. The faded tents from when we camped in the garden; our excavation kit from when we pretended to be archaeologists; a pile of old holiday notebooks, with homework we never finished.

And, in the middle of the shed, under a dust-covered tarp, there she is: Mauro's battered yellow Cinquecento.

He'd gotten it from a scrap dealer, because it wouldn't go even if you pushed it, and then stored it in the shed, waiting to find the time and money to get it back on the road.

Elisa and I would get in and pretend we were driving to imaginary destinations: One day it was Milan, another Madrid, then New York, then Honolulu, or the moon . . .

One summer, I decided I was going to be a mechanic, so I started dismantling it, with Elisa as my assistant. We had no idea what we were doing, but we lost entire afternoons that way.

I cover it up again, overwhelmed by the wave of nostalgia that catches me off guard and, combined with the humiliation of this morning's scene, destroys me once and for all.

On Monday, just before eleven, I go to the village building department to get a copy of the municipal regulations and documents relating to the estate.

The sale is on hold for now, but in case Bingley still wants to get rid of it—Caroline certainly does—I need to get everything we need to present the investment to Bogdanovic.

In reality my heart's no longer in the deal. I'm sad to think that the beautiful vineyard Elisa cultivates with so much passion will become a golf course for snooty billionaires.

However, I made a commitment, and I'm not the type to leave a job half finished.

Plus, now that I'm at odds with Elisa, why am I here if not to work?

When I enter the yellow building overlooking the town square and reach the office on the second floor, it seems I'm the only visitor.

"Good morning," I greet the employee at the reception, a bony woman between fifty and sixty with a bright red bob, glasses pulled down over her hooked nose, and a bored look on her face.

"Wait your turn," she says in a nasal voice.

"My turn?"

"If I haven't called your number, it's not your turn."

"But it's only me." I feel like an idiot for pointing out the obvious.

"Rules are rules," she decrees inflexibly.

"Take a number and wait."

I go back to the entrance, take a number, and walk back in, waving it with a theatrical gesture.

The woman presses the button and announces: "Number one."

I approach the window and throw my number into the bin.

"Good morning," she greets me as if she hadn't seen me two minutes ago. "How can I help you?"

"I'd like to meet with the inspector to ask him for some clarification regarding a property."

"Mmm, a meeting with the municipal inspector, you say?"

"Yeah." Aren't I speaking Italian?

"Do you have an appointment?" she asks, looking at me over her rectangular glasses secured around her neck with a beaded chain.

"I don't, actually."

"You need an appointment," she says.

We're off to a bad start. "So, could I make an appointment, please?"

"Mmm, let's see." She takes an agenda out of the desk drawer and flips through it. "The inspector is free today at eleven, eleven thirty, or twelve. What time works for you?"

It's eleven right now. I don't understand if she's the confused one or if I am. "Eleven is great."

"Who should I say is requesting the meeting?"

"Michael D'Arcy."

"How do you spell it?"

"Is it important? The meeting is now."

"Will you spell it for me, please?" she insists.

I snort, rolling my eyes. "M-i-c-h-a-e-l D-a-r-c-y. Okay? Can I go?"

"Where?" she asks me, as if she's just had a reset.

"To meet the inspector."

"They aren't here yet."

"But it's eleven," I point out.

She turns to the clock hanging on the wall behind her. "Mmm, I think it's ten fifty-seven."

"Are you joking?"

"Please take a seat and wait for the inspector to call you."

I sit on a faded and threadbare armchair with my head in my hands, dazed by the secretary, who has disappeared. "Michael D'Arcy," a voice calls me from behind an opaque glass door covered with yellowed papers. The nameplate says "Surveyor Rubina Gentile."

"Good morning, surveyor," I say as I enter, petrified.

At the desk is the secretary from before.

"Um . . . are you . . . ?"

"Surveyor Rubina Gentile. How can I help you?"

"But . . ." I'm so confused I think I must have hit my head.

"Go on. I don't have much time. I have more meetings after this," she says angrily.

"I'd like to request a copy of the current urban planning regulations and all the building documentation for Le Giuggiole."

"Did you request access to the documents?"

And how would I do that? "No."

"To obtain a copy of public documents, you have to fill out the request form."

"And where do I find this form?" I ask, exhausted.

From a binder, she takes a typed sheet of paper that's practically illegible thanks to the number of times it's been photocopied. "Here. Fill in the property data."

"Do you have a pen, please?"

"Blue or black?"

"It doesn't matter! Blue, please."

I fill in all the requested information and hand it to the surveyor. "Here you are."

"It has to be stamped by the secretary."

"Um, but aren't you also the secretary?"

"Documents are stamped by the secretary, not by the inspectors. And anyway it's not complete."

"What do you mean? I filled everything out."

"You need to pay the two-euro stamp duty."

I breathe in and out calmly. So it's true what they say about Italian bureaucracy! "Okay, I'll go get it and come back," I say, getting up with the cursed paper in my hands.

"Be quick. The appointment ends at eleven thirty," she warns me.

I fly down to the tobacco store, which also sells stamp duties, where I wait patiently while half a dozen grandparents buy their scratch cards, one plays the lottery, and another tops up their phone. I buy my coveted stamp duty and return to my tormentor at the secretary's station.

"Done! Is it okay now?"

She doesn't say anything to me and sticks a sign on the counter that says: "Coffee break. Service will resume at 11:20." Then she looks at me, stirring something that looks like anything but coffee. Peat? Tar?

"Are you joking?"

But she doesn't bat an eye.

Stay calm, Michael. Calm. I pace back and forth in front of the counter, shooting her dirty looks to which she remains impervious.

Once the five minutes have passed, with the precision of an atomic clock, she removes the sign and reopens the window. "How can I help you?"

This must be *Inception*. "I am registering a request for access to building documents," I repeat, exhausted.

"We don't accept hand-delivered requests."

"Then how should they be delivered? By carrier pigeon?"

"By fax."

"Fax?" I've never been this bewildered. "Who the heck still has a fax machine?"

"If you don't have a fax machine, you can use the one at the tobacco store."

"Wait a minute, let me get this straight: I'm here, right in front of you, with this original form I filled out by hand, and you expect me to go back downstairs to have it faxed?"

She scribbles something on a Post-it and hands it to me. "That's the number."

I slap my palm down on the countertop with a crack that echoes down the stairs and then set off on my pilgrimage.

Sending the fax is harder than expected because the line is busy, and I'm starting to think that maybe it's a sign that I should forget about the sale entirely.

When I return for the third time, victorious, the secretary-surveyor is on the phone.

"Did it go through?" I ask breathlessly.

She raises a finger to silence me. "No, Eufemia, I told you, I don't have any coupons left. Yeah, I'm using them all. Two thousand gets me a set of sheets, and I'm getting a coffee set with the rest. Oh, you need thirty-two for the kettle? Listen, talk to Laudomia. She shops for her sister-in-law and should have some extras. Ay-ay-ay, you and Laudomia aren't speaking? What happened? You told her not to water the flowers on her terrace when your clothes are hanging out to dry, but she keeps doing it?"

Tired of her rudeness and indifference, I reach through the hole in the booth and hang up the phone. "So," I exclaim in a very unapologetic tone, "I made the appointment, I filled out the documents request, I got it stamped, I sent it with that blasted fax. Now can I have those damned documents or do you need a blood sample too?!"

"Come with me," she replies dryly, with a sour expression.

"Thank you!"

I follow her back into the surveyor's office, where she fishes out a file from the cabinet and two bundles of crumpled technical standards. "The copier is down the hall."

"Did it really take all that?" I snap, seizing the precious documents.

"You're very rude, you know that?" she tells me.

"And you're not as *gentile* as your name might imply."

It takes me almost half an hour to make copies of everything I need with this photocopier seemingly produced just after Gutenberg's movable type printing press. It's so slow that while the collator works, I entertain myself by reading various leaflets stacked nearby: TAX RETURNS—EVERYTHING YOU NEED TO KNOW; PUBLIC TRANSPORT TIMETABLES; MENOPAUSE AWARENESS; THE CONSULTANCY WILL ASSIST YOU; THE GRAPE HARVEST FESTIVAL: SOCIAL DINNER, RAFFLE, AND SINGING COMPETITION. As soon as my copies are ready, I return everything with a triumphant air.

The surveyor takes them and counts them. "That'll be forty-three euros and thirty-one cents."

I reach for my wallet, but she stops me. "You pay on the third floor, at the treasury."

Hang in there, Michael. The nightmare is almost over. I take the stairs three at a time, but of course the treasury is closed. I knock, but no one opens the door. I knock again—radio silence.

Slow, rhythmic footsteps announce the arrival of a second person who turns out, of course, to be the diabolical Rubina Gentile.

"Let me guess: You're the treasurer."

She doesn't answer, takes out a bunch of keys, and with Olympic calm opens the door, sits at the desk in the small, bare room that smells of must, opens a metal drawer, and looks at me. "How can I help you?"

"Your helpful and delightful colleague in the buildings department directed me here to pay for some copies. Ms. Rubina Gentile, do you know her?" I joke.

"Don't try to be funny. That'll be . . ."

"Forty-three euros and thirty-one cents," I say, handing her fifty euros.

She takes the banknote, checks it's authentic with a marker, and places it in a drawer. "I'll give you the change," she announces in a strangely jovial tone. "Would you like a bag?"

"No, thanks. I can hold the files," I reply.

"It's not for the files," she chirps with a disturbing grin.

And she proceeds to dispense all six euros and sixty-nine cents in one-cent coins.

Exhausted and on the verge of being committed to the psych ward, I go into Mario's bar, frequented by the regulars.

"Give me the strongest thing you have," I say, leaning on the counter as if it were a lifeline.

"You sure?" says Mario.

"Please."

He places a glass on the rubberized mat and takes a bottle of Mr. Muscolo from under the cabinet. "This is the house blend. A two-finger pour will bring someone back from the dead!"

"Just what I need." I down the drink in one gulp and cough, my throat burning. "What's in that?" I gasp.

"I can't tell you, or they'd take away my liquor license."

Someone pats me on the back. "Mario baptized you with his bomb!" It's Max, the mechanic.

"People survive this?"

"In ten minutes, you'll be a new man," he says. "Mario, can you make me a Campari?"

"Listen, Max, what if I said I have an old beat-up Cinquecento I'd like you to fix up?"

"I'd say you're talking to the right person."

"I used to like working with cars, taking apart engines and putting them back together, but I'm out of practice. Could you help me? Paid, of course."

Before I can answer, a gentleman with a very sweaty striped shirt, a nametag with the word *Vanni* hanging from his pocket, and a cap that says "Belvedere in Chianti—Pro Loco" enters with a folder. "Morning, *buccaioli*! Would anyone here like to sign up for karaoke at the grape harvest festival?"

Max raises his hand.

"Our reigning champion!" exclaims Vanni, scribbling his name. "Any other old geezers? This year's prize is a cordless vacuum cleaner! If no one's interested, I'm out of here."

"Wait," I shout. I don't know if it's me or Mario's liquor talking. "Put down 'Michael D'Arcy.'"

"D'Arcy, spelled as its pronounced?"

"Yeah. And Elisa Benetti."

36

Elisa

"Charles has texted maybe five times in the last ten days. Does that sound normal to you?" Giada asks me. We're at the harvest festival, the major fall event in the village. Now that Lucia is at Forte dei Marmi with Elmo, we're down one bartender, so my sister is helping with the drinks. Intemerata is up on stage singing "Sorry, Jesus, if I'm Being Rude," which is pretty much the Italian version of "Oh Happy Day." It's going to be a long night.

"Five messages in ten days? That doesn't seem like very many, but he's probably busy with work."

"Probably," she replies, unconvinced.

"Did you message him?"

"Well, I don't want to seem needy or freak him out, so I don't message him unless he messages me."

"When will you see each other again?"

"After New York and before Hong Kong. He's coming back here for a week and then leaving for Asia from Milan, so we'll have some time together."

"Well, don't worry; sometimes a long-distance relationship just requires some patience and flexibility."

"Maybe nostalgia makes the separation feel more dramatic than it normally would," she concludes with a sigh.

"Hey. Smile," I say, patting her on the cheek. "You're the most beautiful woman at the party, even with your charcuterie apron, and you've landed the most coveted bachelor around. You're the envy of Belvedere."

"Speaking of catches," she says, pointing to the far side of the little square. "Is that Linda I see talking to a boy? Our shy little Linda?"

"Where? What boy?" I ask in a panic, craning over the counter.

"Next to the candy truck. They're eating gummy bears from the same bag. How sweet."

I spot my daughter standing apart from the crowd around the stage, but it takes me a while to recognize her. "What happened to her sweatshirt with the cat-ear hood? She certainly didn't leave the house looking like that!"

"Oops," Giada chirps in a fake innocent tone.

"Oops, what? What have you done?" I ask her.

"She didn't think you'd let her out in that top."

"She thought right!" I exclaim, ready to go cover her up. "Now she can hear it straight from me."

"Where are you going? Get back here." My sister grabs me by an apron tie. "If you want to blame someone, blame me. I bought her the top in Florence."

Pink glitter—I should have known Giada was behind this.

"Giada, are you insane? She's thirteen! What will you do when she's sixteen? Buy her condoms?"

"So what if I do?"

"Well, I was pregnant at sixteen."

"Sounds like you could have used some condoms."

"Very funny. Put yourself in my place, having to play both mom and dad. If I mess up, there's no one else to make up for it."

"There's Mamma and me," she replies.

"You and Mamma are her accomplices. You never tell her no; she wins every battle."

"Okay, maybe so."

"Well then, please don't fuel her emancipation any further. So who is this little Casanova?" I ask, nodding toward the boy with Linda.

"Tommaso Ghirardi."

"Oh, he's one of the boys who came to our house."

"Cute, huh? Seems like a heartthrob."

"People who know they're beautiful always leave a trail of destruction behind them." I know this firsthand, because someone like that screwed me over too. "I have to go over there."

"Come on, let her have a little fun tonight. Linda's always hunched over her books. Don't interfere now that she's acting like a thirteen-year-old for once, or she'll forever be known as the girl who got scolded by her mother at a party. Her social life is already tumbleweeds; she doesn't need to be officially branded as a loser."

I point my finger at her threateningly. "If anything happens, it's on you, just so you know."

"Good evening, ladies," Michael greets us, gliding up to the counter with an annoyingly jovial smile. "Might I trouble you for a glass of wine?"

"I'm doing the nonalcoholic drinks," explains my sister. "Elisa's doing the wines and spirits."

"Tell Michael he has to get a receipt from the register first," I tell Giada, even though he can hear me very well. We haven't spoken since the morning I caught him with his two fuck buddies.

"Brilliant," he replies triumphantly. "Giada, could you tell Elisa I already have a receipt?" And for emphasis he waves the small piece of paper in the air. "A glass of Vernaccia, please."

"Giada," I call to her again. "Tell Michael we're out of Vernaccia."

She looks at me, confused. "But . . . but you're two meters away from him."

He cuts me off. "Giada, tell Elisa I'm fine with any white she has left. I trust her taste."

"Giada, tell him he shouldn't trust me, and he's lucky if he gets a glass of dish soap."

"Oh, guys, cool it! I don't know what I ended up in the middle of, but I want no part of it. Sort it out for yourselves," Giada blurts out, moving out of our line of fire.

"Not serving me wine won't make me go away. I could stand here all night," he exclaims, crossing his arms resolutely.

I rudely fill a plastic cup with hot, flat *pignoletto*, which has been open since six, and slam it down in front of him. "Here."

Instead of telling me it's disgusting, he sips it as if it were nectar from the gods. "Delicious," he says defiantly.

We stare at each other in silence as Pompilia, dressed in a purple leopard-print Lycra dress, takes the stage for her performance.

"I'm singing 'Kobra,' by Donatella Rettore. Michael? Is Michael here? Does anyone know where Michael is?"

With feline reflexes, he leaps over the counter and crouches under it. "Michael? I saw you earlier. Where are you?"

The opportunity is too good to pass up, so I stick my fingers in my mouth and let out a whistle that silences the square. "He's here, Pompilia," I shout. Michael has no escape and is forced to reveal himself as he throws me a vindictive look. But for now, we are one-nil.

"Michael, I dedicate this song to you!" She struts over to the counter like a femme fatale, stands on it, and starts singing, imitating the singer's moves in one of history's cringiest performances.

She seizes Michael by his shirt collar and rubs herself against him as if he were a stripper's pole. Stiff with embarrassment, he mouths to me: "You'll pay for this."

"Thank you, Belvedere!" Pompilia shouts when the song ends, like a consummate pop star. The audience applauds more out of duty than pleasure, and Michael, more relaxed now, puts his mouth close to my ear.

"I hope you had your fun, because now I'm going to have mine."

"Next up," announces Vanni, in his black sequin jacket, "is our English friend, Michael D'Arcy, singing 'Fiumi di Parole,' by Jalisse!"

Huh? "Did you seriously sign yourself up for karaoke?"

He shakes his head. "No, dear, I didn't just sign myself up . . ."

"With Elisa Benetti!" adds Vanni.

A devilish smile spreads across Michael's face. "I signed us both up."

Oh shit.

37

Michael

Joke's on you, babe.

38

Elisa

As I stare at Michael, petrified, the sound of keyboards fills the air, and Vanni's nephew hands me a second microphone, leaving me no escape.

"Do you still remember it?" Michael asks me.

Who could forget? We must have sung it two hundred thousand times when we were kids. Ivaldo, one of the vineyard workers, was a big Jalisse fan. He always used to drive us into the village and had a cassette of "Fiumi di Parole" on repeat in his car.

Michael and I were obsessed with forming a band, so we couldn't resist singing along.

He belts out the first line, and the words have a strange new effect on me.

So, Michael remembers it by heart, too, and we start alternating verses as he keeps me locked under his gaze.

When we sing the chorus together, I shiver from head to toe, hearing our voices in unison after all these years.

It makes me want to smile, but I shouldn't. I can't. I look away to avoid showing my feelings, but he takes me by the hand. When I hear him sing "goodbye," I find myself thinking, *Please, no!* and all my determination fades.

We continue to sing with a kind of distance between us.

I replay all our beautiful moments in my head, reliving the sensations he made me feel but also the intense discomfort of the other morning. I would be nothing more than a game for him, one among many, a holiday fling, and I can't bear the idea of being cast aside.

I almost feel angry in the last verse, my eyes involuntarily blurring with tears.

By the time we finish, everyone in the audience has raised their lighters in the air, and then they break out into an applause like no other at the Belvedere karaoke.

As we stand there, looking at each other in a silence that says everything, we are interrupted by Vanni, who joins us, carrying a Dyson vacuum cleaner festooned with a bright ribbon. "The jury was unanimous! Congratulations!"

"Elisa," Michael murmurs, ignoring Vanni. But I can't stand the tension anymore, so I drop the microphone on the counter and run.

I take refuge in a wooden hut in the park next to the elementary school, my knees pulled tight to my chest, overwhelmed by a tsunami of tears.

I've never been the crybaby type.

I like Michael more than I thought I did, in a way that goes beyond a fleeting animal instinct, much more than a revived lukewarm teenage crush.

I like Michael as a man, even if he's the wrong man. And to say that I like him is an understatement.

I can't be with someone like him, a person who can have whatever he wants, however he wants it. Someone like him would leave me in the dust.

I hear a gentle knock on the roof of the hut.

"Anyone home?" asks Michael, peering inside.

I dry my tears with the back of my hand, relieved the darkness hides my eyes, which are swollen with tears.

"No," I mutter.

"So who just answered, then?"

"I don't feel like playing anymore, Michael. In every sense."

"But I'm not playing," he replies. "May I?" he asks, pointing to the space next to me.

"There isn't room for two," I reply dryly.

"There is if we squeeze." He ignores me and crouches to enter. His presence makes the cabin seem microscopic, our bodies pressing together more than they should.

"That was a low blow from you tonight," I mutter, my throat still catching on my tears.

"I know, but needs must."

"What do you think you got out of it?" I ask.

"Your attention."

"Why do you need that? You already have the attention of every woman in the world."

"But not yours, and that's all I'm interested in."

Every sentence is a gut punch. "Words, Michael. They're just words. Oh, by the way, nice song choice. You've ruined one of my few pleasant memories of us."

"I don't think I ruined anything. In fact maybe I managed to tell you something I otherwise would have kept inside."

"Like what? That you had at least two girlfriends in London? Not one, not two, but three!"

"I didn't think I needed to tell you, because I didn't even consider them to be girlfriends. Sure, I was having sex with both of them at the same time for a while there. Which makes me a classic . . ."

"Asshole," I say venomously.

"It's true; there's no other way to put it. But I'm not proud of it, if you care to know."

"What I care to know is why it would be any different with me!"

"Because, if you haven't noticed, I didn't chase after anyone else. Not Danielle, not Sheila, just you."

"And that's supposed to be enough for me?"

"I'm sorry."

"For what? For making a fool out of me or for getting caught?" I reply harshly.

"For disappointing you. Look, if you need to interrogate me about all my past relationships before you believe I'm serious, then that's something I'm willing to endure."

"I don't have that much time," I snap.

"Maybe I haven't been clear enough, so let me be more direct: I feel something for you, Elisa, and it's not just physical attraction. It's physical, too, but it goes deeper than that. It's something I've had inside me all my life. I'm ready to take a hit from you, but there's something I have to confess. When I was seventeen, I was in love with you and never dared tell you because I was embarrassed. I was an idiot, which is not an excuse but a reality, and I always let myself be influenced by the fact that you—"

"That I was fat and ugly?" I prompt him. "That you didn't want to be the boyfriend of the village loser?"

"That you just saw me as a friend," he corrects me, making me feel stupid and superficial. "I didn't want our friendship to end, so I kept my crush to myself and, like at the end of every summer, I went back to London. But then I realized I'd missed an opportunity, and I decided I'd tell you when I came back the next year. It's just a shame I didn't know that summer would be my last in Tuscany. I couldn't have foreseen the old count's poor health and his son's aversion to teenagers."

I listen to him, my head bowed and my gaze fixed on my knees.

"Believe me, it took me so long to get over you that I didn't have my first real girlfriend until I was nineteen. It wasn't anything memorable, and my second was even less so. With the third one I tried my best, but I still felt nothing and lost interest as soon as we slept together. From then on, I realized that sex with no strings attached was less exhausting and less depressing than trying to fall in love at all costs."

"Careful," I warn him, "you've leaped from 'crushes' to 'falling in love.'"

"That's because I really would give you my heart. I just can't tell if you want it."

"I do want it," I admit, "but I'm afraid you'll take it back."

"You should know that in my eyes, all the women in the world put together are no match for you. I like you because you can piss me off like no one else—and do you know why? Because I'm indifferent to the others. You're the only one I care about. You're in my head. I can't get you out, and I don't even want to. I won't give up on you, even if we have to spend hours screaming in each other's faces."

"What if that's all we can do? Just scream at each other all the time?"

"It's not, Elisa," he objects. "You and I are also this." And I can feel the "this" on my face. He leaves a trail of light kisses on my right cheek, following the wet trail of my tears over to my lips, which, to my surprise, are already open, waiting for him.

Am I forgiving him too quickly? Maybe, but what if, as usual, I jumped to conclusions instead of reflecting on the situation?

"I've seen you cry twice, at most. I'm almost proud of the fact that one of them is because of me," he whispers, his breath against my lips.

"I hate you," I reply, giving him a punch in the chest that he doesn't even feel.

"I know."

"Now kiss me, please."

"You don't need to say 'please.'" His tongue traces my lower lip with a criminal slowness. "If you really want it, you have to come and get it."

39

Michael

Luckily, she kisses me, because I barely manage to contain myself. Why did I do it? Because I want Elisa to decide. I don't want her to feel seduced; I'm willing to give her power. Sure, I teased her, but I left it up to her.

In my head, there's no Sheila, no Danielle. It may be easy to get into my pants but not into my head, not there.

"You're not exactly a pushover, you know," I murmur, as I move my lips from her mouth to that part of her neck just behind her ear, where I breathe in her perfume that drives me crazy.

"I love watching you conquer every inch of me."

"Don't think I always do this. Only if it's worth it."

"Is that so?"

"If you want, I'll show you how we can shake this hut to the ground," I say, lying down on the plank beneath me.

"Am I supposed to believe you like me like this? With this antisex apron from Premiata Salumeria Pianigiani?"

"You couldn't be sexier in a lace thong." I untie the knot behind her back and immediately start unbuttoning her jeans. "But maybe we should take it off anyway . . ."

"We could be arrested for indecent exposure," she sighs, reaching under my hands to stop me.

"They'll finally have something to talk about in Belvedere."

The way she runs her fingers through my hair drives me crazy, the way she wraps her legs around my hips, her muffled moans in my mouth, the way she searches for me with her whole body.

"Do you want us to stop?" I ask her, feeling my point of no return dangerously approaching.

"Yes . . . no . . ." she replies, confused, her lips still searching for mine.

"Yes or no?"

"Maybe . . . I don't know . . . two more minutes."

I can last two minutes thinking about some very boring things: documentaries on armadillos, car servicing, London tube stops . . .

"Is there someone going at it in that old hut?!" a young male voice exclaims from afar. "Get a hotel!"

A thin female voice giggles.

"Maybe we should stop," says Elisa, breathless.

The two silhouettes, which are holding hands, move away in the direction of the swings, so Elisa and I take the chance to recompose ourselves.

"Do you think it's a bad sign that we always get interrupted?" she asks me.

"I really hope not, but it's for the best. I don't think I would have given the greatest performance in this setting."

"Who was that?" she asks me, buttoning her blouse.

"Did you see?"

"No, but judging by how they're kissing on the swings, it seems we've inspired them."

We're about to leave our cave of sins, when Elisa freezes. "That's Linda!" she says, elbowing me in the gut.

"Linda?"

"Yes, my daughter!"

"Are you sure?"

"That's the top my sister got her. I restrained myself earlier, but it's time to put an end to this."

She's ready to sprint over, but I grab her by the waist of her jeans.

"She'll know her mother was the one getting it on in a public park."

"And my lecture will have no credibility since I made a fool of myself and my daughter would feel entitled to do the same?"

"I'm not exactly a psychologist, but yeah, sounds about right."

"So what should I do?"

"Nothing," I reply.

"Nothing?" she asks, astonished. "I should just let my daughter be seduced by that cheap Casanova?"

"I know him."

"You know him?"

"Yeah. You know Linda and I have been speaking English for an hour every day, right? Well, he joined us last week. He's a good guy, all things considered. He has a good head on his shoulders, the attention span of a steamed sea bass, and an unmistakable Tuscan accent. He keeps his lips pressed together to hide his braces, and when he laughs, he hides his mouth with his hand, because even though he acts tough, he's insecure to the core—except that girls don't know this and they go crazy for fake tough guys," I explain, hoping to reassure her. "He's harmless."

"Harmless? He doesn't seem like it to me."

"It's just a first kiss. Your daughter will write it in her diary with a little heart around the date, and in two weeks it'll be a thing of the past."

"First of all, today's teenagers don't keep diaries, and second, you're wrong. After first kisses come first pets, after first pets come first times, and after the first few times you get pregnant like I did."

"Aside from the fact that that seems like a slightly apocalyptic scenario, I really don't think Linda will get pregnant. And she's too smart for that."

"Hey, are you calling me stupid by any chance?"

"Not stupid but maybe naive. And Linda's not naive—she's sharp as a razor blade. Trust her; she's your daughter!"

"I do trust her; it's him I don't trust."

"He doesn't even know how to find his dick in his underwear."

"Maybe you're right," she grumbles, biting her lip. "I'm catastrophizing."

"You're catastrophizing."

"Maybe we should leave. What do you think, Michael?"

"Quickly and quietly," I agree. "Anyway, call me crazy, but I'm happy our first time wasn't wasted on a public park."

"Did you really say 'wasted'?"

"Yes, it would have been a waste," I confirm.

"And what do you have in mind?"

"Something better. Something special." I give her one last kiss before leaving our refuge. "Can you give me a week?"

"I don't know if I can wait that long."

"It will be worth it, I promise," I reassure her.

"You're not very good at making promises."

"This time, trust me."

She pulls her hair back as I tuck my shirt into my pants, and together we emerge from our hiding place.

A thump followed by a dull ache and a wave of dizziness knocks me to the ground, bringing Elisa with me.

"Christ, what a blow!" I say, touching my head.

"Are you okay?" Elisa leans over me, worried. "What happened?"

"I hit my head on the roof. I hope I don't have a head injury."

"Should I call an ambulance?"

"No, no, ask me a question and see if I can answer you."

"Okay." She starts waving her hand in front of my eyes.

"How many fingers?"

"Five."

She looks at me with panic in her eyes. "Oh, my God! Michael, there are four."

"No, there are five," I reply confidently.

"One, two, three, four," she insists, touching her index, middle, ring finger, and little finger. "Four."

"Yeah, but they didn't cut off your thumb, I can see it folded there."

"The bent thumb doesn't count; it's four."

"Then turn your hand around so I can't see it. Are you Italians always so careless?"

"Are you English always so particular? You don't have any cranial trauma, I can assure you. Let's go get some ice; otherwise, you'll have a big bump tomorrow morning."

Two figures appear behind Elisa, who is still leaning over me. "Michael? Mom? What were you doing in the hut?!"

40

Elisa

Getting caught by your daughter making out in a public park has redefined my notion of embarrassment.

She didn't catch us in the act, true, but she didn't need the Parma investigative bureau to know that we were the horny couple in the hut.

I dismiss her question with a very fake smile. "It's getting late, darling. It's time to go home!" I feel like a worm for the whole journey, squeezed into the back seat of the Punto between her and Michael. The cordless vacuum cleaner is resting across our legs as Giada and Mamma comment on the evening's performances.

Back at the estate, Michael and I say goodbye in the "I want to but I can't" style, with a silent promise to resume where we'd stopped in our eyes.

Linda, sulking, flies into her room, and Giada, sitting next to me on the hammock, asks me why she's so grumpy.

"She saw Michael and me doing things," I admit.

"Define 'doing things.'"

"More than a kiss, less than sex."

"Oh, obscene acts in public? You're getting adventurous!"

"In the hut on the playground."

She shakes her head and giggles. "Typical."

"What do you mean, 'typical'?"

"That hut is one of the three classic places in Belvedere where people go to mess around."

"What are the other two, so I can avoid them?"

"The booth for passport photos and the locker rooms at the parish soccer pitch."

"You answer with the confidence of someone who has frequented all three," I observe.

"So have you and Michael made up?"

"Yeah, too bad Linda had to witness it. And I saw her, but she doesn't know it . . . Do you know the boy she spent the whole evening with?"

"Tommaso Ghirardi."

"The two of them were kissing on the swings."

"Awww"—Giada claps her hands happily—"my niece is growing up."

"Not quite the reaction I needed, but yeah, she's growing up before my eyes."

"You should talk to her," she suggests.

"I don't know if she wants me to."

"She comes to me for the easy things. I'm the aunt who always says yes, but she needs you for the important stuff. And this is important."

"Would I even be credible?"

"You are her mother, and you are human. She will understand."

I gather my strength and go up to Linda. In the hallway, I find the pile of clean laundry with Tappo, her teddy bear, on top. I knock, but she doesn't answer, and when I come in, she doesn't speak to me.

"Linda?" Silence. "Look, I know you're awake; you never sleep on your stomach."

"First time for everything. What do you know?"

I sit on the edge of her bed and she rolls away. "I don't bite."

"I'm hot."

"Do you want to tell me why you're mad?" I approach her gently.

"I'm not."

"Then why are you being so short with me?"

"I don't know."

"Do you want to know what Michael and I were doing in the hut?"

"I know what you were doing. I'm not stupid," she grumbles, turning on her side with her back to me.

"And what were we doing?"

"Having sex."

"No. We were doing the same thing you and Tommaso did on the swings, more or less. Maybe more, maybe less, but the same thing."

She rolls over suddenly, her big eyes shining. "You saw us?"

"Yeah."

She dives face-first onto the pillow. "That's it. Now you're never going to let me leave the house again, and everything will be ruined."

"I won't do any of that," I say, running my hand through her soft hair. "But it would be nice if you didn't keep secrets from me, especially if you want me to trust you."

"If I'd told you Tommaso had asked me to meet him tonight, would you have let me go?" she asks defiantly.

"Maybe not immediately. I might have asked why you're so interested in him, for example."

"So you would have let me?"

"I probably would have," I admit, in spite of myself. "But not with that top your aunt gave you."

"It was beautiful."

"Yes, but suitable for a slightly older girl. So, would you like to tell me how long you've been in love with Tommaso?"

"Since last Christmas, when I met him at the school performance. You know how we all had to play that song on the flute? Well, he and I sat near each other."

And I always thought learning to play the flute in middle school was useless! "Did you talk to each other?"

"No. I just looked at him. I didn't have the guts." She takes after me in some things; there's no doubt about it.

"How did you get closer?"

"Once, during recess, I was reading on the steps of the school and he was playing soccer with his friends; the ball went out of bounds, he asked me to throw it to him so I kicked it, and he complimented me on the shot."

"I don't want to keep you isolated, bent over your books all the time. I want you to have a full social life, friends, because these years pass quickly and you'll never get them back, but I also want to protect you from what happened to me, from someone taking advantage of you and making you suffer."

"Will Michael make you suffer?"

"I hope not," I say with a sigh.

"Do you like him?"

"Very much."

"But weren't you friends?"

"Sometimes friends grow into something more."

"So are you a couple now?"

"Not exactly." I wish everything could be so black and white.

"Are you going to have sex?"

Maybe, God willing! "Love, why are you so focused on the issue of sex?" I ask in a cynical attempt to shift her curiosity.

"Because I can't understand if it's a good thing or a bad thing. If it's bad, why does everyone do it? And if it's good, why can't I do it?"

I have to be very careful about my answer. "It's a good thing when you do it with the right person."

"So how do you know when it's the right person?"

Kids with their questions. "It takes a while."

"But if my father wasn't the right person, does that mean it was a bad thing?"

"It was bad not being able to give you the united family you deserved, but it's wonderful to have had you." I hope the sex questions are over. "Can you tell me why I found Tappo in the garbage?" I ask her, holding out the bear.

"I don't want him anymore. I'm too old to sleep with a stuffie."

I look at Tappo's little face, with his crooked eyes, sewn up a thousand times. "So you want to throw him away? He was your friend; he never left you even when you were sick. Do you remember when you had that stomach virus and you held him so close you vomited all over him?"

"Ew, disgusting."

"It was. But he didn't leave you. And he never complained about all the times you sucked on his ears," I remind her, placing Tappo on her pillow.

"I just didn't want Alice, Valentina, and Laura to see my room and make fun of me."

"So you threw away poor Tappo?" I ask.

Linda sniffs, grabs the battered bear, and hugs him to her chest. "Thanks for saving him."

"You know, you don't have to keep him on the bed. We can find him a nice box with a little blanket. Tappo won't be offended if you don't want him on your bed, but if you ever want to say good night to him, you'll know where he is, and he will be happy."

"I'll keep him for tonight," she says, tucking him under her chin. Linda yawns, curling up in a fetal position, ready to fall into Morpheus's arms.

"Good night, Little Cub," I say, kissing the tip of her nose.

"Good night. And just so you know, I'd like it if Michael could be my dad," she says, her voice thick with sleep. "It's fine with me . . . if you guys have sex."

And suddenly I realize this isn't just between Michael and me anymore.

41

Michael

It took me a week of nonstop work, including a few all-nighters, but I finished.

I've planned meticulously for tonight, fulfilling every promise I've ever made—even the ones from fifteen years ago.

I arrive at the annex at the agreed time, and Elisa, dressed in an evening gown, is waiting for me outside on the swing that hangs from the chestnut tree. As soon as she sees me, she jumps up, her hands on her face, which is contorted into an expression of pure amazement.

"I don't believe it!"

I get out of the car and open the passenger door for her. "I hope you cleared your schedule through tomorrow."

"Mauro's Cinquecento!" she exclaims, walking around to take a better look at it. "You got it fixed."

"Small correction: I fixed it myself. Max gave me a hand, but I did the bulk of the work. I have to say I'm quite pleased with the result."

"You should be! It's . . . it's extraordinary. It looks like a model car."

"Elbow grease and sweat of the brow."

"So that's where you've been disappearing this week! Maybe you should consider a career as a mechanic."

In fact, this little Cinquecento L in Positano yellow, with its gleaming chassis, seats smelling of wax, convertible top, and crackling twin-cylinder engine is truly a source of pride for me. I asked Max to get me four two-tone black-and-white tires, while I found a vintage wicker picnic basket with the Fiat logo on eBay: It looks great.

"Now, the question is, will your dress fit in?" I ask, nodding at the vaporous black tulle dress she's wearing.

"I don't know, but I can always take it off."

"I'm tempted to let you, but let's enjoy the evening first. Please," I invite her to get in.

"Wait," she says. "You're missing something."

"What?"

"A pocket square for your jacket."

"They were all in the suitcase I left in the taxi," I explain. "But at least I have this suit."

"Here." Elisa picks a red vine leaf and sticks it in my breast pocket. "Now you're all set. Where are we going?"

"Where I promised to take you fifteen years ago: Florence."

I don't need her to say anything; the smile she flashes me is enough. I drive over the Chianti hills aflame in the sunset, the car radio accompanying us to the city of the lily, as my anxiety about driving on what to me feels like the wrong side of the road slowly dissipates.

We arrive in Florence around half past nine, right on time for dinner. We park in a garage in the city center and dive into the stream of tourists.

"I hope you're hungry. And thirsty," I say, taking her arm.

"Very. But I'm more curious to know why you asked me to wear an evening gown. I hope the restaurant isn't too far away. I'm not used to wearing such high heels."

"It's closer than you'd think," I reply, turning up Via Ghibellina and, after a few feet, indicating an eighteenth-century building with columns at the entrance. "It's here."

"You're crazy," she replies, seeing that we're outside of the renowned Enoteca Pinchiorri.

"I told you it would be worth the wait."

"Not that I can't appreciate this, but two Michelin stars would have been just fine."

"It's three or nothing. What do you say, shall we go in or stand here and stare? I also reserved a visit to the cellar, I know you're dying to look through their one hundred and fifty thousand bottles."

"I wouldn't set foot in there even if I was dead, or at least not without an insurance policy for third-party damages. If I tripped in these heels, I could destroy ten rare bottles that would cost me a lifetime of dishwashing to replace."

"Thank goodness I'm here to hold you up, then."

We enter arm in arm, as she observes everything with her chin lifted and her mouth half open.

"Good evening," I say to the maître d' when we reach the dining room. "We have a nine-thirty reservation for two under the name D'Arcy."

"I'll check right away." He furrows his brow at the computer. "D'Arcy, you said?"

"Michael D'Arcy, yes."

"For tonight?"

"Yes."

"Mmm."

His tone is hardly reassuring, so I ask for clarification. "Is there a problem?"

"I'm afraid I can't find your reservation, sir. Did you use the online form?"

"Yes." To avoid issues with the signal, I went to Max's bar. "I have a confirmation email here."

"Can you show me, please? Maybe I can see what happened."

I take my phone, open the email, and show it to him. "Here you are."

He reads it and shakes his head. "It looks like you booked for two people at nine thirty, but for October tenth."

"September tenth," I specify. "Tonight."

"No, 10/10 is a reservation for October tenth," he insists, indicating the date on the email.

I stare at the maître d', then at the phone, then back at the maître d', and again at the phone.

Well done, asshole is the writing I imagine on the screen, accompanied by fireworks and the blaring of trumpets. I must have jumped ahead a month when I was booking. "Might you have a free table for two anyway? A last-minute cancellation, perhaps?" I ask, anxious that the perfect evening is going belly-up. I really wanted to make Elisa feel special.

"Unfortunately, we're fully booked. I'm sorry for the mix-up, Mr. D'Arcy."

I'm about to insist that they find us a foldaway table, but Elisa beats me to it. "No problem. We'll see you on October tenth. We'll find something else for tonight."

"I feel like an idiot," I say as we leave. "I've ruined everything."

"You didn't ruin anything. I know just where to take you. You'll like it, even if we're a little overdressed. You'll just have to steady me for another ten minutes and keep me from falling on my face."

"It's the least I can do."

We head down toward Lungarno, then turn onto a deserted street with a large crowd at the end.

"You don't need a reservation here, but I assure you it's as good as a Michelin restaurant," says Elisa, pointing to a sign that says All'Antico Vinaio. "The most important thing is to understand where the queue begins and ends."

"Are you sure you want to have dinner here?" I ask skeptically. It's not really a place I'd associate with a romantic evening, rather the kind of place to grab a quick bite between one guided tour and another. Among the casually dressed patrons, the two of us stand out.

"More than sure. Trust me, it's not a fallback."

As we patiently await our turn, she leans back against my chest, and I wrap my arms around her waist, every now and then planting a kiss on her head and breathing in the scent of her hair. In reality, I couldn't say whether kissing her is an excuse to smell her or smelling her is an excuse to kiss her. Probably both.

I watch the customers ahead of us leave clutching sandwiches that are bigger than they are, and I start to get a little worried. With food that heavy, I'll sleep until next Wednesday.

"What can I get for this beautiful couple?" the man at the counter asks when it's our turn.

"Schiacciata with crudo and burrata," orders Elisa without hesitation. "Cut in half."

He cuts a piece of bread the size of a double mattress and shouts "Look at that steam!" The flatbread emits a hot puff and a fresh-from-the-oven smell as it's loaded with a monstrous amount of prosciutto and a whole burrata. "Look how much he's pining for her! Have a good night, kids!"

As our monster sandwich cools down, we stroll to the river, where we lean on the parapet in the light of the Ponte Vecchio, to our right, projecting onto the Arno.

"How is it?" she asks after I take the first bite.

"It's like a drug," I groan, voraciously biting off another piece.

"You know, it would have been nice to see Pinchiorri's cellar, but I must admit I'm much happier here, like this. Plus, look at that," she says, pointing to the sky. "You'd have to go to space to have a starrier night."

True, the evening is perfect, warm, and serene. It would have been a waste to dine indoors. "You're right; this is even better."

"Now let me say something that will shock you: I've never had a real romantic courtship in my life."

"You're joking."

"Never." She licks the burrata mustache from her lip. "When Linda was little, between studying, taking care of her, and the few hours of sleep I got, I didn't have the energy to face an evening out. And by the time she got older . . . let's just say no one ever interested me enough to go on a romantic evening."

"Really."

"It only happened once with a boy I met in a plant pathology course; in the middle of our dinner, Giada called to tell me Linda had a rash and a fever. I rushed home to find my daughter with chickenpox, and I never heard from the boy again. Maybe I should have faked a colitis attack . . ."

"I would like to say I'm sorry to hear it, but I'd be lying."

"How selfish."

"Indeed. If that date had ended happily, it would have been followed by a second, then a third, then you would have gotten emotionally involved to the point of marriage and more children, and then I wouldn't be here with you now. I have your daughter and her timing to thank."

"I'll let her know."

"So you haven't had any relationships since then?"

"Nothing I'd call a relationship. And I certainly don't have the energy to go 'hunting' for one now. The thought of putting on make-up and heels and dragging myself to the clubs every other night of the week is so demoralizing."

I lift her up to sit on the stone parapet, my hands around her waist to keep her from falling backward. She takes off her heels and places them next to her. "Elisa, a single night out would be enough for you."

"If all a girl has is her personality, she needs time to play all her cards."

"You know very well that's not the case for you," I reply, resting my forehead against hers.

"Then what is the case?"

"Here's how it would go: You go out with Giada for an aperitif; a group of men notices you . . ."

"They notice Giada, you mean. She's the beautiful one."

"She may be beautiful, but you have all the charm."

"Cad."

"Will you let me finish the story?" I ask, resting a finger on her lips. "One man in particular can't take his eyes off you because even though your dress doesn't reveal an inch of skin, you're magnetic. It's clear from a mile away you're nothing like any of the other women in the room, that you're a cut above, and for someone like you, he's going to have to work hard. He convinces his friends to sit at the next table and strikes up a conversation. Plot twist: The man turns out to be surprisingly interesting and doesn't seem like a total nutcase, so you're happy to chat. You finish your first drink without even realizing it, so when he offers you a second, you accept. You talk for a long time. He loves listening to you, and even ventures some physical contact; he touches your hand, your arm, and you let him because you like his attention."

"Fantastical but interesting reconstruction. Go on."

"Giada's tired, she wants to go home, and one of the others offers to accompany her. You're undecided between staying and going, because you're having fun and the man has a certain something. The two of you stay and chat for hours until you're the last people in the bar, to the point that they have to tell you it's closing time. On the street, with so much left to say, the man suggests a walk along the river, and as you walk, he takes you by the hand."

"This man is enterprising. Does he have a name?"

"Let's call him Michael."

"This Michael is enterprising," she repeats, her lips breaking into a smile when she says my name. "Keep going. I'm curious now."

"You decide you like Michael, you decide not to be shy, and you tell him. You stop on the Lungarno, he holds you close, and you put your arms around his neck." I guide her gestures to do exactly what I just described.

"Like this?" she asks me, intertwining her fingers behind my neck. "Just like that," I whisper, bringing my mouth closer to hers.

"And then?"

"And then, this happens."

42

Elisa

"And then?"

"And then, this happens," he murmurs, his mouth against mine.

Michael's kisses have become something I can't do without, after oxygen and water. Or maybe even before oxygen and water.

When Michael kisses, he kisses with his whole body, and I feel it everywhere.

Tonight I realized how he really does have the ability to attract every female being within a mile radius.

In Belvedere, it was no contest, but while we were in line for the schiacciata, I noticed how all the women, young and old, single and taken, did nothing but glance at him on the sly. I even caught someone sneaking a photo of him and then—I swear—even a poodle with a pink bow and a rhinestone collar stopped to sniff him and cling to his leg.

You don't see many men as handsome as he is, and at the risk of appearing superficial and vain, being the one on his arm did quite a bit for my confidence. I even enjoyed catching a few envious glances.

I don't think I've ever been envied by anyone in my life, and for once I also feel worthy. I'm dressed like a goddess—Giada pulled out a dress she bought at an haute couture fair, which she got because, she said, "You never know and, in any case, it was such a good deal." I feel better than I have in years, and I'm with a spectacular man who only has eyes for me.

Am I superficial? Very well, then, I'm superficial.

"It seems like my hypothetical evening is going pretty well," I laugh.

"Mine too."

"I'm starting to wonder what Michael and Elisa will do next . . . You interrupted the story just when it was getting good."

"You're about to find out."

If Michael were drafted into the army, he would be a sharpshooter. Every shot, a hit.

In the hottest ten minutes in history, with several breaks along the way to kiss where we had the chance, we reached one of the most central hotels in the city, a stone's throw from the Duomo.

Lost as I am in my fantasies, I absentmindedly catch the words "panoramic suite" at check-in before we step inside the elevator. And elevators, as we know, have that strange something that releases inhibitory brakes. Luckily the ride is short; otherwise, we wouldn't have made it to the room, and it would have been a shame because it is *the* room.

It's not just one of those magazine-perfect rooms—it's more unique than that. "Come have a look," Michael says, throwing open the French windows.

To say it's jaw-dropping is an understatement: The terrace directly overlooks the cupola of the Duomo and Giotto's bell tower. They're so close, I could touch them, plus there's a full Jacuzzi, with wine chilling in an ice bucket and two glasses, all in the glow of an outdoor fireplace. Now I understand the meaning of "panoramic suite."

"You. Are. Insane," I mutter. Lost for better words.

"Too much?"

"Is there a support group for returning to reality after this?"

"I don't know, but for tonight, it's all just for the two of us." Michael holds me, giving me another of his dizzying kisses. "You and me, no interruptions, no setbacks."

"Let me warn you: You'll have to work pretty hard to distract me from all this."

"I can't wait." He lowers my zipper, insinuating his hands under my dress, while I take off his jacket and immediately move on to the buttons of his shirt. "Waiting a week was torture, but it was worth it."

Reluctantly, but in a flash of lucidity, I stop him. "Give me a second, I'll be right there."

I fly into the bathroom to clean myself up. Toothpaste, mouthwash, and bidet. Up to this point everything has been perfect. I want it to continue to be.

I open the kit with the courtesy toothbrush and brush with the same precision I would for the dentist.

After I use the toilet, I'm about to move on to the bidet, when I notice a red stain on the toilet paper.

No!

I wipe again, but the result is the same: blood.

Third wipe, fourth wipe, fifth wipe, blood, blood, and more blood.

My period wasn't supposed to come until next week, but the cursed thing is early. And so sneakily: not a twinge of pain, not one symptom, zero warning. On the other hand, that's how it is. Have a special evening in mind? A day at the pool? A beach holiday? The uterus replies: "I see you want to have some fun? I'll bleed early and ruin everything!"

I feel like crying.

I flush the toilet, put in a tampon, sigh dejectedly, and look at myself in the mirror: I am the portrait of frustration. I want Michael so badly I'm about to explode.

For a moment I think, *Forget my period!* But then I think back to when I read *Fifty Shades of Grey* and the face I made when I read the part where Christian slips his hand between her legs and pulls the blue string to remove her Tampax.

No, I refuse to replicate something so messy on my first night with Michael.

But now I have to tell him.

I wish I could bury myself.

I inhale and exhale a dozen times before I can will myself to step out, my lower lip in an obvious pout.

"Champagne?" he asks me, handsome, bare chested, holding out a glass with a strawberry on the rim. "Whatever you want, we can order it."

"I hope they have Netflix," I say with a tremor in my voice.

He raises an eyebrow, confused. "Netflix?"

"We need to find something to do tonight, since . . . I can't believe what I'm about to say . . . My period came. It's early, a total surprise."

I stare at him for any hint of disappointment that might cross his face, but I can't be more surprised to see him burst into laughter.

A belly laugh that sends him doubling over.

"I'm not joking. I'm dead serious," I say.

With tears in his eyes, gasping for breath, he collapses on the bed and holds out his arms to me. "Come here, Elisa."

I fall into his arms, dejected, and he holds me close to him, my face in the crook of his neck. "Are you mad?" I ask, my stomach churning with anguish.

"I don't care. I just want to be with you," he replies, kissing my forehead.

And I fall asleep like this, to the rhythm of his breath and his fingers caressing my hair.

Pulling up in front of the annex in the Cinquecento—a name that has less to do with the model of the car than the five-hundred-degree temperature inside it—Michael and I exchange a very long kiss, one loaded with promises, unspoken words, hope, trust, and everything else there can be after the kind of night we just spent together, the kind where nothing and everything happens at once. You can make love just by talking, and Michael knows how to give me a mental orgasm with a single word.

Who would have thought that a woman's G-spot was actually in her head?

"I'd better go before my mother calls the police," I say, breaking off the kiss reluctantly. "Harvest starts today. Good thing I have plenty of spare calories to burn." This morning Michael woke me up with a tray of pastries that he personally picked up from the best pastry shop in Florence. He knows how to spoil a woman on her period.

"How long does the harvest usually take?"

"With fifteen people, it takes about ten days; we have to do three passes to collect the best bunches as they ripen," I explain.

"I'll come too," he replies.

"To harvest grapes?"

"Yeah," he insists.

"It's not like in the movies. It's not some cheerful romp," I warn him.

"And what makes you think I want to go on a romp? I think I'll like it, plus you yourself said I have to see how Chianti is made so I can value the property appropriately."

He doesn't even blink. "Of course, but I hardly meant you should become a laborer."

"Shall I call you 'boss'?" he asks me, giving me a playful kiss on the tip of my nose.

"Yes, and you'll have to follow my orders."

"It will be my pleasure."

We say goodbye with a plan to meet at the stables, before I go inside with two objectives: to change and take a painkiller.

In the kitchen I'm surprised to find Giada, already awake.

"Good morning. Why are you up so early? Are you coming to the vineyard too?"

"I'm not, if you can imagine that. I just heard from Charles . . ." Her tone, combined with her dangling sentence, doesn't bode well. "I texted him to see if he wanted me to pick him up at the airport tomorrow, but he said he's not coming."

I feel bad for her. "What do you mean, he's not coming?"

"He says he has tentative commitments in London, and it wouldn't make sense for him to come here before going to Hong Kong, so he's not."

"And when will he come?" I ask.

"He doesn't know." Giada shakes her head disconsolately. "I'm starting to think he doesn't love me anymore . . . if he ever did. I think I've been fooled again."

"Oh, Giada, don't say that." I rush over to where she's sitting on the worn sofa to hug her. She may be my big sister, but when she's sad, she seems more like a stray puppy. "If you want, I can ask Michael whether Charles is just having a hard time going back to work or if maybe he met someone else."

"Don't bring Michael into this. I'll just look desperate. It was so stupid of me to fall into his arms in less than twenty-four hours! Typical of the male hunter: Once he catches his prey, he's no longer interested. Will I ever learn?" Giada is a champion self-pitier. "You should learn from my mistakes: Never give it away like bread. Even though after last night, it's probably wasted advice."

"Actually, it's not."

She cocks her eyebrow at me. "What do you mean?"

"I got my period." I won't add the minor detail that Michael and I traded wild sex for sappy cuddles, lest I put the final nail in the coffin.

"There, good girl, hold back. Women can think straight until they have sex, then they lose their minds; men, on the other hand, are disconnected from their brains until they fuck, and then they regain a cruel lucidity."

43

Michael

Elisa taught me how to identify ripe bunches, how to prune them with the billhook, and how to place them in boxes without damaging the grapes.

It's hard, physical work that I can feel in my legs, arms, and back, and that means I won't be at the gym for at least a month.

But it's fun, and I don't feel tired in Elisa's company.

We work side by side, me on one row and her on the one behind me, and as we work, she tells me about prior harvests, the best ones, the hardest ones, about when her father was still there . . . She barely stops for air between one word and the next.

In fact, this is why I interrupt her.

"Will you stop kissing me? We're working!" she asks in a mock annoyed tone. I know she's not actually annoyed, because she does nothing to escape.

"I'm trying to give you a break."

"I don't need a break."

"You've been talking for forty minutes. Rest your tongue for a minute," I insist, capturing her lips with mine. I love the taste of her. I want to kiss her all over.

"I'm not resting it like this," she laughs. "Hey, are you harassing your boss?"

"A bit."

"I should summon you to my office," she threatens, pointing a finger at my chest.

"I can't wait."

While I'm in the shower—which is cold, as usual, though I'm used to it now—I get a call from Bingley. Because of the connectivity issues, I've started keeping my phone on the bathroom windowsill, the only place it gets a bar, to avoid more unannounced visitors like my exes.

"Hey, Charles!" I greet him, breathless and dripping.

"Michael, am I bothering you?" he asks in a voice that sounds distant and crackling.

"Not at all. I was relaxing in the shower. We started the harvest today."

"What do you mean *we*? What do you have to do with the harvest?"

"I'm picking grapes too."

"You're joking!"

"And get this—I'm actually enjoying it. Elisa taught me."

Charles chuckles. "I told you you'd have your own problems to worry about."

"Did you call to talk about me or about you?" I scoff. Of course he was right, but I wasn't ready to admit it.

"Right. I wanted to let you know I've decided to stay in London. I'm not going back to Italy."

"Ah," I reply dryly. "I, however, would like to talk to you about the estate," I say.

"What about it?"

"I don't know if you should sell: It's a high-yielding farm, it makes excellent wine, it's well managed. There's no need for an owner to live here permanently. You could come every now and then, plus Giada's here, at least until she goes to London."

"Well, you were right about Giada all along. When I left, I restrained myself from texting her, just to see how much she cared to reach out, and guess what? She disappeared. Barely showed signs of life. Even this morning, when I told her I wouldn't be coming back, she didn't show any emotion, she just said, 'Ah, okay, let me know when you're coming,' and that was it."

"I'm sorry, man, I hate to get in the middle of these things, but you know what they say: If you can imagine it . . ."

"You were harsh but fair. I would have jumped into another relationship and been taken for a ride. To that end, I'm in agreement with my sister that we should sell."

"But . . . but are you sure?"

"Without question. I thought you were all for us selling and cashing in."

"I wouldn't want you to make a rash decision," I say in an attempt to temper what, for the first time since I've known Bingley, appears to be unassailable resolve.

"I've thought about it. Don't worry. You've already contacted Bogdanovic, haven't you?"

"Yeah, I spoke to his attorney. He's keen and waiting for a proposal," I share reluctantly.

"Well, then I'm in your hands, Michael. Do you need me or can you manage it on your own?"

I sigh, a weight settling in my stomach. "Leave it to me."

44

Elisa

At the end of the harvest, we have a ritual: Everyone who has taken part—that is, me, Foliero, Carlo, and Angelo, plus the usual eleven seasonal workers who join us—celebrates with a dinner in the vineyard.

Foliero is a master of grilled, bone-in Florentine steak.

We are exhausted but extremely satisfied; we harvested excellent grapes at a higher yield than we expected.

Obviously there's also Michael, our honorary picker, my daughter Linda, and Tommaso, who wanted to earn some extra money for Lucca Comics and Games in November.

She's happy and so am I, although I'm always watching them with eyes on the back of my head to make sure their hands are visible at all times.

Everyone loved working with Michael. He has a great work ethic with a surprising tenacity. It's true that as a kid he liked working with his hands, but I didn't think he was still so rugged and energetic under those designer suits. Did he want to impress me? Why? I'm already here, wobbly in the knees whenever he looks at me!

Like now.

His furtive glances and half smiles when we're in other people's company drive me crazy. They seem to say: *If only we were alone, what I would do to you . . .*

It's a beautiful night, it's almost eleven, and the air is still balmy for mid-September, the little lights hanging between the rows of vines reflecting on the glasses and bottles of wine, while we attack a thirst-quenching late-summer watermelon.

"Does anyone want more?" asks Mamma, the dinner's honorary godmother.

A mass of hands go up around the table, and she shakes her head. "I only asked to be polite. Now I have to go and get it!" she snorts. The industrial fridge where we store the fruit is in the former barn, not very close for those who have to carry a whole twenty-pound watermelon. "Who's coming with me?"

"I'll come, Mariana," Michael offers in a burst of chivalry, leaping to his feet to help her.

"Elisa, can you go with him?" she asks me. "My back hurts."

Mamma has a sixth sense for the dating game, and although I haven't gone into detail about what's been going on between Michael and me, she senses that something is different.

We walk toward the barn, and once we're at a safe distance from the group, our hands automatically search for each other.

"I think your mother sent us a very veiled message," he observes.

"Like all the women of Belvedere, she can't resist the temptation to pair off single people."

"But you're not single," Michael says, shooting me a mischievous look.

"She doesn't know that yet."

"What did you tell her about our night together in Florence?"

"That we went as friends."

"Did she buy it?"

"I don't think so," I reply. "She wasn't born yesterday."

We drag open the sliding door of the former barn, and I peer into the huge chest fridge, bending down to pick out a watermelon.

"Have I told you how nice your butt looks in those shorts?" asks Michael.

"No, but go ahead and have a seat," I reply, happy to have my back turned so that he can't see the smile plastered on my face. "Are you enjoying the show?"

"Very much."

I emerge from the fridge with the watermelon in my arms just as Michael approaches me from behind, his hands pressing into the door frame, leaving me no way around him, his mouth resting impertinently on my shoulder as he slides the strap of my top down with his tongue.

My strength abandons me, and the watermelon falls to the ground in an explosion of seeds, juice, and pulp.

"You're playing dirty," I tell him, returning the provocation, my hands making their way under his T-shirt.

"If it's not dirty, I don't like it . . ." The top button of my shorts surrenders to Michael as he adds, "Do you remember pici night or do you need a reminder?"

"We shouldn't have," I murmur, my lips against his.

"But we wanted to." The second button on my fly leaves the chat, and now Michael's fingers are dangerously close to my panties. "Are you . . . okay?"

Maybe he thinks I still have my period after ten days. "Willing and able," I reassure him. "I think they're going to have to wait for their watermelon," I say, pulling off my top.

He picks me up and heads for the exit. "Fuck the watermelon."

We arrive at his room in a whirlwind of kisses, bites, caresses, and scratches.

He locks the door and presses me against it. "I swear you won't get out of here on your own two feet."

"I swear I'll never want to leave."

In the darkness, I don't know who pushes who onto the bed, probably both of us, with a hunger that verges on desperation, my shorts flying to the floor along with Michael's T-shirt and jeans.

We're not kissing now; we're tearing each other apart. I'm on top of him, astride him, the thin barrier of our underwear the last thing preventing us from consummating our desire, but we're both so ready, I'm afraid we'll explode just by touching.

"You have condoms, right?" I ask him with the last bit of prudence I have left.

"Of course."

"How many?"

"A box of twelve."

"That may be enough."

"Is that a challenge, Elisa?"

"Are you scared?"

"Darling, you have no idea what kind of trouble you just got yourself into."

"Get them," I implore, stifling his possible reply with a kiss. He opens the bedside drawer and blindly feels around.

"My God, where are they?!" he mutters impatiently. "Wait, let me turn on a light."

The lamp dimly illuminates the room, highlighting every muscle of Michael's body, truly sculpted by the hand of Michelangelo. I have to close my eyes so I don't lose my mind.

"Nooo!" he exclaims in dismay.

"What?"

"There are no condoms."

I can't believe my ears. "What do you mean there are no condoms?"

"I left them in the room in Florence."

"Are you kidding?!" I exclaim.

We look at each other with disappointment and dismay. "You're not on the pill, by any chance?"

"Why would I be? I haven't had a relationship since my daughter was in elementary school."

"Say no more."

"And no quail jumping," I warn him.

"Quail jumping?" he stops, confused.

"Pulling out," I explain.

"Ahh, got it. But why quails? How do quails jump?"

"It's an expression . . . how do they say it in England?"

"To leave the church before the singing begins," he replies in all seriousness.

"Seriously?"

"It makes a lot more sense than 'quail jumping'!" he laughs.

"But it's ridiculous," I counter.

"Why? Isn't it funny to think of a man hopping around with a hard-on?"

"Are we seriously sitting here comparing idioms? Let's go get those condoms!"

45

Michael

We leave the villa as if it were on fire and jump onto Elisa's blue Vespa.

"Start the engine," I urge, my helmet still unfastened.

"Damn it. I'm out of gas," she grumbles.

"The Cinquecento! Let's take that," I suggest.

In less than a minute, we're in the car, headed for the village.

"Who sells condoms at this hour?" I ask her.

"The cigarette vending machine outside the tobacco store. It has condoms too."

"Oh. And you know this because you often find yourself scrambling for condoms in the middle of the night?" I ask with a hint of malice.

"Would that make you jealous, by chance?"

"It might," I admit.

"Anyway, when the tobacconist decided to put condoms in the machine, the ultra-Catholic fringe of Belvedere had a fit, accusing him of encouraging promiscuity among the youth, transforming the village into Sodom and Gomorrah. No one talked about anything else for months."

"Not much ever happens here, does it?"

"Believe it or not, no."

"How did it end?"

"Let's just say the tobacconist and the ultra-Catholics settled on a diplomatic solution."

I push the engine of the little Cinquecento to its limits and beyond as I speed toward the parking lot in the square.

"Here they are," Elisa says, pointing to the lit window on the vending machine.

I spot the label glued above the word *Durex*, which sports the image of a long-haired, bearded man sternly pointing his finger in our direction, with the caption "Jesus is watching you."

"That's the diplomatic solution I was referring to."

"Very effective," I note.

Elisa slips a twenty-euro bill into the machine, presses the corresponding button, and we wait.

"Shouldn't they fall down into the hole?" I ask.

"Yeah," she replies nervously.

"But they're not."

"No." She presses the button again, then again and again, but the machine refuses to do its job. "It's blocked, stupid thing!"

"Stop it, stop it, you'll hurt yourself," I say, restraining her from punching the vending machine. "Any other solutions?"

"We can ring the pharmacy."

"Then what are we waiting for?"

The pharmacy has a back door with a little window, like the one prison guards use to check on prisoners in their cells, from which my pharmacist friend peers out.

"Good evening!" he greets us. "What can I get for you?"

"Condoms," I reply quickly.

"Ah, so you're all healed down there?"

"I've never been better, thanks. I'm in a bit of a rush, though." I cut him short.

"So, condoms. I have these super-thin ones, they seem to be popular, people say you can barely feel them."

"Perish the thought. Let's not risk it," Elisa intervenes.

"I have the performance ones, ultra-resistant, if you're really going at it, or fruit flavored for the gourmands."

"Look, normal ones are fine," I explain.

"Tropical fruit?"

"No fruit."

"Stimulants for her? Or a slowing agent for him?" he asks me with a conspiring wink.

"I don't need to delay anything," I declare with a surge of pride. "Just normal, my God! You don't have anything normal?"

"Otherwise," continues the pharmacist, ignoring me, "I have this assortment of forty: aloe, extra-lubricated, anatomical, anti-allergenic . . ."

"We'll take it," Elisa exclaims.

"Excellent choice, congratulations. I always recommend it to undecided shoppers. I'll put it in a bag for you."

"No, that's fine," Elisa stops him, desperate.

"Oh, that'll be twenty-seven euros and forty-five cents."

"Card," I say, pressing my Visa through the little window.

"Actually . . ." he wavers, "we have a fifty-euro minimum for cards. You know how it is. Fees these days . . ."

"We'll take them all," I say.

"They expire, you realize," he warns us.

"I think we'll be okay. Now swipe my damned card, please."

Victorious, with our loot in hand, we rush back to the car and drive off.

"The last time I saw this many condoms, I was twenty-three years old and on holiday in Ibiza with the university club."

"I see, and who should be jealous now?" she teases me.

"In a few minutes, you'll have proof you don't have to be." The car, however, begins to struggle, the engine croaks, then snorts once, twice, three times, and after a powerful jolt, smoke rises from the hood, and we come to a halt in the middle of the road.

"You've got to be kidding me," Elisa murmurs.

"I think I pushed it a little too hard," I observe, deflated. I try to start it again, but the engine doesn't turn. "We can walk back," I suggest.

"Two miles of hills? I hope you're joking."

"You're right."

We look into each other's eyes, in silence, at the limits of our endurance, until Elisa jumps on top of me, throws down the backrest, and we find ourselves in a sort of semi-reclined position. "You know what, Michael? Let's go for it. It's you and me, here, now. I like you. I want you. I can't wait a second longer."

"I'm in."

Where there's a will, there's a way, and somehow we manage to get undressed. Elisa hits the horn with her butt, then I unfold my leg and hit my knee somewhere on the dash.

"Hallelujah, hallelujah, hallelujah . . ." a choir of children's voices fills the car.

"Jesus really is watching over us!" I exclaim.

"You switched on the radio," she replies. "It's Radio Maria."

"Nice to have a bit of music, but is there anything a bit more . . . stimulating?"

Elisa turns the knob, but to no avail. "The receiver won't move. I think the connection's fried."

"Turn it off, then."

"It won't even turn off," she whimpers, on the verge of a nervous breakdown.

"It doesn't matter," I say, unhooking her bra. "We can go to confession tomorrow."

"Good point."

We pick up where we left off, with even more enthusiasm, when the roar of an eighteen-thousand-decibel tri-tonal trumpet makes us both jump.

The beam of two powerful headlights illuminates the cockpit like daylight, Elisa covers herself, and I glimpse the nose of a tractor in the rearview mirror.

"You guys need a tow?" the driver shouts. "I have a hook."

And that's that. Another evening scuppered.

46

Elisa

"There's something romantic going on between you and Michael, isn't there?" Mamma asks me the following morning over coffee in the annex kitchen.

Romantic is the last word I'd use to describe it at the moment, but who am I to parse words? "Let's say it's a friendship with room to evolve," I reply vaguely. If I confirmed her suspicions with a clear and direct yes, she'd start sending out wedding invitations today.

Something else I won't tell her: Michael and I have a high-voltage rendezvous planned tonight, since Giada is taking Linda to Florence to see some pop star I've never heard of, and Mamma and Donatella will be busy at their burraco tournament.

"How wonderful! Between Giada and Charles and now you and Michael, I'll be the envy of the entire village! You're about to become two very wealthy ladies! You even more so than Giada!"

"Your imagination is getting ahead of you." I stop her immediately. I get up and take the folder with all the estate's accounts. "Being a wife is the last thing on my mind. If all goes well, I'll be getting a loan soon."

I was counting on Carletto coming back so I could talk to him in person, but now I'll have to do it by phone, in which case I need to get my facts straight. I may not be a Russian tycoon swimming in gold, but I will offer him what Le Giuggiole is worth, and if our friendship means anything to him, maybe he'll consider the idea.

Mamma mumbles something incomprehensible but which reveals her disapproval of my decision, and I—completely immune to her judgment as I have been since the day I was born—head out.

I have an appointment with the bank director in twenty minutes, but I'm early, so I sit down and observe the people crowding the branch—the only one in the town, obviously.

On the opposite side of the room, sitting on one of the chairs, I'm surprised to notice Donatella, dressed in her tailored suit, fanning herself with a fan.

"If I'd known you were coming, I'd have given you a lift," I say, going to sit next to her.

"Every now and then, I like to take a taxi just to pretend I'm going somewhere interesting," she replies, always in that affected tone of hers. "Tell me, treasure, is today the big loan day?" she asks.

"How did you know?"

"I didn't. I can read," she replies, gesturing to the folder resting on my knees, with the word *loan* written across it in big letters. "Ah, the thrill of debt. I still remember when I was twenty-one and broke and hitchhiking across the United States. I never knew where I'd end up the next day, who I might talk to, what I was going to eat . . . if I even had enough money in my pocket to eat. In the seventies, you could be whoever you wanted and the next day be someone completely different."

"Honestly, I can't picture you hitchhiking coast to coast," I say, trying to summon the image.

"Oh, I've done a lot of things in my life that you couldn't imagine. But there's a time for everything. Certainly the girl who hung out at Studio 54 with Andy Warhol and Truman Capote couldn't have imagined that she would start studying stock market investments dressed in Chanel."

"Do you play the stock market?"

"Oh no. When my last husband died, he left me some shares. I just manage them. I have to speak with an adviser today about where to move a million that's barely yielded anything for a year."

"H-how much?" I must have misheard.

"A million."

"Euros?"

"No, pizzas. Of course, euros, treasure," she confirms nonchalantly.

"But, Donatella, if you're a millionaire, why do you work as a maid? I mean . . . you could have maids!"

"Rich people's lives are so boring. I need to do something; otherwise, I get depressed. And it keeps me busy enough that I can complain about the stress. Complaining is so liberating, don't you think?"

"I'd like to try."

"I envy your loan. It's going to push you to wake up in the morning and use your head to find a way to pay it off. It's very stimulating."

"You know, Donatella, you always make me see things from a different perspective."

"Helmut used to tell me that too," she sighs nostalgically.

"One of your husbands?"

"No, joy. Helmut Newton. I was his muse."

I blink in disbelief. "The nude photographer?"

"He liked how the shadows danced on my skin. It wasn't a sexual relationship, mind you. He was always very professional with me. Oh, they're calling me, hon. I'll wait for you when I'm done so we can go back together." And without waiting for my response, she flits into the financial advisory cubicle.

The director examines my request, scratching his chin. He and my father knew each other, so I hope he spares me some leniency in his memory.

"It's a pretty substantial sum," he observes.

"If it wasn't, I wouldn't be here."

"You'd be running the company?" he asks with a hint of skepticism.

"I've already been running it for several years now." I point to the papers in front of him. "Those figures are the result of my management."

"I see."

"So . . . ?"

"It's unlikely the bank will approve you. Not impossible, but difficult."

"But you are the bank."

"For a loan this big, I have to go through the central office. Even if the business plan is convincing, we'll need something more concrete than that."

"More concrete than that?" I ask, terrified.

"Let's be clear, Elisa, no one lends money to people who don't have money. You need some sort of collateral. But you don't have any, you don't own properties, you don't have an income, and so you can't close the deal." He shakes his head, as if to let me know he's serious. "Are you sure your father would have wanted you to get into this mess?"

"It's not a mess, and he lived for that vineyard. He would be proud as ever if it were mine."

"I would like to say yes, but . . ."

"Don't beat around the bush, please."

"Okay. Your business proposal is beautiful, but beauty isn't everything. It's not a no; it's a maybe."

"And what does this 'maybe' depend on?"

"I need to see customer purchase orders. If we can track the buyers of your products, we can prove the company is solvent."

Okay, the good news is there's a chance they can approve the loan. The bad news . . . now, where can I find some orders?

I leave the director's office in a worse mood than when I left home, but I'm not at rock bottom.

I join Donatella, who I hope will cheer me up with one of her maxims, but I see that she's busy chatting with a village employee.

Rubina Gentile is someone who feels important only because she works in high places, as she likes to say.

"Have you met the new owner yet?" she asks me haughtily, over her glasses.

"Charles Bingley and his sister came in mid-August. They were the talk of the town," I say.

"I'm not talking about the Bingleys. I'm talking about the guy who's turning it into a golf course."

Wait, how does Gentile know about the golf course? "Nobody wants to build a golf course on Le Giuggiole," I reply, feigning ignorance to see what she knows.

"Yes, they do. Mr. D'Arcy came to the town hall three weeks ago to ask for copies of all the property documents and to find out about renovations. He also wanted zoning codes for the golf thing."

"Three weeks ago?" I ask in a small voice. We'd agreed that he would leave the sale alone for at least a month. He promised me.

"Late August," she confirms. "Arrogant guy, very impatient. Now I must go. I'm changing my account because my fees are too high."

Donatella and I get into the car and set off for home, even though I'm in a daze.

How could he?! Michael stabbed me in the back. This isn't what we agreed to.

"Hon, change gears. Are you trying to make it home in second gear?"

"I'm out of my mind," I blurt out.

"I can tell."

"Michael promised he'd suspend negotiations with the Russian for a month and slow down the Bingleys' rush to sell, and I was counting on that time to get a loan so I could buy it myself, but instead he was working behind my back!" I shout. I feel betrayed in the worst possible way. "Evidently business matters more to him than anything: more than promises, more than trust, even . . ." but the words "more than me" remain stuck in my throat.

Donatella doesn't even try to soften her take. "Well, I'm not surprised Michael pushed his friend to sell and cut ties. One night, I brought them drinks in the billiard room and heard him firmly discouraging Charles from dating Giada."

"Are you kidding me?" I ask, hoping I've misunderstood.

"I don't like repeating what I've overheard out of context, especially since they were speaking English, but from what I understood, he was convinced your sister was only interested in Charles for the money and was warning him, suggesting he distance himself."

"So not only did Michael negotiate with the Russian behind my back, he also got between Giada and Charles?!" I have the nauseating suspicion that meddling in their relationship was Michael's way of getting Charles to sell the property to his client.

47

Michael

This manual labor thing is killing me: first the restoration of the Cinquecento, then the harvest, and now it's cooking.

Tonight, Elisa and I will finally be alone, and we intend to enjoy every moment.

I plan to propose something to her, which I never expected from myself.

Of course, before coming here I'd never foaled a mare or bought pads, but I think I'll have to call Saxton to thank him for the vacation he gave me.

I'm preparing pappardelle with a ragù of vegetables from the garden, following an old Tuscan cookbook to the letter.

I had to remake the ragù twice because on the first try I burned the onion and on the second I got carried away with the salt, but my third attempt is more convincing and is now resting in the pan.

I'm working on the pappardelle, but worst case I'll fall back on the dry ones from the supermarket.

If there's one thing I've learned, it's that here in Italy food is love and love is expressed through food; if you love someone, it's worth spending the day cooking for them.

I want Elisa to know I love her. Just in case, however, I also bought some heartburn medication.

"You and I need to talk," she surprises me from behind.

"I asked you not to come to the villa until this evening. You ruined the surprise!" I say, cleaning the flour from my hands with a cloth.

"And I asked you for a month, but instead you continued to negotiate the sale with the Russian," she snaps, and my brain shuts down.

Transmission interrupted.

I would like to tell her that it's not like that, that she's wrong, but the truth is she's not.

"The month is almost over," I reply, clinging to the only extenuating circumstance I have.

"Was it finished three weeks ago when you went to the town hall to ask about zoning for a golf club?"

I gasp without knowing how to respond.

"Yeah, Michael, I found out about it from the surveyor, Gentile. As you know, everyone in Belvedere talks."

"I was just getting ahead on work."

But she jumps straight into a tangent. "I, on the other hand, believe you never seriously considered postponing the sale. You just said what I needed to hear so you could do your business in peace."

"You're wrong. I really did revalue the estate. If it were mine, I'd keep it, but it belongs to the Bingleys and they want to sell it. So if you want to blame someone, blame them."

"Do you think I don't know you're the one behind every decision Charles ever makes? Like distancing himself from Giada?"

Fuck.

"Michael, answer me. Was it you who told him to leave her?"

"Yes," I admit. "It was me."

"I see you're very proud of your puppeteering. Do you enjoy pulling the strings of people's lives? Do you feel some sadistic pleasure in seeing her suffer?"

"I don't enjoy seeing anyone suffer; that's why I wanted to protect Charles. It was clear your sister was only looking for an advantageous marriage so she could leave Belvedere. Charles was naive enough to be the perfect target. I've seen my best friend fooled by all kinds of social climbers over the years. This time I decided to open his eyes before he got hurt, since his intuition when it comes to love is completely offline."

"A luminary of love has spoken! You, who, until the other day, were screwing two women at once! You know nothing about love."

"But that's where you're wrong, Elisa. Because I was right. As soon as Charles put the brakes on his calls and messages, your sister disappeared on him."

"Giada was terrified of asphyxiating him! She was dying of anxiety when she didn't hear from him, but she knew he was away on business and didn't want to bother him! When he disappeared, she thought she was just his summer fling," she screams at me, possessed by anger. "Of course, this played into your hands, so Charles didn't hesitate for a second to sell and gave you carte blanche to close with your client. Well done; your strategy worked perfectly."

"Do you think I'm that smart? Let's pretend I didn't come between him and your sister. I don't understand what three weeks or a month matters to you if Charles wants to sell anyway."

"It matters because I want to buy the estate."

Her response leaves me stunned. "Buy it?"

"Yes. But I need time for the bank to approve the loan. Once I had the money, I was going to make an offer to Charles."

"Excuse my frankness, Elisa, but the Bingleys aren't exactly hurting for money. They won't sell low just to get rid of the property."

"Indeed, that's why it takes so long to get the loan, because I want to make a reasonable offer. I certainly can't get in a bidding war against a Russian billionaire."

"But why do you want to buy Le Giuggiole?"

"If you have to ask, it means you don't understand a damn thing about me," she replies, shaking her head. "Mamma could live out her life in peace here, my sister would have a roof over her head, and my daughter would have a future. Is that enough for you?"

"No, you want to trap your mother, your sister, and your daughter because you feel stuck here yourself," I reply with more malice than I thought I had. "Your mother is close to retirement. If you want to give her peace of mind, you don't force her to look after a twenty-thousand-square-foot property for life. Your sister can't wait to escape Belvedere, and your daughter wants to study in England."

"What are you saying?"

"Didn't you know? No, you didn't. Because your daughter doesn't talk to you. You're so terrified of separating from her that you still treat her like she's five, but she's long past that age." Until now only Elisa had raised her voice, but now I'm joining in too. "Did you know she liked Tommaso Ghirardi? Obviously not, but she told me. Did you know she's applying to go to an English boarding school next year? No, she told me. Did you know she got her period? No, she told me."

Elisa looks at me in shock. "Linda got her period?"

"Maybe now you can see how much you've pushed her away. But she's your daughter, dammit; she can't feel rejected by you."

"I just want to protect her! Nobody knows what it was like for me to become a mother at seventeen. You're all full of lessons for me, but when it comes time to put them into practice, I'm always on my own."

"You don't have to be," I take a step toward her, hoping she understands that I don't want to argue anymore. "I'm here."

"You? You're taking away my house, you're taking away my job, and you're taking away my life."

"Come to London with me," I say suddenly, taking her by the shoulders. "With Linda, I mean."

"London? And do what?"

"I don't know; you'll find something. You won't have to worry about a thing. I'll take care of you," I insist. I had imagined this evening would go a little more like this: During dinner I'd intended to explain to her, in a more relaxed way, that although I believed Le Giuggiole was a valid investment, Charles still intended to sell. However, because she's so important to me and I don't want our relationship to end, I wanted to invite her to join me in London. Proposing to a woman that we move in together after only a month would have been unthinkable for the old Michael, but the new one can't wait. "I have a huge apartment in the city center. I have connections in the most exclusive circles. You'll never be bored. You can reinvent yourself or do nothing all day, and I'll send Linda to the best schools. Why would you want to stay here in this godforsaken place, breaking your back all day, up to your neck in debt, when you can have all that in an instant? I love you, Elisa. Please say yes."

We stare at each other in silence for a very long time, and I hold my breath, awaiting her response.

48

ELISA

If I'd been run over by a truck, I'd be better off. "I didn't think it was necessary to use that many words to offend me, but congratulations, you've broken a record," I say.

"I just told you that I love you," he repeats, more convinced than ever.

"No, you just told me that you don't understand a thing about me and, what's worse, you don't even care. I'm not some beautiful figurine you can use to decorate your precious apartment in the center of London. I'm not for sale, and I'd prefer a thousand times over to die of exhaustion after a day in the vineyard than live a life of comfort dependent on you or anyone else. Everything has a price except dignity. How long will it take, Michael, for us to disagree on something and you to accuse me of costing you the air I breathe?"

"I would never do that."

"It's not a risk I'm willing to take. I didn't do it thirteen years ago. I won't do it now."

"What?" Michael looks at me, confused, and I realize that in my anger I've taken a step too far. "What would you have done thirteen years ago?"

"I had a daughter. With George." There, the die has been cast. I finally said it.

"Say that again?" he hisses icily through his teeth.

"Your brother is Linda's father," I repeat. "He didn't want to have anything to do with her, and I made do."

"Why the fuck didn't you tell me?" Now he's the one shouting, to the point that it echoes in the chimney flue. "I've had a niece for thirteen years and didn't know a thing about it?! I would have given you a hand, I would have been part of her life, I would have taken care of her studies, I would have introduced her to different social circles, have her meet people who matter . . ."

"You just answered your own question: I didn't want anyone to take away my freedom to make decisions as her mother. I didn't want to have to ask permission from whoever was holding the purse strings," I reply.

"You took away my right to have a family," he growls, angrily. "Because, whether you like it or not, I am her uncle."

I'm about to reply, but a thud in the room draws our attention.

It's Linda, emerging from behind the cupboard, her face red and her eyes full of tears. She gives me a terrified look and runs out of the kitchen.

The hidden passage.

"Linda," I call, ready to run after her, but Michael holds me by the wrist.

It's not the firm and gentle grip I'm used to. It's a grip of steel, which crushes my bones and stops my circulation.

"You know, Elisa, no one has ever made me feel as excluded as you have right now."

"Then you must have had an easy life," I reply.

"Maybe, but I'm your family too, and you took away my chance to be a part of it."

"Part of my family? The family whose house you're taking away? And Giada, whose relationship you ruined just to facilitate a transaction? You, Michael, don't deserve to be part of my family, even if we don't live with the comforts you're used to. Now, excuse me, but I have to talk to my daughter."

"Well done, it's about time you started," he replies sharply.

"I don't accept lessons in courage from someone who until the day before yesterday didn't even have the guts to tell the two women he fucked that he was using them."

"Again with these women? You fucked my brother and didn't even bother to mention it to me. Do you truly think you're any better?"

"I didn't fuck your brother. If anything he fucked me, and believe me, specifying who fucked who makes a big difference."

"Really? Because the outcome seems the same to me."

Enough, I can't stand it any longer. "Perfect: You hid things from me. I hid things from you. It's clear that neither of us trusts the other. We were both just hiding. Thank goodness this farce came to light."

"Thank goodness."

"I thank you for your kind offer, but you can keep your high-class life and continue to hang out with the people who matter without me and Linda."

We're facing each other, just inches apart, but it's as if there are miles between us.

Where before there were burning embers, now there's only ash. It will only be a matter of seconds before the wind blows away every trace.

We were friends.

We were enemies.

We were lovers.

Now we're absolutely nothing.

49

Michael

I go up to my room, where, ironically, I find my suitcase waiting for me—the one I left in the taxi when I arrived.

I put on my suit, the only one I've had with me this whole time, and which, among other things, I wore for the evening in Florence with Elisa.

I can still smell her perfume on my shirt.

It's so intense and penetrating that it takes my breath away.

I'm practically wearing our love story, but it doesn't feel like mine.

I could change and wear one of the T-shirts I bought here, but in the end I close the armoire. Those clothes belong to a Michael who isn't me anymore. In London, I wouldn't know what to do with them.

I think of Elisa and me together and then, immediately, picture her with George. A pang tears through my chest. I slam my fist against the bathroom door, and the sound resonates across the ceiling, while the door swings on its squeaky hinges.

The taxi that Donatella called arrives earlier than expected. I don't have time to put on my tie. I dunk my face under freezing water. I don't even dry myself. I take my never-opened suitcase and leave.

In the car I resist the urge to look back. I won't ever be back here, and within a year, there will be a golf club instead of a vineyard.

My gaze falls on the knuckles of my right hand, still clenched, red, and bruised with crusts of dried blood.

I don't feel the pain. I'm completely numb with anger.

I'm only sure of one thing: I plan to send money for Linda to Mariana. Elisa would never accept it, but her mother is too practical not to.

As for the rest, there's nothing else here that concerns me.

50

Elisa

I find Linda sitting on the old swing, dragging her feet in the dirt.

I remember when I pushed her when she was little, her plump little legs dangling in the air as she shouted "Higher, higher" with each flight.

On the way between the villa and the annex, I dried the one cowardly tear that escaped me, but I forced myself not to shed any more. Michael doesn't deserve them, and my daughter shouldn't see me like this.

"Love . . ." I say, approaching her.

"You're a liar!" she accuses me without hesitation.

"Listen, I'll tell you everything." I try to convince her.

"If you're here to tell me more lies, you can save your breath, I don't believe you anymore."

I sit in front of her on the ground, on my knees, and from here I see how her gaze has the same light and the same edge as Michael's. Cruel genetics. "It's true, I wasn't honest, but did you really want me to tell you terrible things about your father and how he behaved toward us?"

"Better the ugly truth than a beautiful lie."

"Clichés are all fine and good, but I was just trying to give you the happiest and most peaceful life possible. How old are you now?"

"Thirteen and a half," she states, as if that half year made all the difference.

"In three years how old will you be?"

"Sixteen and a half."

"And how long does three years seem to you?"

"Well, considering the average lifespan of an Italian woman is eighty-four, and three years is three-point-five-seven percent of eighty-four, I'd say it's not that long," she surmises. She's always been good at arithmetic. I stopped helping with her math homework in third grade.

"That's right, it's not long," I confirm. "Can you imagine becoming a mother in three years?"

Her eyes widen and she shakes her head. "No, I'm too young."

"I was too, but that's what happened to me. And sadly, the person who would have had the immense privilege of being your father abandoned me. He abandoned us. He didn't want to have anything to do with us. I had to choose between telling you the truth at the risk of making you feel rejected or telling you that he died before you were born. I wanted you to grow up certain that you were loved."

"But you didn't want me either. I was an accident."

"From the moment I heard your little heart beating, that thrumming in my belly, I wanted you more than life itself. Does it really make that much of a difference knowing that your real father was a womanizer?"

"No," she moans, "but now that I know, I can see why you've always been so strict with me."

"Protective," I correct her. "I know the same thing won't happen to you. You're smarter than I was, but making sure you're never hurt, not even by mistake, has been my mission since I held you for the first time."

"But would you ever let me study abroad?"

Oh God . . . why? "Linda, I—"

"If money's the issue, I'll find a scholarship. My GPA is perfect, and I'm taking the Cambridge English exam next week. It won't cost that much."

"I don't know if I can be away from you that long," I admit.

"I'd come back for Christmas, Easter, and all summer," she insists.

Now the question is: Can I live with the distance to see her happy, or would I rather have her sad and at home with me? "Can I come visit you?" I ask.

Linda gets off the swing and throws her arms around my neck, sending me tumbling onto my back. "Oh, thank you, Mom! Thank you, thank you, thank you!"

"Now, do you want to tell me why you told Michael about your period?"

"Oh, you heard . . ."

"Uh, yeah."

"Are you going to stop me from seeing Tommaso now?"

"As tempting as that sounds, I won't," I confess with difficulty. "So, how come you elected Michael to be custodian of your secret?"

"It actually happened by chance. But he went to buy me pads."

I must not have heard her right. "Are you kidding?"

"No."

This strikes me in three ways: It makes me laugh to think about Michael choosing period supplies for a teenager, I feel tenderness at the idea of him being so thoughtful, and finally I'm overwhelmed with sadness that that particular Michael no longer exists.

"Mom," my daughter snaps me out of my thoughts.

"What is it?"

"Now that you and Michael have fought, are you going to make up?"

"I don't think so, darling," I murmur, my throat dry.

"But weren't you in love?"

"We thought so, but we were wrong."

51

Michael

"Linda's your niece?" Bingley asks in a voice that's far too loud for the standards of the Oxford and Cambridge Club. We're sitting in one of the lounges at the bar, waiting for our annual reunion dinner.

I've been back in London for ten days, but I've been waiting for him to come back so I could talk to him.

"They can hear you all the way to Trafalgar Square," I say. I told him what happened with Elisa, what I discovered, and how it ended, all accompanied by massive doses of alcohol, not least the glass of Glenmorangie in my hand.

"Sorry, but it's upsetting."

"How do you think I feel, Bing?"

"So, you cut all ties, just like that?"

"With whom have you cut ties?" asks Ashford, the first of our former classmates to arrive and sit on the free sofa.

"A childhood friend he was in love with but then discovered that she had a daughter with his brother," explains Bingley.

"Someone had a child with her brother?" asks Harring, throwing himself into the armchair next to me, his legs on the armrest. "Incest . . . that's a little iffy. Keep talking."

"No, you idiot." My friend immediately stops him. "Not *her* brother, Michael's brother. George!"

"What did George do?" asks Sebastian, the last of the quintet to arrive. Duke stood us up—it's his wife's birthday.

I bristle. "I'm going to say this once, so listen carefully: I went to Tuscany with Bingley to evaluate the estate he inherited from his great-uncle so he could sell it to one of my clients. I saw a childhood friend there."

"Elisa," specifies Bingley.

"I discovered that she'd had a daughter when she was seventeen; the girl is now thirteen."

"Her name is Linda," Bing interjects.

"Something started happening between Elisa and me."

"They fell in love," my friend adds again.

"Oh, and is it quite finished now?"

"Sorry, but you're not being clear."

"In short, we had a fight, and it came out that George is Linda's father, and he didn't want her. Is everything clear now?"

"Incredible, your brother manages to make trouble even when he's dead," Sebastian observes.

"Well, he got her pregnant when he was alive," observes Harring.

"Sorry, can you explain how someone like you managed to graduate?" Sebastian protests.

"I let him copy my work. Sorry, it's my fault," Ashford interjects.

"Okay, so how did it end between you and Elisa?"

"It ended and that's that," I say, downing my whiskey in one gulp.

"He's cross with Elisa because she never told him he had a niece. Elisa is cross with Michael because he wants her to come live in London," continues Bingley, my self-appointed spokesperson.

"And what's so wrong with that?" asks Sebastian.

"She wants to stay in Tuscany and make Chianti," I explain.

"Ah, I missed that part," comments Seb. "You want to take an Italian who's used to working outdoors and lock her up in an apartment in Mayfair to sip tea?"

"No, well . . . there are a lot of things Elisa could do here," I reply.

"Ah yes, between Oxford Street and Piccadilly, there's nothing but vineyards," Ashford says sarcastically.

"In any case, I don't think I can be with someone who hid the existence of a niece from me for all this time."

"Allow me to offer my humble opinion, since I'm the only one here who knows Elisa," says Bingley. "She is someone who wouldn't even ask for help if she were chained to the tracks with a two-hundred-ton freight train speeding toward her. I think she was afraid of making herself look like a money-sucker and would have rather gone to work in the mines. Plus I'd venture she's not particularly proud of having given in to your brother's advances."

"We all knew George. He was a creep, a manipulator, and a narcissist," says Seb without fear of offending the memory of the dead. "He probably promised her the world, and she fell for it. Too bad he didn't become an actor. Such a waste of talent."

"Listen," Ashford says, leaning forward. "Don't focus on the details. Look at the bigger picture. Study a Monet painting up close and it's awful. But from afar, it's a masterpiece. I was in a situation similar to yours with my wife. If I'd taken it personally instead of understanding the reason behind her choice, we'd be divorced now, as opposed to having a child and a corgi breeding farm."

"It's thanks to me you guys got back together," comments Harring.

"That may well be, but Mr. Proudass over there will never bring himself to forgive her," Bingley replies, pointing to me. "Nor to apologize for assuming Elisa would give up her life for one she didn't remotely care about."

"Forgive me if I'm so old-fashioned I want to give my partner a life of ease and comfort instead of letting her kill herself on the farm," I object.

"Patience, friends," Bingley interjects in a patronizing tone. "Michael has never understood a thing about women."

"Oh, so you're all professors now!" I say, taking my aim. "You, Bingley, fall in love with every woman who crosses your path."

"Yeah, you're a lost cause, Charles," Sebastian echoes.

"And you, Seb, realized you loved someone else when you were one step away from the altar, while you, Ash, married someone you barely knew. We shouldn't speak badly of those who are absent, but even Duke is no champion of discernment, given that he was helping who is now his wife get together with her former best friend." There you are. I have something for everyone.

"What about me?" asks Harring, feeling excluded from my blacklist.

"You're practically a primate," I dismiss him.

"A prime mate. Thanks, friend," he replies cheerfully.

"He said *primate*, not *prime mate*, idiot!" explains Sebastian.

"Until very recently, you were all human enough to have a cry on my shoulder, so don't try to lecture me now as though I have something to learn from you."

"You may be right, but you need to hear one last thing, Michael." Ashford and Sebastian look at me as if they've arrived to the same conclusion. "Women do whatever the fuck they want."

52

Elisa

If there remains even a sliver of hope of saving the vineyard, I'll cling to it with all my power.

"The London Wine Fair is October 16 to 21," I say, sitting at the long oak table in the kitchen of the villa. Now that the main house is "uninhabited," we have started spending our evenings there again, and Foliero has joined us.

"The European wine fair," he says.

"The most important European wine fair," I correct him. "And we're going."

"Great, I've always wanted to see it! I know someone who works in the Langhe. She goes every year with her winery and can probably get us guest passes. Tickets cost a fortune."

"Foliero, I mean we're going as vendors."

His jaw almost falls on the table. "You mean, with our own stand?"

"Exactly. It'll be small, six by nine feet." I'd considered how Cosimo and Andres managed to get their perfumes into Selfridges and decided to do the same. Vendor registration closed months ago, so I got on the waiting list, and this morning they told me there was a cancellation for one of the smaller stands. They needed same-day confirmation and payment.

"But it's so expensive!" he exclaims. "How did you get the money?"

"Let's just say my dad gave me a hand." When I registered the winery for the fair, I took one look at the fees and put my father's Vespa up for sale online. When bidders saw a 1973 Vespa Rally 200 Azzurro Cina at auction, offers skyrocketed.

I went to Max to have it valued. I knew it was one of the rarest models—which is why my father loved it so much—but I had no idea where to start the bidding. I certainly wouldn't have imagined I'd get over ten thousand euros.

"I can pay for the stand, the setup, the flight, and the stay for the two of us in an almost decent hotel," I reassure him.

"But why this year? Maybe next year would be better. We'll have wine from the harvest from two years ago, which, if you remember, produced exceptional grapes."

"Next year is too late." I explain what will happen to the vineyard, and he almost cries.

"All our work . . . our beautiful vineyard . . ." he whispers, shaking his head.

"It's not over yet," I reassure him, squeezing his hand.

"My English is a bit rusty. I'm not sure what kind of impression I'll make."

"You don't have to go to the queen's for breakfast. You know enough." Foliero has barely traveled outside of Italy, but his father was an English teacher and forced him to learn it, even if he hasn't used it in forty years. "I need your moral support more than anything."

"Your father would be proud of you, Elisa."

I take a bottle of Chianti that we opened at dinner and pour us two glasses. "Shall we toast?"

We're about to raise our glasses, when Giada opens the kitchen door. "Elisa, crisis alert. You have to come to the annex."

"What happened?"

"I don't know. Linda didn't want to tell me—strangely—she locked herself in your room and is waiting for you. She's been sobbing in there for half an hour."

"What happened, Little Cub?" I ask, taking a seat on my bed. She's lying face down, the mattress muffling her desperate cries.

"You were right. You can't trust men, and I was stupid. I'm not as smart as you thought!" Her sentence is like a blow between the eyes. In three seconds I see the ultrasound monitor, Linda with a baby bump, and the delivery room bed.

I'm not ready, but I can face it. "Linda, remember that we're a family; you'll never be alone."

"I hate Tommasooo."

Of course, who else would be responsible for this? There was no one to go after George for what he did, but if I catch that little bastard around, I'll play him like a bongo, I swear to God. "Do you want to tell me what happened?" I ask her. "I mean, I don't want details. Just broad strokes."

Linda gets to her feet, all her anger on display. "Do you remember how he and I took the Cambridge English exam? He did it to go play soccer in England, and I needed it for high school in London."

"Of course, the exam!" Okay, a story that starts with the Cambridge English exam can't include unprotected sex, right?

"We got our results today."

"And? Did one of you end up failing?"

"Oh no. We both passed. And then Tommaso dumped me not ten minutes later."

"Thank God!" I blurt out.

She looks at me, offended. "Excuse me?"

"Nothing, just . . . How could he have left you?"

"He said he only dated me because I was better than him at English and could help him pass the exam. Now that it's over, I'm no longer of use to him. And I was even dumb enough to sneak the translations to him. If I'd gotten caught, I could have been disqualified!"

"I have no words," I comment, astonished. "He doesn't even have facial hair yet, and he's already that calculating? What an idiot."

"I really liked him, and he took advantage of me! I hope he gets injured and his soccer career goes down the toilet," she curses him.

"That's a very bad thing to wish for," I say, "but to hell with good manners. Let's hope he's stuck on the bench for life."

Giada sticks her head in through the crack in the door. "Can I come in? I brought hot chocolate and biscuits," she announces as she enters with a tray in hand. "I heard everything, and I think this may be the cure we need."

"Why *we*?" asks Linda, taking the cup with the most whipped cream.

"Because chocolate is the best glue for fixing broken hearts, and it can do nothing but good for me and your mother too." My sister sits on the bed with us, the tray in the center.

"What about the biscuits?" asks Linda again.

"The biscuits are the bandages that hold the pieces together while the glue sets," I say.

"How many times can a broken heart be put back together, Mom?" Linda's questions . . .

"As many times as needed," Giada hastens to reply, fearing I'll have a cynical response like *Every time it breaks, it works worse and worse.* "But . . . to put it back together properly, we need something else!"

My sister rushes into her room and comes back waving a CD with a cracked cover. "The Backstreet Boys!" She blows on the disc and puts it in the old stereo on my bookshelf, presses Play, and then grabs a hairbrush and starts singing.

We find ourselves improvising a makeshift concert, complete with choreography, until all three of us collapse on the bed, panting.

"We are a really nice family," says Linda. "Strange but beautiful."

"Strange but beautiful," I repeat. "I like it."

"But I miss Michael a bit. He made me laugh," she says, unaware of the bullet that shoots straight into my chest. "Don't you miss him, Mom?"

"No."

"Not even a little?" she insists.

"Not even a little."

Good thing I promised not to tell her any more lies.

53

Michael

"I was hoping your holiday would make you appreciate a slower pace, but now that you're back, you're working three times as hard as before," Saxton remarks as he passes my office and notices I'm already up to my neck in work. "What time did you get here?"

"Seven."

"If you're not on the edge of a nervous breakdown at all times, you're not happy, right?"

"I won't dignify that question with an answer," I mutter.

"Have a good day yourself," he walks off, shaking his head in obvious disappointment. But he's a stronger person than I am. Work is the best medicine I know for dulling the pain I've been feeling since I've been back in London.

The problem is that I have a tolerance for it now: As the pain increases, I have to work harder to suppress it.

The phone on my desk rings, distracting me from the computer. "Hi, Penny."

"I have a call for you. Can I pass it through?"

"Who is it?"

"Miss Benetti, from Italy."

It takes me a few seconds to realize what I've just heard. Elisa is calling me? Here? I fight with my conscience, which is shouting: *Answer, by God! Answer!*

"I don't know any Miss Benetti," I tell Penny, impassive. As usual my pride gets the better of me.

"Are you sure? Because she says she's your niece."

"Linda?" I exclaim.

"So you do know a Miss Benetti! Of course you do have a very unique definition of an acquaintance . . . like with your girlfriends."

"Look, Penny, if I were you, I wouldn't bring that up. I'm still considering whether to forward your termination letter or not. It's saved in my drafts, ready to go," I threaten her.

"So, what should I do with this call?" she asks, impervious to my threat.

"Put her on."

54

Elisa

No one thought it would be easy, or this hard. The whole world is at this fair, and that's not hyperbole. Getting noticed is an apocalyptic undertaking, especially for such a small winery like ours.

We get the gist by the end of our first day.

Buyers—that is, workers in the catering and sales sectors—arrive at our pavilion after drinking the bigger brands all day. Their tastebuds are already saturated with tastings—which in our field also means they're vaguely tipsy—and drawing them in by offering up another sample is almost impossible.

Conversely, freeloaders abound—that is, everyone who came to snoop around, thanks to free passes from friends of friends—and their sole aim is to drink freely. This second type gravitates around us smaller wineries because they know we won't deny anyone a drink. They pretend to be interested in our story just to get to the thing that matters to them: free swag.

We ordered corkscrews and leak-proof airtight caps with our logo on them.

After a second day that ends with nothing accomplished, I decide to change strategy.

"Listen, Foliero, we need to attract the buyers who matter, but they don't come here, and if they do, they're already too drunk or the ones nearest the entrance get to them first. I'm going to pass out some leaflets at the bigger pavilion."

"It's against the rules," he points out to me.

"I know, but I'll risk a fine. I didn't sell my father's Vespa for nothing."

"Did you sell the Vespa Rally?!" he exclaims, shocked. "Your father would never have allowed it."

"For the vineyard? That and more. Just let me try for an hour. If it doesn't work, I'll come back."

I grab a handful of brochures and go on the hunt.

The bigger pavilion is another planet. There's Dom Pérignon, Antinori, Romanée-Conti, Lafite . . . The first impression is unsettling.

The stands are gob-smacking: One has a string quartet playing, one has a champagne fountain, some have a path through the senses, and some even have sets of towels embroidered with the *maison*'s label as merchandise, packaged in boxes that give off the scent of very expensive essences from three feet away.

My corkscrews, of which I was more than proud until recently, now seem like old junk.

I feel like the little match girl on Christmas Eve.

I fight to overcome a rising wave of self-pity as I try to approach the buyers who seem to matter most.

The problem is that everyone here seems important, and in less than fifteen minutes, I've run out of flyers, so I head back to our stand—whether it's to get more brochures or to hide, I still don't know.

On the way, I'm stopped by a girl dressed in a suit that alone would serve as collateral for my loan. "Here you are," she says in English, handing me a glass of champagne.

"Actually, I'm not a guest. I have a stand," I explain. "It's small," I hasten to add.

"No matter. Just seems like you could use a drink," she replies with a kindness that almost moves me. She takes a shiny bag full of freebies and, before I can object, puts it in my hand with a wink. "Do you see all these brands? They were small once too."

"Thank you," I say, feeling more reassured. "That's what I needed to hear."

I say goodbye the way someone leaves an old friend, and as soon as I turn the corner, I peer into the bag to find a further insult to my humble corkscrews: two beauty kits, his and hers, branded with the name of the winery. A detangling brush, face cream, eye contour cream, miniature perfume, and a mini eyeshadow palette in grape tones made in collaboration with a luxury cosmetics brand. Foliero will appreciate the men's beard and hair kit.

I head down the aisle toward our stand, and when I'm about twenty feet away, I notice two people with their backs to me, both dressed in suits and sober, judging by their posture. I quicken my pace so as not to miss them. When I'm a few steps away, one of them turns in my direction, and I glimpse his profile.

I feel faint.

It's Michael.

55

Michael

It took me a while to make up my mind, but the phone call with Linda kept haunting me in my sleep.

The call itself didn't deliver much news. Linda wanted me to write her a letter of recommendation for Westminster Boarding School.

In the most competitive private schools, there's a sort of unofficial nepotism, and though enrollment is open to all, they tend to favor those recommended by former students, Westminster being no exception.

I'm more than happy to write the letter. I'll also arrange an interview with the headmistress so she can see for herself how much Linda deserves to attend the school.

When saying goodbye, after being very careful not to mention Elisa, Linda said, "Do you know my mom will be in London for the London Wine Fair? She'll have a stand there all week."

Boom!

I couldn't have been more panicked if a live bomb had been thrown into my hands.

I was adamant I wouldn't set foot at that fair even if I was dead, but my pride held out for two days. On the third, after a sleepless night spent tossing and turning, I gave up, and here I am, in front of the Ricasoli winery stand.

Since I didn't know what excuse to show up with, I dragged Sebastian along as a cover. His family owns several international hotel chains, so he can pretend to be looking for new suppliers.

"I have buyers who deal with these things," he objected. "The excuse doesn't hold up."

"But maybe you're a passionate go-getter who loves to do things yourself. Come on, use a little imagination!" I encouraged him. "And anyway, who covered for you with your scary and potentially dangerous ex while you were chasing Charlotte? Me!" I reply. "You owe me a favor."

The result is that at this precise moment he is tasting every single vintage the stand has to offer, because when we arrived, Elisa wasn't here. We had to find a way to wait for her without blowing my cover.

"Foliero, could you let the gentlemen taste the 2015 Gran Riserva. It's our flagship . . . Oh! Michael, I didn't recognize you from over there."

"Hi, Elisa," I greet her. "How are you?"

56

Elisa

I duck into the first bathroom I can find and bless the champagne lady for her gift, because I definitely needed it.

I fix my hair and make-up—or rather, I do them all over again—and generously hose myself with perfume that may be the most expensive I've ever owned. Once I'm satisfied with the result, I head to our stand with the steadiest and boldest stride I can muster.

I'd started off with the equation that being on my feet all day equaled comfortable shoes, which equaled sneakers, but after a day at the fair, I realized I was the only person for whom it added up that way. Even the ticket office hostesses had heels, so I run out to buy a pair at an outlet near Wembley.

Any militant feminist would hang me by my thumbs for my eagerness to conform to the aesthetic standards imposed by the prevailing patriarchy, but I don't want Michael to think I'm suffering because of him.

Because I'm definitely not suffering because of him—just to be clear.

Considering that the best defense is an attack, I'm going for an ambush.

"Foliero, could you let the gentlemen taste the 2015 Gran Riserva, it's our flagship . . . Oh! Michael, I didn't recognize you from over there."

"Hi, Elisa," he greets me. "How are you?"

I try to decode his tone, but I can't detect anything, to my disappointment. "Wonderful," I reply cheekily. "We haven't been able to catch our breath; our stand has been besieged."

"Besieged," confirms Foliero.

"Happy to hear it," he comments.

"What brings you here? I thought you were more of a golf guy," I say, unable to help myself.

"Seb asked me to come with him," he says, pointing to his friend.

"Sebastian Bloom, it's a pleasure," he introduces himself with a distinguished air and a strong handshake.

"Do you know who he is?" Foliero interjects excitedly. "He's the owner of the Bloom International Hotels."

I'm about to have a stroke. The Blooms?! "My pleasure; it's an honor have you here, sir."

"Call me Sebastian. How many bottles do you make a year?" he asks, pointing to the Gran Riserva that Foliero poured for him.

"Twenty thousand," I say promptly. "But this year, we made twenty-three," I immediately add when I notice a slight grimace of disappointment on his face.

"I'm glad to see you're doing well," says Michael.

"Well, we haven't gotten an eviction notice from the new owner yet, so I try to enjoy what I can in the moment." I move closer to him so that Sebastian doesn't hear us. "Even if I end up with nothing, it doesn't mean I can't give my all until the end. Our wines deserve an international showcase, even if it will be the last one they'll ever have."

"No doubt. How's Linda?"

"She's studying, getting excellent grades, and we're looking at some high schools here in England that offer merit scholarships. As you can see, I'm doing just fine."

"I know you don't want any interference from me, but know that whatever she needs, I'm at her disposal. I don't mean financially—that is, not only financially."

"I'll keep that in mind," I say.

We look at each other in silence, with Sebastian and Foliero in the background chatting about the difference between maturation in French oak and Slavonian oak, and I have the feeling that we have a lot more to say to each other, but neither of us has the courage to begin.

"You're busy, so we'll leave you to it," he says. "I hope everything goes well."

"Thanks. Have a good time."

No "goodbye," no "see you soon."

Michael nods at me and walks away with Sebastian, whom Foliero honored with our famous corkscrew and one of our bottles in a wooden case.

"Of course if Bloom put in an order with us . . ."

"Foliero, I visited the bigger pavilion. There is no competition between them and us . . . they're not selling wine. They're selling a lifestyle."

An hour later, without too much enthusiasm and still shaken by the meeting with Michael, I send Foliero on his lunch break.

"Shall I bring you a sandwich?" he offers.

"No, they're disgusting, and I'm not hungry anyway. Take your time. There's not much to do here."

I sit, staring into space, looking but not seeing, lost in a sea of *What ifs* . . . and *But thens* . . . to the point that my eyes start to sting. *Tears, you will not get the better of me.*

I feel a tap on my shoulder, so I rub my eyes with the back of my hand.

"Foliero, you could have taken ten more . . ." But it's not Foliero. "Minutes . . ."

It's Michael.

"Could we have dinner together tonight?" he asks with a nervousness I haven't felt in him before. "With the best possible intentions. I'd like to talk to you."

57

MICHAEL

I wasn't holding my breath, but in the end, she said yes.

I'm waiting for Elisa at the restaurant—I reserved a lounge so we could have some privacy—and I'm feeling a bit rude for not having arranged to pick her up, though I didn't want her to think this was a date.

When I see her, I get up to greet her. "You look great," I say. She's wearing jeans and a blue striped shirt, but she looks gorgeous.

"Thanks, so do you." She sits on the sofa, sending a waft of her crazy-making scent in my direction. "It's very . . . intimate here," she observes.

"I just wanted a quiet space. It's not a date."

"Of course."

"I took the liberty of ordering the tasting menu. The chef's cuisine is quite unique, so you can have a taste of everything and eat what you like. You must be rather hungry, I imagine."

"I'm dying," she replies with a shy smile.

To be brutally honest, I asked for the tasting menu only because it has six courses, and I'd like the dinner to last as long as possible.

"There are some things I need to tell you," I begin.

"Me too," she replies. "About Linda."

"We can agree that Linda is the absolute priority, but first there's one thing you need to know: I postponed the deal between Bogdanovic and the Bingleys until mid-November so that you have time to make an offer. I can't assure you it will be accepted, but at least you have a shot."

"I don't have a loan yet. The bank wants orders as collateral. That's why I'm here at the fair, to find new customers. Anyway, thank you."

We fall silent as the waiters serve the appetizers, after which I hurry to speak again.

"Listen." I reach across the table to squeeze her hand, which, to my surprise, she doesn't withdraw. It does, however, remain limp in my grasp. "I never wanted to be the bad guy in this story. I know how much you care about the vineyard. I'm sorry if I gave you the opposite impression."

"You didn't try very hard to prove yourself wrong, though."

"Neither did you. I must say that you leave a lot to be desired when it comes to communication," I reply, regretting my comment a second later when Elisa glances away, depriving me of the precious eye contact we've maintained so far. "I think I can understand why you hid something as big as Linda's birth from me. May I hazard a guess that my brother wasn't exactly honorable toward you?"

"Is that a sugar-coated way of asking me to tell you how it went?"

Basically. "Only if you want . . ."

"It's a story I don't even like to tell to myself. It was painful and humiliating, and I'm not even sure I can get it straight."

"Call me a masochist, but I really would like to know."

"I met George in Florence, during his year abroad. Lucia and I were window-shopping on Via de' Tornabuoni, fantasizing about what we'd buy if money were no object, and we almost collided with George as he was coming out of Gucci. You and the Bingleys hadn't been to the estate in three years, and he was quite struck by how different I looked. He insisted on buying us dinner at the Palagio, then driving us home in his Maserati."

"My brother always loved living large and showing it off," I comment.

"The next day he reappeared to invite Lucia—my unwitting chaperone—and me to visit Sammezzano castle. It has so many little passages that make it easy to get lost and is full of little nooks where you can hide. He wanted to play hide-and-seek, and of course Lucia disappeared right away and George found me just as quickly, only instead of saying I was 'it,' he pressed me against the wall and kissed me."

Elisa can't imagine, but I'm gripping my fork so hard right now I could crumple it in my palm.

"Am I boring you?" she asks me.

"No," I say through clenched teeth, my jaw tightening. "Go on."

"I wasn't even seventeen, and it was the first time in my life I'd gotten any male attention. I felt so flattered and wanted more. Let's just say I didn't exactly make him chase me." She stops when the second course arrives, waiting for the waiter to leave us alone again. "I made it clear from the start that I liked him. He kept visiting Le Giuggiole every day to take me somewhere, and I always left the house with a different excuse. Lucia stopped coming; we'd made her feel like a third wheel. And so we went from taking innocent strolls around pleasant places to locking ourselves up in his car, on the back seats, exploring the bases one by one until, on what was supposed to be his last night in Italy, I saw fit to mark the occasion by giving him my virginity. Never for a second did he make me doubt his intentions toward me: He was always thoughtful, kind, gallant. He said he planned to come and visit me every weekend and holiday . . . I was so inexperienced, I never could have suspected it was just an act. He insisted on not using any protection: 'Condoms bother me. I can't feel anything. You can't get pregnant your first time, I'll be careful . . .' Telling him no seemed impolite, and so I just trusted him."

"He was very good at selling himself for what he wasn't. That angelic face of his didn't hurt."

"When I found out I was pregnant, still thinking he was Prince Charming, I called him, certain he'd jump on the first flight to Florence to swear eternal love and raise the fruit of our passion together. Instead he wanted nothing to do with it. He told me it was my problem. If I wanted to get rid of it, he'd pay for the surgery, but if I kept the baby I would have to fend for myself. He ordered me never to call him again, and if I dared let you or the Bingleys know that I was pregnant, he'd claim that I was only trying to set him up for money. After that, he changed his number, and I never saw or heard from him again."

I look at Elisa, and I see so much dignity in her that I want to scream. "My brother was always unworthy of the oxygen he breathed. He probably knew that you'd rather cut out your own tongue than look like a gold digger, and he had no qualms about exploiting your weak point."

The waiters take the plates away, and for the third time, hers is untouched. "Now you know everything."

"I'm sorry I was so horrible when you told me Linda was my brother's daughter. I couldn't bear to think of you as one of his victims."

"I've relegated it to a past I can't forget but that I don't want to remember. I only think about Linda and what a terrible thing she was born from."

"I really can't imagine the hell you went through."

"We live in a world where a father who doesn't recognize his children is let off the hook, but if a mother feeds her children a hot roll for dinner because she hasn't managed to go grocery shopping after a fourteen-hour workday, she gets reported to social services. Until society recognizes that parenting is the responsibility of both parties, there will always be girls like me who go to bed virgins and wake up whores, who give birth alone, who raise nobody's children, while the father remains a saint with all the accolades and no burdens and lives his life as if nothing ever happened. You know, when Count Umberto told me George had died, I felt relieved. I was finally free of having to decide whether to reveal his existence to Linda or not. I may be a bad person, but I don't regret any of my decisions. But maybe, if I'd been smarter, I would have made my daughter's life easier."

"Speaking of such, that brings me to the point of this dinner. Linda's surname."

"What's wrong with it?" she asks defensively.

"Nothing. Benetti's a fine name, but I would like it very much, if you agreed, if she could add D'Arcy. I'd like to recognize her as family."

"Michael," she stops me, raising her hand. "I've already told you what I think. I don't want any interference."

"It's only to facilitate—in a very distant future, I hope—her inheritance. My brother burned through everything down to the last cent, but I still own a more than substantial portion of the D'Arcy estate, and I have no heirs."

"Maybe you'll get some."

"And maybe I'll live until I'm a hundred, but I want Linda to have what she deserves. I know you're not interested in my money, but I want to right my brother's wrongs."

"My free will as a mother is priceless."

"It's sacrosanct."

"I'll talk to her about it," she replies in the tone of someone who wants to change the subject.

"I already talked to her."

"What? How dare you?" Elisa is already on the brink of war.

"She called me at the office. She wanted a letter of recommendation for the high school you chose, and I asked her about it. Who do you think told me you were coming to the London Wine Fair?"

Elisa blinks, surprised. "Linda?"

"How else would I have found out?" I lean toward her, my face close enough to hers to feel the heat. "Sebastian didn't ask me to go anywhere—I asked him."

Finally, her beautiful mouth hints at a smile. "So you were there just to see me?"

"Afraid so," I admit.

"So, was I right to dress up before arriving at the stand?"

"Did you dress up just for me?" I imitate her.

Elisa turns her fork on her empty plate. "Afraid so," she says, playing along. And for the first time during this dinner, I feel something akin to relief. "I saw you from across the room, and I went to freshen up."

"We've covered everything we said to each other during our fight except for one thing," I say, ready to go all-in.

"What?"

"I told you I love you."

"I remember."

"And you didn't answer me," I add.

"I remember that too."

"I'd like to know what you think."

She places her napkin on the table. "I think it's getting late. I have another long day at the fair tomorrow."

Nothing. She's inscrutable. I feel like I have twenty keys to open a single lock and not one of them works. "I'll go with you," I say, changing the subject.

"I have to get a taxi; my hotel is far."

"Precisely."

"We said this wasn't a date."

"Indeed, but this is a question of manners. I never let a woman travel alone after midnight."

"Is this something that happens to you often, then?" she asks knowingly.

"Not lately. Don't make me beg you," I reply, getting up. "I care."

In the end she gives in but on her own terms. The taxi ride is heavy with a silence so dense and cumbersome it's suffocating. Elisa keeps her gaze fixed on the window, lost in the darkness. I'd give my right arm to know what she's thinking.

"I believed in it," she says out of the blue.

"In what?"

"Us."

"You don't believe in it anymore?" Suddenly I'm so anxious it feels like someone is holding my head under water.

"I can't feel it."

"Do you want to try?" How is it possible to start such an important conversation just as we're pulling up to the hotel?

"I've learned that I can't allow myself to have everything I want."

As soon as the car stops, Elisa unclasps her seat belt and goes to open the door.

"Don't go," I stop her. "There are things you're not telling me, but I need to hear them."

"I don't want to talk about it." The tremor in her voice contradicts the assertiveness of her words.

"Is that why you came out with this now? Why don't you want to talk about it?"

Finally she deigns to raise her eyes and meet mine. "Michael, what kind of game are we playing?"

"I don't know, but I'm tired of playing it." I can't help but raise my hand to her chin. "If you feel nothing, tell me now, and I promise I'll go. You won't ever have to hear from me again, and in no way will I interfere between you and Linda. But if you have feelings for me, there's no point in us both suffering."

I expect a reply from her, but instead I receive a kiss. Elisa leans toward me, taking me by surprise, pressing her lips into mine in a gesture halfway between relief and desperation. "I love you," she whispers into the kiss. "And I hate loving you because I can't stop. I've tried, but I can't."

"Then don't stop."

The kiss lasts a long time and says all the things we didn't. It is not a sensual, instinctive, physical kiss, the kind that starts on the lips and ends in bed; it's a strange kind of kiss, one I've never experienced before. It goes straight to the soul.

She's the one who pulls away, leaving me dazed. "I have to go," she says. "I'm here another four days. I leave on Tuesday morning."

"Is this an invitation to come find you?"

"Let's just say if you did, I wouldn't mind." She kisses me again, this time just a peck. "Good night." And she gets out of the car and walks into the hotel.

I wait until the sliding doors close behind her and reach for my phone.

Do you have plans tomorrow evening? I'd like to see you again.

PS It's a date.

Elisa reads it in seconds, and I'm left awaiting her reply: Elisa Benetti is typing . . .

58

Elisa

My infamous self-control failed at the most critical moment. We'd nearly reached the hotel, and with two minutes to go, my emotional dam sprung a leak, spilling what I held inside.

I'm not capable of faking it and even less so with Michael. I could see it in my own reflection in the window. I'd be a terrible poker player.

As I'm entering the hotel elevator, I get a message.

It's Michael, and just reading his name stretches my lips into a smile.

Do you have plans tomorrow evening? I'd like to see you again.

PS It's a date.

I stand there, my thumbs hovering over the screen, with no idea what to write. I'd like to say no, just to be the one to call the shots. In military training, snipers compete to see who is most accurate; the one who hits the target "calls" the shot. The better the shooter, the more shots he calls, winning the game. A bit like the competition between Michael and me.

I already gave in back in the taxi. I told him I loved him, I kissed him, I let on that I'd be willing to see him again. I might as well just declare my unconditional surrender.

I can't wait; I write to him. Where are we going?

His response is immediate.

The most exclusive restaurant in London. I'll pick you up.

59

Michael

"Do I look elegant enough?" Elisa asks me as we're leaving the hotel. "I had to buy an evening gown on the fly."

"Don't worry," I say, opening the door for her. "I know the owner. He won't make a fuss."

"I really hope so with what this thing cost me!" There's a bright, cheerful note in her voice, with no edge to it.

"You didn't have to dress up," I reassure her. "That 'Pianigiani Award-Winning Charcuterie' apron suits you just fine."

"We had a great day at the fair today. A few visitors were interested in our wines, and one of them put in a pretty big order. Nothing crazy, but it's a good sign. I wanted to celebrate with something nice for myself . . . it's been years since I bought a dress worthy of its name, as opposed to whatever's on sale."

"Just know this: You're making it very hard for me to keep my eyes on the road." Elisa is wearing a simple dress made of a shiny black fabric, a kind of silk woven with thin silver threads, high-necked and floor-length, but with a slit that goes up past her mid-thigh and exposes her leg, which is mere inches from my hand resting on the gearshift.

"Really? Am I that distracting?"

"I could pull over, but I fear we'd never reach our destination."

"Absolutely not! This could be the only Tom Ford dress I ever own in my life, and I intend to show it off as much as I can. Plus I'd really like to immerse myself in the London that matters and see what your world is like here."

"Tonight might not be the right one for that. I have a special plan in mind, but I'll be happy to show you more of London tomorrow."

"I'm very curious."

"Your curiosity will soon be satisfied . . . and not only that, I hope."

She gives me a smile, the kind she gave me yesterday, and I take it as a green light. I don't want to risk bold moves, but I bring her hand to my lips and kiss it.

We arrive at the city center, where the fog obscures Park Lane up to Brook Street, and I park the car in Grosvenor Square.

"What an elegant neighborhood," observes Elisa, as I help her out of the car. "I don't see any restaurants, though."

"You have to know where they are." I offer her my arm, accompanying her toward the entrance of one of the ancient buildings that surrounds the square.

"Here?" she asks me doubtfully.

"Right here."

"Are we going straight to the chef's house?"

"More or less. Ladies first."

60

Elisa

"You need a gown just to enter this elevator," I observe, noting the rose gold–plated walls molded into the texture of an elaborate brocade. "I hope you booked the right date this time."

"Pinchiorri's was a lesson I'll never forget, but they always keep a table for me here."

"Modest."

"Knowledge is everything in life, and as I told you, it's a *very* exclusive circle."

It's finally dawning on me that this must be one of those exclusive clubs that posh English people like. "Let me guess: members only?"

"Highly selective." We arrive at the right floor, and Michael enters a code on a keypad fixed to the door, which opens the lock.

We enter an apartment that can only be defined one way: white.

"May I?" he asks, removing my jacket. "You've been hiding a secret weapon."

"What?"

"You're wearing the most revealing gown I've ever seen," he comments, staring at the back, which is cut so deep it stops an inch above my buttocks.

"Too revealing?"

"Never."

"I can change if you want."

"I want you to give me a second. I'll be right back." Michael disappears, leaving me alone in a sea of white.

White mohair sofas on which it seems no one has ever sat; a white carpet from which I immediately move away, terrified at the idea of staining it; furniture that reflects the lights to the point of blinding me; and a polished Carrara marble floor that looks like an ice-skating rink. No sign of a life lived. It looks like a house in a real estate catalog.

The sound of two sliding doors behind me draws my attention, so I turn.

"Welcome to Chez Michael," he announces, wearing a black chef's apron, on the threshold of a kitchen that is the size of a small village.

"If I'm your only customer, business must not be going so well." I tease Michael to distract myself from the sight of him, with his shirt sleeves rolled up and his haute cuisine apron, which is enough to short-circuit my hormones.

"It's our opening night. I only wanted the most important guest."

"So you're depending entirely on my reviews?"

"I'm willing to take the risk."

"What's on the menu?"

He holds out his hand to invite me into the kitchen. "I'll show you now."

Unlike the rest of the house, the designer kitchen is dark brown, in a wood that hints of distant lands and a bill with several zeros. A world away from the villa's kitchen, done in masonry and majolica, with its copper vent blackened by smoke from the fire.

He makes me sit on one of the stools at the counter, where he has set the table for two.

"Pici with porcini and truffle sauce," he announces, delivering two plates of steaming pasta on which he generously grates the precious truffle.

"Did you make these?" I ask, amazed.

"They won't be as good as your mother's or as beautiful as yours, but I wanted to cook for you, and this is all I know how to do."

"Actually . . . they're perfect," I say, taking a forkful. "Just right."

"Really? You're not just saying that because you're hungry?"

"I never lie about pici," I reply with my mouth full, unladylike. "So, confess: Did you rent this apartment specifically for the evening or is it the pied-à-terre that you and your friends share for 'special' occasions?" I ask him.

"What do you mean, 'special' occasions?" he asks with a mischievous sparkle in his eyes.

"You know exactly what I mean. So? Have I been caught in your vicious bachelor web?"

"Some of my friends might enjoy the thought of that, but no. This is my home," he announces, spreading his arms wide.

I almost choke. "Seriously?"

"Why would I lie?"

"Did you just move in?"

"I've lived here since my brother died, actually. Why?"

"It just doesn't seem very lived-in," I reply.

"Maybe because I don't spend much time here. I'm always at the office or the gym. I go to a lot of restaurants and clubs . . . I basically just sleep here."

"Alone or with your unsuspecting lovers?" I tease him.

"Alone. I've never brought a woman to my apartment."

"Bullshit!"

"I swear," he insists, placing his right hand over his heart. "You're the first."

"Look, Michael, let me explain the subtle difference between male and female languages. You men think you can make a woman feel special by telling her she's the first, forgetting the fact that this implies others are sure to follow. We women don't want to be the first; we want to be the last."

He starts laughing. "That's good."

"Because it's true."

"So, you're the last."

"And you're an ass." I enjoy making fun of him. "I'll forgive you only because these pici are excellent."

"Oh, good, the hallucinogens I threw in there must be taking effect."

"I'm serious, look at my plate," I say. "I wouldn't have known it was your first attempt."

"Thank you very much," he replies with a hint of a bow. "Of course the bar is so high with you . . ."

"I don't want it to go to your head. But in reality I'm not that surprised. You've always been good with your hands."

"I hope to show you what else I can do with my hands," he replies, winking.

"Are you exposing your ulterior motives?"

"I don't know what you heard, but I was referring to dessert." He gets up from the stool, takes two cups from the fridge, and hands one to me with a teaspoon. "Deconstructed tart."

"You made this too?"

"I did . . . thanks to YouTube," he confesses with that sly smile of his.

"I appreciate the honesty." Oh my God! Honest or not, this dessert is out of this world.

I'm shoveling in a second spoonful before I've even swallowed the first. The coulis of berries blends beautifully with the custard layer below, and with the crunchiness of the shortbread pastry crumbles on the bottom. "You know, Michael, I have to admit you really know your way around the kitchen. You should keep it in mind as a second career if you get bored of finance."

"There's another thing I have to confess: The tart was supposed to be in one piece, except that it broke when I took it out of the mold, so I reassembled it in the cups."

"That's why it's in cups! I thought you were trying to be creative and contemporary."

"The truth is, I didn't even know where the dessert cups were."

"You don't know where things are in your own house?" I ask, amazed.

"I told you I'm never here."

The way he plays with my fingers, intertwining them with his, sends shivers down my arms. "And tell me, how much is the bill for this dinner?" I ask.

He shakes his head, giving me a heart-stopping smile. "It's going to be pricey."

"Luckily I brought my credit card."

"How unfortunate, the machine's down." Our faces are getting closer and closer, and our voices have gone soft.

"I only have fifty pounds with me," I reply, curious about his reply.

"I don't think that will cover it."

"Are you going to make me wash the dishes?" I ask, when the tips of our noses are touching.

"The chef says he's willing to tear up the bill in exchange for a kiss."

"The chef is very cheeky," I say, tugging on his tie. "Does he really think I'd kiss him in exchange for dinner?"

"Oh, no." The deep notes of his voice vibrate inside me. "He's the one who wants to kiss you."

"I can give him a kiss on the cheek."

"Not just on the cheek." He touches his finger my lips.

"Where else would he like to kiss me?"

"Everywhere."

61

MICHAEL

"Where else would he like to kiss me?"

"Everywhere."

Elisa steps back, leaving me momentarily confused. She stands up, puts her right hand behind her back, and pulls the end of the bow that's holding up her dress at the waist—that's right, that diabolical bow sitting exactly an inch above the curve of her butt, which has tormented me all evening. With her left hand, she does the same at the back of her neck, undoing the second bow.

"So, Michael," she whispers as the dress surrenders to gravity and pools on the floor, leaving her naked with the sole exception of her panties. "You'd better get busy."

"You know, Elisa," I say, taking her by the waist and pulling her to me. "You shouldn't provoke me like that."

"And why is that?"

With my finger I take a dollop of custard from my cup and slide it into the hollow of her breasts. "Because once I start, I don't intend to stop." I lick up the sweet trace I've drawn on her skin, and she moans.

"I did well," she replies in a choked voice. "That was exactly my intention." She takes my finger, still dipped in cream, brings it to her mouth, squeezes it between her lips, and sucks it.

"Are you sure?"

"And when you're done, I want you to do it all over again," she takes my face in her hands, touching my lips with hers.

"Darling," I grab her by the buttocks, lifting her against my pelvis. "You'll have to beg me to stop."

We throw ourselves on top of each other, overwhelmed by the explosive mixture of desire and anticipation. Lessing said that the anticipation of pleasure is pleasure itself.

Wrong.

This is pleasure.

It's having Elisa in my hands.

It's having her tongue in my mouth.

It's having her naked body pressed against mine.

But there's no doubt that it was worth the wait.

"Let's go somewhere more comfortable, where I can do everything to you I've been imagining," I say, picking her up as she clings to me.

"Do you at least remember where the bedroom is?" she teases me.

"I can get there with my eyes closed."

I enter the dark room, but removing my hands from Elisa's hips to find the switch is not my priority. I lay her down on the bed, illuminated only by the blue light of the London night that penetrates the window and . . . damn, she looks really good. "My bed has never looked so good as it does with you on it."

"Yeah, but it would be even better if you were on it too."

"I'll undress and join you," I reply, intent on untying my apron knot.

"No," she stops me, kneeling in front of me. "Let me undress you."

Her hands move up and down my chest until they stop on the buttons on my shirt, which she undoes one by one with a disarming slowness. "You're so hot in your chef's outfit. You're the erotic dream I never knew I had."

"Feel free to share any of your fantasies with me."

Her hands move to the fly of my trousers, and her touch has a dramatic effect on me: I love it. I love it too much, actually, and my sprint toward pleasure accelerates vertically—rather literally—so, instead of giving in to her every gesture, I hold myself back.

Once my trousers are off, Elisa hooks the elastic of my boxers and pulls me onto the bed with her. "Now we're even."

"Don't count on it," I reply, lowering her black panties. "I still have a job to finish."

And with her beneath me, I draw the map of her body, kissing every inch of it.

"God, that feels so good," she sighs as my mouth reaches her breast, her nipple between my lips.

"You're beautiful," I reply. I reach over to the bedside lamp and turn on the light.

"No!" she exclaims.

"What do you mean, no?"

"It's more romantic in the dark," she insists, stiffening.

"I want to look at you." I try to make her relax again with a trail of kisses down her belly.

"I don't think so." And before I can get to her pubis, she brings her hands down to cover her lower abdomen.

I sit up. "What's going on?"

"Not every part of my body is beautiful. Come on, trust me; it'll be better in the dark. You'll like it anyway."

"Can you move your hands?" I ask her.

She looks up at the ceiling with a snort and doesn't budge.

"Please."

"Okay, you asked for it. This could ruin everything . . ." she mutters, lifting them without looking at me.

About three inches below the navel, there's a long, thin scar. "Is this what you were hiding from me?" I ask, running my finger over it.

"My C-section scar, yeah," she moans.

"Why?"

"Because men don't like it!" she exclaims. "My last year of university, I was messing around with a Spanish boy from the Erasmus program, and he, well, when he saw it . . ." Elisa holds her index finger up and then bends it. "Instant downer."

"Listen to me," I say, leaning over her again. "I don't know who that asshole was, but I can assure you that this"—I say, giving her a kiss on the far-right side of the scar—"is the best part of you." I continue to kiss her along its entire length. "It's your story, it shows how strong you are, and it makes you even more beautiful."

"Doesn't it . . . depress you?" she asks in a small voice.

"On the contrary." I would like to make her feel how not depressed I am right now, but it seems inelegant to wave such an exuberant demonstration under her nose.

"Kiss me," she begs me.

"I already am."

"On the mouth."

She gets up on her elbows, but I push her back down. "I'm not done yet." I go back between her legs and can't help but smile when I feel her arousal melting on my fingers. As soon as she feels my tongue on her, she arches her pelvis, letting out a muffled cry.

I tease her with another slow caress, and this time she emits a full-throated moan.

The third time, Elisa digs her fingers into my hair, urging me to keep going, and I comply, as if I had no other purpose in life.

She pants, her breath getting shorter and shorter, moving beneath me in rhythm with each lash of my tongue until I feel her twitch against my lips and she announces her orgasm with an "Ooohhhh."

I lie down next to her and look at her, sprawled out on the bed, her breasts rising and falling as she tries to catch her breath.

When she meets my gaze, I read the satisfaction in her eyes, and I can't help but smile smugly. If I had that Spanish imbecile in front of me, I'd give him a good slap.

"Now I know how to get you to stop talking," I say, staring at her silent, half-open mouth.

She turns to her left side and kisses me, then straddles me. "You know," she whispers into my mouth. "I've always wondered if Pompilia is as good as she says she is."

"Do you want me to tell you?" I ask, cocking my eyebrow.

"Is she?"

"Why would you care?"

"Because now," she continues, moving down to my pelvis, "I want to get you to stop talking."

She takes off my boxers, relieving my erection of the forced compression it's been enduring, at least until the first contact with her soft, warm mouth, which sends a shock straight to my brain.

She lowers her head and when she raises it she gives me a fiery look that seems to say *I'm going to kill you,* and I want to reply *I'd be happy to die like this.*

Elisa accompanies the up-and-down motion of her mouth with her hands, and I find myself clutching the sheets so as not to abandon myself completely; otherwise I'd come in no time. I've never had a timing problem, but tonight I've been on the verge of orgasm from the moment she took off her dress.

On the third swirl of her tongue, I find myself forced to stop her. She has nothing to learn from Pompilia—on the contrary. "If you keep this up, you'll make me very happy, very quickly, but I don't want to rush tonight."

I lift her up and kiss her, our mouths tasting of tart and sex, our hands trembling with desire.

"I bought condoms," she tells me.

I reach for the bedside drawer and open it. "Well done, because I don't think this will be enough."

"The variety pack you got in Belvedere!" she exclaims, surprised and amused. "You kept it."

"I wanted a souvenir, but a Duomo magnet seemed too obvious."

"You haven't opened it," she observes, indicating the sealed package.

"Should I have?"

She shakes her head, looking down. "Well . . . it's been a while . . ."

"Elisa," I say, grabbing her chin so she can look me in the eyes. "Who was I supposed to use them with? I didn't want, I don't want, and I won't want anyone but you. I don't want to fuck. I want to make love, because you are neither my first nor my last. You are my only one."

"But I've never made love, Michael. I don't know if I'm capable."

"Me neither." I lean over her and kiss her, but not out of passion or desire. This kiss is an oath. "It's our first time; we'll learn together."

"I missed you."

"I missed you too."

"I want to be yours. Make me feel like yours."

"You already are mine. You always have been."

Our words get lost between one kiss and another, but we understand each other anyway and lose ourselves to the point that we almost forget the condoms.

Elisa is quick to grab one at random and slip it on me.

"I hope you got the extended pleasure ones," I joke.

"Hmmm . . . judging by the smell, I'd say it's the mango."

She sits on me and guides me inside of her with her hand, welcoming me with a squeeze, an internal, intimate embrace, and it almost doesn't seem real that it's actually happening.

Leaning back against the padded headboard, I watch her move and realize I've never seen a more beautiful sight. My worries about whether I can hold out vanish as I lose myself looking into her eyes, gripping her hips and thrusting, while she, with her hands on my shoulders, follows me by rocking her pelvis in a hypnotic back-and-forth. From the way the expression on her face changes like before, I know her orgasm is close, so I make her lie down, reversing our positions.

I bring her to the edge with one thrust after another, and when she begs for a kiss, I lower myself down to capture her lips. She grips me with her thighs and strains against my body as her scream is lost in my mouth. Hearing her voice vibrate in my throat fans the fire inside me, and a second later my scream joins hers, my lower belly pierced with pleasure.

Lying on top of her, my head on her chest, her breasts glistening with sweat, I listen to her heartbeat.

"I want to be yours," I tell her. "Make me feel like I'm yours."

"You already are mine. You always have been."

"Even more."

62

Elisa

After long sleepless hours, Michael and I collapse just before dawn, my head in the crook of his neck, his face buried in my hair, our legs intertwined in a tangle of sheets.

When I've reached my deepest sleep, I wake up with a start to the high-pitched sound of a *cock-a-doodle-doo* at six o'clock.

"What's happening?" I ask, sitting up in bed. "Is that a rooster?!"

Michael grabs my elbow, pulling me back to him. "It's my alarm clock. I got so used to Renato coming to my windowsill to sing me good morning, I can't wake up without it anymore."

"Look, if you miss him, we'll gladly send him to you."

"Do you know what I'm missing?"

"What?"

"You."

"I'm right here," I object. "How can you miss me when I'm so close?"

"Not close enough." He squeezes my hips, pressing me to his belly, making me understand that he wants to be even closer.

"Oh, come on," I say, jumping out of bed.

"What?" he asks, confused.

"Not with morning breath," I say, retrieving a toothbrush and toothpaste from my handbag. "I'm not comfortable with my mouth tasting like a truck stop bathroom." They should stop making romantic films with protagonists who kiss as soon as they wake up, as if their breath smells of roses. Does anyone fall for it? I don't.

Michael follows me by picking up his electric toothbrush. "You're right, in my defense I admit I've never woken up next to a woman, so I'm rather new to morning sex."

"You mean you always left on the sly while the girl was sleeping?"

"More like I've never stayed over."

"How did you manage to get out of it?"

"Work: deadlines, early morning meetings, paperwork . . . Luckily it all sounds so boring that no one ever asked me for details."

We brush our teeth, floss, and double rinse with mouthwash, after which Michael picks me up and kisses me.

"How's that?" he asks, blowing a puff of air at my nose.

"Peppermint and licorice. I like it."

"Good, because it's time for a shower, and I don't intend to take it alone," he says, entering the stall and activating a showerhead that mimics a monsoon rain.

"But I'll be late for the fair!" I object. "It takes an hour on the tube."

"I'll drive you later. You're mine now. I've waited so long for this moment, I don't want to give up even a second of it."

"I don't have a change of clothes," I insist, resisting his hands.

"Go naked, the stand will be mobbed."

"Would you really like the whole fair to see me like that?"

He scrutinizes me with a long lascivious look, in which I read all his bad intentions. "On second thought, no, that's a privilege I should reserve for myself."

"Then I'll need a change of clothes."

"You could skip today. Foliero's there," he insists with a kiss, his caresses also succeeding in their intent to convince me.

"But I can't," I reply with difficulty. "I have to go now."

But when I feel him inside me, my last glimmer of reason is extinguished. "Are you sure?" he murmurs in my ear, his pelvis still as I writhe with the need to feel him move.

"Michael . . ." My voice is barely a whisper.

"Are you really sure?" he tortures me by pushing deeper inside, and the moan he manages to extract from me provokes a smile that announces his victory.

"To hell with it! We can stop at H&M."

Thanks to Michael's inexhaustible imagination, the shower lasts longer than I could have possibly predicted, and now, even afterward, we keep playing with abandon: I shave him, he dries my hair, I tie his tie, and he ties my dress.

"I'm hungry," I say, returning to the living area, the kitchen counter as we left it last night. "Shall we make breakfast?"

But when I open the fridge, I'm disappointed to find only bottles of water, wine, beer, Gatorade, and protein bars.

Even the cupboards are bare. "Sorry, Michael, don't you have anything to eat?"

He shrugs as he absentmindedly scrolls through incoming emails on his phone. "No. I usually eat out."

"Really?"

He looks at me with an expression of pure innocence. "I wasn't joking when I said we were inaugurating the kitchen. Until yesterday, I'd never even turned on the vent."

"Okay, so I guess flour and milk are out of the question too."

"But I have this," he says, opening a door and taking out a mocha. "I can't drink coffee from the machine anymore."

"Better than nothing, but I have to eat something; otherwise, I'll pass out. Is there a café nearby where we can go?"

"There's no need; we can order in on the app. What would you like? Sweet or savory? Why am I even asking? I'll get a bit of everything," and in two clicks, he sends the order.

We use the delivery time to continue our exchange of affections, which, if it weren't for the buzz on the intercom, would have become inappropriate for minors.

We dive into the avocado toast, and between one bite and another, I look around, noticing details I hadn't seen last night when I was wrapped up in Michael.

One thing in particular strikes me: On one of the shelves there's a framed black-and-white close-up of a beautiful girl. It seems like a very personal photo, and even though I trust Michael and the fact that there's no one else but me, if he keeps a photo like that in his house, then that person must have been important to him.

I don't know if I'd be able to hold up against an immortal beloved. In the end, I give in to my fears and ask him. "Who's she?"

"She who?"

"The girl in the photo."

He frowns as if he doesn't understand what I'm talking about, so I point to the frame. "Ah, her! No one."

His response is worrying and hints at a long and difficult history. "Don't you want to talk about it?" I insist, trying not to sound invasive.

"There's nothing to talk about. I didn't put that photo there. It's the stock image that was in the frame when they gave it to me." And to demonstrate his absolute good faith, he takes the photo out of the frame and shows it to me, pointing out the writing on the back with the references to the site from which it was taken. "See?"

"Why didn't you put a photo in there?"

"I always meant to, but I never found the time. Maybe if you send me one, I'll put yours in there."

"I'd rather you take it of me."

"That's a good idea," he replies with a wink that makes me understand what kind of photo he has in mind. "Let's go. The sooner I get you there, the sooner I can see you again this evening."

"When did we plan to meet tonight?"

"We're planning to now. How's nine?"

When I arrive at our booth, Foliero is already rushing toward me, distraught. "Good thing you're here! We're in trouble!"

"Oh God, why? What happened?" I'm already alarmed.

"The wine! We ran out; we don't have a single bottle left at the stand."

Holy Christ! They warned me there might be people who try to sabotage competitors' stands, but I didn't think it would go this far. It's one thing to steal merch, but bottles are a new low! It's like taking away our oxygen. "Have you already reported it to the organizers? Did you ask them to start an investigation?"

"No, but . . ."

"No *buts*, I'll go. You look outside in the bin area to see if they dumped them there."

But before I take a step toward the organizer's area, he grabs me by the shoulders and stops me. "Nobody took anything from us. We sold them."

I'm stunned. "We sold them?"

"All of them."

"Just a minute. Who the hell bought thirty cases at once?"

"It wasn't all at once. There was one man from Harrods, then a very elegant lady from British Airways, a chef, and even a couple in uniform from the cruise line . . . We have three bottles left at the stand."

"That's wonderful!"

"Wonderful?! How are we going to last until Monday?!"

"Let me think . . . The reserves! You remember those two cases we have at the hotel?"

"Yeah, but that's just twelve bottles. And it's not even our best wine."

"For now, go and get them. Giada's coming today, right? I'll call and tell her to bring ten more cases. It will cost us with the airline, but there's nothing else we can do. Now go—"

"Excuse me, are you Miss Elisa Benetti?" interrupts a woman of indeterminate age, wearing a suit that highlights every defect of my own makeshift jacket and trousers.

"Yes, that's me," I reply.

"I'm Mary Glenfield from *Wine Spectator*. Could I disturb you for a short interview?"

I pinch myself. A journalist from the most important magazine in the sector wants to interview me?!

"Ma mi garba abbestia!" I involuntarily spurt out a Florentine expression of enthusiasm as the journalist stares at me, confused. "I mean, for sure," I say.

63

Michael

It was a rough start, but after our cold first encounter, Elisa and I now spend every free moment together, and not just in the bedroom, another absolute novelty for me.

I'm trying to show her more of my life here because, since there's no guarantee the Bingleys will accept her offer, I've become more determined than ever to ask her to live with me. Here.

I asked her once before, but it was bad timing. We were both on the defensive and neither of us were hearing the other properly.

I respect her life, her work, her passion, and how they overlap, but if she lost the vineyard and had to start from scratch, I would like us to be together.

Tonight she came with me to a business dinner, an event organized by the Saxton & D'Arcy partners.

"I hope you're not too offended if I tell you that event was excruciatingly boring. We could have skipped it and gone straight to this," Elisa tells me while we bask in the bathtub, her reclining on my chest, playing with the foam.

"I know they're boring. I never go to them."

"Why did you take me, then? Were you trying to punish me?"

"I wanted to introduce you to Saxton. He's practically my adopted father."

"Did I make a good impression on him?"

"Excellent."

"That's good. Because we could have carved out more time for ourselves since this is my last night. If you hadn't brought me home, I would have dragged you into the closet and taken advantage of you."

"That's not a given," I reply.

"What's not a given? That I would be able to take advantage of you? Look, I too can be very convincing."

"This doesn't necessarily have to be your last evening."

She turns to look at me with a funny ball of foam on the tip of her nose. "What do you mean?"

I swipe off the foam with my finger, and then caress the profile of her lips. "Why don't you stay another week? You don't have anything pressing at the estate . . ."

"What about Linda?"

"Your mother and Donatella are with her, and Giada will be back tomorrow morning."

"But what would I do in London?"

"We're together, you can take in the city, have a break . . ." I try to convince her. "Don't say no."

"If I'm basing my answer on tonight's riveting soiree, it would be an outright no."

"How about we base it on this?" I ask, kissing her.

"Nice, but not convincing enough."

"You're really demanding . . ." my hands search for her under the water and find her immediately as her legs spread to welcome me. "Better?"

"Now we're talking."

"I love you," I repeat, for what must be the millionth time.

"I love you."

"So is that a yes?"

"That's a yes."

64

ELISA

We closed the fair on a high note. I'm satisfied with the impression we made; we got orders. With all that in mind, I'm happy to stay another week in London.

Too bad I don't see Michael as much as I'd like.

He works a lot, leaving at dawn and returning late at night; I spend my days basically alone. He often comes home so tired that we end up staying in, like yesterday, when we were supposed to go to see *Mamma Mia!* in Soho, but I ended up going alone to the early show. Then I surprised him in the office with a takeaway lunch to eat with him. He was happy to see me, but we had to scarf down the food because he barely had any time between his meetings.

He told me he almost never eats lunch, just a quick snack if he's really hungry. I found it sad—not to mention unhealthy—but Michael doesn't seem to give it a second thought.

I spent the rest of my time visiting all the museums, buying the usual souvenirs for Linda, Mamma, Donatella, and Giada; strolling around Hyde Park, which is a few minutes from Michael's house; and doing little else.

It's all beautiful, but I only enjoyed it half as much on my own.

When I tell Michael I've run out of ideas, he gives me his gym membership card, suggesting I indulge in a day of relaxation instead of trying to find more activities.

Maybe I need it, because I keep thinking about home, about Linda, about the vineyard, and I need to turn off my brain for a while; spending an entire afternoon in a place where cell phones are prohibited could be the cure.

Right now, in fact, I'm leaving the sauna feeling pleasantly relaxed, after half an hour of swimming against a current and a reactivating massage.

Wrapped in a terrycloth bathrobe, I head to the Zen bar with heated loungers and herbal teas.

"May I have an orange cinnamon herbal tea, please?" I ask the girl behind the counter, who is the image of serenity.

"Elisa?!" exclaims a woman sitting on the stool to my right with dismay.

It takes me a few seconds to register her face. "Caroline?" It's Bingley's sister.

"Imagine seeing you here! What are you doing in London?" she asks, continuing the conversation in English. She's here, it's her house, her rules, though even in Tuscany, the few times she showed up, she always avoided speaking Italian, which she knows perfectly well.

I adapt and respond in English too. "I was at the London Wine Fair and . . ."

"This is Sophia Skyper-Kensitt and Julia Bromley," she interrupts me, uninterested in my answer, introducing me to the two women next to her, who are focused on their celery and carrots with hummus. "Girls, *this* is Elisa Benetti."

"Ah, the peasant girl!" exclaims the woman with curly hair—I don't know if it's Sophia or Julia.

"Yes," I reply, getting excited, because I couldn't help but notice she'd used the word *peasant*, which I think of as a farmer who works other people's land—so at least she's being accurate, given that the estate belongs to the Bingleys—even though the word also has a negative connotation, and I have the feeling, given her tone, that's more how she meant it. "I make wine."

"We know," replies the other, who is thin with platinum-blond hair styled to perfection. "Caroline told us about you."

"Really? What did she say?"

"Oh, so many things," she replies, giving her blond friend a strange smile. I don't want to make assumptions, but I'm pretty sure I wouldn't have wanted to hear them.

"Anyway, it's a surprise to see you here," comments Caroline with the acrimony that's come to define her. "It's a very exclusive place."

"Do you think I can't afford an exclusive place?" I ask, stirring sugar into the tea.

"Oh no. Except that there's a months-long waitlist."

"I'm Michael's guest," I say, sparking immediate interest.

"Michael?!" Sophia and Julia exclaim in chorus. "Michael D'Arcy?!"

"Yeah," I confirm.

"Oh." Caroline's expression hardens. "How did that come about?"

"I'm staying with him for a week, and he wanted me to have a relaxing afternoon," I reply without going into details.

"At his apartment?!" the other two repeat in unison, amazed.

"Michael is always so generous when it comes to helping the less fortunate," Caroline continues with her digs. "Decent hotels are quite . . . expensive."

"If I can give you some veteran advice," the curly-haired girl interjects, "sleep with one eye open. No doubt Michael will try to seduce you. When a living female being enters his orbit, he can't resist. He may be good in bed, but he doesn't deserve a woman wasting her time on him."

"And you've already wasted a lot," her friend chuckles to her.

The curly-haired woman, however, doesn't take it well. "Not as much as you have," she replies to her through gritted teeth.

"And don't unpack your suitcases," adds the other. "Once he's gotten his fix, he'll ask you to leave him in peace. No woman has ever lasted more than forty-eight hours. I hold the record of forty and only because it was over Christmas!"

"Pay no attention to them," Caroline tells me in a fake friendly tone. "It's just the way he is . . . it's easier to list the women he hasn't slept with yet."

"Like you, for example," I reply, taking a sip of herbal tea. In a fit of morbid curiosity, a few evenings ago, I asked him if there had ever been anything between him and Caroline Bingley. After all, they lived under the same roof until they were adults, and I had my suspicions. Suspicions that he dispelled: "I'd rather die."

Her two friends burst out laughing, and she glares at them.

My composure evaporates. "Girls, it was a pleasure chatting with you, but I have to go. I really needed a relaxing afternoon after ten days of nonstop sex with Michael. You're right, he's really good in bed, and I needed this little rest. Ah, for the record: I don't fall into his orbit, so maybe that's why he's still interested in me. And if I ever do leave, it won't be because he's shown me the door."

They stare at me in silence, their mouths agape.

"I am a farmer, and you might want to thank people like me because otherwise you'd have to pick those carrots and celery yourselves . . . but then, at least then you'd have a way to spend your miserable days."

And having given them the answer they deserved, I get up to leave with an unpleasant sensation of unease, as if I were in the wrong place.

"How many of your exes will I meet this evening?" I ask Michael in the car on our way to his friends' house for dinner.

"Where did that come from?"

"I saw Caroline Bingley with her friends Julia and Sophia this afternoon at the spa, and it turns out they've both slept with you."

"That was back in school. Water under the bridge," he replies. "But knowing them, they probably invented things on purpose to make you jealous."

"I'm not jealous; it just seems that in London there's a new conquest of yours around every bend. I want to know if I need to prepare myself tonight."

"No danger. I've never slept with any of my friends' girlfriends. You can enjoy dinner without fear of treason."

"I don't know if I'm cut out to interact with your acquaintances," I admit with a tightening in my stomach that makes me want to do anything but eat.

"These guys are all really easy, no snobs." He takes advantage of the red light to kiss me. "Everyone will like you."

When a little later we knock on the door of an apartment in a very chic building overlooking the Thames, my heart pounds with anxiety.

Sebastian, whom I already met at the fair, opens the door, and he and Michael greet each other in a sequence of gestures only brothers would know.

"Come in! You're the last to arrive, and we're all starving. It's so nice see you again, Elisa," he greets me warmly, inviting me to give him my coat. "Come on, I'll introduce you around."

The guests are having an aperitif on the living room sofas. "Hey everyone, let me introduce you to Elisa," announces Michael. "And behave yourselves. Elisa, this is Duke and Allegra. And this is Jemma and Ashford, the craziest duke and duchess the United Kingdom has ever seen, and Charlotte is Sebastian's girlfriend. Where are Harring and Cécile?"

"Meeting their wedding planner," Duke replies, pretending to put a gun to his head.

"I'm not great with names, but to make it up to you I brought some wine," I say, gesturing toward the case Michael is holding. "I make it myself at Charles's estate in Tuscany."

"Ah, how beautiful!" Allegra exclaims, applauding. "I'd love to try it. Sebastian was just telling us how delicious it was."

"I'm sure he was just being kind."

"Who, him?" his girlfriend giggles. "He finds something terrible to say about everything. If he speaks well about something, you know he's being sincere. And not only that, last week we had a journalist over for dinner from *Wine Spectator*, who went crazy when she tasted your Chianti Riserva."

Okay, that explains a lot. I have Foliero to thank for thinking so fast.

We take our seats at the table, and, to my great relief, dinner is filled with casual chatter, laughter, and good humor. The boys entertain us with tragicomic anecdotes from university, then Jemma takes center stage with the story of her and Ashford's wedding, a strange tale involving his hallucinating mother, a peyote cake, and the queen. They ask me about myself and my work and are interested in the answers, although after a few too many drinks, I'm no longer so sure I'm expressing myself in proper English.

After we eat, the boys compete at pinball, and I stay with the girls, picking at dessert leftovers around the kitchen island.

"So you're trying to buy Charles's estate in Tuscany?" Jemma asks me.

"Yes, but the bank is still in the process of approving the loan . . ."

"Do you have any photos with you?" Allegra asks me. "I don't mean to be intrusive, but I work in luxury real estate, and this is exactly the kind of property we deal with. We actually manage a Renaissance palace right outside Florence."

I open the gallery on my phone and show her the images. "Here it is."

"How wonderful!" all three exclaim, gathered around a photo of a golden sunset over the vineyard.

"I know, that's why I don't want it to become a golf club," I comment bitterly. "No offense, if any of you play golf."

"I play tennis," replies Allegra.

"I am a champion of skipping . . . the gym," Charlotte intervenes.

"I argue with my mother-in-law," says Jemma. "That burns a lot of calories."

"You said that, in addition to the winery, you want to transform the villa into a farmhouse, right?"

"Yes, but high end," I specify. "It is a seventeenth-century villa, after all. Too bad it costs a fortune."

"I could manage the project," Charlotte says, perking up as if she'd received an electric shock.

"You?"

"I develop hotels for the Bloom Group, and I specialize in restorations. The company also has a foundation for the protection of cultural heritage, and I could include the villa project among my pro bono commitments. You'll still have to pay for the work itself, but I can manage the project and the construction site without any issues."

"Seriously? Are you sure?"

"And I can give you a cost-benefit plan," adds Allegra.

"I was a make-up artist," Jemma chimes in. "But I can promote you. Aristocratic guests are great for marketing . . . In fact, I'll start right away." She takes my cell phone and sends herself the photos.

"What are you doing?"

"I'm sending them to my best friend. Cécile and Harring are getting married next year, and they haven't chosen a venue yet."

"Are you saying they should get married at Le Giuggiole?" Maybe I didn't quite understand her.

"Of course!"

"But . . ." I want to stop her, but I don't know how.

"No *buts*."

"Forget it," Allegra convinces me. "When Jemma gets an idea in her head, there's no stopping her."

"Well, thank you," I say, moved. "I don't know how to reciprocate."

"Give me these, and we'll be even," Jemma says, seizing the two surviving bottles. "I'm having guests for dinner and want to make a good impression on them. May I?"

"Certainly! I'm not taking them home." It seems like the least I can do as a gesture of gratitude. "Tell me, do you often meet for dinner?" I ask hopefully.

Allegra shrugs. "We try to manage a couple of times a year. We're always on the move for work, and Jemma has a baby . . . it's a mess to schedule."

Vanishing hope. "This afternoon I had an unpleasant run-in with Michael's bitter exes, and I wasn't really in the mood to go out. But tonight is the first time I've really felt at ease."

"Girls!" exclaims Charlotte. "Raise your hand if you've had problems with your husband's exes."

All three shoot their hands into the air.

"As you can see," Allegra concludes, pouring me some wine, "you're in good company."

65

Michael

Elisa and I have been living in a bubble, and, like all bubbles, when it bursts, it happens suddenly.

Saturday is ours alone, no work, no commitments, nothing, and we're already in it from the moment we wake up, with breakfast in bed. We're enjoying waffles topped with chocolate syrup when my phone rings.

"Sorry, I know I promised I wouldn't answer any calls, but it's Bingley. He must be back from Paris."

"Even prisoners have the right to a phone call," Elisa concedes. "But don't blame me if your waffle's gone when you get back."

The problem is that the content of the call concerns her, so when I come back to the bedroom, she can't help but notice my troubled expression.

"I was good. I saved you the waffle and the French . . . what's that face? What happened?"

I sit on the bed, repulsed at the thought of eating. "The Bingleys want to sell to Bogdanovic as soon as possible. They asked me to reschedule the meeting with him for this Monday so he can sign the preliminary agreement. I told him that rushing would put Bogdanovic in a position of power to dictate the terms and price, but Charles said it doesn't matter."

"What?!" she exclaims, dropping her still-untouched croissant. "But how? I thought I had until the end of November."

"I know, but Charles talked to his sister, who wants to sell immediately, and . . . you know how he is."

She squeezes her eyes shut as she shakes her head in disbelief. "So everything I did was for nothing?"

"It was still worth trying," I try to console her, though I know the right words don't exist.

She gets out of bed and starts gathering her things and putting them in her suitcase.

"What are you doing?" I ask. "Your flight is on Wednesday."

"Sorry, but I have some loose ends to tie up." She continues to fold clothes and put them in her case without pause. "I could be homeless by Wednesday. I have a family to think about. I can't stay here. Not after this Bingley twist."

"That's exactly why you can and must stay!" I say, trying to stop her. "This is your home."

"My home?" She looks at me coldly. "It's barely yours, Michael."

"I promise you won't regret it. I swear on my parents' grave, I want you here with me. I want Linda here; I want your mother too. I want you in my life."

"Michael." She takes my face in her hands. "I don't want to be in your life. I want to share our lives."

"And we will!" I insist. "Why do you want to go back to Italy when your security is here?"

"Because, Michael, I have nothing to do with this. It's not my house, it's not my pace, it's not my lifestyle." She sits next to me, her hands in mine. "You come to Italy."

"And do what?"

"Anything. I'll have to reinvent myself too, so let's do it together. Let's start again together; let's take risks together."

"Why? I have a life here."

"No, Michael, you have your brother's life, your brother's job, your brother's apartment, to the extent that you can't even see yourself! You live inside boxes: the office box, the apartment box—you even play tennis in a box. You exit one and enter another. When was the last time you felt the warmth of the sun on your skin? Or breathed air that didn't smell like smog?"

"What are you saying?" I blurt out.

"The truth. Your job is boring by your own admission. You only do it to prove you're better than George. There's no need, you've always been better. Why sacrifice yourself for a cause that isn't yours . . . And this apartment? You own it, but it doesn't belong to you. You're nowhere; these walls don't reflect you. You don't even have your own photos in the picture frames."

"Good thing you said you'd stop being judgmental," I mutter, standing up suddenly and breaking contact between us.

"I'm not judging. I'm just showing you what you don't want to see. What are we doing here? You work nonstop, and I wait for you in an empty house. When you come home in the evening, you're exhausted, and we eat takeaway until . . . I don't know, until one of us can't take it anymore?" This time she's the one coming at me, as I'm standing by the window, staring into space. "Going to events because we have to make an appearance? Talking to bores? Me dodging your exes' barbs while waiting for those twice-a-year dinners to spend time with your very busy friends?"

"Oh, sorry if everything sucks. What a hellish week you've had. Maybe you should have gone home after the fair if you're so disgusted with everything I have to offer you."

"Listen to me"—she forces me to turn around, pulling me by the arm—"I don't want to simply be with you. I want to be happy with you. I wouldn't be happy here, but what's worse is that you're not happy either."

"You're asking me to give up everything."

"We'll be together. You and me. The two of us," she replies, more convinced than ever. "Or are you scared?"

She stares into my eyes, waiting for me to accept her challenge as I've always done. But this time it's different. "I can't."

"Michael . . ." her voice trembles.

"I can't," I repeat, adamant. What am I going to do in Italy? Restore old cars? Make fresh pasta? Give English lessons?

She looks away and bows her head, surrendering. "I'm going to shower and get dressed. Can you call me a taxi?"

I feel like we've taken ten steps backward.

66

Elisa

No doubt this is Caroline's way of taking revenge. She had the power and she used it. I, on the other hand, have nothing.

She won.

And with time, she'll probably take Michael from me too.

I don't see how I could feel worse.

One thing is for sure, it will take months, maybe years, to forget him, but if I stayed here in London, I would die inside.

If this is the life he wants, I won't stand in his way. But I can't be with a man who thinks I should automatically leave everything for him, especially when he isn't willing to do the same for me.

London's a great place to visit, I can't deny it has its merits, but it's not for me. I've never felt as sad and alone as I have since I've been here, and I can't allow my happiness to depend on the moments Michael decides to give me.

I quickly dry my hair without bothering to style it and go back to the room, finding it empty.

It's raining outside. The sky, which has been overcast for a week, has finally given way, sending torrents of rain down the windowpanes, making it impossible to see outside.

I'm wearing the last clean clothes I have left: a gray tartan skirt I found at the vintage exchange exhibition in Bagno a Ripoli, a too-tight white sweater that I bought without trying on, black tights with stretched-out ankles I inherited from Giada, and my burgundy Doc Martens, which I've worn and polished a thousand times. I look at myself in the mirror. What business do I have with Michael, with his apartment, with his friends and his life?

I close my suitcase and drag it into the living room, where Michael is standing by the front door already dressed and wearing a tie. In short, ready for another day at the office.

"If the taxi isn't here, I'll wait for it in the lobby so you can go ahead to work," I tell him.

"I didn't call a taxi. I'm going to take you."

"There's no need." And I don't want him to.

"It would take forever to get one in this rain, and it would cost you at least two hundred pounds."

"Fine," I relent. We each stare anywhere but at each other, silently trapped in a devastating feeling of surrender. "I'm ready."

"Okay, let's go."

He reaches out to take my suitcase, and our hands touch on the handle, contact that pushes our gazes to meet against our will.

"So, this is how it ends?" he asks me.

The words have the power to send me into a crisis, draining any strength I have left to reply.

Michael lets go of the suitcase, takes my face in his hands, and kisses me, pushing me against the still-closed door.

My lips welcome him, opening with desperation. I'm holding on to him, my fingers tight on his shoulders and my eyes squeezed shut because I'm too afraid to look at him.

He lifts my sweater, revealing my breasts, which he kisses, and I don't offer the slightest resistance.

If there has to be a last time, let's give it everything we have.

I unhook his belt and unbutton his trousers, and he lifts me against the door, my arms wrapped around his neck.

His right hand finds its way between my legs, shifting my panties to the side, and a second later I feel him inside of me.

My moan is muffled by his mouth.

It's a strange kind of pleasure, combined with a pain stirred by each of his thrusts, but I don't dislike it, so I encourage him by responding to him with the rhythm of my pelvis, telling him to go faster, to go as hard as he can.

"I'm going to hurt you like this," he whispers in my ear.

"Please don't stop." I don't know what I feel, but I need to find a way to turn it off.

"I don't want our last time to be like this." Michael slows down, and the furious sex we were having until a second ago becomes something poignant, rending, as he slowly leads me to the brink of pleasure.

Our bodies say goodbye, uniting in one last, desperate orgasm, which this time pierces us like a blade.

"Loving you is like slow dancing in a room that's on fire," he says, his forehead against mine. "You know you should run, but you want to finish the song and wait to find out what the next one will be, even if you're in flames."

"We're already too burned."

We exchange one last kiss that tastes as salty as my tears, and then we turn and leave.

As I get into the car, a hot, sticky substance moistens my thighs. For the first time, we didn't use protection—neither of us thought about it. And if . . .

"Look, I didn't use . . ."

"I'll take the pill," I interrupt. I'm not sixteen anymore. I'm certainly not used to risky relationships, but at least now I know what to do.

"I'm sorry."

"Don't be; we needed it." We had to feel each other fully for our last time.

The journey to Stansted is prolonged torture. Each of us in their own head, with their own thoughts, with just the sound of the pouring rain on the roof of the Range Rover to fill the silence between us.

When we arrive, he takes my suitcase and brings me inside, and I don't object, even though I'm aware he's making this increasingly difficult.

Once we reach security, we stop. He can't follow me through.

"I'd love to come to the gate."

"What for?" I ask.

"I don't know, in the hopes you might change your mind at the last minute."

"Or you could change yours," I venture, but his silence in return is a tacit no, and our attempt to ignore it fails miserably.

"We could try to do this long distance," he suggests.

"So, what, I'd come here one weekend and you'd come to Belvedere the next?"

"Yeah," he replies, sounding convinced.

"For how long? Six months? A year? And then what? One weekend I won't be able to come, the next you'll be too busy, then we'll argue about not seeing each other enough, then we'll have to decide how to move forward, and we'll be right back here again."

"Can we at least try not to argue? Christ, I've never felt worse in my life, Elisa. How can I watch the only person I've ever loved walk away?"

"I love you too, Michael."

"Then why are we hurting each other?"

"I will always love the Michael I met at Le Giuggiole, the smiling Michael, the Michael who sings 'Fiumi di Parole' with me, the Michael who takes me to Florence in the Cinquecento he restored with his own hands, the Michael who helps me birth a foal . . . but the London Michael, the Michael who doesn't have a second for himself, the guest-in-his-own-house Michael—that's not my Michael."

He lowers his head and tilts my chin with his hand so I can look at him. "I will always be your Michael," he whispers against my lips. "And you will always be my Elisa." He brushes my lips with his. "Always."

The kiss is like a movie, long, intense, passionate, breathtaking. I try to imprint every detail in my memory, the scent of his skin that still smells of aftershave, the warmth of his breath, the softness of his lips, his taste, the velvety vigor of his tongue caressing mine.

We separate with a sigh, and I walk away toward the security line, struggling to counteract the magnetic force drawing me back to him.

I promise myself I won't look back, but I do it once, twice, three times, and Michael is always there, holding me in his gaze.

At least we tried—we owed that much to ourselves. It didn't work out, but it never could have lasted between two people like us.

I put my suitcase on the belt, go through the metal detector, and retrieve my luggage on the other side. Now there's no turning back.

I turn to look at Michael again, now just a speck in the crowd, but he sees me and I see him.

I don't know how long we stay like this, but in the end an agent asks me to go to my gate to make room for the other passengers in security.

After a few more steps, Michael disappears from my sight. It really is over.

67

Michael

I'm physically present at the preliminary sale, but my mind is elsewhere.

I've just been through forty-eight hours of pure, self-inflicted psychological torture: on Saturday I stayed at the airport all morning, doing what I don't know.

Hoping, nothing more.

Hoping to see Elisa leave the departures area as I stared at the departures board with my heart in my throat when the one for Florence started flashing Now Boarding at the top of the list.

Then it disappeared. I waited for her, but after an hour and an untouched cup of coffee gone cold, I gave up and went home.

Her scent still filled the apartment.

In the room, the unmade bed spoke to me of all the nights we spent together, and since then I haven't been able to sleep in it.

On Sunday I nearly killed myself at the gym by exercising to my last breath. Today I woke up on the sofa with a start. I flew to work. I even spilled coffee on myself on the stairs and had to change into the freshly dry-cleaned suit I keep in the office. Now I'm here, in the conference room, with the Bingleys and Bogdanovics, shattered in body and spirit.

My friend taps me on the arm.

"Huh?" I groan, shaking myself out of my stupor.

"I asked if you had a pen," he repeats, waving the one already in his hand. "This one doesn't work."

"Ah, yes. One second." I reach into my jacket pocket, but along with the ballpoint pen, I can feel something else. I pull out the Montblanc, and a leaf comes with it.

How did that end up there?

It's a little stiff, its red color has faded, but it's the vine leaf that Elisa had given me to use in place of a pocket square for our night out in Florence.

Back in London, I'd sent the suit to the dry cleaners, and it's the one I've just changed into at the office.

I turn the leaf between my fingers, thinking back to what Elisa said about the vine: It's strong, and resists even the most impervious conditions, representing life.

Life . . .

"Have you guys ever seen a foal being born?" I find myself asking out of nowhere.

Dismay spreads around the table.

"Michael, dear, do you need a coffee? You're looking rather rough . . ." Caroline asks me.

"This tiny little creature comes out all slimy like a bar of soap. She knows how to stand right away and immediately recognizes her mother. The mare licks her clean and cuddles her, rubbing her face against her baby . . ."

"Very interesting," she comments. "Shall we proceed?"

A strange thing happens. It's as if I leave my body and see myself from the outside: me, standing by while Le Giuggiole is consigned to oblivion. No more grape harvests, no more bottles in the cellars, no more homemade jams or vegetables from the garden, no more Renato singing good morning, and knowing that I was the death of it all slowly fills me with disgust.

The arrangements have been made: Next Tuesday Bogdanovic will sign the final contract and take possession of the estate in exchange for four million pounds—five million euros. One million less than the Bingleys could have gotten had they not been in such a rush to close.

Everyone gets up from the table, satisfied, but Charles stops me before leaving. "Michael, is something wrong?"

"Huh? No, everything's fine," I lie. "I might be coming down with the flu . . ." I don't know if he believes me or if he's just pretending, but he doesn't say anything else.

The evenings have become very long, and what's worse, I'm uncomfortable everywhere I turn.

I sit on the kitchen stool and stare at the empty picture frame—I removed the stock photo—wondering what to put in it.

I haven't printed out photos since high school.

I scroll through the images on my phone, delete a series of screenshots that I needed for work, and look for something to frame.

There's Linda, smiling with her high school acceptance letter, which she sent me a few days ago.

There's the group photo we took at the close of harvest with all the workers.

There's a crooked self-portrait of Max and me with the Cinquecento, filthy but satisfied, taken after we'd just finished polishing it.

There's a photo of Cinta Senese ragù boiling on the fire and Mariana's hand stirring it.

I scroll through the album full of Tuscan sunsets, sinuous hills, rows of cypresses, clear blue skies over the vineyard, baskets full of grapes . . .

There's a shot of Elisa, which I quickly snapped when she wasn't looking, to the extent that she's barely captured in the frame. She's riding her horse through the vineyard and smiling, one of her rare and wonderful smiles that I wanted to keep for myself.

Further back, I find the screensaver images that came with the phone.

Is it possible that I've never taken a single photo here in London? That I've had no moments worth remembering? Nothing important enough to share?

I look around for something to cling to, but all I see is George's house. Now I'm in George's kitchen, I sleep in George's bed, I sit on George's sofas, I work in George's study . . .

"You're a guest in your own home." Elisa's words echo in my head.

Then the fog clears, and it all comes into focus: I never built a life for myself. I adapted myself to my brother's with no plan of my own. I try to imagine myself in ten years but can't bear the thought of myself still here, surrounded by empty picture frames. And what about twenty years from now? What will I do when I stop working?

I suddenly feel poor. My bank accounts couldn't be more bloated, my rental properties are doing better than ever, I'm on the highest rung of wealth in the world, and yet I have nothing. And I do nothing with what I have.

Elisa, on the other hand, has everything I lack: passion, goals, a family, people who respect and love her. And I'm letting Bogdanovic take it all away.

The vine leaf is still here, in front of me, on the marble counter.

The idea is as stupid as it is insane—it's probably even illegal—but if there's any way to fix what I've done, I'll do it.

I fly into the study, power on my PC and scanner, and start looking for the documents I got from the Belvedere town hall . . . I put them here somewhere . . . *Urban and Territorial Governmental Acts* . . . here they are!

I digitize the document with the scanner, but the photocopy is too faded, so the file is unreadable.

I'll have to re-create it word by word . . .

"What do you mean the new zoning plan was approved?!" Bogdanovic's lawyer asks me.

"See?" I hand him a file labeled *Union of the Municipalities of Belvedere and Collalto*. "The municipalities decided to accelerate the approval of their union and needed to homogenize their policies for the newly created territory, which includes a new zoning ordinance for the land falling within the Chianti Classico historical production region," I explain.

"And what does this new law say?" Caroline asks, annoyed.

"That any land with vineyards that are more than thirty years old cannot be subject to substantial modifications, meaning anything greater than twenty percent of the agricultural area, for the purpose of protecting the landscape and environment," I read and translate the article I highlighted on the legislation.

"This means that of the twenty-five hectares of vineyard . . ." continues the lawyer.

"Only five can be transformed for other uses," I conclude. "We didn't think the new law would be introduced until at least the middle of next year, but evidently they were eager to push it through." I try to sound heartbroken. "I wanted to check to be sure nothing had changed and instead I found this update."

"This changes a lot," observes Bogdanovic, in a heavy Russian accent that not even the most expensive English courses with the best Cambridge professors could correct.

"Indeed," I continue, holding the paper in my hand. "We've never spoken explicitly about the buyer's intentions for the property, but since he's an entrepreneur in the golf sector, we shouldn't beat around the bush. I thought it was appropriate to make him aware of the matter because it could affect his decision to buy or not."

Bogdanovic whispers something to his lawyer in Russian, in an agitated and not at all friendly tone.

"Given the facts, Mr. Bogdanovic no longer intends to invest in the property."

"But he's already signed the preliminary agreement," exclaims Caroline furiously.

"I can't build a golf course on so little land," Bogdanovic blurts out. "I need a minimum of twenty hectares."

"We tried to move as quickly as possible, but it wasn't fast enough," Charles replies in a conciliatory tone. "I understand your hesitations in the face of these new conditions."

"I'm not buying it. I'm very sorry, because it's a nice property, but it's no longer useful to me." Then Bogdanovic looks at me. "Thank you, Michael, for your precision. If you hadn't checked, I would have been screwed."

"I've been taking care of your investments for years, Sergei." I say in a friendly manner. "It's my job."

The Bingleys are a little less happy, Caroline in particular, but we tear up the preliminary agreement, and I feel a bit more at peace with myself.

Later that evening, Bingley surprises me with a visit to my apartment.

"Am I bothering you?" he asks when I open the door.

"No, I wasn't doing anything special." I invite him in, gesturing for him to sit on the sofa.

"You skipped the gym today. That's not like you," he scolds me.

"I went on Sunday. I had a credit."

"Royal & Lloyds," says Charles, glancing at my laptop, which is open to a real estate page. "Are you looking for a new buyer?"

"I was actually thinking of selling this apartment and moving. Your idea of a cottage in Primrose isn't so bad, now that I think about it."

"I thought you hated family neighborhoods."

"I think I need a change. Can I offer you something? Water? Tea? Coffee?"

"I'm fine, thanks. I wanted to talk to you."

"About what?"

"Well . . ." he reaches into his briefcase and takes out a copy of the territorial plan that I brought to the meeting this morning. "About this."

"Oh."

"Crazy timing, huh? These guys from the municipality are real killjoys," he observes with a strange smile.

"Totally."

"I was rereading it this afternoon, and I noticed a few grammatical and spelling errors." He shows me several passages that he's underlined with a red ballpoint pen, like an elementary school teacher. "They were in such a hurry, they didn't even correct it."

"You know, Charles—"

"You know, Michael," he interrupts me, "you speak Italian very well, even better than I do, even though I'm a native speaker. You have an exceptional command of accents and an impeccable ear for languages . . . That said, you've always sucked at writing."

"I wrote it," I admit.

"It's obvious."

"I'm sorry, Charles."

"You know I could report you, right?" Charles's tone is strangely ambiguous, and I struggle to discern whether or not he's joking.

"The only way to blow up the sale was to make Bogdanovic lose interest," I explain.

"I won't even ask why you did it."

"Elisa," I say, simply. I know that's enough to get the point across.

"In any case, you may have done me a favor too," says Charles.

I look at him, perplexed. "Oh yeah?"

"I know I could have made a good amount from the sale, but I've never been convinced that Bogdanovic's money is all that clean. I'd prefer zero pounds to dirty millions in my account. He may be a golf course developer now, but I don't know what he did before that, and I have serious suspicions about people who become billionaires overnight from nothing."

"So you won't report me?"

"No. And I won't tell Caroline."

Bingley looks at me, and I see nothing but affection in his eyes, like that of a blood brother—or more.

"You need to know something else," I say. "I was wrong about Giada. It isn't true that she isn't interested in you—on the contrary, she was beside herself when you left. She just didn't text you for fear of bothering you and seeming clingy."

My friend blinks in disbelief. "Seriously?!"

"When Elisa was here for the wine fair, Giada came to give her a hand for the weekend rush. She was hoping to see you, but you were in Paris." If this is going to be the night of amends, I want to make amends for all the mistakes I've made. "She never forgot about you, and I think she's still hoping you'll go back to her."

"Why are you telling me this?"

"Because I know you want to go back to her too and that if you'd known she was in London, you would have come back from Paris immediately."

Charles reaches across the coffee table, grabs my laptop, and places it on his lap.

"What are you doing?"

"I'm looking for the first flight to Florence," he says, typing frantically. "There's one! Tomorrow at ten, only a few seats left. I'll book now."

"Okay, hurry, but log out of my account first."

"Oh no, my friend. I'm not reporting you, but the least you can do is buy me a plane ticket," he replies, his eyes fixed on the screen. "So . . . shall I get two seats?"

68

Elisa

My homecoming was acknowledged quietly, my face was enough to tell everyone that nothing had gone right in London, so they were careful not to mention the sale, the fair, or Michael.

The only good news is that they extended the Internet coverage, so now we have our much-needed Wi-Fi.

For now, I'm continuing to manage the estate without any expectations. What's the point? In a few months, every vine will be uprooted from the earth, and our family will be left to explore other options. A new house. A new job. A new everything . . .

Every so often, my mind flies to London to find Michael, and the pain that spreads across my chest takes my breath away. It's a feeling of loss, of mourning.

His lawyer contacted me with paperwork to change Linda's surname—it's just paperwork, nothing personal—and to open a trust fund in her name, which she'll be able to access when she turns twenty-five.

Michael and I discussed it during our short "honeymoon," and in the end, he convinced me that it would only be enough money to give Linda the opportunity to do something with her life, as opposed to an invitation to do nothing for her entire life. Refusing it now would mean another confrontation with him, and I don't have the strength for that.

"What does *HRH* mean?" Foliero asks as we're going over our accounts at the villa's big kitchen table.

"What?" I ask, distracted.

"I got an email in English that says *HRH*."

"We must have ended up on some mailing list. Move it to spam."

"You sure? My English isn't perfect, but this looks like an order to me."

I get up to stand next to him and look at the screen. Oh God . . . is this a joke? *By appointment of HRH The Prince of Wales*, I read. "Foliero, *HRH* is the acronym for His Royal Highness, His Royal Highness The Prince of Wales." This has to be a joke.

I read and reread the email, trying to tell if it's a scam, though it doesn't look like it.

> The court supplier, at the request of His Royal Highness The Prince of Wales, would like to order a supply of sixty bottles of Chianti Classico Riserva, after Their Royal Highnesses had the pleasure of tasting it at the table of the Duke and Duchess of Burlingham.

My first instinct is to call Jemma, as we've exchanged numbers, to ask for her take.

"I told you I was having guests and wanted to make a good impression!" she explains, speaking very quickly and with that cockney accent of hers that distorts every word. "We practically had to pry the glass out of the prince's hand because he couldn't stop drinking it. With the clay pigeon shooting tournament scheduled for after dinner, we couldn't risk having any victims."

"So the order is real?"

"As real as the poop I just stepped in. Adorable corgis, excrement spreaders with paws. Okay, must go. I have to stop my son from eating liver-flavored dog kibble."

"So?" Foliero asks me with an inquisitive air.

"She confirmed it. The order is from His Highness The Prince of Wales."

"Damn! Now that's an order."

"Yeah, too bad it's probably our last."

Normally, we would have celebrated something like this with fireworks, but with our imminent fate in mind, we accept it with the muted enthusiasm of a consolation prize.

"Everyone, stay calm! Just calm down!" shouts Mamma, who is anything but calm as she bursts into the kitchen.

"What happened? Did the school call? Is Linda sick?" I ask, already in a panic.

"Charles is back!" she announces.

"Mr. Bingley?" asks Foliero, as if we knew another Charles.

"He's just arrived; he's unpacking his luggage. Donatella asked me to go and make up a room for him."

"Is he alone?" I ask with a tremor in my voice.

"Yeah. Luckily his stuck-up sister isn't here." I didn't mean her, but I got the answer I needed anyway.

I sigh for two reasons: the first, from relief, because Michael isn't here; the second, from disappointment, because Michael isn't here. Donatella appears in the arch of the door. "Elisa, Mr. Bingley is waiting for you in the study."

Here it is; this moment had to come sooner or later. My heart quivers, but I'll face this too.

I walk down the hallway that goes around the internal courtyard to the study, a delightful room in all shades of blue that today will set the scene for my execution.

"Hi, Elisa," Charles greets me, his perpetually disheveled red mop of hair contrasting with the furniture's pastel tones. "How's it going? You look well."

"Everything's fine."

"Sit down." He gestures toward the armchair next to the fireplace. "You're making me uncomfortable just standing there."

"I'm not very comfortable either, I confess."

"Oh, why?"

I sit on the edge of the chair, knees stiff and arms folded.

"Well, I know you came to tell me that you've sold the estate to the Russian, and we'll have to leave." He starts to say something but I continue. "We're trying to get organized. As soon as I got back from London, I found a place for us, but the apartment we wanted won't be ready for another two weeks. I realize I'm asking a lot from you, and maybe the Russian won't agree, but believe me, I've done everything possible to arrange to leave the estate as soon as possible. It's just that we've had to work within the limits of our means. I have Linda at school—"

"Okay, slow down," he interrupts me, raising his hand. "What are you talking about?"

"I'm talking about Bogdanovic, who bought the estate to build a golf club. Michael told me about it. And he also told me you were in a rush to sell and had planned to close this Monday. But, like I said, we're ready to leave. We just need fifteen days."

"Did you think I came here to hand you an eviction notice?" he asks, wide-eyed.

"What else would you be here for?"

Charles smiles and I find myself totally lost. "Bogdanovic withdrew from the deal. He's not buying the estate."

"Ah" is all I manage to say, my brain still busy processing the information.

"Yeah."

"Why?"

"He lost interest in the property."

"So it's still yours?"

"Mine and my sister's, yeah. And we still intend to sell."

"Of course."

"I was wondering if you were still willing to buy it."

"Yes. Yes!" I exclaim, leaping up from my chair, wide-eyed. "Of course I'm interested! I'll buy it!"

Charles nods. "I was pretty sure, but I wanted to confirm. Now, you and I have known each other all our lives, and I know you've put your heart into this place. I really would like for the estate to be yours. I won't play games with you on this, but I can't sell below market. Bogdanovic was going to give me five million—do you think the bank would give you that much?"

Ouch. "They said they could do four, according to their appraisal."

"That's a bit low. I know you know the value is there."

"Wait!" I exclaim. "I'll be right back." I fly to the kitchen, where I confiscate Foliero's laptop and return to Charles. "Look, we just got this. It's an order from the Prince of Wales himself for a supply of our wine. Maybe if I show this to the bank, I could get four and a half."

"Four and a half could work. My sister also has to give the okay, and she's more careful than I am when it comes to money. She'd rather look for another buyer than accept an offer that's too low."

"But four and a half would be okay?" I ask.

"Should be fine."

"Oh, thank you! Thank you!" I shout, throwing my arms around his neck. "You're an angel! I'll request an appointment with the bank for this afternoon."

"You're in a bit of a hurry, huh?"

"Like my ass is on fire," I say, jumping up and down. "Of course, let me just say you gave me a shock. You could have called me. There was no need to come all the way to Italy."

"But there was. I didn't come just to sell the estate," he replies with a sweet smile and a dreamy look.

Oh boy, do I hear violins in the air and rose petals falling from the sky? "Oh no?"

"I'd like to see Giada again. I think we had a big misunderstanding that made each of us think we'd lost interest in the other, but instead we were both too afraid to speak up. As long as she's still interested in me . . ."

"Is she interested? She dreams of you every night! Stay right there," I order him. "I'll go wake her up and send her down! Last night she did a hen party mani-pedi session for twenty people. She didn't come home until just before sunrise."

"It's okay, let her rest."

"She'll be wide awake as soon as she sees you. I'll be right back. Ah, Carletto," I say, standing at the door. "Thank you again, truly. Buying the estate is going to change my life."

"Don't thank me," he replies, crossing his arms over his chest. "Thank Michael."

Bang. One shot, one target. "Michael?"

"He's going to kill me for telling you, but if it weren't for him, Bogdanovic would be here, standing in my place today."

I want to know more, but instead I just nod wordlessly.

"Aren't you going to ask me how he is?"

"How is he?" I repeat, petrified.

"Well, first, how are you?" Carletto looks at me as if he were a detective conducting an interrogation. "You know what I'm talking about. Don't be cryptic."

I swallow dryly, terrified. Of course I know. "Not good."

"Neither is he."

"We'll get over it," I say shortly, turning to leave. "We're two adults who have each made our own decisions."

"Or you're two flipping idiots."

"What do you mean you can't approve the loan?" I blurt out.

I'm in the bank manager's office, having arrived all cheerful and confident with the orders from the fair, but after his quick examination of the documents, all my hopes vanished the moment he shook his head.

"You asked me to bring you some orders, and I did!" I insist.

"Of course, Elisa, but the problem is that this isn't enough," he explains. "I was hoping you'd have something better."

"Better than this?! Where . . ." I start looking through the folder. "Here it is." I wave a piece of paper under his nose. "Better than an order from the Prince of Wales? Can you give me the name of another winery you know that has His Royal Highness among its customers?"

"It's only sixty bottles," he points out.

"But in this case, maybe we should look at the quality of the customer, rather than the amount ordered."

"And what guarantee would the quality of the customer give us?"

"Okay," I say, angrily gathering all my documents. "I understand. I won't waste any more of your time. I thought I might have a little support from you, since you knew my father, but obviously I was wrong."

"Elisa, don't take it personally."

"And how should I take it? My whole life is here," I say, waving the folder in front of him.

"I know, but as I said, we don't have enough guarantees, and you don't have a guarantor—"

"Who said she didn't have a guarantor?" asks Donatella, entering the office without bothering to knock. Her pastel suit clashes with the director's sterile gray-black office, not to mention the cloud of Chanel N°5 and hairspray that envelops her. "Sorry, treasure, I would have come earlier but the hairdresser took forever," she says, sitting in the armchair next to me.

"Donatella, what are you doing here?" I ask.

"Le Giuggiole has been my home all these years too, and you, Giada, Mariana, and Linda are my family. I have no desire to go back to living alone in that gloomy Milan apartment my last husband left me. How much time do I have left? Twenty? Twenty-five years? I want to live them well and be where I want to be, and I want to be here with you." She looks at the manager again. "Do I have enough to qualify as her guarantor?"

"More than enough!" he exclaims. He holds out the loan documents, along with a pen, which she eyes in horror.

"I'll use mine, thanks," she says, removing the cap from a Tiffany fountain pen.

"Stop," I say, sliding the papers away. "I really appreciate the gesture and the kind words, but I can't let you do this."

"You need a loan; I need a house," she replies. "And I'm not asking for your permission. At my age, I don't need anyone's permission."

Christ, what a situation. "Donatella"—I sit next to her, addressing her in the gentlest tone I can manage—"you realize, don't you, that if I can't repay the loan, the bank will take all your money?"

"I know, but I also know that that won't happen and that you'll be more than capable of repaying the loan on your own. I don't have any children. If I don't risk my assets for you, who will I do it for?"

"Don't do it at all."

"Don't you remember what I said? Money is boring if you don't do anything with it. At least now I can put it to good use."

"Donatella, I really don't know what to say."

"Say yes!" She pulls the papers out of my hands. "Now, would you rather buy the estate or spend the rest of your life regretting that you didn't?"

I breathe in and out, making peace with my inner demons. "I'll buy it."

69

Michael

When Bingley tells me he sold the estate to Elisa, I feel as if I've begun to atone for all my sins.

Now she's happy, on the threshold of realizing her dream. I, on the other hand, have spent three weeks on the threshold of hell. Saxton asked me to meet with him this evening, and even though I'm not exactly brimming with enthusiasm, I plan to go. I'd be working late anyway. I might as well break up the rhythm for once.

"Michael, come in," Saxton jovially invites me to take a seat on one of the two chesterfield sofas on either side of the burning hearth.

I unbutton my jacket and sit opposite him without saying a word.

"So, I see you continue to perform at the highest levels. How are you able to stay so persistent and full of energy?"

"I know how to manage my limits."

"You're not on any of those strange stimulants?"

"I don't need them. And work keeps my mind busy."

"I understand. Good for you," he observes, stroking his short, white beard. "And what about that woman I met at Barry's event? Elisa, if I'm not mistaken."

"She's back in Italy," I reply distantly.

"Ah, I thought she'd stay; it seemed rather serious."

"A serious relationship, me? You know I'm not the type, Sax." The words coming out of my mouth don't sound convincing in the slightest.

"You've never introduced me to anyone before. I thought it was important."

"It just happened, that's all."

He nods and shrugs. "It's probably for the best, after all." He presses the intercom to summon his assistant. "Eve, bring in the cart, please." And less than half a minute later, she appears with a bucket of ice containing a bottle of champagne and two flutes on a tray.

"What are we celebrating?" I ask him.

He gets up and uncorks the bottle. "You."

"Me?"

"Let's drink to Michael D'Arcy, sole owner of Saxton & D'Arcy," he says, filling the glasses. "I've already started making arrangements to transfer my shares to you."

I take the glass, still unsure of what I've just heard. "Are you retiring?"

"I think you're more than ready to steer this company through the coming decades. Maybe in forty years, sitting here at my desk—unless you want to keep your current office—you'll think back to this moment and remember me."

"Forty years . . ." I repeat, without being able to fathom such a long period of time.

"Or fifty! Who knows when you'll finally wear yourself out," he chuckles. "You know, you were unfocused for a time, but the imposed holiday did you good, you came back tougher and feistier than ever."

"Yeah." I'd like to express slightly more complex thoughts, but only monosyllables come out. And what's worse is that if Saxton had given me this same speech four months ago, I would have jumped to the ceiling for joy. Now, however, I can't feel the slightest bit of happiness.

"Anyway, I won't disappear overnight. I'll stay until January to settle all my affairs, at which point you'll take the helm." He raises his glass in the air and takes a sip of champagne.

I stare at the bubbles slowly rising along the sides of the crystal flute, which reflects the flames of the fireplace, while my mind travels elsewhere.

Forty years.

It's as if the walls of the room are closing in on me, the floor and ceiling crushing me.

Suddenly I miss the warm Tuscan sun on my skin, the smell of the earth, the weight of grape bunches in my hands, the drum of horses' hooves, the commotion of the Belvedere fairs, the crackling muffler of the Cinquecento, "Fiumi di Parole," the *ribollita* simmering on the fire, the scent of freshly baked focaccia, the aroma of the wood barrels in the cellars, the fireflies in the hedge, the clothes that smell of aromatic herbs after a walk in the garden, my face sticky with watermelon juice, Elisa's laughter, her light breath that caresses my skin as she sleeps on my chest, her fingers in my hair . . . It all barrels toward me like a speeding truck.

Here, after a whole day spent in front of my PC, all that awaits me is an empty house and a takeaway meal that no one cooked with me in mind.

"Thank you," I say.

"For what?"

"Thank you, but I don't want your shares."

"I don't understand . . . you don't want my shares?"

"My future isn't here," I reply. I place my untouched glass down on the table and stand up. "I'll give you mine."

Saxton watches in silence as I leave his office.

I return to my office with a strange lightness. I grab my coat, turn off the light, and take the stairs toward the exit.

"I didn't know how else to get through to you," thunders Saxton over the banister, the echo in the stairwell lending his words a strange, godlike effect. "But you finally got it."

70

Elisa

I love to stroll alone among the vines at dawn.

It's mid-November. A light, low fog rises from the ground, the vineyard's wedding veil, illuminated by the milky autumn light.

I walk between two rows of vines along the path that leads from the annex to the villa and reach out to touch the leaves that are turning from red to brown.

Even though it's starting to get cold, I walk barefoot. I want to root myself in the earth. I'm never leaving again.

Le Giuggiole is mine.

I close my eyes and inhale, allowing the fresh, humid air to tickle my lungs. It's my air.

When I reopen my eyes, I notice a blurry figure heading toward me.

The closer he gets, the faster my heart pounds.

I'd recognize that shape among a thousand people.

Michael.

I want to run toward him, but I feel stuck.

The smaller the distance between us, the faster his pace, as he comes closer and closer.

He holds out his arms and enfolds me, imprisons me, holds me close to him, and only when I'm pressed against his warm body do I realize how cold I'd been.

"I realized I don't have a photo of the two of us," he says. "I never put photos in frames before because I had nothing to frame. Now I want us to be in the frame together."

"It'll look great on your kitchen counter."

"There's no kitchen anymore. There's not even an apartment. I brought the frame with me. We can put it wherever you'd like." He bows his head, pressing his forehead against mine. "You were right. I was scared."

"Of what?"

"Scared I'll live the rest of my life wondering what it would have been like. Scared that in forty years, I'll find myself back where I started. Scared of living in an empty apartment forever. Scared of a future without you."

"Are you here to stay?"

"Yeah. With you. Forever." The tip of his nose caresses mine.

"You're not afraid to start from scratch?"

"I rewrote my CV. I'm willing to take any job, even as an intern. I don't know much about viticulture, but I'm good with numbers."

I cup his face in my hands, staring deeply into his eyes. "My Michael."

"My Elisa."

He takes my hands in his and our fingers intertwine, never to unclasp again. "You're cold," he whispers, kissing me.

"Not anymore."

Epilogue

Elisa

Seven months later

"You take one too. Please?" Giada implores after we lock ourselves in the bathroom.

"Why?"

"Because you've already done it. You're an expert, and I'll feel better if you do it with me. Plus, that way we'll know if it's accurate. If my test is negative like yours, it means I'm not pregnant; if mine is positive, it means I'm pregnant for sure. Come on, help me out."

"Do we have to do it today?" I ask, eyeing the time.

In less than half an hour, Jemma's best friend, Cécile Loxley, is marrying one of Michael's best friends at the estate. It's a high-profile event, given that he's a world-famous F1 driver; with all the British aristocracy and international superstars in attendance, Le Giuggiole has become a sort of destination for the jet set. In short, not exactly the time to lock yourself in the bathroom to take a pregnancy test.

We should be out there, making sure everything goes perfectly.

"We have to do it today," insists my sister. "Because yesterday was too early, and I can't handle the wait until tomorrow."

"Does Charles know you might be pregnant?"

"Yeah. We've been trying. We're ready to be parents."

The two of them live in London now, in a cottage that looks like it's from a film. Though to call it a *cottage*—which is what they call it there—is an understatement, given that it has six bedrooms and four bathrooms. At least once a month, Giada comes back to visit us.

"Come on, the sooner we do it, the sooner we're done," she says, taking two sticks from a box that says Babypredictor and holding one out to me.

"The things you make me do . . ." I mutter, sitting on the toilet, my tulle dress pulled up to my waist.

Giada does the same thing after me, and then we place the two tests on the sink.

She tortures her nails while waiting, while I peek out the window at the situation outside: The new swimming pool looks fantastic! Charlotte was right about adding one, and the design she drew up is perfectly integrated with the villa. I was terrified it would look tacky, but it looks like it's always been there. It may have cost three times more than the average swimming pool, but we received a stratospheric wine order for the entire Bloom Group, so the next loan installments are as good as paid.

"The mascara! The mascara!" shouts Linda, charging into the bathroom.

"What happened?" I ask.

"Tommaso and I were sitting on the edge of the fountain . . ."

"I know, I saw you," I comment sharply. "Take a breath. This isn't a freediving competition." Linda and Tommaso got back together—"together" being an accurate spatial description, given that they spend most of the time with their mouths glued to each other's—because he said he left her only to impress his friends but that in reality he'd fallen in love. Years of evolution and males are still stuck in the same place. If Darwin were alive, he'd revise his studies.

"Jemma's dogs dived in like a bomb, and a wave hit us in the face."

Good little naughty corgis. I'll have to reward them with some bones.

"I have to redo my make-up. I look like a panda," she grumbles and opens the cabinet with such vehemence that she knocks everything off the sink, including the tests.

"Nooo!" exclaims Giada, bending over to pick up the two sticks. Luckily my daughter is in such a hurry to get back to Tommaso that she leaves without asking any questions.

"Do you remember which one is yours?" I ask her.

"How would I do that? They're identical!"

In the next minute, the word *Pregnant* appears on one of the two.

"Now we know which one is yours," I say.

"What if it's not mine?" she asks, gripped by anxiety.

"Well, it can't be mine," I say.

"Okay, I'll take the last one in the box," says Giada.

"Look, I have to go downstairs. I'll see you later. Good luck," I say, kissing her on the forehead and going back to the party.

It's a splendid Saturday in June, and the intense blue sky makes the freshly painted villa stand out in the most cinematic way.

I can't help but admire it with pride. Le Giuggiole, by Elisa Benetti . . .

Michael beckons to me from under the wisteria canopy. He holds out his hand and takes me in his arms, swaying us to the rhythm of the music.

"Where did you disappear to?"

"I was with Giada."

"Ah, I see, girl stuff."

"More or less," I say. "Hey, is that Carletto I see drinking wine?" I ask, shocked. "He never drinks alcohol."

"He's dying to become a dad."

"And what do you think about that?" I ask him, not hearing any hints of disapproval in his tone.

"I think he might be on to something . . . I'd like a big family too," he adds, surprising me.

"Yeah, but we have so much to do now with the estate," I say. "The vineyard, the cellar, the resort, the events . . . The vineyard . . ."

"You already said 'vineyard.' By the way, the newlyweds are very happy—you did a magnificent job."

"Not to brag but . . . I know," I gloat. "But I can't take all the credit—I also have an exceptional associate."

"Ah, so is that how I should introduce you? As my associate?"

"Why not? I like it."

"What about 'my great love'? No good?"

"A little much. It sounds fake," I reply, turning up my nose.

"And the classic 'my wife'?"

"It makes us sound old."

"How about 'Mrs. D'Arcy'?"

"In Italy women keep their surname, didn't you know that?"

"But all my friends are English," he insists.

"Okay, fine, as long as I can call you 'Mr. Benetti.'"

He narrows his eyes as if he's thinking about it. "I don't hate it, if I'm honest."

"I've been in your arms for at least five minutes, and you still haven't kissed me, Mr. Benetti," I reproach him.

"Is that cause for divorce?"

"Perhaps. If I were you I wouldn't risk it, Mr. Benetti."

"I'll fix it right away," he whispers, moving closer to my mouth. "But first, say it again."

"What?"

"Mr. Benetti."

"Mr. Benetti," I repeat, brushing his lips with mine.

"Again," he tortures me.

"Mr. Benetti."

And we give each other one of those kisses that promises others, and much more.

In the end, even I, the most diehard antimarriage crusader in all of Belvedere, gave up. Even though Mamma wanted Michael and me to have a live-broadcast wedding with commentary by Enzo Miccio so she could silence her rivals, she had to settle for a civil ceremony, but the outcome was enough to make her happy.

"Do you think anyone would notice if we disappeared?" he murmurs in his *I'll do anything for you* tone.

"In theory we should stick around here . . . The ceremony will be starting soon," I hesitate.

"But . . . ?"

"What about the storage room with the watermelons?" I ask, in the grip of desire. "In the storage room with the watermelons," I repeat decisively.

The moment we take off, Giada strides out of the villa toward me. "Elisa, I have to tell you something."

"Maybe later?" I try to make her understand with a wink that now is not the right time. I'll be happy to compliment her on the baby *later*.

"No," she replies.

"In ten minutes?" I ask, but Michael gives me a look. "Or twenty?"

"Elisa, you don't understand." Giada takes me by the elbow and drags me into the kitchen with such force that I almost trip on my dress.

"You could be a little more discreet!" I protest.

"I took the test again," she says.

"Congratulations!" I exclaim.

"Look"—she puts the stick in my hand—"not pregnant."

"Oh, Giada." I hold out my arms to hug her. "Don't be discouraged, I'm sure next time . . ."

She shakes her head matter-of-factly. "I'm not discouraged, Elisa. Don't worry. But that means the positive test was. Not. Mine."

The calm and poised tone with which she emphasized the last three words hits me.

"But . . . but . . . then . . ." I stammer.

It was mine.

It seems as though my big family with Michael is already well on its way.

Acknowledgments

Like the majority of romance readers, among the classics, *Pride and Prejudice* by the beloved Jane Austen occupies a special place on my bookshelf (in multiple editions) and in my heart. I wanted to pay tribute to this story that has given me so much and which I reread all the time to the extent that I brought some of the elements of the classic to the present day and also to Italy, recombining them.

What if a modern Lizzie Bennet was a single mom?

What if she was the owner of Pemberley?

What if, instead of Meryton, their little world was a village in the Chianti hills?

What if we could enter Mr. Darcy's head?

What if it was a romantic comedy?

One "What if . . ." after another, and *No Place to Be Single* sprung to life.

The choice to set the story on a vineyard was very personal: I owe the life I live today to the work my grandfather Aronne did on his vineyard, to which he gave everything.

He's the first person I have to thank and to whom I dedicate the novel.

I also thank you for reading it. I hope I was good company and gave you a few smiles. Perhaps I say the same thing every time, but because my intent is always the same: to entertain.

Thanks to my entire family, especially our four new grandparents. Without them to help me with the baby, I don't know if this novel would have seen the light of day.

A big thank-you to all my lifelong friends who put up with me to no end: Elisa, Silvia, Azzurra, Lea, Giulia, Paola, and Monica.

I thank my great motivator, Alessia Gazzola: It seemed impossible, but we got to the end of the draft.

Heartfelt thanks to the entire world of blogs, Bookstagram, BookTok, and BookTube for their enormous publicity efforts.

Finally, thanks to Newton Compton, in particular to my editor, Martina Donati, for their help with the Tuscan dialect.

I close with a greeting and a hug, hoping to meet you in person soon at a literary event.

For any news, questions, or updates, you can find me here:

Facebook: Felicia Kingsley official page

Instagram: felicia_kingsley

Blog: www.feliciakingsley.com

Until the next story.

Playlist

You can listen to all the songs that inspired and guided me in the writing of this story on my Spotify profile: Felicia Kingsley A.

1. "Right Now," Sophie and the Giants
2. "Breathless," The Corrs
3. "Cotton-Eye Joe," Rednex
4. "Pummarola," Colic
5. "The Years," 883
6. "There's Nothing Holdin' Me Back," Shawn Mendes
7. "Crash and Burn," Savage Garden
8. "Kobra," Donatella Rettore
9. "Fiumi di Parole," Jalisse
10. "Rosé," The Feeling
11. "Cabriolet Panorama," The Kolors
12. "La Porti un Bacione a Firenze," Odoardo Spadaro
13. "September Song," JP Cooper
14. "Inner Smile," Texas
15. "All or Nothing," Theory of a Deadman
16. "Rewind," Vasco Rossi
17. "Dieci," Annalisa
18. "Broken Strings," James Morrison featuring Nelly Furtado

About the Author

Photo © 2024 Yuma Martellanz

Felicia Kingsley is a bestselling author whose romantic comedies have sold more than 3.8 million copies. *No Place to Be Single*, which was adapted into a film for a 2026 global release, is her second to be translated into English. Born in Carpi, Italy, Felicia loves reading, listening to music, painting, traveling, daydreaming, vintage markets, decluttering, scented candles, and a myrtle spritz. For more information, visit www.feliciakingsley.com.

About the Translator

Hillary Locke's literary work has appeared, most notably, in *Smithsonian Journeys*, *The Washington Post*, *Words Without Borders*, and *Brick: A Literary Journal*. She has translated numerous book-length commercial and literary novels from Spanish, Italian, and Portuguese, while benefiting from the financial support of PEN America, the Vermont Studio Center, the Mystery Writers of America, and the National Endowment for the Arts.